The Lunatic

LAUREN WANTZ

The Lunatic
Copyright © 2021 by Lauren Wantz

ISBN
978-1-954932-18-0 (Paperback)
978-1-954932-17-3 (eBook)

Table of Contents

Part I

Chapter 1

"He has talent, they say, but he was dropped from the moon," Fyodor Dostoyevsky.

They all gathered around the screen with melancholy and concern, though why they were concerned many people would not understand. It wasn't even their own planet, all they had control of over this green and blue ball was the tides and menstrual cycles. But still they were concerned. They had always been rooting for the planet Earth, hoping one day it could be the heaven it had always strived to be, though in many ways it behaved like hell. Another mass shooting, and it went the same as it had done every month for the past several years. The mass shooting would occur, the flags would all go at half mast, the media became a platform for incessant argument and the less than helpful coined phrase of "thoughts and prayers," and in the end nothing would change. It would happen again a month later, in a game of constant amnesia and a divisive failure to save themselves.

"This has gone too far," said Bogomil. "We need to send a representative."

All of them looked at Anglor.

Anglor groaned. "Come on," he said. "Not me."

"You are by far the best equipped."

"How can I change a world I'm not even from?"

Bogomil shook his head. "No, you're not going to change the world," he said. "You are far too naturally pessimistic for that.

But, still you cannot help but to do something, in spite of the pessimism. Your work on Earth will be purely diagnostic- you will simply tell the world it needs to change, you will not change it. You are an artist. That is what artists do"

"How does that help?"

"It helps a great deal. You will be helping people especially. You will make them all feel less alone by reminding them that everyone is lonely."

"Is that all humans share?"

"Regrettably, yes, that and the need for love, but really they boil down to the same thing. And then some humans wish to be free and other humans wish to be enslaved. You are to remind them it is more important to be free, and to let all other men be free as well."

"I would be telling them things they have already been told."

"Yes, but they need a constant reminder. That is why you will never stop working. Their memory is not great."

"Perhaps they just don't listen."

"Yes," Bogomil conceded wearily. "A lot of them don't listen, but there will be people who will, and these people, whether they be a minority or not, are worth fighting for,."

"It's a losing battle…"

"But it was what you were made to do. It is your calling. You cannot help but to do it."

"But what's the point if I can't change the world?"

"Eventually it will change itself, or, if it is capable of being changed by a singular man or woman, it will have to be a human man or woman, not a Selenite like you. And it's not impossible. It has happened before."

"And then eventually Earth returned to its nonsense. The change was evaporated."

"Well, the planet is always rotating. It will always need to be changed, otherwise it will expire. You must remind people of that, the people who will listen, so they are not so afraid, so they know it's natural and going to happen anyway."

Anglor sighed. "Fine," he said. "I will do it. Perhaps Earth is more interesting than the moon…"

"It's significantly more interesting," Bogomil said. "It has humans on it."

Anglor scoffed. "They're too interesting for their own good. They're only interesting because no matter what they do they are bored."

"Don't be so cynical," Bogomil said.

"That's another thing," Anglor went on. "Why should I help humans when I don't even like them?"

"Those who don't like people wish to help them more than anything, to at least make them likeable."

Anglor groaned and decided to stop arguing.

"We're going to drop you on the planet now," Bogomil said.

"Alright," Anglor conceded.

"I should warn you though," Bogomil continued hesitantly. "The people of Earth… they're going to think you're mad."

"What?!" Anglor cried. "Then how the hell am I going to get people to listen to me? No one's going to listen to someone they think is insane!"

"That's the point. You're going to prove you're sane."

"Why are they going to think I'm mad?"

"Because you're not from Earth. You will not abandon our customs and way of life when you reach Earth, you will act still like a Selenite, not like an Earthling."

"Why?"

"Because they need a new point of view. That's partially their problem. They only know human wisdom, human knowledge, they have never met any other intelligent life forms. You must show them a different way to live, the way we live. That's really why they'll think you're mad, not because you actually are, but because you will have a perspective so unique at first it will seem like insanity for being so unprecedented."

"This sounds like a suicide mission."

"So? We commit suicide every six months."

"What's the point of being original on Earth? Here I'm just like everyone else."

Bogomil smiled. "No, you're not."

Anglor sighed again. "I thought everyone on Earth was mad," he said.

"Exactly. You'll be the mad one for being the sane one. And eventually people will listen to you. Come now, enough talking, let's get you off the moon."

"Alright."

Then they walked to the edge of their cold rock in the sky and Bogomil very gently pushed Anglor off. He fell face first into the ubiquitous void of space. He saw very few stars, and the ones he did he knew were dying. The sun was dying, someday the moon would die, too, and just because they decomposed at a slower rate than humans didn't mean they still weren't dying quickly. Time is not how humans perceive it. Everything is happening quickly, and nothing is old, everything is still practically new, particularly Earth. Nothing is old but everything is dying, and dying quickly. Life on Earth dies the fastest, though, though Earth itself does not die as quickly, and will probably outlast these people who for the time being foolishly think they're its master, when really they are only actors that the Earth is allowing to use its stage so they can entertain their audience, which is themselves, as if they are always looking in the mirror. Otherwise they cannot affirm that they exist.

Anglor fell for a long time, he fell for lightyears, and he saw almost nothing on the way down. It felt like freedom, though, this falling, falling through a great emptiness, head first into a void. He fell sluggishly, the dark matter of space pulling on him as he went down. He didn't mind the lack of oxygen, he had been trained to live with that. He had been living in space his whole life, it was going to be strange to leave it. He didn't know what would cushion his fall, if anything, but as he was falling, into the great, cosmic loneliness, he felt truly free, though being free meant he had to fall alone. That was fine. He didn't want to drag anyone down with him. He felt like lucifer. He was plummeting downwards into what was both heaven and hell. At last he reached Earth.

He fell into the ozone layer, then he fell into the stratosphere, then he fell through the ordinary sky. The people of Earth thought he was a mere comet, they thought nothing of it. Eventually he fell into the ocean. He looked around wildly at what would be his new home and suddenly felt an incredible weight. He looked down into the water. There were weights on his chest.

'Well, I suppose I am due for my bi-annual suicide,' he thought. He let the weights pull him down, drag him into the ocean.

A woman screamed. "That man is trying to drown himself!" she cried.

Meanwhile Anglor was underwater, patiently waiting for his half death. With his eyes closed underwater he looked so serene, like an angel or a martyr. Suddenly he felt several pairs of hands pulling him up, taking the weights off.

"Why are you stopping me?" he asked, bewildered. "I was due for it, otherwise the weights wouldn't have been on my chest."

"What the hell were you thinking?" a lifeguard castigated. "There are kids here!"

"I don't understand why you're mad," Anglor said flatly. "It happens every six months."

"What, suicide?!"

"What else? I'm sorry, I'm not from here."

Where are you from?"

Anglor pointed blankly to the sky.

"I'm sorry," the lifeguard said. "I'm going to have to call an ambulance, and they will probably put you away for a while."

"Put me away where?"

"A mental hospital."

"What's that?"

"A place for people who are sick in the mind, not the body."

"I assure you I'm perfectly healthy…"

"You just tried to drown yourself?!"

"Where I'm from we commit suicide every six months in order to be reborn."

"Where the hell are you from then, another looney bin?"

Again Anglor pointed vaguely to the sky. At last he and the lifeguard got to the shore. There waiting for him were about ten police officers.

"Come with us," one of them said.

"You're arresting me?"

"No, we're taking you to the emergency room."

"What on Earth for?"

"You tried to commit suicide, sir."

Anglor groaned but he complied. He had heard stories about how brutish and violent Earth policemen could be, so he didn't want to start a fight. Really they were frightened, frightened of anyone who was not like them. So many people feel that way. Anglor somewhat understood. He was frightened of Earthlings, but perhaps for better reasons than they were frightened of him.

The police handcuffed him, put him in the back of their car, and drove him to the emergency room of the local hospital. There they told him he was being pink slipped, which meant he would be put on an involuntary psychiatric hold for 72 hours, but Anglor learned quickly that it was always longer than that. A psych ward is just like anywhere else, it even resembles most a high school-the introverted eccentrics are always deemed more mad than the loud people who like regular things. They are in fact even picked on, picked on by the staff. They are shot up with one of the worst drugs invented, Halidol, which makes you feel like your head has dissipated into thin air, into an asthenic strand of oxygen. Anghlor found out all these things quickly. He thought it was strange that he was regular on the moon but mad on Earth. Different cultures, he supposed.

When he got to the psychiatric ward it was two in the morning, so they had to admit him quietly.

"Why are you here?" an overworked and surly male nurse asked him wearily.

"I tried to kill myself, but it's not what it seems."

"What do you mean?"

"Well, you see, where I come from we commit suicide every six months so we can be reborn."

"And where do you come from?"

Anglor gulped, but still he did not want to tell a lie. "I'm from the moon," he said glibly. "I'm a Selenite."

The nurse gave him an odd look and started writing things down. "There's no life on the moon," he said.

"We're too small to be seen."

"Then why can I see you?"

"I grew as I fell."

"Fell? From where?"

"The moon."

The nurse tried to hide a scoff. "What's your name?" he asked.

Anglor didn't want to lie, but for some reason he didn't want these people to know his real name. He thought of an Earth name. "Michael," he said. "My name is Michael."

"All this about the moon," the nurse said. "Is that a joke or do you genuinely believe it?"

"I'm telling the truth," Anglor said stiffly. "I'm not insane, I' just not from this planet, I have different customs than you humans do."

"Right," the nurse said. "I'll show you to your bedroom. You're not from the moon, Michael."

"You have lived too long in the world of the possible. You've forgotten the beauty of impossibility."

"I've been living too long in the world of the mad," the nurse said under his breath. "I've forgotten the beauty of sanity."

Still Anglor heard him. "There is no beauty in sanity," he said, still stiffly, and followed the nurse to his bedroom. It was a small room, nothing in it but two beds and a bathroom and a window with slatted blinds so you couldn't really see out of it. Anglor tried to anyway. He looked out of the window, peeking through the slatted blinds, and saw the moon, a beacon of light in darkness, a solitary, lonely rock in the sky, but it was not as lonely as the people on Earth. That's what allowed a place like this to exist, this mental hospital. Anglor sighed and tried to fall asleep, covertly looking at the moon as he did. He was homesick already. The Earth could never be his home, because it had already reneged his tenuous freedom. He was about to discover what it was like to be an Earthling, here in this mental hospital. He was about to learn the key difference between humans and Selenites- Selenites killed themselves in order to be reborn, humans kill themselves to die, because they feel they cannot be reborn. Anglor was about to find out what that was like. He as about to wish to kill himself the human way, for death, not rebirth, a feeling which he would only have on Earth, a feeling that only exists on Earth.

It would be the only thing he had in common with humans.

Chapter 2

Anglor was unable to sleep. The tap water was running in the bathroom and the bed was stiff and cold. He thought he could feel ghosts all around him. He was a man who by the custom of his planet killed himself every six months, but he had never felt closer to death as he did now. Death was all around him, beckoning to him, telling him to commit his last suicide. He wasn't supposed to commit his last suicide until he was one hundred, and he was only thirty nine, but he yearned for it. On his only few minutes of Earth they had already completely stripped him of his free will. He felt that he really was mad.

He rolled wearily out of his sleepless bed and went down the hallway. A nurse was sitting in a high back chair on her phone.

"Excuse me," Anglor said.

"Yes, Michael?"

"I can't sleep."

"You can hang out in the dayroom until breakfast time. It's unlocked."

"Okay, thank you."

Anglor went into the dayroom and looed at the impassive, blank dry erase board. He decided to draw on it. He picked up the markers and began his work of art. His back hurt, but he ignored it. This was always the perfect way to ignore pain, because it was invented by pain. He worked on it for about an hour until the other patients started to wake up and the nurses made the two pots of decaffeinated coffee that was all the residents of this mental hospital were living for at the moment. Anglor got a cup of coffee as well.

"Did you draw that?' one of the patients asked, pointing to Anglor's drawing. It was a picture of a strange, amorphous, blob like alien.

"Yes," Anglor said.

"It's good," the patient told him. "What's your name?"

"Michael."

"Hi, I'm Cheree," and the woman shook his hand.

Michael smiled at her warmly. "If you want I can draw you a picture, too."

"Okay."

Then the nurses started to gather everyone for breakfast. Anglor got in line for breakfast with Cheree and he felt more exhausted than he had in his entire life. It was a long way to fall, and this was the pit he had ended up in. He was learning quickly all about Earth. He was learning that it was rock bottom.

'All the doors of the hospital locked as soon as they were closed, so Anglor had to hold the heavy door open to let everyone through. Then they had to walk down a long corridor and hold the door open for the kitchen as well. The nurses were desultory and often unkind, but not all of them. A few of them were actually quite kind, but it was a minority. The kitchen was a large room with eight or nine round tables to sit at. After Anglor got his breakfast he sat with Cheree.

"I'm sitting with you," he sang playfully, "cuz I'm made out of glue."

Cheree looked at him and laughed. "Well, at least that'll keep you from falling apart."

Anglor smiled and began to eat his breakfast.

"Are you bisexual?" Cheree suddenly asked.

Anglor nodded his head. "Yes," he said. "Everyone where I come from is bisexual."

"Where's that?"

"The moon."

Cheree chuckled. "Cool. I can always sense when someone else is bisexual."

"You are too, I presume?"

"Yes. I'm married but I also have a girlfriend."

"That's awesome."

Cheree laughed. "I'm a prostitute," she went on. "I wish I could say I was a big baller, but really I only ever break even enough to buy my dope."

"That's how it usually goes."

"Yes, it's awful, I need to stop."

"'The money that is stolen from the prostitute will go back to the prostitute in turn.'"

"Who said that?"

"Jesus."

'You guys read the bible om the moon?"

"We read everything on the moon. That is one thing we respect about humans, the artwork they can create. We try to emulate it, but it's not the same, because we're not human."

"I thought your art was pretty good."

"Well, I live on Earth now, so I am in a great deal of pain."

"And you weren't on the moon?"

Anglor sighed. "I realize now I never belonged there. But I didn't know that until I came to Earth. And I don't belong on Earth, either. Here, let me draw you your picture."

Anglor took out a piece of paper and began to draw.

"What is it?" Cheree asked, peering over his shoulder to look at the drawing.

"It's a showerhead with a body," he said.

Cheree irrupted into laughter. "I like the way your mind works," she said.

Anglor smiled and continued the drawing.

"Oh my God," Cheree said, still giggling, "it's got muscles and a vagina."

Anglor smirked almost lasciviously. Being in this hospital had made him realize how alone he was, something he was inured to previously, but now he was fully aware, and he wanted someone to hold onto however briefly. He wanted a lover. Everyone in here did, and all the patients fell in love with each other left and right. It was simple, they were lonely, and wanted to love someone for a moment, not very long, but a moment. They were alone and suddenly, when they were brought into this new world full of other people who were like them, people who were at last no longer being hidden from each other and who belonged together, for a moment: in other words, they were all horny. They were looking to forget their troubles for a little while in the folds of the flesh of someone they didn't have to love and who didn't have to love them, but who understood. This was what all the people in this hospital were after much more than love, and which was granted them in their fellow lunatics- understanding.

And Anglor got caught up in this too. He had never realized before that no one had ever understood him, but now he realized it painfully, when he had finally found people who did, or at least if they did not understand him, appreciated his twisted, tormented, and unusual mind. This would be the closest thing to home on Earth, not the hospital, but the people in it, and it would be best that once this ordeal was over with he never saw them again. He was just like everyone else in the hospital, he only needed to be loved for a moment, then he could move on in loneliness just as he always had, and carry with him the memory of this loneliness being satiated for a moment, and no longer, for they all knew the longer it got the more bitter it got. It was the opposite of wine, though it intoxicated one just as deftly, the hangover was much worse.

Another patient looked over and Anglor's drawing for Cheree. "It's both a man and a woman?" he asked. Anglor nodded.

"Which man and which woman?' he asked.

"Any."

"Oh. Sometimes I take it too literally. This speaks to me though, though I can't explain why. I barely understand it. But it speaks to me."

"I think it speaks to everyone in here," Cheree said with a twinkle in her eye. "Though none of us know why. Are you bisexual, too?" she asked the other patient.

"No, but I can endure the thought of being bisexual. It doesn't offend me or anything."

Cheree smiled at the boy. Anglor's heart sank. She would fall in love with this other man instead. He didn't know why he felt so moderately crushed, though. He was only looking to have sex with her, he wasn't exactly ready for a love affair. It had been years since his last romance, which was short and bitter, full of miscommunication and grossly indulgent self love on both of their parts. Anglor didn't think he could do it, he didn't think he could love.

At last it was time for their smoke break, the few minutes every day that was all the people in the hospital were living for. Anglor sat next to Cheree and the man who could endure the thought of being bisexual, but they both ignored him, so Anglor sat and smoked his donated "community cigarette" and tried not to fall over because he was so tired. The cigarette didn't last long, it felt like it was gone in a moment, just like everything else in this world where time never moved and when it did it was at too little a distance to notice any change, this world where things were preserved in their insanity as if they all were not humans but wax statues of what had once been human, melting outside in the sun as they smoked their cigarettes, deliquescing into the muddy grass, waiting to be buried underneath it.

For a moment as Anglor sat there everything went white. He shook himself a little bit, then the color of the world returned.

"I need to sleep," he groaned, but he was sure that if he slept he would die. He looked at the other people around him, the other patients. He was indeed like them, so maybe he was mad. These people were strange only in that they were more noticeably flawed than other people. They really weren't any more flawed, though, they were just unfortunate enough to be unlike other people in that they could not hope to hide it, and, as they got older, no longer wished to hide it, but relished in it almost obnoxiously, being naked all the time.

"Go get some sleep," Cheree said, and put a hand on his shoulder. It was true. Anglor was like this people, he was more noticeably flawed than an average man, so perhaps he really was mad. And perhaps mad was not such a bad thing to be. He went to his room to sleep but when he closed the door he felt more alone than ever. Cheree was just a passing fancy like any other, passing on from this world into the next, if there was a next world. 'Life is a game and death is the end of that game,' Anglor thought sadly to himself. 'And no one wins. All you can do is lose.'

Chapter 3

In a few more days Anglor was released from the hospital. He was glad to be gone. These more noticeably flawed people got under his skin after awhile, they had no answers, they were not beacons of light or hope or beacons of anything, they were merely desperate people who had found rock bottom to be the only home they could live in, the only place they could survive. Anglor found out in the end, they were not special, in fact they were just as narcissistic as anyone else. But he did find the so called sane people of Earth even harder to relate to. They were completely benign, people who lived on a plateau where there was no sky to try to grab, just an endless plane, they made the Earth seem flat. And Anglor slowly found that in spite of the fact it was Earthlings who had invented art, it was harder to be an artist on Earth than anywhere else.

Most Earthlings no longer wanted art. They had traded it for entertainment, they had rid themselves of erudition and culture, of wisdom, for mere spectacle, for a pleasant but meaningless diversion. And this was the kind of thing that sold now. Real artists, people who truly had something to day, had something to say no one wanted to hear, because it did not make them forget themselves, it in fact reminded them of themselves, and no one wanted that anymore, even if it was life affirming. They wanted explosions and tight rope walkers walking over fire. They wanted someone to risk their life to entertain them, they wanted nothing more than mere panem et circenses, and indeed with the wealth of this in America they had ceased to rebel. They had giant phones these days, which they could look into like a mirror, but instead of seeing their face they saw an entire bored world dying for entertainment, and in the end people confused this for their reflection, for who they really were. Who they truly were though they had already abandoned for convenience.

So It was hard to be an artist in this world. It seemed so strange to Anglor. This was the world that had invented art, and yet its people were hostile to it, while every other idiotic invention, a toilet that wipes you ass for you, a coffee maker that could make coffee in thirty seconds or less, a phone that did your thinking for you- all these purposeless inventions were greeted with much fanfare because people thought they would make life easier, not more meaningful. That's what they wanted now. Art made life more difficult, particularly for the artist, so no one wanted it anymore. Art made life more difficult but in a sublime way- it made life more difficult because it gave life meaning. It made life more difficult so it didn't become so easy it resembled death, which is exactly what Anglor found was happening in America today. He loathed it. He felt all his talents were being wasted. He had to except at the end of the day that he still did it because he loved it, a pity prize really. And his love for art hardly payed the rent.. Eventually he had to get a job.

Working on Earth was quite different than working on the moon. On the moon all types of labor were valuable, but on Earth the labor was senseless and draining, and you were treated like a dog. There was a caste system, and people who had to work low paying jobs were seen as a new kind of pariah, though without their labor the capitalism of the country could not move,. Anglor felt very out of place at work. He got a job at a local gas station, third shift, and all he liked about the job was that he was alone. He would draw when he had a few minutes to himself. America was so strange, he decided. The people here were willing to barter all of their selfhood to be accepted, and they had no other dreams, only to be like other people and therefore liked by them. It was the same with the job, and Anglor found himself caught in this trap, as well. He would break his back with senseless labor only so the other employees would let them in their clique. It was a popularity contest like any other, and Anglor found that was all America was, a popularity contest that never ended until death, and even then you needed a crowd at your funeral.

And of course Anglor could not make it into the upper echelon here in America. He was not willing to barter enough of his self-hood. After all, it was all he had, and he did not want to give all he had to other people not out of compassion, but hoping they would have compassion for him. He didn't need their compassion that badly. He was perfectly adept at feeling sorry for himself, that was the way he saw it. He was a decent worker, though, in spite of it all, but he did find it overwhelming. He had panic attacks almost nightly at work, then he would go outside to smoke a cigarette and he would look at the moon. He wondered what was happening there, but he already knew the answer. Nothing was happening there, nothing had ever happened there, it was just a dead rock in the sky with dead rock people on it. On Earth something was always happening, and yet the people were all bored as if nothing was happening, but something was always happening. It's a strange choice people have to make. They either are bored or in the midst of a great tragedy.

Anglor didn't know why there couldn't be an in between. He disliked both, and equally, he disliked being bored just as much as he disliked being in a great tragedy. He thought perhaps they were the same thing wearing different masks. They were both death. Either alternative in life was death. Maybe it was only like this on Earth, but Anglor felt it was the same on the moon, which had preserved itself by doing nothing for millions of years. It was much more peaceful than the Earth, but that was all. It was no utopia, it was just a place where people do nothing, like heaven, like the great endless plateau, a landscape with not a single thing on it. That is the closest thing to utopia, an eternity of idle boredom. Humans could not possibly live like that. They would make something happen no matter what, even if it was an atrocity. That is why Earth would never be a utopia, because human beings cannot stand being bored. That's fine, though. Utopia is actually quite a trite thing.

Heaven is infinite boredom and hell is never ending tragedy, these are the two choices we have to make, and human beings, who cannot stand being bored, would much prefer hell, in spite of how they claimed they were trying to get to heaven. And then there was Anglor, an outsider, who disliked both, who didn't want to be either idle in heaven or tormented with labor in hell. He must have been somewhere in between, the in between that did not exist.

Then Anglor needed an apartment, too. He found an advertisement in the paper, 'woman with two bedroom apartment wishes to rent out room.' He called the number and met the woman the net day. He approached the apartment slowly. There was a sign on the door written in uncial lettering that said 'Maria's Place.' He knocked on the door rather timidly, so at first the occupant couldn't hear him. He cleared his throat and knocked a little louder. The door opened and a girl answered. She was neither strikingly beautiful or strikingly ugly, but she was not average looking either. She looked completely unlike anyone Anglor had ever seen, and her eyes, they were full with at once melancholy and furor, a great ague of the mind, an intense passion that came hand in hand with the melancholy but which fortunately, the melancholy could not drench, not completely, it would always be a part of her, a great staple of her personality and her looks. It almost made her beautiful, but mostly it made her intense, a thing many men were afraid of, so she was also used to being alone, this great passion in her eyes being wasted in privacy and solitude, but still it was there. It burned bright as ever even when she was alone.

"Hello," she said with a timidity that did not match this incendiary intensity in her eyes.

Anglor cleared his throat. "Hi," he said. "My name is Michael. I'm here to answer your ad."

"Oh, alright," she said sleepily. "You want to live here?"

"Sure."

"Come in and have a look. The bedroom on the right would be yours. I want two hundred dollars a month to make this economically viable for me. You know, ad valorem and whatnot. I can't afford this place by myself anymore, and I don't want to move. I hate goddamn moving."

"So do I," Anglor said mysteriously, and went to look at the room. It was big enough, the apartment was big enough for two people to live comfortably.

"My name's Maria," she said suddenly. "Michael, you said?"

"Yes."

"I'll have to do a background check on you. No offense. You seem like a perfectly nice guy, but then again so did Ted Bundy."

"I've been admitted to a mental hospital before," Michael said honestly.

"What's it like?' she asked.

"It's awful."

She paused for a moment and thought about it. "Well, that doesn't bother me," she said at last. "I appreciate your honesty. Besides, weirdos are always more insightful anyway."

Anglor chuckled. "Thank you," he said. 'Even though you called me a weirdo."

"You'll find out soon I'm not that normal either. I'm not mentally ill, but there is something different about me."

"Yes, there is," Anglor conceded.

"Do you like it?"

"I do."

"Well, I'm sure I'll come to like whatever is different about you too…"

"I'm from the moon," he whispered under his breath.

"What?"

"Nothing. It's an old Russian phrase. People used to say about odd people that they were dropped from the moon. I was dropped from the moon. It didn't want me anymore, and the Earth didn't want me either. At least when Lucifer fell he was able to lord over hell, a place he was needed and wanted."

"Well, most of us aren't fortunate enough to be the devil."

Anglor smiled at her and noticed the anfractuous curves of her wild, unkempt hair and thought perhaps she was beautiful, but in the most absurd way. That made sense, though. Beauty was the most absurd thing to occur in nature, even more absurd than ugliness, which was much more natural.

"I like you," Maria suddenly said firmly, as if it were a conviction. "Even if you were dropped from the moon. I won't bother with the background check, I know I can trust you. Where did you learn that phrase anyway?"

"What, dropped from the moon?"

"Yea. Are you Russian?"

"No. I learned it from, a Dostoyevsky novel."

Maria laughed. "Well, he would know, wouldn't he? If anyone was dropped from the moon it was him. I suppose people said that about him often. Maybe that's the prerequisite for doing anything exceptional, that first you have to be dropped from the moon. Maybe no one who's made history has been from planet Earth."

"I think they were from planet Earth, they just didn't feel comfortable there, so they had to make it better, for themselves, so they could live there."

"Well, you can't live anywhere else, not even you, who was dropped from the moon. You're stuck here now."

"It would appear so."

"And you're going to live with me. I feel like you're soft all over so I have to protect you."

"Thank you."

Maria smiled at him gently. "That's how I can tell you were dropped from the moon," she said. "Because you're soft all over. People who have never fallen, who have been stationary on this planet all their lives, are hard, desiccated in their hearts, all their authenticity dead and buried along the straightened arrow of time and the curving, dangerous road of life, just so they could go on. It's a good thing to be dropped from the moon, it's a good thing to be soft all over. Don't ever let life take that from you, as it will insistently try to do so."

"Thank you," was all Anglor could think to say.

"Would you like some coffee? I'm about to make some."

"Sure."

Maria went into the kitchen to make the coffee and they were silent for a moment, as comfortable a silence as can be expected from two people who have just met. But Maria still felt the need to break it.

"So, how long have you been crazy?" she asked.

Anglor smiled at her wickedly. "Only since I reached Earth."

The next day he moved his stuff in, but to Maria's shock he didn't have anything to bring with him.

"Do you know where I can get a bed?" he asked mildly.

Maria looked at him bewildered. "Were you homeless before this?"

Anglor shrugged. "Somewhat. I was staying at a seedy motel."

He had nothing. He had fallen with nothing, as all people who fall do.

"You poor thing," she said. "There's a mattress store a few blocks from here, we'll go get one. Have you got the money?"

"Yes."

"…Because if not I can pay for it."

Anglor laughed gently and put his hand on Maria's shoulder. "Don't worry about it," he said. "I have the money, I have a job."

"Okay, good. I guess I should have asked you that before I let you move in. You will be able to pay your half of the rent, right?"

"Of course."

So they rigged up Maria's car with zip ties and got the mattress. It was the only thing in Anglor's room. He thought it was the only thing he needed.

"Well, I guess that was an easy move in," Maria observed.

Anglor smiled but didn't say anything. Maria opened her hand and beckoned him to take what was in it. It was the key to the place. Anglor smiled again and took it genially.

"Thank you."

"I'm taking a real chance on you," Maria said somewhat stiffly. "Please don't let me down."

"I won't."

"I mean, you not having anything, that's a little unnerving. It's like you just appeared here suddenly, it's like you really were dropped from the moon."

And the next month passed and Anglor paid his share of the rent and Maria's mind was put at ease. They got to know each other as only two people living together can do. Anglor found out that Maria was a voracious reader. She read about a book a week, no matter how big the book was, and she and Anglor would often sit on the couch together listening to music and both reading, though Anglor could not do it as fast as she did. It was a pleasant ritual, though, a form of silent intimacy as true intimacy must always be mute.

Maria was indeed a strange girl. She picked up other people's habits almost like a vacuum of personality, like a moth that picks up traces of people as they're leaving. She mostly picked up habits from old lovers. She would take on their tendencies and that way they would stay with her forever, even after they left, so she could be her own memory of them, until she was a walking museum of lost people's eccentricities, nervous habits, jokes and phrases. She missed people very easily, even people who in the end had tried to ruin her, which they almost did each time, but she had a stash of herself she always kept hidden, like a bit of the soul kept in a safe where it would be untouched, so she was always able to get up and get moving and get on with her life being almost ruined. But still she would have this person's tendencies, she kept that always as a pity prize, having too many people inside her, having loved too many people and a lot of them having sunk too deeply into her.

She also smoked a lot of weed. Often, when she wasn't reading, she would smoke several joints in a row, as if they were no more than cigarettes. Anglor tried it once and it made him feel strange. It made him feel like he was no longer part of his body, and all a human being has to show for their existence is their body, a warm body with the closest thing in it to resemble a soul being a brain, and this is also an organ, the ghost in the machine being another machine itself. So when Anglor no longer felt like he was part of his body he felt he no longer existed, that he was just some kind of passing wind. He could still think but he didn't even feel he was connected to his brain any more, so he had no idea how it was he was able to think when he was so disambiguated. He didn't know this is the best way to think. He felt like soul without body, which is of course impossible. People think the soul goes on without the body, they do not realize it is only another organ, and it expires like any other organ, and is even an organ that can be removed and the body it came from can still go on living, if you can even call that living. If you remove the brain you certainly die. That is the real soul, this machine within the machine that at once orders and takes orders from the machine it is so deftly enclosed in, and which is the only part of the body that can produce things that are immaterial, thoughts being like unspoken words lost in the air, ideas beings like images only the mind could see, not the eye, a kind of inward psychosis. Sa Anglor felt he was just a brain. Just a big brain floating in the air the no one can see, a ghost that is always thinking beside you. No body in sight. Then when he got past this phase of the high he immediately felt a deep sense of self-loathing.

And there were days when Maria couldn't get out of bed. She would lay there thinking herself, trying to have the same sensation Anglor loathed, of having no body, and sometimes she would cry, though quietly, trying not to have Anglor hear her. He did, though. He went to her bed, a little self conscious. He'd never been to an Earthling's bed before.

"What's wrong?" he asked her as she was sobbing silently.

"This world is so sad," she said. "I don't understand how everyone isn't always weeping."

"Because they have to go to work."

Maria scoffed but didn't say anything. She continued crying. Anglor put a warm, heavy hand on her shoulder.

"Despair is otiose," he said.

"Well, so is happiness."

Anglor sighed. "You smoke too much marijuana, Maria. It's fucking with your mood."

"I know, but it's the only way I feel comfortable doing nothing, and everyone has to do nothing."

She had stopped crying though. Perhaps all she needed was someone to talk to, if only for a moment. Perhaps that's why she made the advertisement to begin with. She didn't need money, she was lonely. Anglor understood. There was something about the Planet Earth that made everyone feel lonely. Perhaps it was due to constantly rotating in nothingness, everything always changing but always staying the same, still being life inside the womb of a great void, being the children of an abyss, the only difference being the seasons, a cosmically diurnal vicissitude. And Maria was one of those people who felt everything, though she kept it to herself, that being the sunken prize her lovers could never get to, and it was no prize. It was a great bane, but it was all that made her feel like she was part of the world, the only thing she shared with it being its despair. Anglor could understand this. There was nothing else in this planet he could relate to, either, and he had only known this great despair since he had arrived.

"I have a little extra money," he said softly to Maria. "We can go out if you'd like."

"How can I have fun when most people in the world are dying from some casual atrocity?"

"What did you read?" Anglor asked.

"Nothing. I watched the news. That teacher who opened fire on his students."

"I'm sorry, Maria."

"America is sick. It has some kind of cancer."

Anglor nodded. He knew what she meant. "We'll you're not," he said. "You're not sick."

"What makes you say that?"

"Because you're still strong enough to weep over these things."

At last she worked up a smile. Anglor would come to find out in these next few months that she was quite a depressive character, with or without the marijuana. He hated to admit it, but it was hard to live with. Some days they'd both be home and he wouldn't see her at all, she being in her bedroom with her headphones on actively ignoring him and relishing almost self- indulgently in her loneliness and despair that was supposedly her gift to the world, her way of placating it, but really this despair was all she had to give to the world because it was all the world had been able to give to her, and really it did not give it to her, she took it from it, claiming the melancholy of the masses was all her own. But perhaps that was true. Maybe all despair is is some kind of commiseration, but with what no one knew. Perhaps commiseration with the devil, the fallen, the lost, all the people who were wasted on the trite confines of life, of Earth. Anglor managed to get Maria out of bed this time, though, and they went out to eat.

They both lived in a squalid land depressive city called Dayton, Ohio. It was a strange city. It was populated by many artists but the city itself was dying so deftly it already appeared dead, as if it were on life support, and no one cared enough to pull the plug. No one was sentimental about the city and wanted it to live, it was just no one cared if it lived or died, so it was left there on life support, with no family to at last begrudgingly agree to euthanize it. Heroin was trafficked heavily around here, and it was one of the worst places in the country for the addiction. The people in the city were on life support, too, and as the same phenomenon, no one caring enough to pull the plug, not even themselves. Anglor supposed they all felt like Maria did, that in the midst of the tsuris of the millions it was impossible for the sole individual to be happy. He supposed they felt not only Dayton, but the whole world was on life support, and they could not pull the plug as they wished to, so they pulled the plug on themselves instead, disconnected from their own minds, having given up on a world that had initially given up on them, getting no sympathy from anyone, not even themselves. See, drug addiction is always based on self- loathing, the desire to become as worthless and morally ambiguous as you feel you are.

Anglor tried not to think of it, though. Maria's depression was catching, and he got the feeling that he didn't have time for that, that even though he would live to be one hundred, there was not enough time in the world for that. So he took Maria out to eat, a nice, eccentric restaurant called the Spaghetti Warehouse. His nictitating eyes welcomed Maria into something like intimacy, the act of at least having a friend. She accepted the invitation with a weak smile. He wanted to tell her, 'don't commiserate with the devil anymore. He made his choice.' But she was supposedly commiserating with the world. It was the same thing. The world had made its choice, too. Anglor wanted to explain this to her, but it was always the same problem. The words were only valid in his head, as soon as they came out of his mouth they were corrupted.

"You feeling better?" was all he managed.

"A little," Maria said. "Getting out of bed is the hardest thing. After I'm over that hurdle the rest of the day is comparatively easy."

"Good."

"But I'm always depressed as soon as I wake up. It's like I'm disappointed that I didn't die in my sleep."

"Do you want to die?"

"Sometimes. I have reasons to live but I often forget them. Then I feel they can't really be too important if they're so forgettable."

"That's not true," Anglor said. "It's just that depression makes you forget everything except yourself, who you remember painfully, but as if you were already dead, as if you are nothing more than a memory of yourself."

Maria nodded. "I sometimes think I was more likeable when I was a teenager."

Anglor chuckled. "I doubt that. All those hormones: puberty, existential crises. You were probably a complete mess."

Maria laughed in turn. "Yes, I was. I just wish I could be young again."

"You are still young."

"And I'm afraid to be old."

"Why?'

"Because if I forget my reasons to live again even when I'm old, I might as well just die. And what if I'm still alone?"

Anglor sighed. "You won't be."

"How do you know?"

"I don't know. I don't know anything for certain."

She smiled at him wistfully, twirling one of the fake flowers on table in her hand. "Then don't make any promises," she said.

Anglor grinned at her weakly in return. "I suppose that applies to love more than anything. We do not know how long forever is. It could be no more than a year."

"You're strange," Maria said, still playfully. "I like you."

"I like you too, Maria."

"I just wish it wasn't so hard to get out of bed. I just feel ridiculous sometimes, living the same day over and over again. I feel like I should be able to die intermittently, then come back when I'm bored of death, and go when I'm bored of life."

"Then what do you do when you become bored of both of them?"

"I don't know. I suppose that's the halfway point to sanity. But still it's possible to only get half way."

"For some people that's as far as they can. And that's alright. I think some people actually need a little insanity, to keep everything from, becoming too dull."

"My insanity *is* what makes everything dull."

"You're not insane, you're just depressed. Insanity has a lot more verve to it."

"I suppose so. The thing that's so strange about it, I can't make art out of it. I mean, I thought that was what art was for, to express abstractedly how depressed you are to make the depression abstract as well. But it already is abstract, so I can't get it out into art. I can't even put it into words. Maybe that's all grief is, an inability to express grief."

"You're an artist? You never told me that."

"Sometimes. I don't take it too seriously, though, not like you do. I don't take anything seriously."

Anglpr shrugged. "Well, that's ok, I guess."

"I don't take anything seriously except my depression. It's like it's my boss."

Anglor tried to smile at her but couldn't. He drank his beer in silence, wondering what it was he was supposed to do, how he was supposed to make this planet feel less alone, starting with this girl. He found he couldn't express it either, it's magnitude was far too great for only one mind. He would have to make art out of it for the rest of his life, and still he would not be able to say it all. That was one at once good and deleterious thing about the planet Earth, there was always something to write about, too much to write about. He guessed it was a good thing that there were several writers in the world, but even if everyone was a writer, and everyone wrote about all they could in their short lives, still not all of it would be expressed. This was a good thing in the sense that it always gave someone with a restless, disconsolate imagination something to do, but it was a bad thing because even though there was so much of it, so much to write about, something no single generation of artists could tackle themselves, but all the artists through the length of time, it was also nothing, all these things to write about, all these issues to try to manage with oneiric, abstract imagination, really it was all nothing. They were writing about nothing at all in their fruitless quest to try to elucidate everything. It was trying to make sense of nothingness, something that has to be senseless in order to survive.

"What's wrong?" Maria suddenly asked. "Now you seem depressed too."

"It's nothing, I'm just thinking."

"That's how it always starts out, thinking, until you can't do anything else but think."

"What else is there to do?"

Maria nodded. "That's the sad part about it. Those people who never think but constantly divert themselves, they're the closest thing to happy humans know, and they're not happy. They're just as restless as everyone else, restlessly trying to avoid thought."

"Maybe you're right," Anglor said. "I try not to think about it."

Anglor was beginning to hate his job more and more. After it was discovered he'd break his back just to be liked they did indeed break his back. With each shift the work load was multiplied, and eventually Anglor couldn't keep up. He was nonplussed beyond belief, he was running and looking for a place to hide. He ran into the bathroom and locked himself in. Then he grabbed the box cutter and slit his wrist with it.

Once he had done it he immediately regretted it, but he was looking for a way to relieve the tension. It wasn't his six months due to commit suicide in order to be reborn. He had done it only after three months, and of his own volition, and not to be reborn, but to die. Ever since the mental hospital, the feeling of being stripped of free will, he had suddenly wanted to kill himself to die, and once he had had that feeling he could never shake it off completely. It would come back to him with semi regularity. It's always like that. Once you want to die you may not wish to die permanently, but the idea will still strike you from time to time, for the rest of your life, after you have broken the seal and wanted to die at least once.

Anglor looked in the mirror with his wrists bleeding profusely, his hands shaking, covered in his own sanguinary goop, and he cried "look what the Earth has done to me!" Those who try to save the world are those who are destroyed by it most. A customer walked in. Anglor went to go help them even with the bleeding wrists. He thought if he just acted like it wasn't happening then it wouldn't be happening. The customer gasped and suddenly Anglor became light headed. The customer dashed away, not bothering to call an ambulance or anything, and Anglor slowly blacked out.

When he awoke he was in the Emergency Room. Maria was standing over his bed.

"I'm, jealous," was all she said. "I don't have the nerve."

"Fuck you," Anglor whispered back in a tired, hollow, anechoic voice.

"You'll be alright. They're going to send you back to OHP though."

"Where?"

"Ohio Hospital for Psychiatry."

"That will make me want to die even more."

"At first, but eventually they'll give you the right medication…. How are you going to pay me rent now?"

"I'll get another job."

"Perhaps you should get on SSI."

"What's that?"

"Disabilities."

"Maybe I'll become a prostitute."

Maria laughed. "You're not good looking enough for that," she said teasingly. "But it doesn't matter. I don't mind if you can't pay me rent for a few months."

"Really? What made you change your mind?"

She grabbed him by the hand, lightly touching the fresh garish scar that was on his left wrist. "You're my friend," she said. "I have to protect you."

"I promise I'll get back up on my feet quickly."

"Maybe you shouldn't. Maybe you need to lie down for a little while."

Anglor smiled up at her and squeezed her hand. "Thank you, Maria," he said. "For everything."

Then the doctor came in. "The ambulance is here for you," he said. "We're sending you to OHP."

Anglor nodded and started getting his stuff ready. Maria deftly kissed him on the cheek, in a very clandestine manner. Then she drifted out as if she'd never been there. Anglor sighed as they put him on the stretcher. It was a long way to OHP, which was in Columbus, about thirty miles from Dayton. Maria had given him her Ipod so he could have music to listen to on the way. He neurotically listened to the same song the entire way there. He had been in the emergency room for eighteen hours without food, and his stomach started to groan. He had been pink slipped again, he was on an involuntary psychiatric hold. When he finally got to the hospital the same nurse who was there last time was checking him in again.

"Oh, Michael," he said. "Why are you here?"

"I tried to kill myself to die instead of kill myself to be reborn," and then he took off the bandages and showed the man the scars.

"Okay," was all he said, without any surprise. He had seen this many times., and eventually it had worn his compassion down into little particles he then swept away. This was what he was like now, surprised by nothing, so the joie de verve of life was gone after having seen too many people actively try to die, having gotten to that sad point where they were more frightened of life than death, though they were frightened of both. Death was so much easier, though, and that seems to be the divine quest of people on Earth, to make things easy. If things weren't easy you were doing something wrong, you were wrong, if your life was difficult you became hard and insensate, blind to both life and death, carrying on for no reason whatsoever, just doing it because it is what you have always done, being used to society shunning you for not having an idyllic life that meant even less than a tragic one.

"Your room is this way," the nurse said, directing him to another uncomfortable bed. "You have a roommate this time," he said.

Anglor looked in on his roommate. He was fast asleep, but he was a tall man who was, like Anglor, blessed with absolutely no pulchritude, who had a long beard and drooping bags under his eyes. Anglor went to sleep in the bed next to his, but still he could not sleep. In the next room he could hear two people fucking, the nurses doing nothing about it, so he put a pillow over his ears and tried to drown it out.

The next morning he was exhausted as he always was the first night he entered this place, and the same old feeling came over him, that he had no free will. In fact, that was why he tried to kill himself off schedule, so he could get his free will back. His job was taking it from him as well, and to our young aspirant felo de se, free will was everything, it was the only viable reason to live or die. Without it he didn't think one was human anymore. And the people who tried to take free will were worse than the people who gave it up willingly in their quests for an easy life. Anglor felt life had to be a little difficult, because often the closest we can get to meaning is in complexity, though everyone will try to simplify it away, everyone will try to cure it with clichés.

That's what they did in the mental hospital, too. Every night there was an AA meeting. Anglor was perhaps the only patient on the ward who didn't have a problem with addiction, and he figured that was only because he hadn't been on Earth long enough, he was somewhat of a newborn. But people who have lived on Earth their whole lives, their only consolation was the bottle, and AA was trying to take it away from them, because it was killing them, but most of them did want to die. It was a way to make life simple that in the end made it unnecessarily difficult with the way it obliterated everything., especially consciousness.

But AA did try to cure it with clichés, as if it were a stereotypical mother and house wife. Anglor couldn't see that ever working on him, because he loathed clichés, he loathed people's instinctive urge to make the complex so simple it didn't mean anything anymore, of trying to put life into a box where it would be contained like some zoo animal, so you can only be its spectator, it was keeping life prisoner in the bounds of a false simplicity, a half truth, something uttered flippantly, without much thought, that was what people were trying to turn life into. Anglor figured the AA people thought all the clichés would work because if life was simple why would anyone need to drink? But life wasn't simple, far from it, and one could never hope to make it simple, in fact, to wish it to be simple is only to make it more complex, because then you are fighting against its nature.

Besides AA meetings there was nothing else to do but draw. Most people colored in adult coloring books, with quite deft precision and anal retentiveness, but most people on the ward were not creative. He was the only true artist, he was the only person who could draw things that came from his head like Athena, though much more ugly, and the other patients marveled at it. "I just don't have the patience to do something like that," they would say, and Anglor would smile.

"It doesn't take patience," he would say, "only suicidal tendencies." But the more he stayed in the mental hospital the more he found to his dismay that crazy people aren't really special, that most of them are of average intellect and average taste, they seem like everyone else, the only thing different about them being that they want to kill themselves, and they were more anomic than most people, having been turned rotten not from the inside but the outside, the society they were in degenerating rapidly and degenerating the people in it as well, dragging them down with it, and both were at fault, people for destroying society and society for destroying people Anglor grew tired of them all. He was tired of America and he was already tired of Earth. He was sent here to help people but only found that he couldn't help himself, and he didn't think the Earth was capable of changing. The moon wasn't capable of changing, either, being a mundane utopia where nothing ever happened, so all they had to do was watch the Earth, where something was always happening, no matter how deleterious. The people here had adjusted to atrocity, and easily, too, as a survival mechanism, and that was the real madness.

Anglor started talking less and less. All his sentences became lost to aposiopesis as he'd start a sentence and then it would rapidly fade into a pathetic morendo. There was nothing to say, and yet there was too much to say, as well, but he didn't want to say it anymore, he didn't want to say anything at all. So he spent most of his time at OHP in silence, or starting sentences he couldn't finish, because the medicine had made his thoughts disjointed until they could only be half formed conceptions, bastard children of the mind whose father had abandoned them after only having partially created them, so they had to limp off deformed into the ether, back into non- existence. But in spite of this his art was unharmed,. He drew voraciously now, after being unable to completely think or to completely speak.

Slowly he adjusted to the new medication and it started to get better. He was able to read again, which he wasn't when they first put him on the medication. It had initially made him feel that half his brain was thoughts but half these thoughts were nothing but air, and the other half of his brain, he didn't even know what it was since it had become so atrophied. But he adjusted, as people do at all costs. They even adjust to adjusting, realizing it's all you can do to live. They even adjusted to things no one should adjust to, things that should be anathema to anyone of sense. Anglor had even adjusted to this damn mental hospital, and the was the saddest thing, knowing in his mind that he would always be insane, so long as he was on Earth.

And so far he hadn't helped anyone except maybe Maria. He tried to think of Maria as if she were the whole world, and really if he could heal her he could heal anybody. She came to visit him a few times, not everyday, but enough to where Anglor could see she gave a damn about him, and he deeply appreciated it, because at this point he didn't give a damn about himself, he thought he should leave himself at the side of the road, refuse that would take centuries to biodegrade, but at least he wouldn't have to carry it around anymore. He would be the Earth's problem then, the Earth would no longer be his problem. But maybe it was already like this, the world being contaminated by humans just as humans were contaminated by the world. But they invented the world as it is now. They simply contaminated themselves, the Earth before them was just lush verdant fields and blue sky and animals that were able to kill one another for the only good reason to kill something, to ingest food, and no one being angry about it, all things on Earth realizing this is just how it is. Nothing killed members of its own species, that was also a human invention. It was the same with the rotten society. We are being destroyed by our creations as a reprisal for destroying them.

Eventually they let Anglor out, but it was the same as last time. They kept him for quite awhile. He knew not to mention he was from the moon again. This they called progress. To be considered sane you have to lie your ass off, and not tell them what you know, to pretend you know nothing, and then you will appear normal. Anglor was beginning to accept that on Earth he was mad, though. He realized that on Earth any modicum of talent or genius had to come with handicaps, because no human being can be Godlike. And for the time being Anglor was human. It was incredibly painful and awkward even for people who had always been human, having a head full of nothing but desires and all of them being conflicting, many of them even being harmful. The whole species itself was mad. Often he thought the people who were deemed insane were only the people who could not adjust to these conditions, and Anglor felt this smacked a little bit of sanity.

They let him out and he went back home to Maria, the only place on Earth he felt safe. She picked him up from the hospital and they drove home quietly, stopping for something to eat on the way which of course Maria had to pay for. She didn't kvetch, though, as Anglor expected she would. She was mostly just worried about him.

"Sorry about what I said in the hospital."

"What?"

"That I was jealous."

"Oh," Anglor said, and continued masticating his food.

"I meant it, though," Maria went on. "I really was jealous."

"Well, as you can see it didn't really work out for me."

"I'm glad it didn't."

Anglor smiled and grabbed her hand. "Me too…. I think."

"They brainwashed you into wanting to live, didn't they?"

"Yes, but that's okay. Anyone in any profession does that, particularly advertising, marketing. Life itself brainwashes you into staying alive.. You have to stay alive in order to buy things."

"It's just that no one knows if non-existence is better, because no one remembers it, and you can't ask someone who's dead, either. So I think wanting to die is just an insatiable curiosity, wanting to bite the forbidden fruit of not being alive and no longer buying things. It's just wanting to know what it's like, if it is better or not."

"But if it's not better you can't go back."

"I think you can't even tell the difference."

"Probably not, since you've lost all consciousness."

Maria looked down at Anglor's hand covering her own. It was rugose and pale, covered in lines as if he had lived through the whole century. She gently placed it off of her hand. Anglor smiled weakly and withdrew it completely. He had always felt sorry for Earth women. The things they had to put up with from men, and the way they did it just because they knew they had to continue carrying on the species- they never thought of their own lives, only of their children's lives, and in that way they thought only of the life of the entire species, them being the vessels of this life, only requiring men for the moment of ejaculation, to fertilize the egg. But what they had to put up with from men to continue this species, it would be unendurable to men, who were to women barely symbiotic parasites, something that fed off them that they endured because of their sperm, so they could continue continuing the species. And then childbirth. The incredible pain, all the blood. No woman enjoyed it, they simply did it because they knew they had to. They had a strange sense of purpose that way, while men did not. Men rather floated around aimlessly getting whatever they wanted and ejaculating. They did not have the same direct and sedulous way of women, who knew if there was a God he created them for a reason, and not only the reason of childbirth, but many other reasons. Men just felt they were able to own whom or whatever without having to claim any responsibility over it.

'In this brief moment Anglor hated himself for being a man. But he was not an Earth man. He was a Selenite, so his body was a little different. He didn't have a penis but rather a gaping proboscis in his mid section, that also fertilized eggs and got women pregnant, in a similar viviparous situation that mammals and particularly humans had. It was also a little saprogenic, just like it was on Earth. The existence of life must be paid for with decay, and as the child grew in the erumpent belly the mother slowly began to die, this being the catalyst to her eventual non-existence, this taking years off her life, this being a great sacrifice of biology that no one hailed anymore because it had been the norm since the species existence. It was like that on the moon, too. He felt very sorry for women. They were all martyrs to the species, to the continued existence of human life, and he wasn't sure they enjoyed any of it, even the rearing of the child, though of course they always loved the child, bringing it up wasn't pleasant either, the child being as much of a burden truly alive as it was intrauterine.

Anglor wanted to apologize to Maria, for being a man. But he didn't say anything. He just sat watching Maria watching him, though they were both so shy to the point of scopophobia, they still watched each other, as if they were two mirrors looking into each other, so of course there was no reflection, only a half assed mise en abyme of glass and light, a hollow refraction, a false eternity in a Gorgon stare. They looked at each other and saw nothing. They were both hollow, an empty chamber for one another's echoes. Anglor sighed. He was a barely symbiotic parasite to a woman who was caring for him like he was a child. But he did feel like a child. He felt like a newborn on this planet, he felt incredibly vulnerable and anaclitic, trusting no one but his mother figure, Maria. He had heard about Freud. He was sad to feel that the man had been right, that we are all disgusting incestuous creatures who care only for sex and murder, starting with the confines and delimitations of the family, then in adulthood projected onto all of society, in the acts of sex and death, fucking and world war. Society was like the father, and we its Oedipal inhabitants want to murder it.

As Anglor thought of this he threw back his glass of wine down his palate and thought to himself spitefully, 'screw you, AA. This is the only consolation life has to offer.'

"Did they make you find a higher power?" Maria suddenly asked, almost reading his mind.

"They tried to. I take it you're not religious?"

"No, only extremely masochistic women are religious, which is unfortunately most of them, but that's what they've been taught to be,"

Anglor nodded and didn't say anything.

"Every religion has a misogynistic element to it," Maia continued.

"Don't worry," Anglor said stoically. "They're just jealous."

"Who?'

"Men. Men are jealous of women, white people are jealous of black people, heterosexuals are jealous of homosexuals…."

"Why do you think that is? Why would they be jealous? I mean, it's much easier to be a straight white man than to be a woman, black, or gay."

"They're jealous because they have had to fit in the same mold their entire lives. People who aren't like them fit into no mold, no matter how much they try to make them with the ubiquitous cruelty and power of stereotypes. Believe me, Maria, we only ever enslave people we are envious of for being too free."

Maria nodded. "I think you're right. Maybe all prejudice is envy. But they are envying people who have much harder lives than they do."

"Well, that is the price of talent, as well as freedom. Talented people are never what people expect them to be, they are never the norm or the imagined construct of what the masses think a talented person should be. They are generally neither rich nor good looking, they usually have nothing except their talent. I imagine the second coming is going to be an asthenic black man with glasses who got his ass kicked everyday at school…"

"I doubt the second coming would be American. He or she was probably already barrel bombed in Syria."

Anglor laughed and continued downing his wine. "It's strange. You're right, no one should be jealous of these people, whose lives are much harder, but then again, they should be jealous, because these people are unique, original, and have something that is inherently missing in the people who envy them, the people who otherwise have it all."

"What is that?"

"The fact that they are unexpected, not so mundanely predictable. The fact that they have a rich well of life going through their veins, the fact that they are truly alive, perhaps in desperation and privation, but this only makes them more vivid, more pulsing, more alive. The fact that they are everything we are erroneously taught are lesser, but we find are much greater, who go on now matter how much they have been cheated, exacting no revenge besides being themselves, exactly what people envy of them."

Maria grinned. "I like those people."

"So do I."

They went home and to their separate beds as usual. Anglor had trouble sleeping again. His bed at home really wasn't that much more comfortable than the one at the mental hospital, but eventually he slept, and his dreams were disturbed. He dreamt he and Maria were trying to fuck. Trying, but they were having trouble doing it because they were both covered with spikes, and every time they tried to touch each other they would stab one another with the pricks, it was like they were copulating pieces of barbed wire. But they needed to fuck for some reason, though Anglor didn't know the reason, he didn't know the reason why anybody fucked except to feel a little less alienated for a moment. So they fucked in spite of their long spikes, and as they fucked they both impaled each other, and they died right there on the bed. Then, as they bled to death together, the spikes finally disappeared, they were finally free from the foibles that made it hard to get close together, but it didn't matter much now because they were dead, but would at least never feel the need to get close to anyone again, try to get close to anyone when they were covered in defensive spikes. It was a terrifying concupiscent *liebestod* of suicide achieved through sex, as often both Anglor and Maria's only wish was to die. But at least they had gotten close to one another first, though that was what had killed them. Anglor rolled over lazily as he woke up, still half dreaming, and thought to himself 'these damn spikes,' but they were all he had to protect him.

He woke up and tried to shake off the nightmare. Maria was in the kitchen making coffee, listening to miles Davis' "Blue in Green," on repeat. She always did this when she was feeling lonely. She said the song expressed loneliness perfectly. It was the damn spikes again, that were making her feel this way. Hegel had said something about it before, that they were the origin of distant politeness. He stayed in bed for a moment and just listened to "Blue in Green." Maria was right, it did express loneliness perfectly. That was the one thing Anglor could not express in art, besides all his drawings of aliens which if he were human would have represented a complex, cosmic loneliness and alienation, but for him, being a Selenite, was just homesickness. Maybe they were the same. Maybe humans miss outer space, as well, missing the time when they were nothing more than bits of stardust and the refuse of nebulas.

Maria sometimes tried to write, but the problem with her writing was that she had read so much often she got moments of cryptomnesia where she would write things that had already been written, but she did manage to say it in a different way. She liked to write while she listened to "Blue in Green," almost relishing in the loneliness, becoming one with it. It was the only time when her spikes didn't bother her. It wasn't better, or even particularly pleasant, it was only easier. Anglor grabbed his coffee and sat next to her lighting a cigarette. She didn't say anything to him. Anglor thought about how strange life is. It is a poison we never want to stop drinking- no matter how hard it gets, no matter how unsatisfying it remains, we always want more of it, as if it is a food that will never make us full, that doesn't even taste good, but which we keep eating because it's the only thing on the menu. He sighed and slumped down on the couch.

"You alright?" Maria asked.

He waved her off dismissively. "I'm fine." They were simply sharing loneliness together, listening to "Blue in Green." It was the loneliness of the Earth, that was really green in blue, a few continents and land masses all moored in a world full of ocean, and Anglor was not sure what prevented it all from drowning, especially considering how suicidal it was. Anglor wasn't sure why it never committed suicide, threw itself in the larger ocean, what made up most of the Earth. He read somewhere that deep sea fish were the largest habitat on Earth, a bunch of monsters living in darkness, unsure when the next meal would come. That was most of the planet. That was most of its human, too.

Anglor got the hint that Maria didn't want to talk and he headed back to his bedroom with his cup of coffee. He was soon due for his biannual suicide, but he didn't know how he was going to be able to do it without being sent back to the mental hospital again. He would have to do it when Maria wasn't home, and hopefully he would be reborn by the time she got back. It was important, though, he knew he had to do it. If you skip your biannual suicide you won't live to be one hundred, but the more Anglor thought about it he wasn't sure he did want to live to be one hundred, he wasn't sure he wanted that much of the food that never makes you full. But it was tradition,. It was what he had done very six months since he was born, and at the moment he missed home too much not to abide by its rules. If he stopped acting like a Selenite he would soon become an earthling, and he didn't want that. His suicides were what separated him from humans.

And besides, though tradition was often hollow at least it made you feel you belong in some sort of tribe, a shibboleth, however empty, but still one that lets you know you're part of something, even if it is miniscule and idiotic, with tradition at least you are not an outcast. So Anglor began planning his suicide. Tradition was something not worth being honored that you have to honor anyway, if you want to belong, and Anglor knew he did not belong on the Earth, the green in blue loneliness, so he at least wanted to still belong to the moon, his home that had sent him here with seemingly no other ostensible reason than to torture him.

He also applied for disabilities, so he wouldn't have to work anymore. Human work was very difficult for a Selenite, but he still needed to pay Maria rent. As he was in his bedroom musing suddenly there was a loud, obstreperous noise coming from his closet. He opened it. It was Bogomil.

"What are you doing here?"

"What's wrong with you?' Bogomil said sharply.

"What?"

"You actually tried to kill yourself?"

"You guys are watching me?"

"Yes, we are. Is the Earth really so bad?"

"It is. But at the same time it's wonderful."

"Then why did you slit your wrists?"

"Working here is particularly agonizing."

"You need to get it together. You're supposed to be a beacon of hope to these people…"

"How can I be a beacon of hope when I am hopeless?"

"It's tricky, but it can be done, It's called martyrdom."

"Which is the same as suicide, only a holy one."

Bogomil sighed. "Not all martyrs have to die," he said.

Both of them suddenly became stock still as Maria knocked on the door. "Michael?" she called. "Who are you talking to in there?"

"I'm on the phone Maria."

Then she left without saying anything more. Bogomil was silent until her footsteps were across the other side of the apartment and he continued in a harried whisper. "Listen," he said. "You have an obligation to this planet…" "Why? I'm not even from here."

"You live here now, and anyone who lives on Earth has an obligation to it."

"Why? It doesn't feel any obligation to us."

"That's because it's a large rock, it doesn't feel. And it doesn't need to be obligated to you, you need to be obligated to it, and for yourself, if you want to make the place bearable to live in. That's the only reason it's not at the moment, because people don't feel obligated to it, they act as if it will always be here."

"But I'm not always going to be here…"

"Neither are the people on Earth. No one is born inherently with a purpose, you acquire it by accident, just like you have acquired this obligation to Earth. It is harboring you right now. Whatever harbors you you are in debt to."

"But I don't want to be here."

"No one does. If you don't like this planet you have to change it, because I'm telling you now you'll be here for awhile."

"Is the Earth even capable of changing?"

Bogomil sighed and eased up a little bit from his sanctimony. "I don't know, Anglor," he said. "I honestly don't know. But we must still try."

"Why do you care so much?"

"Because I think this planet is the only planet that has potential for being truly beautiful. The moon is different. The moon is just a cold rock with microscopic creatures on it. It will never be paradise."

"The Earth is not paradise."

"No, but it should be. It deserves that."

"Do its people?"

"Most of them honestly do. The regular people, not the people in power…"

"Some of the regular people are just as hateful."

"Yes, because that's what they've been taught to be. In their hearts they're really not, though. They have just been corrupted by the powers that be. They are, admittedly, not very intelligent. But they are not bad, not really. Most human beings want to be good, honestly they do, it's just society stops them from doing it. Society wants them to be indifferent."

Anglor at last sighed as well and gave up his argument. "Okay," he said. "Okay."

"It's your job to let them know it's okay to be good, though it will leave them vulnerable, but you have to be so in order to be good."

"Do you really think they'll listen to me?"

Bogomil shrugged. "I have no idea. But if you at least try you will be absolved of all of humanity's sins, though you will commit many of them. Everyone does, though. It's an instinct. You have to learn evil firsthand if you want to be capable of good…"

"Most humans do neither."

Bogmil smiled. "But you're different, aren't you?"

Anglor chuckled. "Of course I'm different. I'm not human."

"I find you incredibly human. I always have. That's why I chose you for this. And I mean that as a compliment."

"Why? Why do you think I'm human?"

"Because you will always be strange everywhere."

"Great."

Bogomil chuckled again and put a hand on Anglor's shoulder. "I have to go now," he said. "But I have faith in you. Just no more extra curricular suicides, okay?"

"Okay."

Then Bogomil disappeared through the wall, as Selenites are able to do. Maria knocked on the door again. "Come in!" Anglor roared a little brusquely.

"Not on the phone anymore?"

"No."

"It sounded like an interesting conversation. I didn't know you had other friends."

"He's not really my friend."

"Then what is he?"

Anglor looked dazedly into the empty space between his bed and the window, as if he were grateful that there was nothing there. "My boss."

"What?" Maria said, bewildered. "You got a job?"

"More like an assignment."

"What is it?"

"I'm supposed to make the world a better place."

Maria smiled at him sanguinely. "I'm sure you will," she said.

Anglor smiled back. "There's more coffee if you want some," Maria went on.

"Okay," he said, and he was suddenly very happy when he realized they were not always covered in spikes, that sometimes they were able to be vulnerable with each other, without breaking one another when they were most delicate. Anglor felt incredibly relieved. They were two depressed people living together, and while they could not make one another less depressed, they were able to make themselves feel wanted, at least by someone. Anglor knew Maria wasn't right for him because she was an Earthling, but at least they felt comfortable around each other, comfortable enough to remove their spikes.

Anglor went in the other room to receive his coffee. Maria had at last stopped playing "Blue in Green" and had put something else in the CD player. They were feeling slightly less lonely. For the moment the wish to die was abated, abated the only way it can be, with companionship, the only other thing that can abate it being perhaps purpose, though purpose is hardly a comfort, it's just a reason to keep going. And Anglor's purpose was forced on him, inherited unwillingly, but now that he thought about it, it was a reason to go on, and he realized there is nothing else viable to do with one's life on Earth than what he had been assigned.

He was due for his six month suicide. He had planned it out well. He had bought a small revolver from a gun store in Dayton and waited patiently for Marias to go to work. He put the gun against his temple. The cold steel felt good there, as if it were the cure for a headache, the headache of existence. But Anglor didn't want to completely die, not this time, he was merely honoring an ancient tradition, so he did not feel completely like an Earthling, though Earthlings often survived suicides, as well. But they were not reborn from it, they were simply disappointed in themselves, and already plotting the day when they would try it again. He let the cool steel of the gun relax his temple for a moment and then he quickly pulled the trigger, like tearing off a band- aid. The other residents of his and Maria's apartment complex heard the gunshot, but they didn't do anything, as Anglor was counting on, they simply locked their doors.

Maria arrived home shortly after, and saw the presumably dead body with the gunshot wound to the head. She covered her hand over her mouth so no one could hear her scream as tears flowed out of her eyes. She gently picked up the body and inspected it.

"You really did it this time," she whispered. "I'm sorry. I was too focused on my own depression, I didn't know yours was so bad."

But as she held the body it slumped on the ground, and an odd sigh came out of it.

"Anglor?' Maria asked tentatively, her eyes slowly locking at all the blood and bits of brain on the wall. "You can't really be alive."

Then the body started to convulse and out of the small bullet hole in the temple something began festering. Maria came to look more closely. Out of the bullet hole she could see a single eyeball swiveling around, observing its surroundings. Then another matching eyeball came up. Then a whole face, Anglor's face.

Maria did not even try to mask her scream this time. Everyone in the complex must have heard it, so more locked doors. Maria screamed and screamed and began to piss herself as slowly, out of that small cranial bullet hole, a full body crawled out, Anglor's full body He crawled out of the bullet hole completely, then shook himself a little bit, trying to get all of the blood off him. It really did look like he had just been born, he didn't scream though, as people often do both coming into the world and going out of it. He merely looked mildly at his reflection in the mirror. He noticed he was completely naked, covered in blood, and then he heard Maria's scream.

He quickly covered his proboscis like genitals and apologized.

"What the hell is going on?" Maria asked shakily.

"I was due for it," Anglor said. "My six month suicide in order to be reborn."

Maria with a shaking hand removed Anglor's hands from what she supposed was his penis. She saw the proboscis, the sucker mouthed hole at the top, the vermiform shape, and she whimpered a little bit. "My God," she said. "You really are from the moon."

"I'm surprised you reached that conclusion so quick," Anglor said as he began washing the blood off his body stridgel like in the sink. "Most Earthlings think it's impossible."

"Well,' Maria said, at last calmed down. "I've come to learn anything is possible. Anything except God."

"Well the universe is much more amazing than God. Believe me, I've seen it. But it's also mostly lifeless."

Maria grunted. "Take a shower," she said. "And get some clothes on."

"Yes Ma'am."

"What are we going to do about the body?"

Anglor chucked and winked at her. "What body?" he said, and Maria looked for the cadaver that was there only a moment ago and it was gone.

"So, it's the custom on the moon to commit suicide sometimes?"

"Yes. Once every six months, in order to be reborn."

"So last time…"

"No," Anglor said with the quiet lassitude of shame. "I really meant it that time."

"Has that ever happened to you before?"

"Again, only since I reached Earth."

Marisa paused for a minute and then gave Anglor a towel to cover himself with. "Your penis is even more ugly than human penises."

"Thanks."

"So…Why are you here?"

"On Earth?"

"Yes."

"Honestly, I'm not sure. My instructions were not clear, but I'm supposed to make this planet better somehow, more inhabitable. I think I'm supposed to give humans a lesson in forgiveness."

"So you're like some kind of alien Jesus?"

Anglor chuckled. "I'm not like Jesus," he said. "I don't intend to be crucified. I'm not going to teach forgiveness by being unforgiven. Or maybe I am, and maybe I will be crucified, but not literally."

"How are you going to do it then, this lesson in forgiveness?"

"The only way I know how to. With art."

"Was Jesus from the moon, too?"

"I thought you were an atheist."

"I am, I'm just wondering now if every messiah has been sent from outer space."

"I'm not a messiah."

"You've been given a messiah's job."

"Yes, but I can do it without actually being a messiah. It is the task of a regular human being."

"But you're not a human being either," Maria rebutted, gesturing mildly to the towel that was covering his grotesque penis.

Anglor sighed. "I'm just like anyone else on Earth," he said. "I don't know why I'm here, I just know I have a job to do. "He then looked around and saw a bit of his old brain sliding down the wall. "Christ," he groaned and gestured towards it. "My head is so full there's no more room for a brain. And yet it's empty."

"Blame the media," Maria said.

"Blame America."

"Blame Planet Earth."

Anglor sighed. "And the bit of intelligence I do possess I owe to my insanity."

"Well, that's your brain." Maria also watched it slowly sliding down the wall. "You better clean this up."

"I will, don't worry. That's part of the ritual."

"I wish I could kill myself so casually."

"You have drinking and smoking."

Maria laughed. "You're so clever, Michael," she said, and then paused. "Michael," she said, as if tasting the word for a moment to see how it felt. "That can't be your real name."

"No, my real name is Anglor."

"Take a shower," she said. "You're covered in your own blood, born from your own womb…"

"My brain."

"You're both Zeus and Athena. Born out of your own brain…"

"Reborn out of my own brain."

"Does that mean you're not mad anymore?"

"For now. Until I have to be reborn again."

"You do it so easily," Maria said. "For earthlings it's extremely difficult. And when we shoot ourselves in the head we don't come crawling back out of it."

Anglor looked puzzled at his fingertips, thinking. "I imagined myself," he said slowly. "That's how I came to exist."

"Better than being imagined by anyone else. Everyone else is exactly like their parents, that's why everyone is the same."

Anglor chuckled. "I'm going to take a shower now," he said.

"Good. I need it after you…I pissed myself."

"I'm sorry, Maria."

"I really thought you were dead."

"I was. You have to die in order to be reborn." Then Anglor quickly turned on the hot water in the shower and Maria changed her pants. As Anglor showered he thought Maria was like a fire, something that can keep you warm but which you still can't get too close to, something mesmerizing and pleasant but also dangerous. She was something that killed martyrs, though unknowingly, she was just the tool for it, it was the judge, jury and executioner who really killed the martyr, but Maria was the crucible in which they burned. She was quite a muse. Anglor knew she didn't want to be a muse, though, she wanted to be an artist, but she was too flame like, she was too much like destruction, her sorrow would one day burn the world. Perhaps it already had.

He watched morosely as the blood he had been washing off his body went down the drain. 'There goes the last memory of my old body,' he thought to himself, then he looked at his body. It looked the same, just fresher, the skin softer, no more rugose hands, as if he were a grown up infant. He was glad every time he became reborn he didn't come back crying like humans do when they are first born, as if they are mourning the loss of the womb, a home they can never return to and will soon forget completely, their new home being reality, the world of the living, a hostile, cold environment where once you are done being a baby you are then at the mercy of ubiquitous indifference. Anglor thought he should have screamed like an infant when he fell to Earth, but he was too busy watching the stars. It was better that way.

Anglor got out of the shower and dried off, then started cleaning the blood and bits of brain from the wall. He picked up a piece of his extant cerebrum and laughed to himself. "It's hard to believe this is my soul," he said. Maria was in her bedroom preparing to do her laundry. Anglor looked at her. She was beautiful in an arcane way, in an abstruse way, a kind of intellectual beauty, not made for every man, but acroamatic, for a special erudite few.

"I'm done with the shower," he called. "I'm cleaning up my brain."

"Good," Maria said. "It does get tainted sometimes."

Anglor shrugged. "It gets filled with garbage. I'm glad I'm able to be reborn every six months. I do not envy you humans with your one life."

"Maybe only once makes it more special."

Anglor raised an eyebrow. "Does it?"

"Not at all."

Anglor got on disabilities, and was able to pay Maria rent again, without having to work. This was good, because this way he could focus on art, the world's only salvation. He decided that was his job, especially considering it was his reason to be on Earth, and he found it was a good reason. And it was strange, since he had been on Earth his art had gotten better, more passionate because he was in more pain. On the moon his art had been lifelessly idyllic statues and the like, Apollonian art, as Nietzsche would have it, but since he had been on Earth his art had become Dionysian, not the casual, easy going, and heartless art of the cultured bourgeois, who had nothing to mourn, but the art of a true artist, someone who mourned everything, and it was dark, savage, baleful and surreal- it frightened some people. That's how Anglor knew it was good. He was no longer making art for the comfortable, he was making art for the damned. This was what happened to him as an artist after he had hit rock bottom, in other words, landed on Earth. It was no longer for the bourgeois, it was *epater le bourgeois*, and yet it was not for the common man, either. It was for other lunatics, for other artists.

He got better and better at this new kind of art that was grotesque and unsettling, and he had a little bit of success. He sold some paintings and he was put in a few art galleries. He did not know it yet, but fame was right around the corner. It came slowly though, as it always does to someone who has truly earned it, it only ever comes quickly to someone who has fallen into it by mere chance, someone who is not truly talented. Jean Cocteau spoke of the evil of instant fame, that it is an idol we should stop bowing down to, it is a false idol. In fact, it is Faustian, it comes at the price of the soul, and Anglor was slowly coming to find out that those who are willing to sell their soul really had no soul to begin with, so it is an empty gift, and that is why the devil is so impoverished. These were the people who became famous instantly, their name up in lights with a mere flipping of the switch. To those who have earned it, though, those people spend many years in poverty and darkness, unable to sell their soul because they have one, unable to make much money or eat much or do anything except their art, their greatest misery and their sole salvation. This was the route by which Anglor eventually found fame, not by stumbling into it blindly, but by building his own ladder to it, which was incredibly difficult to build, and even more difficult to climb, for it went so high and still it did not reach to heaven.

He went about fame the right way, the respectable way, the way that you do not become just an extravagant chattel of the public, but as someone people could genuinely admire. And this road is incredibly long, so long you think you'll die on the way, but people like Anglor, miraculously and against all odds, make it to the end, they achieve the desired goal walking along the proverbial road less traveled, which is anfractuous, thin, tenebrous, and perilous, and, as I said, incredibly long. Then when people like Anglor get to the end of this road they realize it only keeps going, and they are relieved, for they have been travelling this road for most of their lives now, and they know no other route, no other road to travel., and no other way to live. There will always be more art to create, which means there will always be more struggle, more sweat, and more work to be done, enough that it can fill someone's entire life. It would be many a long, arduous years before Anglor was famous, and many people would write him off as a loser, someone who couldn't even make it to the bottom of the ladder, but he wouldn't mind. He knew how he had to live, and that was as an artist and nothing else, he could not be an attendant at the gas station at the same time. And he found he liked a quiet life, it kept him from being unnerved.

The amount of money he got from disabilities was not very much, though, and often at the end of the month he was penniless. He thought perhaps he should get another job. This was a bad idea, he came to find. He really couldn't work, because he wasn't from this planet and couldn't comprehend this menial borderline slave labor. There was many things still about planet Earth he could not understand, although he had been here about a year now and felt it was his home for the time being. Really he didn't think anywhere was his home, not rock bottom, Earth, and not the heavens, outer space and the moon. He began to realize that he was a drifter even when he was standing still, because he did not belong anywhere. But there's one thing about Earth- if you want to inhabit it properly you need to have money, so Anglor got his job at the gas station back.

So of course it wasn't long until he had to return to the mental hospital. He was at the emergency room for another eighteen hours. They would not let him go to the psych ward because he was not suicidal, which means one has already made a plan to commit suicide. Anglor thought it must have been a little late by then. 'No wonder so many people kill themselves,' he muttered to himself. It felt like the doctors didn't give a shit, that no one gave a shit about the mentally ill. Eugenics is alive and well in America, that's why Anglor made a pittance and had to get that horrible job again to begin with. And America had done a number on him. It had convinced him that he was actually mad, not just an alien.

Maria sat by his bed at the hospital again. "I told you you shouldn't have gotten that job."

"But I have no money."

"Get on food stamps, that way you can at least eat every month. And buy cheaper cigarettes."

"Okay," he said.

"It'll be alright, Anglor."

"Shhh," he said. "They still think my name is Michael."

"Do you miss the moon right now?"

"I never get homesick."

"So the Earth is better?"

"No, it's not, but it's not worse. At least this civilization is alive, though it is extremely corrupted. Everything is dead on the moon. That's why it's so peaceful, it's like a tomb in the stars. The Earth is like a menagerie in the sky. It's full of life. That's its problem. There's too much life, all competing to stay alive."

"So you don't like either?"

"They are two polar extremes. In fact, the Earth is the polar extreme of the whole universe. Animals don't know this, but humans know this, that's why they feel so alone, they know what an anomaly they are and what an anomaly they are living in."

Maria chuckled. "You're the philosopher."

Anglor grabbed her by the hand. "It doesn't matter how insane they think I am," he said. "I know I am living my life well, and I regret none of it, even the madness which is the price I have to pay for it."

"You talk like you're dying. And you're not mad, Anglor, you're just from the moon."

"Oh yea."

"Have you already forgotten?"

"No, it just slips my mind sometimes."

"Don't get too used to the Earth, okay."

"Why?"

"I would give that same advise to all the people who live here, the people who have lived nowhere else, which is all people except you. I'm not only saying it because you're an alien. I think Earthlings should do the same."

"Why? They have nowhere else to go."

Maria sighed but didn't say anything. The doctor came in. Anglor was being pink slipped again. Anglor sighed. "This is a nightmare that keeps really happening."

"I'm sure it does feel like that," the doctor said tacitly, then left the room.

Anglor groaned and rolled over. "At least they're not taking me to OHP. They're taking me to a place called KBMC. It's closer."

"Do you really think it's going to be any different?"

"No. Probably not."

Maria squeezed his hand. "If it's a nightmare you'll wake up. If the earth is just a nightmare, you'll wake up from it. Be glad. Human beings don't get that option."

"They die," Anglor said. "That's how they wake up from the nightmare, by going to sleep."

"Jesus," Maria groaned. "You utilize far too often the part of your head that screams."

"My mouth?"

"Your brain."

"Well, what other part of my head am I supposed to utilize? I have nothing else."

The doctor then walked in with a stretcher and two paramedics. They loaded him on the stretcher and Maria politely looked away. For a moment she was crying. Anglor was dead silent. In the ambulance ride over there the paramedics asked him an enfilade of questions he found he couldn't answer. He just shook his head docilely either yes or no. He thought of Maria. She was a nice woman, and she was exactly like him, she was built to endure abuse, they both were, because they were both those extremely rare people who are truly passive, and such people are always abused, and have a higher tolerance for it than anyone else due to their peaceful nature and their inability to lie. But since both Maria and Anglor were this way they were lucky to live together, they would never abuse one another. They had managed to create a refuge from normal people, who are always abrasive and will always take advantage of someone they perceive to be weaker than them, and built a safe haven of two people who would let the other live as they chose, who were not, unlike everyone, apt to criticize everything about each other. Anglor thought of this and realized they were both quite lucky that they found each other, due to their high tolerance of abuse, and the fact that because of this high tolerance or abuse they themselves were never abusive. They were always victims because they lwere martyrs, martyrs of passivity, of silence acceptance of people and their flaws, sometimes even their evil, who knew they did not have the luxury to be cruel to people as people were cruel to them. In fact, often they didn't even feel the urge.

As Anglor thought of this he realized he had only been this way since he reached Earth. On the moon people are not interested in each other enough to abuse one another. He realized his passivity was a mostly good quality, especially due to its rarity, but it would only cause him great pain, and he was tired of his back being bent. He would have to change eventually they both would if they expected to survive. And Anglor was supposed to change this Earth. He thought perhaps the best way to do it was with passivity, but he would have to make this passivity a conviction, he would have to herald it with confidence, he would have to be firm about it. He realized people like him and Maria, the ones built to endure abuse, were actually the strongest people there were. It is always what we misapprehend as weakness that is actually strength. It was something worth fighting for, but Anglor realized he would have to stop silently accepting other people's evil, though he knew he could not change it, he shouldn't allow it either, allowing it was cooperating with it. He would have to do something he hated doing, he would have to fight. But he knew he had potential for bravery, it's always the shy ones who do, who behind their quietude is a salvo waiting for its detonation, a storm of incredible passion, of violent fougue. That's what was brewing under the surface, like a volcano underground, like the dead about to rise. Many shy people eventually decide to stop wasting their lives that way, even though it is painful and against their nature to act any other way, eventually they step reluctantly and nervously under the spotlight, ready to prove their bravery that has been dying inside them behind the shyness, but which now, if the shy person doesn't want it to die, must come out. The ambulance quickly arrived to the ward, and Anglor was deposited there. He immediately went to his room and a nurse brought him some food, but he wouldn't eat. She interviewed him for a half an hour but he would barely respond. "Did you try to kill yourself, Michael?' she asked.

"No. Not this time. I just had a manic episode."

"Well, try to eat a little," and then she left, and Anglor was relieved. He immediately threw the food in the garbage and got in bed. He groaned as he did. He always felt he was in a state of nullibiety when he was in these kinds of places. In fact, he felt that way on the Earth and also on the moon. He came from space, which is truly nowhere, then he came to the Earth, what he called rock bottom, which was less nowhere but it was still nowhere, and then in the mental hospital, which was like space, truly nowhere. He felt like he was in a void everywhere he went, probably because everything was in the universe, and the universe was mostly a void with a few planets and nebulas scattered about. It was a void that came out of a void, and there were even more voids contained in it, black holes and what not. The least void like thing was the Earth, and yet Anglor felt it was an abyss like any other, just one with life on it. He felt as empty as space, he felt he was something ne could simply look through, that you could look at him and see his heart and his brain, the only thing that wasn't visible was the soul, if he even had one, or if souls even existed as anything more than a metaphor for the personality.

Anglor rolled in bed, and groaned again. "It's a long way to tomorrow," he said. At least it was for him.

*   *   *

Chapter 4

He slept without dreaming, as only the drunk, the dead, or the truly in despair do. He woke up but didn't get out of bed, he just stared at the wall. A nurse popped in. "You have a positive thought group in five minutes, Michael," she said. Anglor just nodded his head at her. He was now somewhat of a veteran of these places, and he knew you had to go to the group if they were ever going to let you out. Places like these you had to lie your way out of, and then when you get out you have to never think about it, never think about how the path to so called sanity is through a falsehood of yourself, a pretense at something you can never be, And eventually you just start being yourself, which people will accept begrudgingly, at last you'll feel free to be eccentric. But Anglor wasn't at this stage yet, he was not comfortable enough. This is perhaps why people have to go to the mental hospital several times, particularly shy people.

Anglor at last got out of bed and walked to the bathroom. He could hear echoes in it. He knew where he was, every mental hospital had one. It was the well of forgotten ideas, a hell that was the size of the Earth, but could still fit into this tiny psychiatric ward. They were invisible, the forgotten ideas, but one could still hear them echoing hollowly out of the well, begging softly the words "mother. Father," for they were, since the moment they had been forgotten, eternal orphans. Anglor brushed his teeth and tried to ignore the soft pleading of "mother. Father," but it was too pitiable to overlook. He thought these forgotten ideas were much like human beings, only half made and then forgotten by whatever only partially created them then left them uncreated, as nothing but echoes, forgotten for all ages, absorbed into the brain as another immaterial bit of thought that didn't matter, then forgotten, as if they were only phantoms that walked the mind's halls then disappeared through the walls of it, invisible and mute, nothingness that almost became something until it was disregarded. People echoing out of a void, old ideas, begging for mom and dad, the orphans of humanity while humanity is the orphan of the Gods, though they died of an Oedipal murder-human beings killed the Gods, then lamented their absence, self-made cosmic, divine orphans.

Another nurse knocked on Anglor's door. "Time for positive thoughts group, Michael," she said.

Anglor grunted. "Be there in a minute."

He went to the group. "We're going to do a little project," the occupational therapist leading the group said. "I want you all to take a piece of paper and write down some positive adjectives about yourself, things you like about yourself, and then we'll share them with the group who will add more adjectives."

Unfortunately the group didn't know very many adjectives. Anglor quickly learned that apparently everyone in the world is "smart, funny, kind, etc." He didn't want to write such a self-congratulatory thing, so instead he grabbed the piece of paper and started writing a short story. He had never really written before, but he found it quite enjoyable, that it was no different from drawing, that really it was drawing with words.

"Michael, you look like you've got a lot written down. Just share one thing with us," the occupational therapist went on.

"I didn't write down positive adjectives about myself," he said. "I wrote a short story about a person like me and I gave them some nice attributes, though I'm not sure they're attributes I actually have, but I suppose that's what's fiction is for, isn't it? To make ourselves seem better than we really are because we're in a better world."

"Umm," the occupational therapist said. "That's not really what this group is about."

Anglor gave an aporetic shrug. "I don't see how clichés can cure me when clichés are what made me sick to begin with."

"I'm not sure I understand."

"None of you do," Anglor whispered under his breath. "They taught you everything in college except *Einfuhlung*."

"What did you say, Michael?"

"Nothing."

"Well, give us one positive adjective about yourself."

"I'm intelligent," Anglor finally said begrudgingly. "But that's part of the problem."

The occupational therapist ignored the second part. "Good," she said "Now, does anyone have anything to add? Any positive adjectives about Michael?"

"He's interesting," a young woman added.

"He's smart," another person said, though Anglor had already mentioned that.

"He seems creative," the young woman who had called him interesting said.

"Thank you," Anglor said dully. He didn't believe any of them. When the group was done he threw his short story in the garbage can, ignoring its piteous pleas of "father," as he threw it amidst the waste. Naturally, he went back to is room to read. Someone softly knocked on the door. It was the girl who had told him he was interesting and creative in the positive thoughts group.

"What is it?" Anglor said dully, with his usual anhedonia. The girl put out her arm and his short story was in her hand.

"You shouldn't throw it away," she said.

"Why not?"

"You don't know it right now because you're too depressed to realize, but you need it. You need it even more than it needs you."

Anglor scoffed. "It doesn't need me."

"Yes, it does. Art always needs its medium."

"So, I am just a tool for some invisible force to manipulate me?"

"We all are," she said softly. "You're lucky it's art, inspiration that uses you, not war or politics or fate or anything else horrible like that."

"Fate manipulates me, too."

"No one even knows if fate exists, or the soul, or eternity. We can only speculate on these things, for they are not of the realm of the human but of the divine, another thing we can't be sure exists."

"It doesn't," Anglor said stiffly. "None of it exists."

"But art exists," the girl said persistently, still pushing Anglo's short story to him with her hand. "We know it exists, so you might as well let it use you, to be the plaything of eternity, which perhaps only exists in art. Why not? You have nothing else to live for."

Anglor sighed and at last grabbed the short story from her. "You should finish it," she said.

"Why? It's just another story about another lunatic in a lunatic's home."

"It's good to live things twice," she said. "Then after the second time you can forget it. That's one of the many reasons art exists…."

"To forget things?"

"To forget painful things by remembering them."

"What's your name?' Anglor at last asked her.

"Melanie," she said.

"Melanie," he said, as if he were trying on the name. "Sorry I've been an ass," he continued. "I'm just not feeling well. I promise you that's not who I really am."

She smiled at him gregariously. "I know," she said, and then she left. Anglor smiled and picked up the short story. He decided he was going to finish it after all.

In a few more days he was at last able to come home. Maria picked him up as always and they stopped by the bookstore. Anglor felt worried about nothing, as if everything was going to be alright, a feeling he felt rarely, so on the slight occasions that it was with him he tried to enjoy it as best he could, before the dawn of the next morning when reality would set back in. He realized the catamnesis on his case was growing to the size of a Tolstoy novel but he didn't care. He was with Maria right now, and they were at the bookstore, and they both cared about each other immensely, and that was enough for right now, it was enough to have one person in the great wide world care for him.

They browsed the books and Maria got coffee. They sat in the café a little while, talking about nothing, which was actually quite nice, because Anglor got tired of feeling he had to be philosophical all the time. He had read somewhere that philosophy always says the same things. He thought it was Jacques Lacan who said this, and he realized it was true, and yet this same thing was something you could say into eternity and it would still be new, though you could not get an answer back, that this same thing, forever abstract and philosophy being a futile attempt to reify it, could be said forever and still not change, but be different each time, but still not quite be the truth, in spite of how many minds had reiterated it in the quest for innovation So why did philosophy attract him so, if he was merely going to say the same thing, in different ways, that perhaps thousands of minds had already said? But it was always different, it was the same thing but brought about from different perspectives. It was truth as analyzed by a different mind each time, which made it no longer be truth, as soon as it was the scansion of a human being. It was like the soul, as soon as it was made visible it did not exist anymore, was not truth anymore. But still Anglor thought philosophy was necessary, though it was an incredible burden to all of humanity, it was still necessary through its innate sorrow the attempt to make sense of everything, and the ability of the human mind to ruminate on truth, though it could not actually find truth.

At the bookstore he had gotten a philosophy book. He had bought Kant's "Critique of Pure Reason." He wondered if it would say the same thing, the thing he had always known. That was what was so good about philosophy, it told you what you already knew, and at last made you certain of it: it told you nothing is certain. It told you everything you've known since you were in the womb, every *ennoiai* you had almost happily forgotten through thoughtlessness and now you were at last reminded, whether happily or not, it is still important to remember things, particularly ancient knowledge, and not forget too much. Anglor drank his coffee happily. Sometimes he even preferred coffee to alcohol. That was one good thing about the Earth, the fodder and potation was good, though all of it was addictive. That was one good thing about the Earth- there was always something new to try, though many things once you tried you would not be able to give up easily. Anglor knew what it all was, an attempt to fill the emptiness, constant diversions, a thrill that was brief like any thrill to for a moment forget the much longer monotony of life, but these things would never be enough, nothing would ever be enough, the hole was too large, the gap between life and death too short, and the thrills even more brief. That's why it was all so addicting, because it wasn't good enough, because no amount of it can cure the ill it only temporarily soothes, the natural restlessness of the human being.

He calmly drank his coffee and avoided Maria's eye. It was too late- once you decide to become a philosopher you can never go back to being a normal person, you have to be a philosopher the rest of your life, you can't undo it, it will not let you go. He thought of one of Virgil's historical phrases. It was *facilis descensus Averni*, the descent to hell is easy. He thought of this phrase and couldn't decide if it was right or wrong, he couldn't decide if anything was right or wrong. The descent to hell is easy, it is in that once you've decided to do it nothing will stop you from doing it. It is in that it's much easier to fall than to rise, but falling is much more painful, so is the descent to hell, it's so easy, easy enough that anyone can do it, but it's also much more difficult, much more painful, though the fall is so easy to achieve, often you can merely stumble into it, it is also much more difficult, much more difficult than winning, though not everyone can win, but everyone can fall to hell- in short, pain is certainly not more simple than pleasure but it is easier to attain. Anglor thought about his fall to Earth. It was indeed easy, all he had to do was plummet through space, almost too passively, but it was also very difficult to be lost from the world you came from and have to fall to a world where you know you will not belong, for no one belongs in Hell, and no one belongs on Earth. He wanted to disinter Virgil to tell him this, that the descent to hell was not so easy, though it was. It takes only a very short period of time to fall, and it is a very passive act, being motionlessly at the mercy of gravity, but these long plummets into the annals of hell, it is like falling down a long, winding staircase where every step downwards breaks you. It is as long a road as any other, though it takes half the time. Anglor knew it was easier than rising to heaven, but also only because it was more accessible- it wasn't a life of idyllic ease, in fact it was a life of constant degradation and tutelage, but it was easier to attain- that's all. It is easier but it is also much more difficult. Anyone can fall, but it is not a simple life that cushions the fall. It's not easier, it's just easier to attain, often you can attain it when you don't want to, merely by reaching out your hand and then suddenly you are descending with rapid speed into a world where everything is difficult, particularly pleasure.

"What are you thinking about?" Maria suddenly asked, and Anglor was snapped out of his reverie.

"What?'

"What are you thinking about?"

"Nothing."

"It's impossible to think about nothing."

Anglor chuckled mirthlessly. "I'm a philosopher," he said. "I think about it all the time. In fact, there is nothing else to think about."

Maria laughed at him and finished her coffee. "I want alcohol," she said.

"So do I."

She pointed at the television they had both been ignoring. "We are in the age of entertainment," she said. "And we have never been more bored."

"Indeed," Anglor said. "How about that alcohol?"

"There's a bar around the corner. Let's go."

Anglor nodded, and they paid for their books and left for the bar. It was empty and Anglor was glad. Besides the alcohol he didn't like the bar so much, he spent most of his time there drawing on napkins and avoiding eye contact, He and Maria sat down and ordered a pitcher of beer. "Do they have alcohol on the moon?" Maria asked.

"No. We don't need it there."

"Why not?"

"The people there are not as sad. I'm beginning to realize that makes them empty, though. I almost like Earthlings better, well I would if they weren't so hostile."

"Mmm," Maria said while chugging her beer. "Yes," she said, once she had removed the beer from her mouth. "We are hostile people. We are particularly hostile to people who are different, too, though they are our only salvation."

Anglor groaned. "I don't want to speak philosophically anymore. I want to be an idiot for awhile."

"Keep drinking and you will be. It's karaoke night, are you going to sing?"

"God no."

"I'm going to."

"Are you a singer?" Anglor asked, his interest suddenly piqued.

"Yes, I am."

"I'm sure you're very good."

She shrugged. "I'm not bad. You'll find out soon."

So they spent their time at the bar waiting for Maria's turn to sing karaoke while Anglor of course, drew on a napkin and avoided making eye contact. He didn't even talk to Maria very much, who was incredibly nervous and wouldn't stop drinking. Anglor was nervous and couldn't stop drinking either. Public places like these always made him nervous, he supposed that's what the alcohol was for, but he got the feeling he was surrounded by people who were incredibly regular, and incredibly regular people can be incredibly cruel, without even realizing it themselves, because they have always been told they are good, no one has ever broken their heart by telling them they were bad. At last it was Maria's turn to sing, and she quickly downed the rest of her beer and got up on the small stage. Anglor was thinking a bar was perhaps not the best place to go to right after one has been released from a mental hospital.

Maria began singing. Anglor didn't know the song, but it was quite beautiful, and so was Maria, though her body was so strange, svelte and corpulent in all the wrong places, she was still beautiful, and her voice was indeed good. She was an apt cantatrice, with a voice so tender it almost sounded like it was always breaking, like it were made of glass. It was an incredibly vulnerable voice, with gentle affettuoso, that sounded like it was begging, begging not to be broken again.

"I wanted to paint the blues," she crooned gently. "But it was too long and I was too late. The blues had already painted me."

Anglor liked this song. "I wanted to paint the blues, the subtle tones and the warbling voice, but it was too long and I was too late, the blues had already painted me. I wanted to paint the blues, the somber faces too tired to frown, the sluggish groaning, the anguish when the sun comes up, but it was too long and I was too late, the blues had already painted me. I wanted to paint the blues, everything inside of me, but it was too long and I was too late, the blues had painted me hollow, there was nothing left inside of me."

Anglor sighed into his beer. This was the perfect song for Maria, who was particularly marked by depression. Then Anglor thought of himself. He knew by now that by Earth standards, he was insane, but he didn't think he was entirely lost. He didn't think he was a raving lunatic, he wasn't hopelessly dereisitc, in fact often he was quite rational. 'Maybe that's the problem,' he thought to himself. 'Maybe being too rational is its own kind of insanity.' Still, he was grateful to have this kind of insanity, the kind where you knew nothing was real instead of not knowing what's real. He was a sane insane person, and he was even trying to engage in some kind of noesis with his art, though his art was abstract and absurd, and herein lay Anglor's problem, the surreal was quite real to him, and so far no one, not even the doctors, had been able to prove him wrong.

"I wanted to paint the blues, the quiet frustration, the aching of days, the menacing quickness of years, but it was too long and I was too late, the blues had already painted me old."

Anglor sighed once more and pulled out of his pocket the short story he had written in the mental hospital. He had already finished it, but now he wanted to edit it. It was written in blunt pencil because that is all you're allowed to have in the mental hospital. Anglor thought it must be a very dedicated person who would slit their wrists with a pen.

'I wanted to paint the blues, that ancient feeling that will always be around so long as we are, but it was too long and I was too late, the blues had already painted me and I was no great work of art, I knew then that no matter how much you create you are still created, it was too long and I was too late, the blues had already painted me. It was too long and I was too late, I'd already been born."

Maria was then finished and everyone politely clapped, though they were all secretly thinking that the song had ruined the mood and they held this against her. Maria knew this and she didn't care. She had to express herself somehow. She had to admit the truth, and admitting the truth to a room full of strangers that did not give a damn was easier. She resumed her seat next to Anglor and attempted to regale him, until she noticed he was working on something.

"What is it?" she asked.

"It's a short story."

"What's it called?"

"*Verloren und Wiedergefunden.*"

"What does that mean?"

Anglor smiled sanguinely, thinking of Melanie. "It means lost and re-found."

"How nice," Maria said. "But then art is always able to be re-found, it's never truly lost."

"Because you cannot lose the eternal."

Maria scoffed. "Nothing Earthly is eternal," she said. "Art is eternal compared to us, its master, but it is not eternal in regards to the universe. It is part of civilization, and civilization will die someday, too."

"But we still have the art of Ancient Rome, though that civilization died."

"I don't mean when just one civilization dies, I mean when all civilization dies."

"And then a new race of men will be born and they'll find all our art."

"You have too much faith in art."

Anglor shrugged. "I have to have faith in something. Everyone does. Even atheists I think believe in synchronicity."

"Maybe," Maria conceded. "I have faith in nothing, and that's why I'm so down all the time."

"Have faith in yourself."

"Why?'

"Because there is nothing else to have faith in."

She sneered. "That and art."

They were silent for a moment. Maria kept looking at a young man at the end of the bar, who was completely absorbed in his drink and nothing else. "Look at that guy," Maria said.

"Why?"

"Because he hasn't said anything all night. People who don't talk much are either really interesting or really boring."

"Perhaps he is interesting, but I still don't want to get to know him."

"No," Maria said mysteriously. "I don't really either. He just caught my eye. Let's get out of here."

Anglor sighed with relief. "I hate the bar." - They both walked out of the bar, but they were stopped by the quiet man who was either really interesting or really boring. He handed Anglor a piece of paper.

Anglor went to open it but the man stopped him. "Read it later," he said. "Here is not the place for it. Here everyone is trying to forget."

Anglor nodded and put the piece of paper in his pocket, then they walked out.

"That was weird," Maria said.

"I guess he's really interesting, after all."

"Funny. You don't usually find someone like that at the bar."

Anglor nodded. They didn't read the piece of paper until they got home. Anglor opened it up and it was in French.

"L'etants sommes rien,

Et delire c'set reel.

Je manqué eternite

Un reve c'est reel

L'etant sommes reves, reves sommes delire.

Reel c'est reves

Reel c'est delire et

L'etants sommes rien

Toujours c'est delire

Je manqué eternite,
Je manqué rien
Nous sommes le parvenir."

"What the hell does that mean?" Maria asked.

"Beings are nothing, and delirium is reality. I miss eternity, a dream is reality, beings are dreams, dreams are delirium. Reality is dreams, reality is delirium and beings are nothing. Everything is delirium. I miss eternity. I miss nothing. We are the end."

"You speak French and German? How? You're not even from this planet."

"In school I took a course on Earth languages."

"You guys have schools on the moon?'

"Yes. It is the only Earth institution we agree with, though even it has been corrupted here, particularly in America, but I've found teachers are the only authority figures that aren't an imbecilic menace."

"It's an interesting poem. Do you suppose he wrote it?"

"I suppose so. I can tell he's not a native French speaker, though. The grammar is terrible."

"Why do you think he wanted us to read it?"

"I'm always amazed at the workings of human beings. I never really know their motivation for anything."

"That's okay. Half the time we don't know what motivates us either. It's a nice poem, though, though a bit clunky."

Anglor turned over the piece of paper in his hand. "Look, there's something else," he said.

"What?"

"Something in German. 'Die seligkeit von seelenmord.'"

"What does that mean?"

"The bliss of soul murder."

"Bliss?" Maria cried in disbelief. "People have been trying to murder my soul my whole life, I can assure you it's not blissful. It hurts."

"Perhaps he means the bliss of masochism then."

Maria scoffed. "My father was a masochist," she said. "My mother caught him paying a dominatrix to whip him because she wouldn't do it. He hanged himself and left a suicide note. All it said was 'the shame.'"

"Yes, I suppose masochists do feel great shame, but everyone is ashamed of their desires."

"And they should be."

Anglor scoffed. "Don't be so hard on your father. Being ashamed is useless. It will never stop you from still desiring the thing."

"My father was a masochist," Maria said again. "When he kicked over the chair and his neck snapped he probably thought it felt good."

Anglor held up the poem to the light. "Do you think we'll ever see this man again?" he asked.

"Why? Do you want to?"

"I want to know what he finds so blissful about the murder of the soul."

"Some people think it's nice to feel nothing, I suppose."

"Then he's not a masochist, or even a sadist. He is something that wants to be dead."

"Or already is."

Anglor shook his head. "The shame," he repeated. "The immense, incredible, irrefragable shame."

"Of what?"

"Being."

"Do you think it goes against God?"

"No. I don't think anything goes against God, for in order to do that it would have to go against nature, and that's impossible, even for humans."

"You don't think murder and war and things like that are against nature?"

Anglor shrugged. "Nature allows it."

"Then she is a bit too permissive. That's the real shame my father was talking about."

"I'm sorry he killed himself."

Maria then shrugged also. "I guess he didn't like pain as much as he thought he did."

"What about your mother?"

"She's alive but deteriorating. She lives in a nursing home in California. I call her on the phone sometimes. My family was very wealthy, you see."

"That's why you're depressed. See, either too much money or too little money makes people insane."

"Indeed. That's why art thrives most in either fortune or desolation."

"And fortune and desolation is all we know, we haven't found the in between. So art is always thriving."

Maria chuckled again. "You really do love it, don't you?"

Anglor nodded.

"Well, that's a good thing. Everyone has to love something, otherwise there is no point."

"There is no point anyway."

"You switch from hope to despair quite easily, don't you? And the only time I hear you speak of hope is when you're talking about art."

"It's my only hope in hell."

Mara opened up the poem and examined it again. "I want to meet this man," she said.

"We'll meet him. He's a crucial interstice of our destiny."

"How do you know that?"

"A feeling."

"What do you think is the difference between thoughts and feelings?"

"There isn't any."

"Maybe a feeling is just a violent thought."

"Indeed. Then love is the most violent thought of them all."

Maria paused for a moment and looked into Anglor's face ruminatively. "Have you ever been in love, Anglor?"

"Hasn't everyone?"

"Have you?"

He sighed at last. "No," he said. "I haven't. On the moon we have outgrown it."

"No wonder you don't get homesick."

"Odysseus in the Odyssey used the Greek work 'nsotos' to describe how he missed his home. I'm assuming that's where the word nostalgia comes from. That's a violent thought I've never had, nor ever want to have. I think I feel the same about love, too, because in the end it becomes nostos, missing a home that was doomed to be temporary anyway."

"Not always."

"But most of the time. I avoid nostos, I avoid becoming too attached to any home or lover. When I leave the Earth and go back home I won't feel nostos towards the Earth, either. That is the upside of having no home, not having to feel nostalgia."

"Don't feel bad. Most people don't like Earth, either, but until I met you I thought it was the only place to live."

"The moon is really no place to live. All we do is watch Earth. You are far more interesting than we are, perhaps because of your violent thoughts."

"I suppose that's a compliment."

"It is and it isn't. Sometimes your violent thoughts are much too violent."

Maria rolled her eyes. "I can't help that I'm human, Anglor, anymore than you can help being an alien."

"I know," he said.

"Maybe now that you live on Earth you will fall in love."

"I don't want to, particularly not with a human, no offense. People are stupid and that's what makes them cruel, *amathia*. I think love is the same way."

"You think love is cruel because it's stupid?"

"Yes. It mirrors people."

"Bloody hell," Maria said. "Even I don't feel so dim about it. Love can be quite erudite sometimes."

"When it's a poet in love, but intelligent people can be just as cruel as stupid people, and not accidentally like stupid people."

Maria waved her hands up in the air flippantly in defeat. "Believe whatever you want to believe," she said. "But this time I think you're wrong. You're awfully jaded for someone who's never been in love before."

Anglor just shrugged. "I've observed it a lot. It seems like it can ruin people."

"You have to take your chances on Earth. Being alone too long can ruin you, too."

"You get used to it."

"Now you're going to claim you don't feel loneliness."

Anglor looked down, ashamed. "I do feel loneliness," he said softly. "In fact I feel it more than anything else. That is my cardinal violent thought."

"Then fall in love, trade it for another violent thought."

"One that's even more violent."

"Loneliness is too benign. You're an artist, you're passionate."

"But in many ways I am also quite benign."

"You've become the loneliness. That's bad."

Anglor scoffed. "Who are you to give me advice? You're lonely too."

"But I'm ready to become un- lonely."

"No you're not. No one is ever ready for that."

"Well, I would like it."

"You think so, but then when it happens it will make you uncomfortable."

Maria smiled at him patiently. "I've been comfortable for too long," she said. "I could use a little bit of discomfort. Getting too comfortable is quite like death, stagnation."

"Well, since you want it so bad I hope it will happen to you…"

"But it will probably happen to you, because you don't want it."

"I don't want anything."

"That's the same as wanting everything."

"Maybe I already have everything."

"Then it's not much."

"No, it isn't."

"We should go to bed in our separate bedrooms."

"Do you want me to sleep with you?"

"No. Your penis is too strange."

"That's not what I meant."

"Good night, Anglor."

After that they went back to the bar several times to see if they could run into the man who had written the poem. They were never able to find him, and eventually they gave up. Then they ran into him. He was in the grocery store, buying a large box of wine, which was the same thing Maria and Anglor were doing.

"Alcohol seems to be the common bond here," Anglor whispered to Maria.

"It often is." They walked up to the man and stared rather rudely.

Anglor cleared his throat, as if that would dispel the strangeness of it all. "We liked your poem," he said.

"Good. I wrote it for you."

"What's your name?"

"Does it matter?"

"Well, I'm Michael, and this is Ma…"

"Your name's not Michael."

And then they were silent again. 'This is just what I need in my life,' Anglor thought to himself. 'A discerning alcoholic. A drunken haruspex.' The man quietly looked into Anglor's eyes and shook his head slowly.

"*Le Pudeur,*" he said, "the shame."

"What are you so ashamed of?"

"The same thing you're so ashamed of. The same thing the whole world is ashamed of."

"Which is?"

"Itself."

"If you didn't want to meet us then why did you write that poem?"

The man shrugged. "I wanted someone to know the truth. You seemed like you wanted to know it."

"That's not the truth," Anglor said stiffly. "What you wrote is not the truth, it's just the way you perceive things."

"Well, what else am I supposed to write if not my perception?"

"Nothing, there is nothing else you can write. Still, it's not truth."

"Then what is?"

"I don't think we'll ever know."

"*Le pudeur*," the man repeated.

"Indeed. What are you doing?"

"Juts going home to drink alone as usual."

"Come drink with us."

The man smiled. "Sure," so they went to Maria and Anglor's to drink together. They quickly discovered this man whose name didn't matter was no dilettante when it came to consuming alcohol. Anglor and Maria, who were also hardly advocates of temperance, struggled to keep up with him. The wine was sapid and cold, a pleasure to the palette, but it quickly dehydrated them and they would have started to drink water instead if they weren't trying to impress this older, veteran alcoholic.

"This makes me forget the shame," he said, and he downed a whole glass of wine in one sip. "And other times it reminds me of it more. It is only half an antidote, the rest of it poison. But even the poison tastes good, in a bitter way. Paracelsus would have appreciated it."

Anglor groaned and poured himself another glass from the spout coming out of the box. "It's the waters of Lethe in a cup."

The man chuckled. "No," he said. "Not quite. The waters of Lethe heal memory, this only stultifies it, and you have to pay for it, you have to pay dearly for forgetting."

"I suppose you do," Anglor said, and also drained his glass, imitating the man's panache in misery as he did it. Maria was slurring her words and trying to sing the song she had sung at the bar, the one about the blues painting her.

"And the blues is no great arrtisstt," she crooned.

"No," the man said. "But it makes good artists. It is simply the genitrix."

"I don't ever want to be a mother," Maria said through hiccups. "I don't want someone to have to live here just because I'm lonely."

"Yes, people are created by loneliness, even with parents who are supposedly in love. Obviously they are not enough for each other if they need a *tertrium quid*."

"So that's what keeps the human race going- loneliness, that is our life instinct!"

"And it is also our death instinct," the man with no name said. "The two really aren't that different. Life cannot be created without death, and there can be no creation at all without destruction. Loneliness creates everything, and it destroys everything."

"The blues painted everyone," Maria began to sing. "And the blues is no great artisttt."

"*Le Pudeur*," the man repeated.

"Damn the shame!" Anglor said, and threw his glass of wine down. "I can live without it!"

"Can you?"

Maria was in the corner, the most drunk of all of them, and she looked out the window with a manitc, mystic air in her eyes. "Loneliness created love," she said eerily. "For that we are in debt to it."

The man with no name snorted and drank another whole glass of wine "You're right," he said. "We will always be in debt to it."

"It tells the truth, too," Anglor said.

"Sometimes," the man with no name replied. "But it's capable of lying like everything else, like consciousness, like love."

"I love love," Maria said through more hiccups. "But it is an unrequited affair."

"Yes," the man with no name said. "I used to be quite a romantic, but now I am only a cynic, because of all the unrequited affairs, because of the loneliness I am in debt to. I pay it back with ingratitude, because it often feels like love missed me. But no, it didn't miss me, it hit me very hard, it missed all the people I wanted to love."

"I think the blues painted love, too," Maria said. "I think it painted everything."

"And it's no great artist," the man finished for her.

Maria threw her head back and laughed. "Tragedy is comedy," she said, "and comedy is tragedy."

Then Maria abruptly passed out. Anglor carried her to her bed and tucked her in, like a lover, but he was merely a caretaker. He didn't want to be a lover, he didn't want to feel *nostos*, it was bad enough feeling *Pudeur*.

"These damn violent thoughts," he whispered to himself. He had never really had them until he reached Earth. This planet had a way of making people alive, then of course making them dead. Antithesis is semblance, Anglor supposed, all opposites are just mirrors reflecting a vacuum in between them, reflections of nothing reflecting nothing, a vapid way to create a void, the acting of deepening something that was already hollow. It was a silent echo chamber, echoing silence, proliferating nothingness. Anglor finished putting Maria into bed, sighed, and went into the other room to drink some more, although everything was already coruscating in a menacing, carnival like blur.

Anglor sat down in front of the man with no name and poured himself another glass of wine. The box was almost empty now.

"She alright?" the man asked.

"She's fine."

"Poor Maria," the man said. "She thinks every one eyed man is Wotan."

Anglor shrugged.

"You know," the man said. "The three of us are too depressed to be wise, like we try to claim we are."

"Yes, that's true, but this depression is a step up on the way to wisdom."

"What if we never get to the next rung of the ladder, the one that leads us closer to wisdom? What if we stay on this step on the way forever? What if we will always be depressed?"

"Wisdom is impossible to attain, anyway. That's why philosophers are philosophers for the rest of their lives, because the wisdom they seek doesn't come until death. They seek for it in vain in life."

"This is what I mean," the man said. "What you just said, that can't be wisdom."

"You're right, it's not."

"Get to the next step on the way, get out of this step to wisdom, for this one is the most dangerous, this is the one that if you indulge too much will never let you out, and then you will never become wise, then you can never complete your mission."

"Excuse me?"

"Yes," the man said, and drained his last glass of wine with a strange elegance. "I know why you're here, and I know where you're from."

"How?"

"I watched you fall. You were like an angel, I thought you were going to save us all, not wallow in the mire of a drunken depression."

"I'm just not used to Earth yet."

"No one gets used to it, but still, we make do with it."

"I'm sorry if I've let you down."

"You haven't yet," he said. "It's not too late."

"It's always too late here."

"Pessimism is perhaps just as unrealistic as optimism, though it often doesn't seem like it. You're right, it is late, your very coming here is late, but we are in something of an eternity- not a real eternity, that can only be found in a vacuum, but we will be alive for the foreseeable future, in spite of our acts of destruction, we have been given the time of the universe, which is not infinite, but unbounding- though we hardly deserve it. But it gives us enough time to redeem ourselves, however late. Perhaps that's why we have been given it."

"Not individually of course," Anglor said. "Individual life is hardly eternity, it is its opposite."

"Still, there is something eternal in it, for you especially, being an artist. You should know you are incredibly lucky for that."

"You're right," Anglor almost whispered. "I am. But what you say about human beings being given the time to redeem themselves, does that mean when they do redeem themselves that will be the end of them? And if deep down they know this, they will choose never to redeem themselves, because humanity's only goal is to survive at all costs."

"Perhaps if they do redeem themselves they will truly be eternal. They won't have to merely survive anymore."

"I doubt they see it that way. I doubt they even know the difference."

The man smiled at him. "Someone who's so misanthropic can only be a human themselves."

"But I'm not human."

"But you are, incredibly human. I am not surprised that I would find such humanity from an alien."

Anglor finished his drink and went to get more wine only to find the box was finally empty. He lit a cigarette instead. "I fell just like lucifer," he said. "From heaven to hell, only to find there's not much difference between the two."

"You fell from the sky, you didn't fall from heaven. Either heaven or hell can only be found on Earth."

Anglor sighed and dragged lissomly on his cigarette. "I don't want to be a philosopher anymore," he whispered, but the man heard him.

"It's too late," he said. "You are too deep into this well to crawl out of it now."

"At least is truth at the bottom of it?'

The man shrugged. "We don't even know if there is a bottom."

"Tell me your name," Anglor demanded.

"It's Mark," the man finally admitted.

Anglor groaned. "I need to sleep. I'm drunk."

"Go to sleep then. I'll make myself comfortable on the couch."

Anglor splayed himself out on the floor and looked at the ceiling as if it were a sky full of stars. "Mark," he said. "How did you find me?"

"I just happened to be at the bar and I recognized you from the time you fell, and when you hit the ocean the weights were on your neck."

"I guess it's necessary that people think I'm insane."

"Better than them finding out you're an alien, but people will be hostile to you either way."

"Yes," Anglor said through another sigh, and a last closed his eyes.

The next morning when Anglor and Maria at last woke up each with individual raging hangovers Mark was gone. He didn't leave a note, and Anglor was relieved, he would be relieved if he never saw the man again, but he knew this was impossible. Synchronicity in its infinite but blind wisdom seemed to have placed Mark here for a reason that synchronicity did not know, because it never knew its reasons, though there were always reasons. Humans had to interpret them instead, the organized aleatory nature of the universe did not analyze it before it meted it out, it merely threw it into the Earth flippantly like garbage in a disposal, something it didn't want anymore, yet sometimes it was almost a miracle, because it was created by God, which is the randomness of a cold, mostly empty and violent universe. A randomness that seemed to conform to reason, though, and almost to a higher purpose, in spite of how blindly it did it.

Maria began to make them both coffee. Anglor sat on the couch Mark had occupied only the night before and he could smell his scent on it. It was rather pleasant.

"You need to get famous soon," Maria said. "We need the money."

"It always comes late," Anglor said. "It's like love. But then it's not like love at all."

"Better or worse?"

"I don't know. A little bit more hollow."

"You don't even know yet."

"I have a feeling. Success is the false idol people in America worship much more than Jesus Christ, who was never successful. All he did successfully was die."

"Well, He said Himself He didn't come to save the world."

"I didn't either."

"Then why are you here?"

"To remind the world it can only be saved by itself, that everyone on Earth must be its savior, not just one man."

"It's true that they don't seem to know that. Most people are just trying to get by, though, they are too demoralized to change the world."

"That is the fault of the powers that be, who are benefitting off the so called way of the world, who do not want it to change…"

"So you want a revolution?"

"No, revolution is always violent…"

"Then what do you want?"

"I don't know," Anglor groaned. "It's not what I want to begin with. If it were up to me I wouldn't give a damn about this planet…"

"Just like its people."

"… But I have to be better than that. I have to want better for the world, and I do, it deserves more, I just don't know quite what that more is. I've become just like everyone else, so adjusted to a corrupt system that I can't even imagine anything else. I don't know how I'm going to change anything, maybe I'm not going to change anything, but pave the way for the people who can."

"Do such people exist?"

"They have before, they're dead now. And I know what you're going to say, that noting really changed, but that is because this is an eternal battle, that will last as long as human beings do. We must fight for whatever is right every single generation. It is dialectic like that."

"That's what Karl Marx said."

"And he was right."

"But look how his revolution ended."

"Please, Maria," Anglor whispered. "I'm pessimistic enough about this as it is. Don't make it worse."

"I'm sorry, I'm just confused about what your mission is, if it's not to save the world."

"I'm confused about it, too. I'm just supposed to upset the order of things a little bit, and make people think more, think about how *they* can change things. I am trying to get this planet to have a little hope in itself, make it realize its potential if only it gave up some of the conveniences and some of its bad habits. I'm merely an orator."

"Just like Jesus."

"I'm not dying for anybody's sins, I'm just making people aware of them. They have become so inured to them they don't even realize they are actively participating in them, and it's not even really their sins, it's the sins of civilization as a whole, of its id, which seems just as active as its ego, and just as obvious."

"Hmmm," Maria said. "It seems that you do understand your mission."

"Somewhat. I don't know how the hell I'm going to do it, though. Since I fell to Earth I've felt just as confused and misguided as any Earthling."

Maria put her hand on his shoulder. "You'll figure it out," she said. "I think maybe that's part of your mission, becoming human first."

Anglor breathed in deeply and then let out a big gust of air into Maria's face. "Perhaps," he said. But he wasn't feeling well. His head hurt and he was nauseated. He kept imagining some of the strangest things. By far the most welcome though was the one where he was descending into a pile of lissomly waving black veils. They were so inviting for some reason, and he stuck his head in them and they covered his eyes. Everything was black and he was falling, falling through the darkness, as if he were in space again. He wondered if it was death calling him, as it often did, though it would never take him, it just wanted to remind him that someday it would, that everything, even a Selenite on a very important mission, had to die, and by the looks of it Anglor thought perhaps it was a pleasant experience, that perhaps there was a moment in death where everything was peace, where you forgot everything including yourself, and just one second before becoming eternal nothingness your mind is at last empty, and at last you are content, no longer concerned with Earthly things, no longer concerned with anything at all. He went towards the black veils, he stuck his head in, and they wrapped around him like the warm embrace of a woman, and for a moment he didn't feel anything, no more violent thoughts, no more thoughts at all. Perhaps you can only become enlightened at the moment of death.

But his reverie was quickly ended when Maria spoke to him again. He felt himself pulled by the scruff of the neck backwards away from the veils, and their glorious simplicity was gone, and he was again in a world of the dizzying chaos of sensation and perception, where there was too much noise and life, where everyone was competing to scream over the intense din of their own paltriness, their meaningless conversations that filled the Earth until it was nothing but voices saying nothing, as if it were a violent wind, these violent thoughts that always get mistranslated into words.

"Anglor!" Maria suddenly yelled.

He quickly snapped out of it.

"Where were you?" she asked.

"I don't know," Anglor said. "Somewhere else. Somewhere easier."

"I thought you hated people who strived only for the easy."

"I don't know. My head hurts."

"Lie down. I'm making coffee."

"You think coffee is a panacea."

"It isn't?"

Anglor laughed and lay down on the couch. "That guy finally told me his name."

"What was it?"

"Mark."

"Such an ordinary name for such a strange man."

"We have no room to judge on being unusual."

"I like being unusual, though," Maria said. "That way it feels less like I was some mass produced object."

"You're an Objet d' art."

"And you're an Objet Trouve. And I'm glad I was the one that found you."

Chapter 5

Anglor was due for his bi annual suicide again. It was amazing to him that a year had already passed, especially since he had been depressed. Life only feels long when you no longer want it, and when you do want it, there's never enough of it, it is always too short. That's how time works, so Anglor was surprised the time was moving as fast as it was, but the more he thought about it the more he realized he didn't want it to be rapid, either. He didn't want it to move slowly or too quickly, he wanted something in between, which is of course impossible.

He warned Maria this time before he did it, and when she came home to find him hanging in the closest she was perfectly sang froid.

"Hello, Anglor."

He didn't say anything, he was still dead. His purple caput mortuum like head was tumid, grotesque and silent. As he was hanging there he thought about the skeleton, he thought about how there's a part of your body that is already dead that walks around inside you. Maybe the soul was the same way- the soul was the knowledge of the eternal; even in the midst of a temporal world: in other words, it was the knowledge of death, it was the clock that timed the body's decay, it was the eternity we measure ourselves against to find how insignificant we are, the eternity we try to aspire to but which can only be achieved by death. Humans make themselves eternal through sexual reproduction, to replace themselves with another, to leave some of their genetics behind before they die. So the human version of eternity, the eternity of cyclical vicissitudes and machine like duplication, can only be achieved with death. If we weren't going to die we wouldn't even feel the need to reproduce, but that is the closest we can get to any kind of eternity, as a species, as a genus, but never as individuals. And so we must be recycled, we must create duplicates and then ourselves expire.

"I still don't understand why you do this six month suicide thing," Mara went on. "You say it's to be reborn, but you never change. You're always the same. It seems more like hollow tradition to me."

Anglor still didn't answer, he merely drooled on the rope around his neck.

"Ah," Maria said. "I know why you do it. So you don't feel human."

"Isn't that why anyone commits suicide?" Anglor suddenly choked out. "Cut me down, will you?"

Maria grabbed a swiss army knife from her back pocket and slowly cut him down.

"That and of course *le pudeur*," she said.

"They're the same thing."

At last Maria freed him from the rope and he choked for a moment to clear his throat but slowly his face became less purple. The rope burn were still on his neck, though, garish and obvious.

Anglor rubbed his neck and cleared his throat some more. "This is the worst form of suicide," he said. "Hanging yourself. It truly hurts afterwards."

"Then why did you do it?"

"There are only so many ways to kill yourself. Shooting yourself in the head is the easiest, but I didn't want you to see me crawl out of my own head again. I could tell it gave you a fright."

"Yes, I'll never be able to get used to that. Let me get you a glass of water."

"Thank you."

Maria came back with a glass of water and Anglor drank the whole thing in one gulp, then gave her back the empty glass. "I'm in something of a kenosis," he said.

"A what?"

"It was when Christ renounced his divine attributes to suffer like a human. That's what I'm doing, though I didn't renounce anything divine, I renounced all that was alien in me, all of my selenite, to suffer like a human. That's integral to my mission, to suffer like a human, and I found all I had to do to do it, to achieve my kenosis, was arrive on Earth. As soon as you reach Earth you suffer like a human, it was the same for Christ, being one of the few Gods who lived on Earth for awhile, that's all He had to do to renounce His divinity, and that's all He had to do to suffer. It has been the same for me."

"But why is suffering integral to your mission?"

"Because you cannot help humans unless you are somewhat human yourself, and humans suffer, that is what separates them from animals and Gods. Some people are born to suffer, as if it is their purpose, as if it is their divinity. When Christ suffered like a human that was when He was truly divine, that was what made him a God. It might be the same for me. I might be here just to suffer, and people can interpret from that what they will. Maybe I am just here to know what it's like to be human."

"You don't strike me as a martyr."

"Everyone who wants to save humanity in the end has to be a martyr."

"But you don't want to."

"I didn't at first, but now I do, now that I know how much you suffer. Now your people have my pity."

"So that's all it takes, huh?"

"That's all it takes to change the world," Angloir said, "the right person suffering. Now that I know why I'm here I don't mind being here, though I am only here to suffer."

"So that's why we're all here?" Maria asked in a bewildered, quizzical rage. "To suffer?"

"I never said it's why everyone is here. No person will ever be wise enough to know why the entire human race exists. It has to be enough to know why you personally are here."

"But this is a reason you prescribed to yourself…."

"Who else is supposed to give me the reason? There is no one else. And I didn't necessarily prescribe it to myself. It was handed down to me by fate."

"You don't even believe in fate."

"No, but I do believe there are natural laws which make no sense and which act almost as fate."

"It doesn't make you angry?"

"It did at first, but now I see a glimpse of reason in it, though the reason is probably accidental. At least I know why I'm here, though this place is certainly not my home. I never knew why I was on the moon, but I never questioned it back then. I can never go back to that. I was living a lie, I was living thoughtlessly. Even if the truth is uninviting, it is the truth, and once you know it you can never un-know it. You simply have to try to learn to live with it."

"Or change it."

"I don't believe that anyone can change that truth, that some people are born merely to suffer."

"I see no divinity or higher purpose in suffering," Maria said. "I see only suffering in suffering. That was Christ's biggest lie, that it means something."

"It must have meant something, we all remember him."

"Maybe for some people."

"And we are lucky. It makes the suffering a little easier, knowing it's for something."

"For what?"

"Humanity."

Maria scoffed but didn't say anything. Anglor massaged his neck slowly, trying to get rid of the rope burn. He was lucky he was a Selenite, and therefore healed ten times faster than human beings. Bodily, that is, not mentally, emotionally or spiritual. That takes all thinking beings a long time., because in the meantime you cannot stop thinking, because you possess memory, the blight of mankind but also the only thing that makes them more than an animal. We have to be grateful to it even as it is ruining us.

The rope burns slowly faded from Anglor's neck. It was as if it had never happened, but he felt strange this time, he felt like he had actually been reborn, and not just in the technical way, coming back from the dead, but in the actual sense that he was now a new, better person, ready to fulfil his obligations, and not warily, not out of a sense of begrudging necessity, now he actually respected this necessity, and knew the importance of what he had to do. This was also a feeling he had only felt since he had been on Earth, though it was the first pleasant one, but suddenly he was full of purpose. He had finally escaped the longest most treacherous way on the road to wisdom, the depression, or, as Hegel would call it "The Unhappy Consciousness," the way on the road that is hardest to traverse, and which often people never get out of it, never reach wisdom or at least the human version of it, and sink into the quicksand, the traps that lay on the way, for good.

Anglor realized at last that intelligence was not necessarily wisdom. He still believed one had to be intelligent to be wise, but still, they were two different things. Wisdom was intelligence with a heart and eyes, that could see and feel everything. He was looking forward to reaching it, or the closest human beings can reach it, and he though that though it was denied human beings in its fulness, it could also only be attained by human beings. There are no Gods, and Selenites are too boring for such a thing. So only humans can be wise, and they cannot be completely wise. Complete wisdom is a vague dream in the sleeping head of the universal consciousness, it is unconscious, it is only an idealistic idea. Humans invented it but they could not attain, because it was not real, it was only a pleasant hallucination dreamed of for the first time centuries ago in Ancient Greece, by a man with a death sentence, walking the Earth, just like Christ, who finished what Socrates started by reminding mankind wisdom must walk hand in hand with kindness, that its heart is more important than its eyes, that it is wiser to be understanding than discerning. Anglor thought bleakly that what he learned from this is that wise men get executed.

But he didn't mind. He had been executing himself every six months since he was born, he was used to it. He was no stranger to death, for this was also a part of wisdom, and perhaps that's why wise men get executed, for not being frightened of death, and the common people, the demos, are too jealous of that to let him or her live, so they test them, to see if they really aren't frightened, and then when the people find they were telling the truth, that they really weren't frightened, in a couple hundred more years they are worshipped. Devotion like that always comes late, posthumously But whether you are frightened of death or not, you still have to die, so you might as well be unafraid, accepting it as nature's law, a law that will never be able to be broken, and be gracefully executed.

Anglor thought of these things and sat on the couch and lit a cigarette.

"You do seem different this time," Maria suddenly said. "More peaceful."

Anglor simply nodded.

"I don't understand you now," she admitted.

Anglor smiled. "No one will understand me now," he said. "Not for thousands of years."

Anglor managed to get his art in a few of the galleries in Dayton. He never got his own gallery, as some lucky artists do, but he was working his way up to that. He never enjoyed the day of the show. He always did his mandatory four\ hours of volunteer work which was the price for being allowed in the gallery, though many of the artists in the show didn't do it. Anglor always did it, though. He thought it was the least he could do for them letting his shit art be hung up on the wall. As it turned out, the volunteer shift was the most fun part of the show. The rest of it was spent with Anglor spending too much money on wine and standing alone, looking at everybody, and when he got bored of that, sitting alone and reading, wondering when the bus would come so he could go home. Last year someone had even sat on him while he was reading, as if a book is now something that can make you invisible in public. If it was Anglor liked reading even more, though he did not particularly like being sat on.

Maria never came to these events anymore. She did the first time, but it was an effort to get her out of the house, as it was for Anglor, and the week of the show was very stressful and it was little payback for all the work, but he still kept doing it every year because he knew he couldn't complete his mission if he didn't first become a famous artist, or at least one of some note. He was at the front of the building, checking people's id's and then giving them the requisite wristband that proved they were at least twenty one years of age. The alcohol was not free, even to the artists, and Anglor drank several glasses of wine as he was checking id's.

He was jealous of the other artists. Many of them were better than him, but that wasn't the reason he was jealous of them- he was jealous of them because they were able to have fun. Even with his copious amounts of wine Anglor wasn't able to have fun, and he was certain his art that was in the corner by the restroom wouldn't be noticed by anyone. Fortunately, this year he was wrong.

After he was done with his volunteer shift and he stood alone drinking and waiting for the bus, a man approached him. He was a rather odd man. He had a face just like anyone else but on the side of it was tattooed another face. It looked exactly like a photograph by Saul Steinberg. The man came up to him and Anglor grew nervous, then chugged his glass of wine and tried to drink more of it, but was disappointed when he realized it was empty. The man approaching him had a proud, vaunting swagger, but in his two faces he looked helpless and unsure of himself. "Hello," he said, and when he spoke two voices came out, one sonorous bass and another of a higher pitch, castrato type voice, and the two voices did not work in harmony- it was a horrible musical dissonance that came out, as if it were a group of unpracticed singers. Anglor shuddered a little bit when he heard it.

"Hello," he said reluctantly in return.

"Are you Michael Smith?"

Anglor nodded. He had tried to give himself the most normal name possible, so no one knew he was either insane or an alien.

"I rather enjoyed your art work," the two dissonant, clashing voices said, as if they were competing with each other, though for what they were competing Anglor couldn't say. Perhaps the man's soul. "My name is Zweifle, Aaron Zweifle, and I am an art procurer."

Anglor's ears suddenly pricked up and his eyes widened. He felt like an empty, cold opportunist but this is what happens to you when you're hungry. He thought of all Earth people's cruel expressions. "Kill them with kindness," "catch more flies with honey," as if goodness were only a utilitarian tool to get what you want. It's been that way since the birth of religion, the bribe that keeps people if not good, at least perfunctorily decent, with the promise of Heaven. Few people were actually good, and many did good only for the hopes of reward, divine or otherwise, at least that what's the expressions denoted, that kindness was a trickery, the tool of an opportunist such as Anglor was at this moment, a form of manipulation, the honey that catches the flies being more like a spider disguised in sweetness. It was a smile with a scowl writhing underneath it, graciousness that had taken root in the heart of sadism and grew flowers of evil there, beautiful things that were actually only parasitic weeds.

And this was how Anglor felt right now, that he was taking part in this game, but he had to. He had to acquire creative success because it was the only way out of the vicious cycle of doing nothing but being born, then working, then dying. Anglor cleared his throat. "It's nice to meet you," he said, and shook the man's hand.

"Your art is very interesting to me," he said. "It is full of imagination, very abstract, and a bit monstrous. I like that."

Anglor wanted to roll his eyes at the way the man went on like an art critic with his two voices, but he suppressed it and thanked the man instead.

"It has such a sense of love in history in it, like a good work of literature."

Anglor laughed and lit a cigarette. "Love in history," he repeated. "I'm still not sure how it's possible. In fact, I think love gets sacrificed to history."

"Why?" Zweifle asked curiously, cocking his head like a maieutic child.

Anglor shrugged. "That's the only way we don't feel insignificant. If we have a history we are a people and at the very least we have noticed ourselves, and can talk about ourselves. It makes us feel important, and barely any people have to take part in it, most people just watch, now even on television, but it makes the whole human race feel like it matters, with the sacrifice of a few hundred thousand for the glee of the billions. My opinion is we have to find another way to feel significant. History runs with the arrow of time, the arrow of entropy, it only gets more and more chaotic. I think we have to kill it, murder history, and stop it from happening at all. It always demands blood, and mostly consists of war, and, as I said, we often give up our right to love for it."

Zweifle laughed and lit a cigar. "Do you think that's really possible?" he asked, "to kill history?"

"No, history is like a hydra and it is always growing, but that's what all my artwork means, and hopefully a few intelligent people will agree with me, and hopefully one day they will make the world instead of being ignored."

"Hmm," Zweifle said. "Well, it's not like it was before. Thanks to the television you mentioned people are so far removed from history they can love in spite of it, particularly in America, though perhaps literature suffers because of it."

"That's not good either." Anglor said solemnly. "If people are that removed from history they will never kill it, and what about the rest of the world? Many countries do not have the luxury of being removed from it, they have to live directly in it, and instead of killing history, history kills them. That's what people don't understand. Killing history would be a great luxury, and the Americans, who are so far removed from it, in the space between themselves and the television, have the power to do it. I regret that most of them are so far removed from it they don't care, but I know a few people do."

"Obviously you do."

"I do. I think it's very important to kill history. In our naïve, vainglorious quest to be significant we will not only destroy ourselves, we will destroy everything. We already have."

"Hmm," Zweifle said again. "Because we in America are still able to follow the whispers of our own personal will, even amidst the will of history, we do not realize how destructive history is. You're right, it's an untenably spoiled outlook, and you're right, most people in the world don't have such luck. Their personal will is destroyed by the will of history until it is no more, and they become merely a toy of the epoch."

Anglor nodded and didn't say anything.

"If that's what your artwork is begging the world to do it's even more important than I thought. It is unlike most art., which is essential to culture. Yours is essential to civilization."

"I   wouldn't   say   that..."
"I will help you," Zweifle said again, with boisterous magnanimity in both his voices. "I will help you kill history. I believe in what

you're doing, I believe in you. I own an art gallery, and I want you to be next month's feature artist. I will make you my personal cause, because I quite like you. You have a quest in life. So few people are still like that."

"Thank you," Anglor stuttered out. "Thank you so much."

Zweifle waved a dismissive hand but the face tattooed on him smiled of its own will and Anglor shuddered again. "Don't fawn over me," he said. "Perhaps one day I will have more reason to be grateful to you, if everything goes as planned."

Anglor smiled. "I hope so," and the two shook hands.

"You know," Zweifle said with both faces smiling sickly, "if it works, if you do kill history, what are you going tc make art about?"

Anglor scoffed. "I'm not a man that makes profit off of doom," he said. "Art flourishes just as well in good times as it does in bad. The world will always need art, even, well *especially*, if it becomes a utopia. Art is the only way we know ourselves. When times are hard we use it to cope and to teach the world a lesson, to make it stop acting the way it is, and when times are good we use it to flourish, to achieve self- actualization."

Both of Zwefle's faces were still smiling. "You have too much faith in art," he said.

Anglor shrugged and sighed at the same time. "That's what people tell me."

Chapter 6

Maria was helping Anglor get everything ready for his opening. The show was called "killing history," and Anglor had written a brief manifesto in the lobby of the gallery that was hanging in a frame. Anglor was very stressed and Maria was attempting to soothe him, though she knew the link between them, the thing they had in common, was that they were both inconsolable. Maria went through the lobby door to go to the car and get more of his paintings to hang up on the wall, but she stopped to read the manifesto.

"History is an incubus and it has impregnated us too long. Our biggest fear is being bored, and so we let history run its course of destruction so there will always be something on the television. We must stop this. We must become bored. They say idle hands are the devil's plaything, but I think it is actually entertained audiences, with the devil on the stage, pulling a bloody and mangled rabbit out of a hat that is history, and we clap at the illusion, the illusion that we are significant, important, and then we happily keep our hands idle so long as our minds are ensnared. We must stop living like this. It is gluttonous and pathetic, and people get hurt because of it. History is the devil on the world stage, and it has many victims, it turns the Earth, a paradise of life, into hell, a chamber of death...."

After that Maria stopped reading it and continued with her task of getting more of Anglor's paintings. She looked at the door to the gallery. It said "Michael Smith" on it, "Killing History." She shook her head. Such a normal name for such an extravagant man, who hates history and hates entertainment, yet he is also on the stage, pulling a different rabbit out of a hat, offering an alternative illusion to the run of the mill prestidigitator's lies. She did not think he was the devil, though, though he had fallen like him from the stars, like an asteroid, something that had the force to destroy an entire species, perhaps due to his mission to save it. Maria wondered if people killed history what would they kill next. If they killed the past they would probably then become bloodthirsty for the future, and murder it as well. She supposed they might as well. It was a menacing thing, the future was, full of promises but one always got the feeling that not only were they empty, the future itself was empty, and you'd be living in it alone.

Maria went around the corner to smoke a joint in the alley. She saw a sign there, it said "pray for our nation." She shook her head. 'Damn,' she thought. 'Things really are going wrong if even the religious nuts know they are.' She puffed on the joint. The smoke was caustic and made her cough, but still it felt good. She felt every muscle in her body relax and got a soothing kind of tired, a tired where she could still go about her day without passing out, but which also let her be more like a shadow among her life, something fading, so it did not feel like she was participating completely, more like she was watching it, analyzing it with indifference, without a heart, completely detached, free. She liked that feeling, it was nice, she liked to be removed from it all.

Once she finished the joint she went back into the gallery and hung Anglor's paintings.

"Do you still need me?" she asked him.

"No. Take a break. Relax."

She nodded and went into the backroom where there was a television. The back room was more like a dank storeroom or a cellar, somebody's half hearted office, or a place to relax occasionally. She lit a menthol cigarette. The biting cool hit the back of her throat and she exhaled. This felt good, too. As long as she could always be smoking something she was alright. She turned on the tv and languidly drew on her cigarette, trying to savor it. Everything was slow right now, as if time were but a fly caught in molasses. This was nice too. The news was on. Putin had dropped a nerve agent on Syria and now President Trump was retaliating by also doing airstrikes on Syria. Maria shook her head. 'So here we are again,' she thought. 'America is sticking its dirty fingers in yet another country's civil war. We must be incredibly bored to keep doing this, fighting in wars that don't want us.'

More news. Trump's head of Veteran Affairs was under investigation. Manafort was under investigation, the whole team was corrupt. Then a little bit about the Rohingya refugees. Maria smoked her cigarette rapidly now, with a little bit of anxiety. She remembered when the Prime Minister of Myanmar had briefly talked about the genocide, and was completely dismissive about it. She didn't understand. This woman was a Nobel peace prize winner, and she didn't care about these people. She didn't understand how this happened, and it happened often, that one race of people, without having done anything, inspire so much hate even from so called rational people. It is a mass delusion, Maria thought, but she did not understand how so many people caught it, as if it were a delusion that was contagious. How an innocent group of people inspires such bloodlust she did not understand, and it was merely by them existing, there was no other reason, and certainly not a rational one, but this happened a lot. It happened to the African Americans in America, it happened to the Jews all over the world, it didn't make sense. She supposed all she could blame was mob mentality, the yearning of all people to belong in a large group and to do it the easiest way possible, by hating another group, so there didn't have to be an actual alliance, something based on a real connection between many different individuals, but instead the hatred of an easily made scapegoat, so people could belong together at the exclusion of others.

The news continued. Some actress from the show *Smallville* was mow the Madame of a sex cult which wouldn't let people leave it. Maria cringed and at last changed the channel. She remembered the sign "pray for our nation," but she didn't remember how to pray- (she knew there was a certain way to do it correctly, but she knew that most people didn't know it and that she was one of them,) and she thought perhaps the nation needed something more substantial than prayer, the whispers to a deaf God. She finished her cigarette and immediately lit another one. 'Perhaps Anglor's right,' she thought. 'Perhaps we do need to kill history, before history kills us, our own morbid invention, an Oedipal murder.'

Maria lit another cigarette, she changed the channel again. Another new channel, although this time she did not see news. She saw the devil dancing on the stage, in front of a red curtain that would never fall. As he danced he destroyed cities, genocide came out of his fingers, dictators were born from him and slowly waltzed with him, him in the lead, the dictator following his every move in obedience, another puppet, while the audience then danced as the dictator danced, obeying his every move, more puppets. They all threw flowers at the devil, as if this stage were a grave, and it was indeed, a mass grave, with the devil dancing over it. Maria felt sickened and at last turned the TV off. She dragged on her cigarette with rapidity, trying to get that image out of her head. 'It's just because I'm stoned,' she thought. 'I don't even believe in the devil.'

But as she tried to get the image out of her head worse images still came flooding the corners of her mind, the places she often avoided but which took their vengeance out her negligence of them in dreams, and sometimes, like right now, when she was stoned. She thought about the Rohingya Muslims, and she thought about Hannah Arendt. Hannah Arendt had described refugees and victims of genocide as "worldless," and now suddenly Maria knew what that meant. It was being told by the world that it didn't want you in it anymore, that you not only didn't belong in it, they would not allow you to exist there anymore, but of course there was no where else to go. They were not so fortunate as Anglor, who could return to the moon at any time, everyone else could not escape Earth, even when Earth was ejecting them, even when the entire Earth, not only one's native country, is no longer home anymore. It would be like being homeless in your own house, this state of being worldless in the world.

Maria thought she understood it a little bit. She had never felt like Earth was home, but then again, no one was trying to kick her out of it, no one was trying to force her not to exist. She supposed being worldless was being completely free, but an aimless freedom, the freedom of being adrift in the sea with nothing to hold onto, the loneliest freedom, where you cannot believe in anyone anymore, after having been victim to humanity's darkness, the kind of freedom you are forced into, the kind of freedom that no one would ever choose, a freedom without free will, which should be impossible, but regrettably isn't. It is the state of being lost in a world that no longer wants to find you, the freedom of being discarded from your right to the world, which everyone is supposed to have inherently.

Maria took a particularly arduous drag off her cigarette and started coughing violently. She didn't want to think of these things anymore. She thought of all these worldless people in their long procession into nullibiety and the devil laughing like an imp in the background, herding them through the stage and behind the curtain where no one knew what waited for them.

Anglor stuck his head in. "Are you alright?"

"Fine."

"I heard you coughing."

"I'm fine."

"The show's about to start, want to join us?"

"Sure," Maria said, but really she did not want to. She was very happy for Anglor, but she was in a peculiar mood tonight, even before she had smoked the pot. She didn't want to be around all these ineffectual, stuffy, empty headed ersatz intellectuals and their opinion of art which they thought should he respected, but Maria didn't know how they could be respected because none of them could make art, they only studied it and renounced it. And she was right. As soon as the doors opened in came flooding the young drug addicted intelligentsia with their Supreme hats and skinny jeans, all smelling of Marijuana even worse than Maria was, some of their noses bleeding, all of them talking loudly and in an affected drone of preciosity, all of them afraid they wouldn't be heard, though they had nothing to say except what Rotten Tomatoes review of the latest movie was and what they thought of the new Kanye West album. They were all particularly dilettantish and empty, and Maria was disappointed in them. Young people were supposed to save the world each generation, but these young people just did drugs, watched Netflix, and droned on and on about media all day, practically enslaved to it, borrowing other people's opinions all day, very few of them having touched a book since college, and all of them checking their smart phones almost every ten seconds with anxiety, as if if they didn't carry their link to the entire world in their pockets all the time they would no longer be a part of it, as if it was a mirror that reminded them they were still young and still alive, and without it the felt they didn't exist.

But their older counterparts were even worse- all fat men with PHD's going on in the same drone about Fellini and comparing Anglor's art to Wassily Kandinsky or Adolf Wolfli, and just a touch of Cocteau and Modigliani, saying how delightfully art brut it was, smelling of old pipe tobacco and speaking about art in a way that was erudite but with deliberate effect, as if they knew everything about art as compensation for the fact that they couldn't understand it, and they could make or break an artist, and they usually chose to break them, though they themselves were not artists and never would be, they would never know either the joy or the agony of creating, and so while they held all the power, as if they were the pimps of human creation, they were always lagging behind in time, they were nowhere near as ahead of time as an artist, who always moves through time rapidly, living always in the future even when the future has yet to arrive, so these pimps could not really comprehend the artist, and they never knew he or she was any good, they never knew when something truly special had nascently arrived, because they were stuck in the present, most of the time the past, and if they had come across a starving Chagall or Modigliani in the modern world they probably would have sent them a rejection letter. They were not who they thought they were, all they knew about themselves is that they were educated, because that's all there was to them. They were executioners in suits and ties, ready to either cut off the artist's head or to make him or her a millionaire, and they always did both things to the wrong people.

Maria sighed and went back into the alley for another joint. Anglor was pretty much inaccessible all night. People were asking him questions and giving him champagne and patting him on the back like business men while he had to explain himself over and over again as the answer to the impertinent, cliché question "what does this *mean*?" a question Anglor asked nothingness each and everyday but which he felt was apropos of nothing when talking about art. And just like nothingness, Anglor didn't have an answer for it.

Maria smoked her joint in the alley again when she caught Mark out of the corner of her eye walking into the gallery. She gestured for him to come over.

"Hello, Maria," he said.

"Wanna smoke this joint with me?"

"Sure," he said, and grabbed it wand took a hit.

"What are you doing here?"

"I wouldn't miss it for the world."

"It's extremely boring, and the building is full of assholes."

"Well, those are the people that make you famous."

Maria took another it off the joint then passed it back to Mark who did the same. "Do you really think he'll become famous?" Maria asked.

"I do," Mark said somberly. "It is written in the stars for him."

"I hate the ink in the stars. It's too permanent."

"Oh, Maria," Mark said while billowing a cloud of smoke out of his mouth. "Nothing is permanent."

Maria shrugged. She looked across the street. Jehovah's witnesses were knocking on every door, trying to sell salvation. "Jesus." Maria said, groaning. "These days Heaven is an advertisement."

Mark laughed and passed the joint back to Maria. "You're different from most people," he said. "You can bear loneliness without making it someone else's problem. You don't cling to people in the hope it will end."

"Because I know it won't."

"But most people are not like that. They'll do anything to make them less lonely. That's what God is for."

"How is that any different from a schizophrenic that likes the voices in their head because they keep them company?"

Mark laughed heartily. "I see why you see it that way. We all have our imaginary friends, imaginary lovers, and so on. It's no different than keeping yourself company, just a different version of yourself, one you invented, and that's God, he's another version of the whole human race trying to keep itself company by talking to itself. You would be amazed what people would do not to feel lonely. They do not all accept it as you do, but both of you are sad, becoming inured to it just as much as doing compromising things in a futile attempt to end it."

"You're an asshole, Mark."

He chuckled and took the last hit off the joint and assed it back to Maria. "That's a roach," he said.

"I have a bowl"

"You stoners really do suck the life out of a joint."

"It costs money you know."

Then at last Anglor walked outside. Maria smiled at him warmly as she packed the bowl and Mark gave him a friendly pat on the back, which was unusual for Mark.

"How's your big night?" Mark asked.

"Draining. Let me hit that bowl, Maria."

She passed it to him. "So many assholes in there," Anglor went on. "All calling me 'delightfully droll. Like Marcel DuChamp or George Grosz.' I can't take it anymore."

"It's not what you thought it was?" Mark asked.

"I just didn't think I'd have to do so much talking. I was hoping the art would speak for me."

"Most people don't listen to art."

Anglor shook his head. 'Then how are we going to kill history?"

"They'll listen to *you*, " Mark said.

Anglor shrugged and passed the bowl to Mark. "I do appreciate you guys coming, though."

"I wouldn't miss it for the world," Maria said as she lit a cigarette.

"You did miss it," Anglor said. "You've been out here the whole time."

"I'm sorry. I don't like crowds."

"Neither do I, and I wasn't really expecting one for *my* opening, but a lot of people came. I should be happy but I'm not."

"Why not?' Mark asked.

"Because I don't think anyone is listening to me, to me or my art. I think they're just here to look intelligent, and I'm just here to reassure them that they are, but I don't think they're intelligent. I think they've just spent their lives reading to feel interesting, not to actually be interesting, but to play at it. I think they know to be truly interesting you have to be alone a lot."

"It's never what it seems," Mark said. "And regrettably these people are who your future depends on."

"No," Anglor said definitively. "I have always made my own future, and I always will. I depend on no one for it."

Mark smiled and passed the bowl to him. "Because you are truly interesting," he said.

Anglor smiled and hit the bowl. "It's nice to be around you two," he said. "You understand. That's extremely rare."

"Well, you know," Mark said, "the magic of life comes and goes. Sometimes it is gone for a very long time, and you want to die, pining for what's become emptiness in your life, but it will come back, you just have to ride through life becoming stale and impotent for awhile until it returns, because it will return."

"Sometimes it doesn't stay for very long," Maria said almost petulantly. "And the stale, impotent life as you call it lasts much longer."

Mark shrugged. "There is nothing else to live for."

The next day Anglor was in the city paper. He remembered talking to the journalist, Zweifle had introduced them. He read the article. It was a nice eclat, and said very kind things about his artwork, and also spoke of his message to kill history. His picture was in the article, standing with Zweifle while all four of his eyes were looking shiftily at Anglor. He got out of bed. Maria was already awake, which was unusual. Often she never even got out of bed. She was making coffee as usual, they rarely actually ate breakfast. Anglor showed her the article.

"Very nice," Maria said. "It seems the night was a success." Suddenly Anglor's phone rang. He picked it up.

"Hello," he said.

"Michael, it's Zweifle."

"Hello," Anglor said again.

"Did you read the article?"

"Yes, I did. It was very flattering."

"You're about to go on tour, kid. I've gotten you a slot for a gallery in Columbus."

"Th…Thank you," Anglor stuttered out.

"This is the start of a beautiful friendship," Zweifle said, and then the phone clicked as he hung up.

"What was that?" Maria asked as she brought out the coffee.

"Zweifle wants me in a gallery in Columbus."

"Oooo," Maria said. "Branching out."

"I don't want to do it again," Anglor admitted, "but I have to. I don't know why I feel this way. It should be an honor."

"I don't know. Maybe you're just still waiting on 'the magic of life,' like the rest of us."

"What if it never comes?"

"According to Mark it will."

"And then I'm destined to lose it again."

Maria shrugged. "That's the way it goes. We have to share it with the billions of people who live on this planet, we can't hog it all."

"I think it forgets a lot of the people on this planet, thinks some of us are negligible."

"It does, but we are Americans, it won't forget us. It will come to us in an advertisement."

Anglor dropped his head in his hands. "I feel like a criminal for that, "he said.

Maria patted him on the back. "It'll pass," she said. "I remember when I was in high school. I was big into philosophy, all of my friends were. That was just what we liked, philosophy, marijuana, and masturbation. I remember those times occasionally, though not often, but I remember them right now. I used to spend all my waking hours trying to answer some very difficult questions. I was never able to answer them, but they haunted my mind, I could never stop thinking about them. I couldn't decide if unity as a whole, some collective conscious, or individuality was more important. I used to argue it with myself for hours, unable ever to make a decision, because they both seemed equally important though opposed to one another. And then I became an adult and I ceased to care- I never think about it anymore. Now it is enough just to make it through every single day. Now it's the bare minimum that counts."

"That's sad," Anglor said. "It seems you gave up the magic of life."

"I just don't have time anymore. Besides, it was maddening."

"You have plenty of time," Anglor said flatly. "We all do. We all do nothing all day and think it's business."

"Aye," Maria said. "That's the horror of adulthood. All the things that were important to you when you were a kid aren't important anymore, are overshadowed by a greater anxiety, and then suddenly nothing is important to you but merely surviving, and you are living for nothing but you keep on living because it would be a sin to die, but living for nothing I think is an even greater sin."

"It's not a sin, it's an accident."

"Well, most sins are."

Anglor lit a cigarette and drank his coffee. "Zweifle is a pimp," he said wearily. "And my works of art are his prostitutes."

Maria shrugged. "Unfortunately that's how it works."

"I am trying to rid corruption by working hand in hand with it. I'm trying to defeat the devil but first I must sell my soul to him. It's so backwards."

"Enough with the shit about the devil. He doesn't exist, only human beings and their demons do."

A train went by and they were both silent. They lived far enough away from the tracks that it was not a thunderous roar, more like a distant sound of melancholia, as if it were the past trying to communicate with them, mourning its own death, mourning that it was no damn good and only hurt.. It was a very lonely sound, and Anglor and Maria listened to it. It was the sound they would have made if they could.

At last it passed and they began to talk again. "I love that sound," Maria said.

"I do too. It sounds like freedom."

"The years of growing old have offered me little wisdom, but it did teach me one thing: there is nothing else but solitude."

"That's sad and comforting at the same time. I need a drink."

"There's a bottle of whiskey in the cabinet."

"Oh thank God."

Anglor went into the kitchen and poured himself a drink. Straight, on the rocks. 'I'm going to have to quit this one day,' he thought to himself as he drank in one long, flourishing gulp. 'I can't live like this forever, but for now it's nice. It's like I'm mourning that soon my youth will be at an end., though not consciously. It's masqueraded as so called fun.'

"Do you want one, too," Anglor called from the kitchen.

"I suppose so. You know it's only noon."

"I know and I don't care."

Maria gave him a quizzical look. "What are you upset about?" she asked.

"Nothing. This is just not what I thought it would be."

"What?"

He brought Maria her drink and sighed rather loudly in her ear. "My mission. Suddenly it feels cheap. I feel like an empty demagogue."

"It will get better. This is only the beginning."

"But usually the beginning is the best part, and then after that it will become stale routine."

"Maybe with what you're ding it's the opposite. Maybe it will only get better."

Anglor sighed again and drank. "Maybe," he said., but he didn't have much faith in the word.

Maria put her hand on his shoulder gently. "Balzac said our worst fears lie in anticipation," she said. "Our greatest hopes lie there as well."

Anglor laughed and finished his drink. "It's too early to be completely drunk," he said. "Stop me from getting another."

"Okay. It's going to be a long day today. It's summer. The days are longer."

Anglor sighed and looked at his empty cup, wishing there were still alcohol in it. "It doesn't matter," he said. "Whether the days are long or short, they're intimidating either way."

Anglor's opening in Columbus went very well. Even more people came than they did the last one, though it was the same type of people again. It was exactly the same. Maria didn't mind helping to set up but as soon as the enfilade of hipsters and aged professors came in she snuck out back to get high all night, while Anglor was at the mercy of these people and their impertinent questions, telling him how his artwork made them feel, which famous artist they could equate it to, and what was his inspiration for this piece? And how long did it take him to draw it? And so on and so forth.

Anglor was in a twilight whirl of these questions and what seemed a never ending glass of champagne. As soon as he ran out someone would pass him another, and he would accept it mutely, like a baby being given a bottle of milk, and by the time the opening was over he was black out drunk and puking in a trash can. Luckily no one saw him do so except Maria, who had seen him do this many times.

"Where am I?" he asked her dazedly, completely vulnerable.

"Heaven," she said, and she gently put him in Mark's car where he passed out on the back seat. Maria then went in and spoke for him the rest of the night, and acted exactly as he had. She drank herself through the whole thing. But the night was still a success. They went home, Maria and Mark chain smoking on the highway in Mark's car while Anglor was unconscious in the back breathing out of his mouth and making a quiet whistling sound. It wasn't long before Anglor got another opening, this time in New York, which he was actually excited about. He had always wanted to see New York City, even when he had lived on the moon. He had forgotten for awhile that he wasn't human.

The gallery in New York was an even bigger success, with a crowd neither Anglor or Maria could stomach. Again it passed in the drunken blur that was the cure for anxiety, but Anglor was growing very popular. Punk Rock kids were now walking around with T-shirts they had made themselves that said "Kill History," in big, white, grimy lettering. Anglor was very pleased when he heard this. Young people are our only salvation, but they always fail us because eventually they grow old. So goes time. It wasn't long before Anglor at last became a household name, among certain circles, but he was glad he was popular with the youth. Of course everything he owed to Adam Zweifle, though.

The gallery in New York was by far the most stressful one, though both Anglor and Maria were glad to see the city, it had much more pulse than the small town they lived in in Ohio, which had always been old and dying, even right after it was born, that was a place for people whose simplicity made them eager to participate in brutality, a population of people that was more like a mob, in their aging, dying city, where they worshipped the geront and hoped the future would never touch them and their imbecilic comforts. New York was much different. Progress beat through the city like it was its heart, that if the future happened anywhere, it happened here, daily, and the people were much more but less like a mob, more like a herd without a *poimen,* so they were free to do whatever they wanted to without God, and mostly they just went to work in the busy city that had grown used to its anxiety, but it was a city throbbing with all types of life, all of them desperate to make it in a city that was almost by necessity cruel, and which felt like a microcosm of the whole world, the whole world in one city. It was much more interesting than Miamisburg, the small town Maria and Anglor lived in.

By far the largest crowd showed up to Anglor's opening in New York City. This time Maria couldn't even sneak away, almost every time she did someone would see her and ask if they could hit the joint, and often times it was a whole group of young people and Maria would concede reluctantly because she had always been a passively acquiescent person even though that was rarely what she really wanted. So she ended up staying in the gallery this time, drinking as much champagne as Anglor to alleviate the incredible heat from all the bodies packed in there, but it was a more interesting crowd than the other two openings. Maria thought she saw someone from almost every ethnicity here, and that made her happy. The conversation was of average volume, but there was so much of it that it became a roaring buzz, like a herd of bees in the room. It was a healthy vibration, like a heartbeat. Maria didn't have a panic attack this time, because everyone in the room seemed so alive, in the most variegated city in the world, a place that was truly no one's home, but which accepted everyone, though begrudgingly at first, it was still a place anyone could live.

There was one piece in the gallery that people were particularly attracted to. It was just a picture of the Earth behind glass, but when you went up to it you could see your own reflection in it, your face spread across the world. It was called "The Mirror." Maria stared at it and was only reminded for the umpteenth time that she was not strikingly attractive. But it went deeper than this. This mirror, the Earth, it aggravated her noogenic neurosis. She thought about the Earth. It had blue skies that looked like a vast plateau of tears, then red skies that looked like God was bleeding, and immense oceans that rolled with the vagaries of the moon, the cold rock Anglor was born on, and she thought of all this and marveled that her face should be there, that her consciousness demanded to be apart of the world for her consciousness to exist, when the Earth shouldn't be marred with her. The Earth was so beautiful, naturally, as it had created itself, before humans had been born here and polluted it with skyscrapers, shopping malls, concentration camps.

Maria wished she couldn't see her face there, she wished she couldn't see anyone's face there- she realized a visage on the surface of this rock was a scar, a marring. "My God," she suddenly whispered to herself. "How beautiful the world would be if only we weren't here!"

Part II

Chapter 1

And so at last Angor was famous, and of course he didn't feel anything. They were backstage at the Bill Maher show where he was soon to be interviewed. He was already having a panic attack. He had taken two valiums and was starting to pass out. Maria shook him and gave him a huge cup of coffee. "You can't blow this," she said.

"I want to blow it all away," Anglor said through a slur and Maria rolled her eyes.

"This is your mission, it's your reason to live."

"Give me a glass of water, would you?"

There had been an annoying stage hand who kept explaining in grotesque details what the Omega Point was, another obscure intellectual just like Anglor had once been, doing his work in the dark because his whole life was in the dark, writing by candlelight, *et lux in tenbris lucet*, the only light in such a dim world, this light being the ambition, the hope that one day you will get to step outside the wings and at last on the stage, into the sun. But Anglor already had, and he found it was too bright to look into, that your own life could blind you this way, and he missed writing by the dim candlelight, he missed being a naïve kid who thought he knew what he wanted, but we all want things that turn out to be hollow when we get them, because that's just life, it's dissatisfying overall, and dreams do come true but not in the way you want them to, and next is the disillusionment, the bitterness, that life can only offer you a diluted, impure version of your ideals.

Anglor began to sweat profusely and he started fanning his face. "It's so hot," he groaned.

The irritating stagehand returned. "You're on in five," he said. "Stand here."

But Anglor didn't want to do it. He didn't want to deal with Bill Maher's overly aggressive intelligence or practiced sang froid. He didn't want to ask questions that there were no answer to. Suddenly he heard Bill Maher call his name from the stage and the roar of applause and he walked across the stage sluggishly, as if in a dream where he was being pulled along by a string, and he hoped the string would lead him somewhere, but it never did, it just pulled him until he didn't have much free will, and the only place it could take anyone to was the end.

Anglor sat down in his chair and waved politely to the audience. He was sweating so hard you could actually see it, even the camera could see it.

"So," Bill Maher said with his usual preciosity. "The man who wants to kill history. You know, I'll be out of a job."

"Do you really like this job anyway?" Anglor said warily, and Bill Maher roared with laughter.

"Fine point, fine point. I do appreciate the money however."

"You can find that anywhere."

Bill Maher half chuckled and half scoffed. "So, what made you decide you were an artist?"

"I'm not an artist," Anglor said dejectedly. "I'm just a lunatic with a pen."

"Well, that's an artist."

After he said this Anglor began to loosen up a little bit, but he was still pouring sweat and he couldn't speak without stuttering. The interview went on and Anglor did the best he could, but eventually he couldn't take it anymore. "Please," he implored. "Let me go."

"What's wrong?" Bill Maher asked.

"I'm not cut out for this. I'm having a panic attack." Then everyone at home got the television screen completely blue with the heinous beeping and the sign that said "technical difficulties." Anglor was rushed off the stage. He was coughing furiously and vomited in a garbage bin back stage. He felt like his clothes were suffocating him, so he kept trying to tear them off and when they would not budge he screamed in agony and grabbed the pair of scissors that was sitting on the table nearest him.

Maria wrestled them away from him as he tried to plunge them into his skin. Anglor screamed again and tugged at his clothes more. "I can't breathe!" he yelled.

"Let's go outside," Maria said gently. "Get some air."

"Get this tie off of me, it's like a noose!"

So Maria removed Anglor's tie and he crashed into a chair where he panted furiously. "Call an ambulance," he said.

"What?"

"Call an ambulance. I have to get out of here. I need to go to the hospital."

So the ambulance came and as they tried to strap Anglor in he thrashed violently and screamed more. The paramedic to the left of him deftly injected him with Ativan and Halidol, and after a few more minutes of struggling he at last grew limp. "I wanna go home," he kept pleading softly.

Then the ambulance took off and Maria bit back tears as she got in her car to meet them in the emergency room. All she could think of was when Anglor had shot himself in the head, and she realized in that moment the exact definition of a lunatic- it is a man crawling from his own head, desperately trying to get out.

Chapter 2

Anglor woke up in another mental hospital, unaware of where he really was or even the name of the facility. Somewhere in New York. The place was extremely crowded and most of the patients were homeless, so they did not want to leave. Most of them had no idea who Anglor was, they had not heard of the great Michael Smith, and he was glad. He rolled over in bed. He felt as if he was hungover, his head seemed to be in a rage at him, as if he had abused it too long, never mind how much it had abused him. He got up and pissed, then crawled back in bed, hoping he could sleep away the headache. There was a knock on the door.

"Breakfast, Michael," a nurse said.

"No," Anglor groaned. "I need more sleep."

The nurse nodded and walked away. Anglor fell into a spot of his pillow where he had salivated excessively the night before. He didn't even care. He shut his eyes.

"You're doing a very good job," a voice said from the corner of the room.

"Bogomil," Anglor groaned out. "Leave me alone."

"I just wanted you to know you are performing admirably. People will really think you are insane."

"I'm not acting, Bogomil," Anglor said sharply. "I really have gone mad."

"Well, that's even better."

"Why?"

"If people think you're mad they'll know you're humane. Besides, the only way to wisdom is through immense suffering,"

Anglor rolled over in bed, away from Bogomil. "Is wisdom even worth it then?" he whispered.

"It is," Bogomil said firmly. "Everything worthwhile comes at a heavy price, you know that. Since you've been on Earth you've had to pay for being an artist with madness. Think while you are suffering so that you will soon acquire wisdom, that it will end and when it does you will be stronger and more intelligent, older in the way people are supposed to age, with wisdom. Think of wisdom as an *et lux in tenebris lucet*, a light in the dark, for you cannot help these humans if you are not wise, and you cannot be wise if you don't suffer. This is the very reason fate gives people pain, and those who waste it, who waste their pain, grow old without wisdom, and so they die afraid."

"That makes sense," Ajnglor barely whispered.

"Don't waste your pain," Bogomil reiterated. "Use this at every opportunity as wisdom, the only fruit on a tree that is otherwise covered in thorns."

"Okay."

"Because," Bogomil went on. "If you don't use it to make you stronger it will kill you." And then he disappeared. Anglor tried to sleep a little more but he couldn't, so eventually he got begrudgingly out of bed and into the shower, about to start the day in the mental hospital. After he showered breakfast was over, and all the patients were scattered randomly about the ward. He saw an old man sitting on a couch and he decided he would sit next to him. The man seemed solemn, like he wouldn't bother anyone.

"Michael Smith," the man said as Anglor sat down.

"Hello," Anglor said wearily back, wishing the old man could hear his thought that the only reason he sat down next to him was so he wouldn't talk.

"I quite like your art," the man said.

"Thank you."

"I'm a novelist," he said.

Anglor raised an eyebrow. "Really?"

"Really."

"How did you become that? I still don't know how I became an artist. I don't understand how any of us become anything, the series of random events that have to happen to make it so, it's overwhelming to think about."

"Indeed. Mine was quite simple, though. I was going to kill myself, and so I wrote a suicide note, but the suicide note became a whole novel, and halfway through it it became a reason to live."

"I suppose that's how I became an artist, too. But if it worked, if we both found a reason to live, what are we doing here?"

The man coughed rather violently and waved Anglor's question off. "Most of these illnesses are life long," he said. "Sometimes it just happens."

"What was the novel about if halfway through it was no longer a suicide note?"

"When it stopped being a suicide note it became a plea, much like your plea for people to kill history, though my plea was that we make the world less into a place that makes people feel the need to write a suicide note."

"Then you would have never become a writer, and you would never have had a reason to live."

The man chuckled. "We all have to convince ourselves to live," he said. "Life itself will not convince us. The reason has to be from within, not from without."

"I already know this."

"But you've forgotten. I'm here to remind you."

Anglor sighed and relaxed a little bit in his chair.

"Have you ever published?"

"Only self- published, unfortunately. None of my books were ever best sellers, or even noticed. But that's ok. It was still worth it to write them, though I'll never be famous like you."

"It was essential that I became famous…"

"It was essential for me, too, but it never happened. I always wanted to make a living off of writing, it was the only job I could ever stand, and Social Security doesn't give me shit…"

"I know how that goes."

"Don't forget how lucky you are. The rest of us are wasting away in obscurity."

"Fame is an empty promise," Anglor said.

"That may be so, but you're still paid to do the work you love. Most people are paid to do the work they hate and which degrades them. Your work doesn't do that."

"Neither does yours, even if you didn't get paid for it, it was still your work."

The man smiled. "Yes, it is. And I can rest easy when I die knowing that I only ever did the work I loved, that I never made room for the work that I hated and which would degrade me. When I die I can rest easy knowing that though my dreams were never fulfilled, at least I dedicated my life *trying* to fulfill them. Most of the time we don't get what we want, Michael, and what we are given in its stead often feels like complacently settling for a lesser thing, but we don't necessarily have to settle for it, though if we don't we will be given nothing. Perhaps that's better."

"Perhaps. What's your name?"

The old man extended a hand and Anglor shook it. "My name is Adam," he said. "I am the world's first man."

"I'm the world's last man," Anglor said. "We are both lonely then. It begins and ends in loneliness."

"At least we have our work. Believe me, there is nothing else. We are lucky that this nothing else we have we actually enjoy. Most people have a nothing else they can't stand. And still there is nothing else. But there is really nothing else besides art, except maybe love, but I think they are essentially the same thing.'

"And they're both madness."

"Sometimes. But they are also man's only reason. Man's only reason is his insanity."

Anglor chuckled but didn't say anything. A woman slowly approached them.

"How you doing, Eleanor?" Adam called to her. She sat down next to him.

"This place doesn't make me want to kill myself any less."

"Indeed," Adam said Anglor also agreed. Then another man approached them, a young, lean Italian. Her put his arms around Eleanor's waist.

"Get the fuck off me." Eleanor said sharply.

"Come on, sweetheart," the Italian man said in a slow drawl, with an accent. "It's no harm. Just a little bit of lingam in the yoni, mentula in the cunnus."

Adam picked up his cane and wielded it wildly in front of the young man, "You better leave her alone," he said, then bopped the Italian man on the head wit his cane. "Go on now!" Adam yelled "Fuck off!"

"*Vecchio uomo,*" the Italian man spat, but he walked away.

"Are you alright, Eleanor?" Adam asked.

Eleanor dragged slowly on her cigarette. "It's bullshit," she said. "I'm the one who got raped and I'm the one who ends up in the damn nut house. And all these men here are so thirsty. They haven't had sex in years. Why is that? Why is it that every pathetic fucker who hasn't gotten laid in years comes crawling to me as if I'm the patron saint of pity fucks?"

"I'm sorry, Eleanor," Adam said, but she just waved him off. It was true, she was raped, and all these men in here kept making a move on her and every time they did it a deafening alarm went off in her head. An elderly man about Adam's age had done it, too, and when he did Maria whited out for a second and fell on the pavement and hit her head. There was a bandage there. Anglor looked at her. She was indeed beautiful, zaftig in all the right places, and she walked around with it begrudgingly, this femininity of hers that she had never wanted, never asked for, but which fell upon her upwards from the most lubricious abyss of hell. All it meant was that you often had to have sex when you didn't want to, because men wouldn't leave you alone, and it was hard to tell which ones would take no for an answer and which ones wouldn't. But Eleanor was tired of it all. She wished she were ugly, she wished she never had to have sex again. The femininity, the sexy, jaw dropping *Ewig Weibliche* of hers was a bane.

"I wish I were a lesbian," she said. "I don't understand how these guys get horny in a mental hospital. This is the last place I would wanna get laid."

"They're animals," Adam said.

"Who is this handsome fellow?" Eleanor asked, pointing to Anglort with her cigarette.

"This is Michael Smith, the artist."

"Oh yes, I've seen his art, it's good," but she said it very off handedly, not that she wasn't sincere, but that Anglor was just another man to her, and therefore another potential predator.

Anglor sensed this. "Don't worry," he said. "I won't hit on you. I've never had much of a sex drive."

Eleanor softened at this. "Me either," she said. "But it's always been required of me."

"I'm sorry."

She shrugged. "It's not your fault. It is that Italian man's fault, though."

"It's ridiculous," Adam went on. "They act like they've never seen a woman before."

Anglor laughed and put out his cigarette. He was grateful for these mental hospitals that let you smoke. They were few and could only be found in big cities, but they also had the most desperate patients, people who had been struggling with addiction their whole lives, the majority of the city that the tourists never noticed, the poor who stood no chance in this big apple that had several worms eating through it and which these unfortunate people had all swallowed and it acted like a tapeworm, so no amount of ingesting or imbibing could ever be enough. It was just like the mental hospital in Columbus but worse- it was worse the bigger the city was. Still, Anglor liked cities, they were still full of life even with so many walking dead, and he would rather spend his time with these people than the people back home, who also had an addiction problem, but hid it better. Big cities and small towns, these are the places you're most likely to become addicted to drugs, from either too much glamour or too much ennui. You had to either deaden or heighten the senses.

Then the smoke break was over, the best part of the day was over, and it only happened once a day, and you were blessed if you even had cigarettes. Anhglor was grateful that Maria was bringing him cigarettes every visit, though she was amazed at the price. Adam went back to his room and it was just Anglor and Eleanor. They were both very timid with each other.

"I saw your freak out on Bill Maher," she said. "It was on the TV here."

Anglor didn't say anything. "I would have done the same thing," she added.

"It was just too much."

"Can I watch you draw?"

"I don't really like people watching me…"

"Well, will you draw something for me?"

"Sure."

"I like you. It's been awhile since I met a man I liked. You seem so gentle."

"I'm just fragile."

"I like that, too, it's what makes you gentle. But I don't want to be your mother."

"I don't need a mother. I don't need a lover, either.'

"Oh," Eleanor said, as if surprised.

"I'll draw something for you, though." And he sat down and quickly sketched her out a picture. It was a man with many faces holding an invisible guitar. It was called "The Guitarist." He didn't know what else to draw here.

"It's nice," she said as he gave it to her. "You are good, you know."

"Thank you. I'm always the prom king in the mental hospital because of my damn art."

"I'm the prom queen everywhere I go and I hate it."

"Yea," Anglor said softly. "I hate it, too. I hate being here."

The nurses gathered everyone for lunch and Anglor didn't see Eleanor anymore. He sat down and ate lunch with Adam and they were both silent. Afterwards, after a lack of anything better to do, Anglor took a nap.

He had a dream. He and Maria were going to school, art school. There was a gallery the teacher walked them through, but Anglor and Maria were strange. They had both been crucified by the teacher. They were no longer on their crosses, but both their wrists still had nails in. Anglor went up to Maria and begged her to remove is.

"It's going to hurt," she said.

"I don't care." And so Maria slowly removed the nails. It did hurt, and there was a lot of blood. Anglor felt as if he had slit his wrists, he felt as if he had committed suicide again. They were surrounded art, and Anglor looked at it and realized it was his art. His head began to spin and Maria laid down on the ground, her nails still in her wrists, and beckoned to Anglor. He lay down on top of her and she put her arms around him.

"You understand," he whispered to her. "You were crucified, too."

Then he woke up in bed and almost screamed with a shock when he found Eleanor in his arms.

"What are you doing?" he asked. "We'll get in a lot of trouble."

"Who cares? It's the end of the world," and she kissed him rather violently.

"Stop, Eleanor," Anglor said as he twisted his lips away from hers. Eleanor paused for a moment. At first she looked into his eyes like she was really hurt, then her expression softened.

"I'm sorry," she whispered. "I don't know any other way to show affection. I've always been taught sex was the most important thing to give." And then she threw her face into Anglor's chest and wept. He held her.

"Christ!" she suddenly yelled. "We are the smartest creatures on the planet, perhaps the entire universe, and we're dumb as hell!"

Later it was visiting hour. Maria came to see him and brought him the much desired pack of cigarettes. He told her about his dream and she smiled eerily.

"Other than that are you doing okay?"

"Yea," he said. "I think I'd rather be here than on TV."

"I thought it was a bit much that they sent you back to the mental hospital. I would have just given you some Ativan and sent you home."

"They thought I was suicidal because of the incident with the scissors."

"But you weren't?"

"No. I was just trying to take the edge off."

"Well, that's a bad way to do it."

"It's no different than drinking, it's just that drinking is socially acceptable…."

"Because it helps people socialize."

"Whatever makes people feel normal I guess."

Maria smiled. "No one really feels normal. They only pretend. Normal is not a real thing, there is only strange. Everything is strange."

"Therefore nothing is. That's the sad part. When everything is so unusual that nothing is unusual, everything becomes permitted. Genocide becomes permitted. I often think it's permitted even more than murder."

"Because it's an act of war, and war is socially acceptable because it makes some people, the people who rule the world, very rich. Murder's not ok, but mass murder is, so long as it is in the name of the country or God."

"People in America have confused the country for God."

"Well, it's the closest thing to God we have."

"It's a false idol," Anglor said rather obdurately.

Maria smiled again. "I know," she said. "Everyone thinking God is on their side, that's what creates war, but God is on no one's side. If He exists He is neutral."

"And we always think people who are neutral are cowardly, but that's not true. They're just sane. But we can't comprehend neutrality. We always have to have an opinion to avoid feeling empty, so we can feel relevant, so we can vainly and stupidly think we're apart of this world, that we have a say in it, when it is just as neutral as God."

"It only makes us more empty, I think, unless you truly believe what you say. You're reminding me of that piece of art you did, 'The Mirror'"

"The one that gave you a panic attack?"

"That's the one. I just feel sometimes that I shouldn't be here, that I'm trespassing on something sacred, like I'm always walking on a burial ground."

Anglor sighed. "I feel that way sometimes. I also feel like my life is already over, that it has been for a long time, and now it's just dragging out its ending."

"You feel that way because you're famous."

"Maybe. We should move here, Maria, we should move to New York. We have the money now."

"Why?'

"Because I don't want to die in Miamisburg. That place is the reason I think my life is over, because every day is the same there. If we move I can feel like I'm starting over, I can feel like my life is beginning again."

"Why don't you just kill yourself and come back to life again?"

"It's not the same."

Maria paused for a second. "This was your plan all along, wasn't it?"

"I'm supposed to change the world, and in order to do that I'll need to be in it. The world is in New York. Nothing is in Miamisburg, it's more of an abyss than an actual location."

"I'll think about it," Maria finally conceded. "If it would make you happier."

"I don't know if it will make me happier, but I feel much more alive in this city than I do at home."

"Your home is the moon."

"Not anymore. When I get back I'll be a complete stranger. I've been on Earth too long."

Maria paused for a second and lifted an eyebrow at him. "You mean, you want to stay here?"

"No, I don't, but going back home isn't going to be easy. I'm changed irrevocably now."

"It's never easy to go back home," Maria said. "I think it's even harder than leaving it. Everything stays the same for so long, then you leave, you come back, and everything has changed in a blink of an eye."

"The moon never changes, but I have."

"That might not be a bad thing."

Anglor laughed about that and hugged Maria on her way out. visiting time was only about an hour long, and you were only allowed to have two visitors at a time. Luckily Anglor only ever had one, and he was grateful for this rule. He didn't need a hoard of people to see him this way, completely dejected, and having to slowly gain back the will to live, which you always leave behind when you first enter the mental hospital, which is a propaedeutic to being there. Another smoke break, and Anglor was glad he had his own cigarettes.

He sat with Eleanor and Adam again,. They were his friends for the time being, for you simply cannot get through something like this alone, but then when they were all released they would never see each other again, never want to see each other again, for it would just be a reminder of the time they were non compos mentis and had to be kept away from society for it, for their own safety. But at this moment they were very close friends. At this moment they were all they had, all that was keeping them somewhat sane, or at least so they could make a pretense of being sane, enough to get out of here The mental hospital was not a place where you were allowed the luxury of being lonely, because sometimes loneliness is a luxury, but in here if you decided to remain lonely you would not get better, you would only have to return rapidly. The brief friendships are what get you out, and for some people it is nice. For some people they have more friends in here than they do the outside world.

Anglor dragged on his cigarette languidly, trying to savor it, for all the cigarettes in here seemed to burn at light speed. Eleanor kept looking at him from the corner of her eye.

"Thanks for the picture," she said.

"No problem."

"It really is pretty good. Now I can go home and say I met the great Michael Smith."

Adam laughed. He was also trying to smoke his cigarette slowly. There was a man only a couple feet beside them who had his head lowered and was talking to himself in French. Everyone knew he was talking to the voices in his head. He caught Anglor's eye, then walked up to him.

"Alors," he said. "Vous etes un genie?"

Anglor shrugged. "Pretendument."

"Vous manqué meconnaissance?"

"Quelquefois."

Chapter 3

The news was on. This was the only time that all the patients in the hospital gathered in the same room, besides when they went outside for smoke breaks. All these mentally ill people were somewhat political, and divisively so, as well. There were people like Anglor who were die hard liberals and then there were people who were avid Trump supporters, in spite of the fact he wanted to take their health care, but still, everyone was political. They realized that though these things seem distant in America, they still determined your life, and the lives of mentally ill people were always affected by politics, for they were one of the groups of unfortunates that were debated over. Besides, there were many different types of people in this hospital- black people, gay people, immigrants, all people who had to know politics because it made them nervous, because it was always determining their destiny, their fate was unwillingly in its hands, particularly now. And of course it was the history Anglor was hoping to kill. So they all gathered for the news and were silent when it was on, most of them keeping their mouths shut about their opinions on it to avoid argument.

It went on as usual. A hopeful new director of the CIA who wanted to get rid of torture, several Palestinian protesters killed at the Gaza Strip, North Korea refusing to show up at the summit, things like that. Then it got to another topic. Tom Wolfe, the writer, was dead. Anglor felt his stomach sink and his spirits fizzle out. He always hated when an artist he admired died, for they were like kinfolk to him, and they were like teachers, they taught him how to do his work, they were the only people who could teach him, the ones who had really done it, not a professor, but an actual artist. And he did always feel a spiritual connection with them, as if they were actually mentors, and often they had abated his loneliness in the small hours of the lonely dark of insomnia and hypomania, they had all made him feel less strange, and he felt he was in debt to them for that, for regular people could not make him feel that way, only the greats. And Tom Wolfe was indeed one of the Great's. He had gotten an obscure book of his short stories only a week ago, due of course to synchronicity, the prescience that one of his masters was about to depart. The universe had provided it to him, so he went to his room and read the book.

Not long after it inspired him to write his own short story. He called it simply "Loneliness," and he wrote it for Maria, who was markedly lonely, to the point that it was a part of her personality, a portion of the makeup of her being that she could not shed. She was particularly easy to neglect emotionally, she always had been. Perhaps because of how self-sufficient she seemed, but she only seemed that way. Loneliness had actually made her quite dependent, but her stoicism hid this way, the mask of indifference, *unglauben*, often confused people into thinking she was content, content to be alone, but really she was always restless. Anglor knew her well enough to know this, so he had written the short story for her, to prove to her that he understood her, for he was crucified, too. He was damned to loneliness as well, for committing some ancient crime that had left his memory eons ago, so he did not know what he was guilty of. Perhaps it was just strangeness.

When Anglor got out of the hospital he took to working rabidly. He realized work, at least this kind of work, was all there was to life, all life had to offer him, and if he did not do it he would not survive the strangeness of life on Earth. He had known for a long time this was the way it had to be if you were going to make a career in art, you actually had to make art, and not every now and then, but always, everyday, until the point that there is almost nothing else in your life. It has to obsess you, you have to be devoted to it. You have to crank it out all the time, even if fifty percent of what you're cranking out is shit, you still have to crank it out, you cannot just sit around in idleness and wait for the muse to strike you, or she will leave you for neglecting her- she demands complete devotion, all your attention, and more than that, she demands that you toil for her, sweat for her, give your entire life to her. And, if you do only practice your art on the accession of your fancy, soon you will stop practicing art all together, and you will become a stranger to yourself, and life will have lost the only meaning it begrudgingly provided you, because you wasted it, because you did not engage in it everyday.

People like Anglor had to. It was his only reason to live, and he had to be reminded of it constantly unless he would lose it. Besides, he was so full of frustrated neuroses, he had to get them all out each day, and at the end of the day he had, and he felt comfortably empty, and he was able to sleep, but then the neuroses came back to him in his sleep, through dreams, and he had to get them all out again the next day. He realized his mind was something that needed this constant maintenance, or it would easily lose itself again, it was the only way he could keep a hold of it, as if on a leash, before it began to have a leash on him, and then all became ruinous at that point.

Besides, he was married to his discontent, his *unbehagen*, for to become content would be sin- to become content would be to become complacent, it would mean an end to the work, and the work was all there ever was and all that ever would be, without it he would just be a shell ready to explode at any moment. No, he could not be content. The discontent was very important to help him work. No one who is content wants to create art, and besides, how could he be content, when the world was still on its self- destructive path, when history was not dead yet? It would be unfair to be content, unfair to all the people who are caught in history's vagaries and vicissitudes, who are being crushed and mangled under its wheel as it turns into centuries. It was not fair to be content in a world where most people do not even have the privilege to be restless. Besides, he had not finished his mission. Until then, when he had finished what he had come here to do, when he was back on the moon, could he be content and again make idyllic art that didn't really men anything, and was only aesthetically pleasing. But Earth demands you be discontent, otherwise you are not listening to its ancient scream.

Anglor only wished at times that he had chosen his mission, that he had not been sent on it by other people. You always put more of your heart and soul into something you choose, something that comes from inside you, not outside of you, and Anglor had always been better at working under his own direction, perhaps because of his problem with authority, or his reclusiveness, or a mixture of both, but he felt all work, all missions, should be autotelic. But he had chosen to be an artist, that was his, and he did think now that if he had been given the option to choose this mission, if it were not chosen for him, he would have chosen it eventually, because day by day it was dawning on him how important it was. He had something important to do, so he could not die. He had even stopped his every sixth month suicide. For the time being he was not a Selenite, so he did not feel the need to follow their customs. Right now he was an Earthling, a human, and he had already been reborn when he landed on Earth. Of course, anything born or reborn on Earth is born or reborn with incredible character flaws, but these insufficiencies were also important, these character flaws dire to the makeup of character, because perfection is a dream we can't really even conceive- perfection is never being born at all, yet alone reborn, it is that state, that *me psunai,* the *effes,* that we cannot even imagine because it is so contrary to our existence for it is non- existence. Anything that is born must be born imperfect, the universe itself has to be imperfect, and the Earth, because otherwise there is no room for improvement, and therefore no reason to truly live, that's why perfect things don't live, that is why they are in the darkness we cannot reach for too many moments in the light, or even only seconds, for your conception of this darkness is shed as soon as you are born, and the rest of your life is slowly remembering it, this is called philosophy, and then one day you remember it completely, this is called death. Philosophy is getting ready for it, so it does not take you completely by surprise, this remembering.

Still, a live thing can never fully conceive of it. This is why philosophy is so theoretical in nature, why it cannot be quite as empirical as science. But Anglor believed more in philosophy, for it allowed the conception of a soul, a *seelenauffassung*, which science did not speculate much on. Even if the soul was only a metaphor, it still seemed to Anglor like the most important part of a person, and if it didn't exist we would all be lost, so perhaps it doesn't, and that's why we flounder so in time. If one is born without a soul they are born with an imperfection too large to ever remedy, they are born a psychopath, people who will always exist but which no one knows why. They are the worst mistake in nature, but they are born in each century, several of them, and they probably always will be. They were what got in Anglor's way of killing history, they kept it going, they worshipped it only because they often made it, controlled it, because deep down they were just as upset as everyone else knowing that there is no reason for them, they just are, and all they can do is irrevocable damage. They feel the missing of their soul, and they collaborate with death to avenge it. They know they will always be missing something essential, and it has made them against nature though nature too created them, as it creates everything, without reason, but other people can attain a reason from life. The only reason the psychopath can ever know is death, that is his only logic.

And why does nature make such a thing, something that wants to destroy it and tarnish the Earth, just to be noticed, just to be part of history, who will settle for notoriety as a means of fame, like Herostratus? But it seemed they were destined for such negative fame, they could not help but to be psychopaths, but they were still bad men. Anglor was never destined for fame, notoriety or otherwise, he had to force himself into it, he had to spit in the face of the odds, he had to work without stop, he had to never surrender until at last fate begrudgingly surrendered to him. This was much more difficult but much more dignified.

Anglor had decided to take a break., He had been drawing all day, so he got online and read the news. Another school shooting in Santa Fe, another psychopath getting his fame, history happening in the present, fully alive, nowhere near being killed. And it was thanks to the people who did nothing about it, Anglor realizing he was one, though he wanted desperately to change it, he had no idea how. He had fame but still he had no power. Other people agreed with him that history needed to be murdered, but they, like him, did nothing about it. All they did was post political memes on Facebook. Anglor's soul sunk inside itself, as if burrowing into a hole, but it was the hole, long and narrow and deeply rooted in the ground, with no end in sight. He remembered that this was the reason he had been sent to Earth, and America in particular, because there was a school shooting, and still in his presence on the planet it was happening nevertheless. He felt he was to blame. He believed in collective guilt, though it didn't seem to ever absolve itself, it still could not be forgiven because it never stopped.

Anglor hung his head in shame, in collective guilt, in *le pudeur*. He was failing miserably at his mission. Then Maria came home at last and they talked about it for a little bit. Their neighbors they were acquainted with were going to a party, and they had been invited. Maria said it might take his mind off of it.

"I don't need to take my mind off of it…"

"Well brooding will never change it. That's the failure of collective guilt, it doesn't make anyone collectively do something about it."

Anglor hung his head in shame again, realizing she was right, but still, he felt collectively guilty. Christ had endured all of the sins of man on his back, was that collective guilt or collective innocence? Should Anglor do the same thing, or is Maria right, is martyrdom foolhardy? Because did it really change anything? It did not even change men's hearts, all we remember is the man, and not as flesh and blood, but as a legend, might as well be a myth, something glorious that nobody learned from, and they would repeat the mistake today, if it was a mistake. Supposedly he had to be crucified. Supposedly he had to take collective guilt and accept it all as his own, the one man who was innocent. Is that the solution? If so we are screwed, for such a person does not exist today. He may have never existed at all. He may have been the perfection of man that only exists in man's imagination, though it could be a reality, if only people would act on it.

But Anglor reluctantly agreed to go to the party, though he was moody the whole time. It was raining and the night was dark, it was relaxing, and it was the perfect weather to nurse Anglor's solemn despair. He sat in the corner chain smoking and binge drinking and not saying anything. The people at the party talked about normal things,. Where they went to high school, things to do in town, memories of when they were young, and what kinds of liquor makes you "shit fire." And then of course the topic of Santa Fe came up.

"I don't want to talk about it, though," the man who brought it up said.

"I don't want to talk about it either," both Anglor and Maria said at once, because these days, people thinking of him as some idol of the intellectual, he was always expected to have a political opinion, which he usually did, but he did not always want to talk about it. And Maria was so easily depressive, she didn't even want to think about it, or she would be in the same state that Anglor was in, which she had only narrowly avoided, by the rare mercy of her mind. But still, they talked about the school shooting.

"I don't think there's any solution," someone said, and almost everyone except Anglor and Maria agreed. Anglor began to glower. 'this is pathetic,' he thought. The solution was quite obvious, and even if it wasn't, you think people would still make an effort to find it, instead of almost happily giving up like that. Adults almost always fail their children, but this was more than Anglor had ever seen before, more than he could tolerate. He thought they would at least try to stop them from dying. And people called him a pessimist, yet here these regular people were being so fatalistic in the face of their children being in danger just so they didn't have to get rid of their damn guns, just because they had prescribed themselves to a certain political party they always had to agree with, no matter what, or said political party would not find them respectable anymore. In short, because they were brainwashed, because they were always happy with their stupidity, because it made them comfortable, and they would not even trade it for the safety of their children. Anglor almost smashed the ash tray on the table out of anger but Maria saw him make a fist and she gently grabbed his arm.

He knew the problem. It was because it had not happened to them and their children specifically. There is an incredible error in human thinking, particularly in America, that those who suffer must suffer because they are guilty of something, that they in some way deserve it. People do not seem to realize suffering is blind to a person's character, that it crawls into all of us at some point, and we deserve this suffering even less than we deserve our good fortune. Along with simple mindedness came a lack of empathy, in many ways it was cruel even as it asserted its innocence in ignorance. Anglor couldn't stand it anymore. All these people had lived in Miamisburg their whole lives, and they were the run of the mill puppets of the Republican party, the people who were simply enough to go along with any barbaric cruelty, and Anglor looked at Maria and she knew what his stare meant. He was saying to her 'We have to get out of here.'

Maria looked back at him and tried a weak smile. "Okay," was all she said, but it was enough for Anglor. At a time like this he could not speak his mind, he was outnumbered and he didn't want to be hated, even for something he believed in. He still needed this simple, cruel people's acceptance. He thirsted for acceptance everywhere, and would take it even from the most debauched people, which were usually the only people kind enough to offer it. He felt like a coward, but he kept his mouth shut. He realized anyone who spoke their mind all the time would be an intolerable asshole, and yet that is who we all secretly are, full of malicious thoughts we conceal beneath politeness, judgment, censure behind a smile, and envy in a compliment. It is not always this way, but Anglor realized most of the time we are around other people we are pretending, pretending that we are not full of contempt, that we are likeable. It is only with ourselves that we can truly be ourselves, because we do not know how to judge ourselves, whether we like or hate ourselves we are wrong, and we admit to our own minds things we could never admit to another person about how inadequate we are. This is why certain people love solitude and certain people hate it, it all depends on how much you do or do not want to be who you truly are. But the most important thing to learn in life is how to face yourself, and many people never learn it.

So they smoked weed as usual. Anglor was becoming like Maria, he needed drugs to relax, but, unlike Maria, he didn't feel the need to be relaxed all day. He thought too much relaxation made life meaningless, that there was some amount of stress and anxiety you actually needed and was good for you, though too much of that also takes its toll. But it was important to do the work you loved, it was not important to do the work that was just a fill in for existence and which you were utilizing just to get by. Everyone could live without that type of work, though they have become so inured to it they think they can't. Anglor remembered when he was on disabilities everyone would ask "don't you get bored?" they did not realize there was life beyond menial employment. It made Anglor sad. Capitalism had truly brainwashed the normal person. He told them he still worked, it was just a different kind of work, one that actually interested him, and it was work even when he didn't get paid for it. This was something else people didn't understand, one, that you can enjoy your work and it is still work, and that it can even still be work if you don't get paid. "That's just a hobby," people would say. Which irritated Anglor to no end, and he would respond back sharply, "no, it's work.' And it was indeed, hard work, too.

Though Anglor didn't feel the need to be relaxed all day, there was always the end of the day, the diurnal anticlimax of life, when all your business suddenly becomes nothing and then you are bored. Anglor could not relax like other people. He always had to be busy, and then when it was time to relax he felt frantic, restless, so he took to drugs the same way Maria did, and not always only Marijuana. Sometimes he took seconal and valium to sleep. He had trouble sleeping, often it would take two and a half hours lying discontentedly in bed before he could get to sleep. He was glad he didn't share a bed with anyone, they would be sorely irritated with him. He had a way of annoying people just by being himself, full of compulsions and eccentricities, no one until Maria had ever been able to live with him, and he was amazed by her quiet patience, a golden quality many people took advantage of like they were children.

They listened to awful music, some kind of supposed rock and roll that was petulant and facile in its sense of despair. He realized depression in unintelligent people was almost callow when put into words. Anglor was glad his despair was a little more intellectual, though this made it a real despair, at least it had some meaning to it, at least you could put it into words that only an unfortunate few would understand but which the whole human race knew, though perhaps unconsciously, and often it was truth that people refused to recognize though deep in their mind they must have known it to be true. It was a snobbish thought, but it was how Anglor felt. He was glad his despair was legitimate, that it was somewhat more mature, though this meant it was not passing like the callow despair he saw in the average man but was a part of his mind that was vexing but integral, that he could not get rid of if he expected to be himself. But at times he also thought that the despair of the average man was actually quite great, quite deep, but average people could not recognize it because if they did they would be ousted and condemned form the comfortable conformity of being average. It would be a sin to admit any discontent, because being average is all about contentment, being average meant you had to be ashamed of anything other than a numb, sterile so called happiness handed down to you in advertisements, children, and modest homes, in average lives that never deviated. Anglor at last realized they weren't to be envied, though society was always persisting they were, but really society had only deemed these people happy so it could manipulate them better.

Anglor felt relieved when he realized this, and also sorry for regular people. He thought to himself that he was alone most of the time because he had to be, that was the only way he could get his work done. He had always envied people who weren't lonely but it was slowly dawning on him that no such people existed. He was just a little more lonely, or more aware of his loneliness. But the whole planet Earth was lonely, being the only known life in the universe, and even all the life seemed too far away. That's why people didn't kill history, because we are all too distant from each other to feel much for one another. That is why empathy seems so scarce, and is only the quality of the most sophisticated minds, though it should be easy, it should be easy to know how suffering feels, seeing as it escapes none of us. But there is a great distance between all of us, even those we are close with, the gap created by our completely separate minds and beings, which can often not be filled, even by love, at the end of the day one is oneself and another is simply another, too far away, impossible to reach beyond individual consciousness.

Anglor considered this as he looked at his neighbors. They lived right down the hall, but they were world's away, Anglor being so different from them, but it was nice that they accepted him anyway. They seemed to think his strangeness had something charming about it, which it did, though often people neglected that. They suddenly got on the topic of slavery.

"First we kept black people as slaves," Anglor said caustically. "Now it is Mexicans."

"Oh, that's not true," someone said.

"It is," Anglort almost violently insisted. "Hispanic immigrants in prison are doing forced labor, and even Hispanics who are free have to work for much lower wages than whites. They are our slaves, and yet the current administration doesn't even want them to come over the border. You know, they're separating families at the border, too, children lose their parents. How would you feel if that was your kids?"

No one said anything, until Maria piped up and said "I don't want to talk about this."

"I don't either," Said Anglor, and downed his beer in one gulp.

"My father killed himself," Maria suddenly said. "He was listening to 'Wouldn't it be Nice?' by The Beach Boys when he hanged himself. He never forgave himself for losing my mother, and he couldn't face the world news everyday anymore."

"I'm sorry, Maria," someone said.

She shrugged. "As I get older I understand him more. I understand why he killed himself now. It was because there are still slaves."

There was an awkward silence and Anglor squeezed Maris's shoulder.

"How did we get on such a gloomy subject?' someone said. "Let's talk about something else."

Anglor and Maria nodded, also wishing to talk about something else, as they had the entire night.

"So, Michael," the same helpful man said. 'Why did you become an artist?"

This was also something Anglor didn't want to talk about. It was like a television interview again, although at last he had gotten used to those, although not without valium. "Well, it's simple. I wanted a way out," Anglor said honestly.

"A way out of what?"

"They cycle of American labor, and there are only two ways out of this, becoming a criminal or becoming an artist, and being a criminal isn't really a way out, so I decided to be an artist."

The man chuckled, not really having understood what Anglor had said. "Right on, man. Can I see some of your art?'

This question actually brought Anglor great joy. He loved it when someone was interested, so he pulled out his sketch pad he took with him everywhere now and the neighbor flipped through it.

"Hey," he said. "You're pretty good. Some of this you must have done when you were in a pretty bad mood, huh?"

"Yes," Anglor said. In fact he had done one when he was in a bad mood yesterday, when again he had made the mistake of watching the news, and learned of the laws of arbitration preventing workers from filing class action suits against their employers, and about Mark Zuckerberg and the Cambridge Analytica Scandal. Anglor had learned about these things and got that horrible feeling again, the feeling that it was no longer just the stuff of a cautionary novel anymore, that now dystopia was a reality in America, as it had been in Russia and Germany. So he felt distraught, because he had always feared dystopia, even when he lived on the moon, and now that he had the feeling he was actually living in it, he was depressed, disappointed Laund afraid, afraid for the present now, not just the future. So, he had drawn to calm himself. He drew a picture of a twisted, distorted, and subtly screaming face with a bird like figure coming out of his head, watching him, and called it "The Average Citoyen of Dystopia." He showed this one to the neighbor.

"I was in a very bad mood when I drew this one."

"Why?'

"Because some of my favorite novels came true. They were good as fiction, they are horrifying as reality."

Chapter 4

Anglor went outside to grab a bite to eat. He looked around at his surroundings he saw everyday and which never variated, but still he looked at them everyday, hoping for a change, hoping something could surprise him. All that was different was that the flag was at half mast, and that wasn't even that different. It often was. He saw it and he felt a strange twinge in his heart, the feeling of both mourning for a nation, along with disappointment that he and many of its citizens had failed it, and that was why the flag was hanging flaccid and pathetic halfway down its pole, a symbol of a nation that was no longer marked by freedom, but by tragedy.

He went and got his food, but he ate it listlessly, not really enjoying it. That had been the one good thing about Earth, the food and the wine, and now it all seemed tawdry and tasteless, benign. Then he walked back home. It was an obscenely hot day, and Anglor could feel himself sweating through his deodorant. Luckily the walk was not far. Miamisburg was such a small place, nothing was really far from anything else, but this did not alleviate the loneliness. He went home, turned the air conditioner on full blast, and sat at his computer to read the news. An article by the satirical news website "The Onion," popped up, it was about the football players who kneeled during the national anthem being fined. The article headline was somewhere along the lines of "Players Must Stand to the Flag whose Patriotic Spirit is Subservience." 'Jesus,' Anglor thought to himself. 'The Onion gets more like real news every day. Not only are we living in dystopia, our dystopia is a satire!'

He got off the computer, feeling dejected and strange. Everything in America was failing right now, even its intelligentsia. It was because of the complacency the powers that be always encouraged and which citizens gladly took part in and were happy with because it meant they could be comfortably lazy. And Anglor thought sadly to himself that the youth had gotten this way, too, the only salvation we've ever had. And the intelligentsia of the youth, as well. They had noticed that some people in America were so uneducated that they didn't feel the need to become more educated, they became complacent in their intelligence due to comparison, they had ceased to realize that intellect is something that has to be constantly nourished or it will die, and it was indeed dying in this complacency by comparison, people who thought they were scholars in comparison to the masses, and so they had ceased to become scholars. They were still intelligent, but they were not letting their intelligence grow and thrive, they were leaving it as it was, only half formed, pubescent, not fully matured, because intellect is just like us, it always has to be maturing, it always has to be getting older, so it will become wisdom, and that is the most important thing for intelligence to eventually become, that is its main goal. And now we have all these young people whose incipient intelligence they will not nurture enough to grow, now we have an entire generation just like the last one where most of them will not become wise, but always be just intelligent enough, not realizing they are barely separated from the masses because they have let their intelligence wither and now are barely intelligent. People seem to think that's acceptable, though. Just enough intelligence to get by, to be a pseudointellectual, while a real intellectual is so strange these days they are degraded to a madman.

Anglor felt very sad for America and all that was happening to it. He did not know why he'd landed here from the moon.

He had wanted to help the entire world, not this country that was by far the most spoiled and ungrateful. But he did feel something strange in himself that he had felt ever since he'd landed on this rock, he felt like the entire world was somewhere within him, was within all of us, and so we are all capable of saving us. This sense of the entire world existing in our being Anglor thought was something all humans were born with, and the horrible divisiveness of nationalism came later. Those who did not care about the world did not care about themselves, for they carry it around in themselves, we all do, though many of us lose touch with it when we lose touch with our curiosity. Even a bit of the universe is in us, as well, that's the nothingness, the hollow feeling, which sometimes swallows the Earth in us. But none of us are one person, we are all everyone, and that is why we are so confused by ourselves. We all have a bit of the saint and a bit of the psychopath in us, and if you pay attention to yourself, if you listen to the great bounty of love and the wasteland of hate in your heart, you will understand all things human, even Anglor, who wasn't human, and this was wisdom, being everyone on Earth. It was an incredibly difficult task, to carry so many heads on your shoulder, and all those heads amounting to the world, but this is what humans were born for and if they do not achieve it they are wasting their existence. That is worldliness, not someone who has travelled a lot, or even someone who has read a lot about the world, though this is a necessary step to worldliness: worldliness is actually being the world, being the whole world in one hell of a hodge podge personality, but in it is an understanding of all aspects of the human, even the evil aspects, and it teaches you a very important thing- how to forgive the world, and eventually, how to forgive yourself, and the inadequacies and evils of them both.

Anglor didn't want to just forgive them, though, he wanted to get rid of them completely, and his heart sank a little every time when he thought this was perhaps impossible, but it was worth a try. It would certainly be impossible if no one tried, and that was the only reason why it had been impossible, because no one tried, because again they were manipulated by those who hold in their hands the means of production who need war- they had told all the citizens of the Earth it was impossible, and the citizens of Earth had agreed with them partly out of complacency, and partly because they thought pessimism made them intelligent. Anglor didn't understand why people agreed to be manipulated so easily, maybe just to feel loved, but Anglor didn't want to be loved that badly. He wanted to help this poor withering planet, and he realized the only way to do it was ignore the powers and the masses that wanted to manipulate him and crush him into complacency and fatalism, for this was the only way "saving the world" could become possible, to first stop thinking it was impossible, to give up our habit of violence and being comfortably manipulated, for that is simply abetting violence, eventually we will no longer be able to claim innocence in it.

Anglor thought of this and drew up another declaration on how to kill history. It was a brief slogan, "it's only impossible if you say it is," followed by words in bold print and underlined: **<u>Don't make it impossible.</u>** Don't become comfortably numb to the world, for that is becoming comfortably numb to yourself. Don't accept things as they are, for many people are being hurt by them, for they are rhadamanthine and cruel. Don't inherit despair from masters who want you to leave everything as it is for everything as it is has made them rich- don't let the few benefit from the tutelage and even death of the many. In fact, since Anglor had been poor, he was beginning to think the lower classes were actually much more educated than the upper classes. The upper class was frivolous, vapid, cold Lund vacant. They never thought about anything, whereas a poor man is forced to ruminate about everything because his life is always ready to destroy him, because a part of him is actually quite righteous, so the devil is always on his tail. The upper class are devoid of all things except money, there is nothing else to them, and they read no more than anyone else does these days- they are not wealthy because they're intelligent they are wealthy because they are inordinately cruel, always willing to turn a blind eye to suffering because they have never known it. They don't give a damn about anything except themselves and their social circle, and what expensive bars to populate. They are vacuous to the point where you can see through everything they do, and it is always aimless, happily idle, without any purpose and not even wishing for one, for they are paid in generous sums not to have a purpose, but to be totally feckless and inspired by cruelty because they are secretly so bored. They know they have no reason, and they do not care. They are smiling, extravagant nihilists who do not care that their lives are worthless because everything is always within their reach. That's why they and their lives are so empty, because everything is easy, but they don't mind, they don't mind being so inutile, because they are paid for it well, paid to be a person whose whole life is an advertisement for America's supposed prosperity and ease, that only these few empty actors know and enjoy gluttonously, never feeling ashamed, because no one has ever taught them shame, nor even pride- they have only been taught arrogance.

The lower classes are much different. They have an almost brutal, primitive, and direct intelligence. They understand just about every human condition of degradation because they have seen it all, known it all, therefore they are more capable of sympathy, for most of these hardships they've seen they have some personal knowledge of, many times they have been through it themselves. They know about mental illnesses, they have heard about almost all of them, whereas if you try to talk psychology with a rich man you will be speaking a foreign tongue. Many of their white people have grown up around all kinds of races and are therefore not racist. They certainly watch the news, and they of all people truly know what the government is like, they have a very good grasp of politics because they are always politics' victim. They by necessity have vast street knowledge, and they also certainly know the law, again because they are always victim to it.

There are of course many simple people who are racist and hateful, but it is odd to me that I have seen almost all of these people being friendly to a black person. Of course the old psychological rule, that one makes exceptions, but I have the feeling that many people stand behind racism simply because it is a tradition, a tradition, like many, that is archaic and barbaric, immeasurably, generalizing, and blindly cruel. Many traditions have been like this, that is why progress intends to destroy them. But people hold dearly to their traditions, no matter how barbarous they are, and not because they truly believe in them, but because they are so familiar, and make life seem stable. I think that's how some people feel about their racism, that though it is absolutely irrational and absurd, "it was they way they were raised," and they will not give it up for the sake of progress because they always want everything to remain the same- in essence, it is someone trying to be a child forever. And children are of course not racist unless their parents teach them to be- it is people who always want to remain children and therefore have never lost their excessive and naïve faith in their parents. It is almost as if hatred brings them some kind of nostalgia for the so called simplicity of their homes. It was a longing for the past that more resembled a fear of the future, a fear of progress and its threat that it will make you irrelevant. But the past is always relevant, in that we need to keep it in the past, not resurrect it into the present as we have done, and the future, god knows what it has in store, so everyone is afraid of it, but when the past is barbarous and the present a sickening, facile re- run of it, like a poorly made sequel of a television series that was already subpar, there is nothing left to look forward to. No one holds onto the present like they should, even when it is rewarding, people always cower into the past or become too over inflated with some false ambition, a *spiritus lenis*, and obsess over a phantom like future, no one cares for the nonce, and at the moment I can't blame them, but only because it is too much like the past.

Nostalgia is a false longing, a longing for something one should never long for, it is the act of romanticizing a horror through the passing of time, romanticizing a war, slavery, economic depression, an old lover that was fickle and unkind, friends who were as false as false prophets, things that are remembered to the point of a religious ceremonial, but which are much better off forgotten, and if not forgotten, at least not held dear, for there is no such thing as a simpler time as these racists seem to think their racism denotes, it is in fact a time just as complex as our own, like all time is. The past is a rusted pot gathering dust that through the blindness of nostalgia has been bedizened into the finest samovar, but beneath that patina it still exist as it truly is and always was, something broken, intractable that can never be fixed, can never be redeemed even by the nostalgia that has hallucinated it as something fine, something precious. The past is just as deleterious as the present, and the future is so unknown we will never be able to grasp it, so what are we left with? The lie that the past was easy.

Anglor sat and wrote this all down on his new proposition, that nostalgia, or *toska*, was what was preventing us from killing history, and once we let go of this thing that was not only erroneous, but actually quite painful, the stab in the back of memory as it creates new wounds over the old ones through recollection, will no longer be necessary. But Anglor had the feeling people wanted to hold onto it. We always hold onto dead things as if they are life, therefore, we always hold onto the archaic, the extant, the mistakes of all our combined generations made immemorial through entropy, and often we abandon truly living for a corpse- the past.

Anglor wrote all these things down then decided to read. He had observed Tom Wolfe's death, now he wanted to observe Thomas Wolfe's death, though he had died in 1938, many years before Anglor was even hatched from a head on the moon. He had forgotten that. He had often forgotten now that he was not human. His kenosis was working. He had always liked Thomas Wolfe, because he felt a great sadness radiating off his language, an incredible loneliness that was too disconsolate to leave the man, that was a part and the function of his personality. He got the feeling Thomas Wolfe lived a sad life, and a short one too. It was too painful, too lonely to go on much longer. He had known desolation, he had known the indifference of God toward the suffering of men, and he truly knew the suffering of men, everyday his loneliness had showed it to him in perfect clarity, which he turned into eloquent description hoping he could rid himself of the image of this eidolon, this wretched dybbuk, and then at least manage his loneliness, at least be able to talk to himself everyday and thereby talk to the world, the lonely world, which was a good listener because it never answered. It was the cold impassive rock that kept all our sorrows contained within it, and you can speak to it but it won't speak back, though eventually, if your suffering is noble enough, it will grant you some small amount of notice- people may start to read your books, your one sided conversations with the world, like any player on the stage in front of an audience, but a dead audience, one that does not move, but you can rouse them back into life if you're rousing enough.

This was what eventually happened to Thomas Wolfe, after he was dead. And his books were large and onerous, but Anglor was well versed enough in literature to know this meant they were good- he knew all the best books are a burden, a burden to read and an incredible burden to write, but if you are writing it you are also shedding the burden a little bit like an old skin you want to get out of, like a mind you want to drain a little bit of its persistent and overbearing, multitudinous thoughts. Anglor always thought Maria would make a good writer, she certainly read enough, and she was quietly thoughtful, and though people didn't understand her she understood people. That was the first step to becoming a writer, understanding and even trying to pardon a race that would never dare to so much as try to understand or pardon you.

Anglor knew it must have been incredibly hard work, just as hard if not more than art, but he felt Maria needed to do something, something to shed the dead skin of her despair, or eventually it would become like a coat she could never take off, and it was getting warmer outside.

When she came home he'd talk to her about it. She walked in the door and Anglor greeted her with a smile.

"I've been thinking, Maria," he said. "I think you should write a novel."

"I don't have the time" she said gruffly and sat down to smoke a joint.

"Rough day at work?"

"Yes." Maria was a waitress, one of the most vexing jobs in the world, and Anglor wanted to tell her she always would be if she did not become a writer. But he was not one for deciding other people's lives for them.

"You write a new manifesto?" she asked as she drew on the joint languidly.

"Yes. It's strangely optimistic, and though I believe what I am saying, I am pessimistic about it. I'm always pessimistic."

"Must be nice to be right all the time," Maria said acerbically, and Anglor's face fell.

"I don't want to be right that badly."

Chapter 5

More bad news. ICE had lost 1,475 migrant children to Arizona. Children were not only being separated from their parents at the border, they were also being trafficked and kept in cages. Then it came out that border patrol has been Draconian for years, abusing many human rights, raping women and denying children medical care, and of course beating people. Anglor felt sick. He knew Trump was an evil man, but he didn't think he would abuse children like this. Then of course there was the Santa Fe shooter. They were blaming it on a girl, a girl who had supposedly rejected him. So it was an obscene instance of rape culture as well. Anglor again thought that it would be good fiction, but was a terror as it was actually happening. He turned off his computer in disgust, because everyone had to restart their browser in order not to be hacked by the Russians.

"These times are absolutely mad," he said. "We are being run by mad people, and not the right kind of mad people." Anglor didn't understand if people would listen to lunatics like these why no one would listen to a lunatic like him, who still had a certain sense of rationale, who felt he could see the world clearly because for years he didn't speak and only watched it. Now it was his time to speak, and the few people that were listening just posted his message on Facebook. Everyone was still opinionated, but the spirit of rebellion had seemed to commit suicide because on the other side was offered inane comfort. Anglor cursed under his breath. It wasn't working. No one was killing history. Everyone was outraged but no one knew what to do. Anglor didn't know what to do either. He felt like a false, empty prophet, who only had words, meaningless words, that could easily be disregarded like almost all words are, even the words of Christ, he had no actual action.

But deep in his heart he knew an artist could never be a revolutionary, that though he was political he was a passive kind of political, someone who made people aware of the facts and tried to show how meaningless it all was, and absurd, he was merely someone who tried to make other people think about it the way he was doomed to think about it, but he was not the kind of public figure who actually changed things- he was merely an artist. He tried to kill history by drawing it, by making it into something surreal, which it is, by turning this harsh reality that seemed to be based on fiction back into fiction, in the world where it belonged, not the real world whose chaos is at least supposed to be manageable, sensible, a necessary part of freedom, not something that can infringe on freedom. Still, his job was important, even if it didn't change things, it paved the way for people who could. Still, Anglor wished he could do more. He had always felt limited to only the artistic, he had always felt that otherwise he was completely helpless and naïve, that he could do nothing else.

He had to take a shower and get ready. He was meeting up with Zweifle for another gallery opening. He hoped to himself a foolish thought, that if all he was ever destined to be was an artist he hoped he could be an artistic martyr, he almost longed for his crucifixion, which was simply the bedizened longing for his death. And he felt maybe by torture he could be purified, that maybe he could forgive himself for his failure if is failure at least was paid for in blood. And he felt martyrs really did change the world, as he wanted to do. Martin Luther king and Joan of Arc certainly did. Often Anglor wasn't sure if Christ did, or maybe his promises were destined to come late, or, as he alleged, after death, but Anglor didn't believe there was anything after death, just a great and conquering darkness one can never leave, the last cannot be first there, because there is no first or last, there is nothing. But Anglor didn't know if this was a fact or an opinion, but based on what little evidence there was, he thought it was probably a fact. He thought of death often, how it makes us all pure in the end, how it returns us to where we belong, back into the belly of nothingness, back to the only place that is anyone's true home. With it we forget the violence of humanity, and even the violence of our deaths, in it we are returned to peace.

Maria was sitting next to him, smoking a joint as always and reading. Anglor was drawing, not a very good picture today, but at least he did it. Tomorrow he had another opening, in Columbus again. He had made all the plans with Zweifle. He was beginning to feel sorry for Zweifle. His second face seemed to be quite a burden, almost as if it were heavy, a weight to be carried that eventually, after many years of struggle. broke the back and killed the man. We all live with this, though, but on Zweifle it was on the face to visibly see, the rest of us kept it buried in the heart, though it made it harder to love while it lived there, there was nowhere else to hide it, the soul rejected it, if there was a soul. Anglor again felt that old familiar feeling where he was incredibly sorry for mankind, as if mankind were some prisoner sentenced to death that was certainly guilty of his crime, but still you did not want to see him die, still something about his guilt made you feel sorry for him, just as sorry as you were for his condemnation. It was almost Stockholm Syndrome for Anglor, empathizing with the thing that was going to kill you, for you realized you needed to die. Perhaps all condemned men feel this way- perhaps all of humanity feels this way.

Maria was deep in her book but Anglor wanted to interrupt her. He wanted to talk to someone, though Maria was hardly sociable when she was reading. She was a true reader, she got absolutely absorbed by the printed page, and she did it avidly and voraciously, she would do it all day if she could. It relaxed her, and often it confirmed that a part of her was sane, that there was reason behind her depression, although this made the depression much worse- it would have been better if her sorrow was completely irrational, but no sorrow is completely irrational, it always has some basis in fact. Anglor could only hope happiness was the same way, but he had never felt it long enough to be ale to tell. It passed through like a premonition, like a brief chill up the spine, something that feels titillating but unnatural, strange.

"Maria," Anglor said weakly.

"Yes?"

"Talk to me please."

She kindly sat the book down. "Are you alright?" she asked.

"I don't know. I feel...odd."

"What's bothering you?"

"Everything."

"Everything bothers me too, but what can we do?"

"We have to do something."

Maria just shrugged. This was the kind of surrender that made Anglor so angry, this was why nothing ever changed, but he was feeling it too at this moment, and that was dangerous. When everyone gives up we have certainly walked right into the door of totalitarianism, in a world where all we will ever do is give up, allowing our will to be crushed like a mode of only semi consensual sex, a half rape, something we gave into almost willingly just to no longer have to fight. But we always have to fight, particularly for our liberty and our peace of mind, and unfortunately Anglor felt in recent times that people cared so much about peace of mind that this is why they so easily gave up, to not have to sacrifice it, and yet they were sacrificing it, they just didn't know. As long as all they had to worry about was their own lives, not the lives of others, certainly not the lives of nameless strangers, or even the life of the community. That was what allowed these things to happen, this general disinterest of the public in any existence but their own.

"I feel like we are not in the real universe," Anglor suddenly said. "I feel like we are in the parallel universe where everything is backwards."

Maria shrugged again. "We don't know any better."

Anglor slowly exhaled some air through his nose. "You're supposed to be making me feel better, not wrangling me into your despair."

"If you want a therapist you can hire one," Maria said flippantly, and continued reading her book. "I'm tired of the way we communicate," she suddenly added. "As if we're characters in a novel. I don't feel real anymore when we have these discussions."

"Did you ever?"

"Leave me alone, Anglor."

Anglor sighed again. "I'm sorry," her said, but he didn't really feel guilty or remorseful. He felt he had only told the truth. Maria was just as complacent as the rest of them, with the convenient excuse of her depression. He hated this generation, he hated the state Americans had landed themselves in, the one where they were willfully controlled and frightened. But he didn't want to blame the people, he didn't want to blame the victims, even if they had allowed themselves to be victims with their obdurate fear of change. Anglor could only think of the shame, the great shame of being human, which means you are something malleable and pliable and willing to go along with anything, able to adjust to the most iniquitous circumstances just for the sake of survival, and rather than take your own destiny in your hands, to rather let it be a great wave that beats you senselessly against the rocks, but at least you do not have to move, at least you do not have to fight it. If you did fight it you would probably drown, but at this point Anglor would prefer that, he preferred death than obsequious acceptance of fate and the evils of the times it has brought along with it. He thought that perhaps death was what made free will possible, and that was why it is necessary. If we were immortal we would constantly be resigned to fate, until the day of our death that would never come. And Anglor had the feeling we would still get old, but without any wisdom, it is death which the living borrow wisdom from, and of course one day we have to give it back- then we become completely wise, then we can remember all that we have forgotten, which is just nothingness, but the rest of it was an illusion, a representation of a thought, which in the end is nothing more than an opinion. Anglor thought of all his artwork. They were the same. They were nothing but opinions presented in an abstract way, an abstraction of his opinions, an abstraction of his thoughts, if there was any difference between the two. The world as it is is probably just as nothingness as death, it is our minds that have given it form, our opinions which have molded it to our purposes, bent it to our will, and that is why the place is such a horror show, for all that we will is philautic- we yearn for eternal life, that is why we have children, we yearn for wealth, that is why we start wars, we yearn for glory, that is why we fight them, and we yearn for a lack of free will, that is why we have enslaved other and then eventually allowed ourselves to be enslaved as well, enslaved in the mind, because we also wanted to give up thinking, so we could not recognize this horrible world that we created so haphazardly, to the vagaries of our will which in the end was our will to surrender it. We made the world this way, and therefore only we could fix it, Anglor believed.

He wanted to tell Maria all of this, but as soon as he was about to speak he lost the words. That was why he was an artist, so he didn't have to speak it, he could just represent it, a representation of a representation, a mere mimesis of a thought or an opinion if there was any difference. Just opinions in the head all day, distortions of facts, as scarce as they are, for the laws of nature will never be enough for us- we will always demand that we conquer them, and then in the midst of all our achievements one day we give them all up just so we can be regular, which these days means interested in nothing but your own insignificant, private affairs, your *idios*, eventually we all give it up to one day be comfortable idiots, still riding on the broken back of slavery and the works of others that has brought us this convenience and therefore whose talents were a waste, wasted on people who care only for comfort, who have happily given up free will. These people did neither harm or good, but if you do nothing you are doing harm, if you are doing no good you are doing harm. The majority of America was doing harm this way, by doing nothing, by doing no good and merely supposing that because they are so benign they are doing no harm, but that was erroneous Anglor believed. Anglor believed they were doing immense harm simply through abetting.

And as he lookesd art Maria he realized she was the same, that through her depression she was doing no good or harm, and therefore doing harm, that she had given up, surrendered her free will to her depression, and he wanted to shake her out of her stupor, because he knew she was capable of so much, of so much more than just smoking weed and reading books passively. He wanted to tell her, but again the words would not come out. He shook her a little by the arm, and put it as simply as he could.

"You are so much more than your depression has you believe," he said. "And you could be so much more than who it's falsely told you you are."

She smiled weakly. "I'm wasting my life, aren't I?'

"It's an easy thing to waste. We forget how rare it is because we see it all the time."

Maria smiled weakly. "I think I could have done without it," she said.

"Well, it's much too late for that."

"Maybe I'll become a philosopher. What is a philosopher anyway?"

"Someone who thinks about thinking."

"And that's not a waste of life?"

Anglor shrugged. "What else is there to do?"

"And what is a genius?'

"Someone who constantly fails but in a unique way."

"So they're not a genius about everything."

"No, nor are they even a genius all the time. *Nemo potest personam diu ferre fictam.*"

"What does that mean?"

"No one can wear a mask for long."

Maria smirked. "That's why we don't live very long."

"Throughout the ages we live longer and longer. I don't know if that means we're more genuine now or if we are just able to wear the mask longer, if we've adjusted to it somewhat."

"It doesn't matter how long we live, life will still always feel short."

"Yes, probably."

"Medicine and progress cannot make immortality. And the longer we live and the more comfortable we are the more we waste life."

"You're right," Anglor said. "Life means more when it's a struggle, it means less when it's full of ease."

Maria nodded and began to roll another joint.

"Can I have some of that?" Anglor asked.

"Of course. We have some beer in the fridge, too."

"Thank God," Anglor said, and got up to grab himself a beer. He opened it and sat down next to Maria. The potation fell down his throat with ease, the panacea that was also a poison, but which made you forget for awhile that life now consists mostly of enthymematic arguments on the internet, because everyone is not only divided, they are divided publicly, people do everything publicly now, even the most intimate things such as loving and grieving, no one feels validated at all anymore unless the world and of course Big Brother along with it is watching. But so long as they feel the world is watching, they'll let Big Brother see in, too, as long as they are seen and heard among a multitude of screaming voices who in their contest to be noticed by a world that is perhaps as indifferent as the universe it lies in, only drown each other out into a whisper, into a loud indistinct mumping of oblivion. Anglor didn't want to take part in that anymore.

"Tell me how," Maria suddenly said to him. "Tell me how not to waste my life."

"I can't tell you anything,." Anglor said. "All I know is how not to waste my life, I have no idea about other people's lives."

"Well, all you do is work."

"I love my work though."

"More than you love any human being?"

"Honestly," Anglor said falteringly. "Yes."

Maria shrugged. "I don't know if that's healthy or not."

"It's probably not, but I can't change it."

"Let's invite Mark over and get shitfaced."

Anglor sighed. "If you wish."

"You don't want to?"

"I have to get up early tomorrow to meet with Zweifle. He's only in town for a day."

"Do you still want to move to New York?"

"Yes. You can have Mark over if you want, but I'm going to bed early. I've had enough of this day."

"How do you do it?" Maria suddenly said. "How do you get up and work everyday even though you're depressed?"

"Because there is nothing else that can un- depress me. I always wake up feeling bad, but then I get up and draw and it's like nothing else matters, not even the depression that's inspiring it."

"It must be nice."

"You could find something like that, too. You need to."

"I'm not really creative…"

"Have you been a child before?"

"Well, yes…."

"Then you are creative, you've just forgotten it."

Maria tried to force a smile. "Love is just a dream," she said. "And one day I'll wake up from it. Then I'll be free."

Anglor smiled at her sadly. "I've never met anyone who wanted to be free that badly."

"I just don't want to live in an illusion."

"Then you can't live in life, either.'

"I already know that," she said solemnly. "I'm just one of those people who were never supposed to be born."

"Everyone is like that."

"I'm not like everyone, though."

"No, you're not, but no one really is. That's why people are so eager to participate in a mob, because it alleviates the loneliness of individuality. But a mob is always cruel. It's better to be lonely and not hurt anybody."

"Yes," Maria conceded. "Maybe lonely people are kinder."

"It's easier to become wise when you're lonely, too, though it's not goods for your physical health. It's really not good for your mind either, but you get so bored that way you have no choice but to take up philosophy, with all the time you have to think."

"I've been lonely my whole life. I've always been a philosopher."

"All philosophers have always been philosophers. You're born that way."

Maria nodded towards him in agreement and got on her phone to text Mark. "It's better with you here," she said. "It makes it less lonely, but I am still lonely. It's a part of who I am."

"It must be part of you if you wish to be an individual, and it is a quiddity of humanity in general, I think. But it is no sin. It's just part of being young and then growing old. It's a part of all of us, it's just that people like you and I can't abandon it, can't forget it in a bar or in any kind of crowd. Everyone is lonely, but the wise are the most lonely."

"Is it worth it then?"

"I have been told it is, and besides, we have no choice. It chose us, and we should be grateful, it chooses very few, but the condition for rarity is loneliness. I wouldn't want to be like other people, though, I wouldn't want to be a part of a mob. A mob's only goal is to kill something innocent."

Mark then texted Maria back. "He's coming over," she said stoically.

"Do you think it will alleviate the loneliness?"

"It never goes away, but that's good because if it's around all the time sometimes you don't notice it. You adjust to its ubiquity."

"It almost becomes a friend."

"It does, but not a real one, an imaginary one, though because it's imaginary it never sells you out."

"It's hard to find," Anglor said slowly. "But there are real people who won't sell you out, as well."

"Like you" Maria said with a smile and patted him gently on the cheek. Anglor smiled back.

"You make it better," he said to her. "You really do. You don't make it go away, but you make it better. Oddly enough, in a way, I don't want it to go away."

"Why not?"

"Because this isolation of mine links me to the rest of the world. It makes me understand people more, in an abstract way, though in a direct, objective way I cannot understand them at all. But I do understand them when I'm alone, I just don't understand them when I'm with them."

"That makes sense."

"Few people would say that. That's what makes you so special."

They embraced briefly and then Maria fired up another joint. They waited for Mark. He came quickly and of course brought a box of wine with him. Anglor and Maria looked at it eagerly. They were more than ready to get drunk. Anglor hadn't been sleeping well, his dreams and minds were haunted by whatever border control was doing to those children they were locking up in kennels. Sometimes he would think of it and a wave of disgust and horror would suddenly come over him and he could not move. It was too awful to even think about. America really was in the hands of a tyrant now, and a tyrant is just a terrorist who terrorizes the whole nation, and mentally as well, it is being in the hands of an abusive husband but the abused wife is an entire country. How one man can do that much destruction, Anglor would never know, how one person could dominate a people like that, it didn't make any sense, but many things in this life don't make sense, and it's better if you do not try to rationalize them but accept them as the anomaly they are. To rationalize them would mean to pardon them. It is better to be bewildered, to feel like life itself is what makes you lost, than to comprehend the character of such evil, even if you are a genius and understand the motives of all people and therefore plead their case before justice and fate- still we cannot excuse all of them. Some of them already know they are damned and drag along with them all of us like we are their refuse deep into Hell with them, for fear of being in hell alone, though this hell was of their own making, they fashioned it for a nation. We must crawl out. We must make him be in the loneliest part of hell, we must make him sit alone in eternity until he finally recognizes himself. If the devil is on the stage at least do not be a part of the audience.

Maria, Anglor and Mark drank steadily, not at blitzkrieg speed as they often did, and certainly not slowly either, but they each always had a drink in their hand and they drank with almost regimented regularity.

"So," Mark said to Anglor. "How's fame treating you?"

"I mostly just work, which is fine by me. I keep having this dream that I'm a character in a play and I know none of my lines. I think this is a version of me going before the public to pretend I'm sane, but I don't know the right words, I don't know the things that sane people say. I feel like I'm not fit for the world stage because of this."

"No one is really fit for the world stage, but still you find the occasional person on it, whether they deserve to be or not, and most of them play their parts- the play the parts of politicians and tyrants, and then of course there are the artists like you, and I think only the tyrants and the politicians have rehearsed their lines, a bunch of speech that they don't mean. The artists have no idea what to say unless they say it in their art, and they mean it. This is more valuable. Let your work speak for you, you are much more eloquent in this mode anyways."

"Okay."

"And you don't have to pretend to be sane, that, in the end, is what makes people insane. Plenty of famous people are crazy."

Anglolr smiled and drank some more of his wine. He thought about being an artist. It was the odd state of being someone who has too much to say but who speaks little. All of his conversations were with himself, all of his conversations were the seemingly endless soliloquy of thinking, of having to truly listen to yourself, and he had to save them for his art- he could not waste them in regular conversation, which was just as immaterial as ideas are when they are merely thoughts, when they haven't been recorded in the artist's medium yet and are just reeling in the ether of your skull. He didn't like wasting thoughts to the air like that, as spoken words or as ideas he left inside his head, which, like any prisoner, would escape somehow, often in the form of insanity. Art was how he spoke, in the act of actually speaking he always fell short, he didn't know his lines and he didn't dare ad lib, the words were just *vox faucibus haesit*, stuck in his throat like some kind of internal irritant, the burden of having to speak when he had already said all he could, and he was not out of thoughts but he was out of words.

Maria put on some music. It was Edvard Grieg's *Berceuse*. They liked the music. It was eldritch and haunting but it was calm in its discord, as if saying, this is how my mind works, with complete chaos that I can organize into art. What an at once happy and miserable insanity that is, one of constant striving and constant suffering then constant regurgitation of this striving and suffering into the idea, into some kind of inspiration, and then whatever ghost is haunting your mind is silenced until the next one takes its place, and you must write again. It is as if your head is a museum, the haunt of the muses, and one has to get the art in the museum out into the real world before the museum, the head, gets too full, before the thoughts that are always capable of being priceless works of art ate for being abandoned to the ether in the skull and then become madness. It was difficult to be so strange, Anglor knew this, because you have to be alone all the time, and eventually you spend so much time talking to a deaf humanity, a multitude that never answers the questions and the demands of the artist, that eventually, after having wasted time on something that moves and answers, speaks and understands, at a much slower rate than the artist speaks to it, you forget completely how to speak to human beings, you know only how to speak to humanity, which for the first few years is only talking to yourself, it is the essence and telos of solitude, and the artist's loneliness, trying to speak to a world and then forgetting how to speak to the individuals of the world, only knowing how to query the masses that you are no longer a part of, and perhaps never were, and that is why you are so strange, that is why you speak to the hard rock of the Earth and realize you are speaking to yourself, because you have no one else to speak to, around people you have nothing to say.

"What is success like?" Maria then asked Anglor.

"I don't know what success is like."

"That's because you're above average. Both of you are," Mark said. "And above average people always fail. It is the average people who succeed. Above average people are almost forbidden success, because they mist strive always, they cannot become part of the emptiness and vanity of success, they must be obscure, they must be well versed in the art of losing everything, because truthfully the world does not want them, it is so cowed by them this intimidation turns into jealousy, disgust and hatred, and it is people themselves who will not allow above average people to succeed. And it is also the world, the very world that the above average person intends to revive from its slumber, because the world, nature, knows that if the above average person were to succeed they would no longer be above average, because all their ambitions, all their dreams that keep them going through their marathon of failure, will die at the first sign of content, and the world knows it needs the above average person, so it will not let them wither in comfort, and people like the above average person to fail so they can feel erroneously that they are better than the above average person, though deep in their hearts they know it's not true. Deep in their hearts they know this above average person has something they do not, even though overall the average person has much more than them, there is still this one thing the above average person possesses that the average man will never be able to touch, so they are incredibly envious.."

"Impressive speech," Anglor said, and poured another glass of wine. "If only we had never eaten from the tree of the knowledge of good and evil, we would know nothing and that would make us happy. Then we would all be average."

"Below average, I'd say," Mark quipped. "The tree of the knowledge of good and evil was basically the tree of the knowledge of fucking. That's what the parable is about. As soon as man figured out how to reproduce he figured out how to die. That was the punishment, but it could have been no other way. Nature made us eat that fruit with its seeds of procreation and then its reaping of death. It had to happen, because in all of life the only two things we really have to do are copulate and die. Nature just had us eat the fruit so we could feel it was our choice, but it was no choice, we would have had to eat that fruit, for destiny is only human error, and this was an error we had to make in order to be in accordance with nature."

"You're on a roll tonight, Mark," Maria said. "But personally I don't believe any of that shit. We didn't disobey God to fuck and die in accordance with destiny, we were born with that being the only knowledge we had."

Mark chuckled and drew a deep gulp from his glass of wine. "Perhaps we are born with a lot of knowledge," he said, "and it is only getting older that makes us forget."

"Perhaps, Socrates," Anglor said, and Mark laughed once more.

"Ars non discitur," Mark said. "Art cannot be taught. You have to be born that way, and it is an odd thing to be born as. Even when you were an infant you were strange, Anglor."

"Perhaps."

"You use that word a lot."

"It's the only word I know."

"Why?"

"Because I'm a philosopher."

This time Mark roared with cynical laughter and Maria smirked. Anglor wondered for a moment if he even liked his friends.

"Yes," mark said. "The artist, the writer and the philosopher are all the same many headed being, and you all answer in nature's mute stead, and you all say 'perhaps.' When you were born and you were screaming that's the word you were crying out."

Anglor finished off his glass of wine. "You go on like a philosopher, too, Mark."

"But I'm only an amateur, not a professional like you. Do you know why?"

"Why?"

Mark scoffed. "Why!" he cried. "The other cardinal word of the philosophers. You all talk to yourselves, and your eloquent conversations are just asking and answering yourself 'Why?' 'Perhaps.' That's why you're a professional and I'm an amateur, because you're an artist, and you need to be an artist to be a philosopher, and you need to be a philosopher to be an artist."

Maria poured herself another glass and irrupted suddenly, "I don't want to have this conversation anymore. It seems to go in a loop."

"Yes," mark said. "It's an ouroboros of a conversation, but that's philosophy for you."

"I don't want to be a philosopher anymore," Maria whispered, as if she were saying something very intimate, something she was ashamed of.

"It's sad," Mark went on, while Maria rolled another joint. "Philosophy was invented because science and religion, no matter what truth they spoke, were not good enough. Then we found philosophy wasn't good enough either. That's our problem, we will always want more, more truth, because as it is we will never have enough of it because we cannot own it completely, not with science, philosophy and religion combined."

"Well," Maria said. "There are many different truths, and we cannot know them all, and more than anything we can't know a single truth, something that unites them all, this will forever elude us. We can't find it in philosophy any more than we can find it in science or religion. Still, philosophy is important, even though it isn't a perfect doctrine of a united truth, this perhaps doesn't exist. It is important though because it teaches us to be solemn and stop wanting for what doesn't exist."

"Then why don't you want to be a philosopher anymore?" Anglor asked almost facetiously.

Maria shrugged. "No human being is truly cut out for it, and once you've been drawn into its web you can never get back out of it again, you can never un learn the dim version of truth it has taught you, and you become strange forevermore after that, like someone who has seen a war returning to civilian life, you know too much to keep pretending, to keep pretending there is even such a thing as normalcy or sanity. It isolates you a little bit."

"So do all the noble pursuits," Mark said solemnly, and drained his glass of wine with sad, impotent bravado.

"I think about the devil a lot," Maria suddenly said. "I don't believe in him, but I'm frightened of him, I'm frightened of the ideas he represents, for these things are indeed terrible, and though

I fear them so much I also realize I am a part of them and they are a part of me. This makes me fear myself, and this is perhaps one of the few rational fears that exist, and it is more terrifying for being rational."

"This is a civic responsibility, though" Mark said, "to realize what you, being a human, are capable of, and to be frightened of yourself, that only means to be self- aware. This will make you less likely to participate in the deeds of the devil, which is really just the collective id of human beings, if you know how apt you are to participate in them. And then maybe you can rid this devil at least from your soul, though to rid him from the universal soul, that is much harder, that is what Anglor is trying to do with his murder of history."

"Perhaps he is an irrevocable part of human nature," Anglor mused. "And we need him as much as God."

"We need him so that we may make the decision to be rid of him," Mark said. "We need him just to destroy him, and build our character without him."

"What about the people who keep him?"

Mark smiled an ancient and mysterious smile that old age had at last granted him, a smile of patience and knowledge amidst the chaos of entropy, life and dying. "God only knows what happens to them," he said.

Chapter 6

Anglor met with Zweifle again to set up a gallery in Dayton. It was the same incredible amount of anxiety for a night that would last only a few hours and would fade rapidly in the fog of drunkenness Anglor needed these days to feel even a modicum of relaxation in the chaos of his life. The only time he didn't feel disorganized and confused was when he was working, it was better even than being drunk or high, because it was a few moments of being in control for a person who for the rest of their lives were helpless to fate and violent vicissitudes, then helpless to life's stagnant ennui that people not as strange as him called comfort, of life going well, but to him was just as deleterious as the chaos, perhaps even more so, but when he was working he felt neither, he at last had the blessed in between that doesn't come so easily to others who do not have these gifts of talent. It was the one thing he had over the masses who were less passionate than him and therefore less insane, and sanity makes you so odd you can easily adjust to life without thinking about it much. Anglor realized that most people didn't have a driving passion, they just settled into things that were comfortable and adequate, enough to make a living, but they had no idea what it was like to actually *need* your work, often more times than you need company or love. They didn't know this great bane or this great, rare and intense pleasure of afflatus, something that rarely touches mankind but when it does it does so violently, with a nonpareil sublimity, a kind of drunkenness on your sobriety of mind, that is clear and rational in the delirium of creativity. Anglor was grateful he knew this, though it came at a heavy cost- it came at the cost of being awkward and hard to know, hard not to be alone.

Anglor and Zweifle at last finished getting everything ready and so they sat down for a cigarette and a glass of wine. Anglor dragged on his cigarette slowly, with the leisure of having completed a taxing, arduous task.

"How do we do it every time?" he asked Zweifle. "How do we not just fall over and give up?"

"If there's one thing human beings do well is work," Zweifle replied. "You're right, it is almost miraculous, but if there is ever work to be done we do it and we do it well, in spite of all the odds against it. That's the only reason we've survived so long as a species. In fact, I think if we ever do have to face some apocalypse we will prevent it at the very last minute, then appear before some stage, some onlookers, with smiles on our faces, as if nothing had just happened, as if it were easy."

Anglor laughed easily. "It is odd," he said. "We do our work well even if we hate our work."

"Well, in America we are taught work is our only self worth."

"Yes," Anglor said wearily. "I am the same way, even though I do a different kind of work, I still get all my self validation from it."

"It's better than getting all your self validation from someone else. That's our problem, that's why we are so lonely, because we are all madly in love with ourselves, we have to be to survive, our selves are always our biggest concern, our need for self- preservation is at the bottom of all of our other needs and impulses, human survival requires narcissism, and narcissism is perhaps the loneliest thing in the world, but it is man's natural state, it's what he needs to continue living."

"I suppose you're right," Anglor said, then put out his cigarette and immediately lit another one. "The way I look at it the past is completely useless. I think we are in Hell, and that means we cannot look back, we have to look forward."

Zweifle chuckled but his other face was crying He wiped it almost manically and sighed. "Damn this second face," he whispered in shame, the same way Maria had said she didn't want to be a philosopher anymore.

"Perhaps I can get it off you."

Zweifle snorted with doubt. "How on Earth could you do that? I was born with this damn thing and I will die with it, like a mental illness, like any other birth defect. I try to look forward in Hell, but I have no control over the second face, it is always looking back."

"Come here," Anglor gestured to him, and pulled a knife out of his pocket.

"Will it hurt?" Zweifle asked like a small child.

"No more than always having a second face."

Zweifle moved closer to Anglor, obviously nervous and aporetic. Anglor began to carve the second face out of the skin as gently as he could, but Zweifle flinched the whole time, and bled more than Anglor expected, and the face went nowhere. So Anglor threw the knife aside and tried to pry the face out of the skin with his fingers. At first it held tenaciously to the skin, like a parasite, but Anglor was slowly able to lift it, like pulling away a decal. As the face lifted from the skin of the face it was living off of it bled, and Zweifle squirmed a little bit from the pain, but after a few more minutes, Anglor completely removed the face. His hands were covered in blood and more of it squirted out of Zweifle's at last singular face and he cried with glee. Anglor had murdered the second face of a nebbish, benign man named doubt, he had murdered history.

"I'm free!" Zweifle cried with glee, and pulled a handkerchief out of his pocket to wipe off his face. The second face was on the floor at his feet, as if he were at last its master, not its slave, and it screamed for a moment out of its garish mouth and then was blown away by the wind, like the past.

"Now you can look forward all the time," Anglor said.

Zweifle was beaming. "Oh thank you, Michael," he cried. "Thank you!"

The show went on as it always did, between deep anxiety and intoxication, and the usual crowd showed up, the young pseudo- intelligentsia of Dayton, Ohio. Anglor grew sad to think that with this generation, so buried under technology and media, even intelligent people didn't read anymore. He looked to Maria. At least she did, everyday. He looked at her some more. The poor thing was not a beauty. She was overweight, flat chested and had a strange, intimidating face mostly covered by large glasses and the hat she always wore in order not to make eye contact with people. Anglor had written a large sign he put in front of the gallery. It said **Mord geschichte. Ist est unrecht!** No one asked him what the words meant, they walked right past it after looking at it for only a moment with complete indifference towards things they didn't understand. He supposed it was better than people who were frightened of what they didn't understand, and he supposed that was the disappointing difference between average men and this pseudo intelligentsia that was the closest thing to an intelligentsia we have now, in spite of them being mostly a *phainomenon Agathon*, a mere appearance- the average people were afraid of what they didn't understand, and the ersatz intellectuals who had taken over intellectualism for being much more in number, a true intellectual being almost an endangered species now, didn't give a shit about what they didn't understand, and with this arrogant sang froid they were not only a mere appearance of intelligence, they were a picture of "cool," which has always only been mere appearance, and always will be. Their indifference was vaunting, as if to say that they were too much greater than the world to take part in it, though they had never, like true saints, actually worked to renounce the world for salvation, they had simply discarded it casually, and only for the sake of appearing interesting for being so disinterested.

Then at this opening there were actually a few normal people. They were bewildered. Anglor got a feeling that the young "cool" intelligentsia was bewildered as well, that they were actually always bewildered, bit they hid it underneath their indifference so they didn't feel they owed the world anything, a world that had deeply disappointed them and discarded their dreams, a world that actually treated their parents much better, and if they ever appeared that they cared, if they ever let their buried confusion surface, they would lose the only war they had won, which was pretending not to care, pretending that the incredible nihilism of their generation didn't bother them, and they could live with it no problem. They were never able to admit that really they were forced to adjust to it and when they did their childhood was brutally murdered in front of their eyes, and they wanted to weep but it was important not to weep because their faces had been forced by the zeitgeist into an ill fitting mask, one that could not produce tears or really any emotion. Everything else became buried under it. Anglor for a moment decided to ease his criticism of them. He actually felt sorry for them.

And of course normal people were intolerable. A woman who for as far as Anglor could tell, appeared only to escape the ennui of her *durchscnittlichkeit* for a moment and to get drunk in public was looking at Anglor's work almost with disgust.

"It frightens me!" she cried.

"That's why I make art to begin with," Anglor, who was standing behind her the whole time, said. "To make people like you afraid."

The woman stared at him wild eyed with fear. Anglor angrily rolled his eyes at her and walked away. He was tired of people being afraid of him because he was insane when he was on Earth and his art was strange, he was strange. People never realized he was actually quite gentle, and the only person he was ever a danger to was himself, and that was because while he was going through his kenosis, his being human for the time being, he would have to be a danger to someone, besides just being a danger to the whole planet, and it was better to be a danger to himself than other people. He thought that was all mental illness was, a choice to become a masochist instead of a casual sadist. And people were very afraid of him not because he was a danger to them or even himself, they were afraid of him only because he and his illness were so abstract, and they feared abstraction incredibly for its resemblance to confusion and death. They failed to realize they lived in an abstraction, that their senses, their perception, their aisthesis, and their entire being was an abstraction, that the whole world itself was an abstraction. They could only deal with the normalized abstractions, the objective ones, the accidental ones. They could not deal with the deliberate, subjective ones. They could not force themselves to see the world through a so called insane person's eyes because they were too afraid that it would have some truth to it, that through the abstraction of Anglor's art they would have to realize the abstraction of everything, and they would feel alone and disoriented- this world that they had worked so hard to simplify, they could not handle the fact that in spite of their clichés it was as abstruse as ever, and always would be.

Anglor realized there was a stigma on intelligence in America. Every intelligent person he'd met here had been an outcast at some point. He realized it was because American society hoped its population would be stupid to be more easily manipulated, and it did this successfully by making ignorance a virtue, and intelligence a sin- it did this by making the unintelligent masses the accepted ones, and by alienating anyone who tried to pick up a book, by telling them because they had tried to get a real grasp on the world they were no longer allowed to be a part of it, that they would have to spend their lives alone, and American society took up this role eagerly, relieved that they were allowed to be as stupid as they wanted and they would be loved for it, while the intelligent would be hated and misunderstood. They did not realize they were puppets, and Anglor often wondered if they found out if they would even care, so long as they were the righteous ones, so long as they were the acceptable ones, so long as they belonged to the masses and the illusion that they weren't lonely.

Anglor groaned with disgust. He looked at the piece of art that had scared that woman. It was one of his prop pieces. It was set up like a Matrushka doll- it was a world, and when you opened that up there was another world, and when you opened up that world there was another world, and so on and so forth until you got to the last world and opened it there was a man, a doll, alone and screaming, as if in a cage, trapped within these worlds within worlds and knowing there was no escape, that all you could do was scream, and the worlds within worlds you were prisoner within would not hear. You were lucky if even other people heard you. The loudest screams are always silent. But they are not silent, it's just that people are deaf to them.

Anglor looked at this piece of art and sighed to himself. "She's right," he admitted. "It is frightening."

Chapter 7

After the show Anglor was of course drunk but he wasn't so drunk he had blacked out or vomited, so he was doing better than he normally did at these things. They decided to have an after party. A girl named Liza had invited everyone back to her house. Maria, Mark and Anglor decided to tag along because they wanted to continue getting drunk, and they were sure this Liza girl had more weed, as well. They went to her house it was strange. There was a huge portrait of Rosa Luxembourg right next to an equally large picture of Dolores Ibarurri Gomez. Liza saw Anglor looking at it and smiled.

"La Pasionaria," she said.

Anglor nodded. He looked more closely at Liza. She was wearing a blood red beret and a T- shirt covered in paint. He looked around and saw her paintings. They were good. There were many books in her apartment. Anglor saw a copy of Heidegger's "Being and Time," on top of the coffee table, that was obviously what she was reading now, but besides that there were many other books- Hemingway, Goethe, Balzac, Hegel, etc., and there was a book of Marc Chagall's painting also on the coffee table, and a big Wassily Kandinsky-esque painting in the middle of the room. Maria's eyes widened. These were the types of books she liked to read, as well, and she immediately ran over to Liza to talk about them. Meanwhile the rest of them got drunk and high. There was cocaine there, too. Anglor decided he would try it. It was an odd feeling. He snorted it and immediately his throat felt dry, then in a few more moments he was incredibly happy, more happy than he had ever been in his life- he could feel his soul soar above his body, as if he were dead, but he'd never felt so alive. He felt this way for about five minutes, and then it was gone, just like any other happiness, and particularly this one because it was synthetic. So he snorted another line.

He overheard bits and pieces of Liza and Maria's conversation. Liza was pontificating a little bit. "Ousia," she went on in an affected voice. "Dasein. This is being, and you can't have being without thinking, you know the old line by Descartes, so with being is *dianoein*, thinking, and then with thinking comes, *dianoia, vernunft*, reason, and then eventually with reason comes the most beautiful thing of all, knowing yourself, therefore knowing humanity, *gnothi sauton, sichkennen*."

Anglor barely suppressed the need to roll his eyes but he looked over at Maria and she was completely enraptured by it. He sighed. He always suspected Maria had some Sapphic tendencies, though she never spoke of them. Anglor was of course Bisexual, everyone on the moon was, but he never talked about it either. No one ever fell in love on the moon, they merely procreated. Love was an entirely human invention, that was their redeeming quality, Anglor thought. He drank more beer. He was very drunk but the cocaine was waking him up, making him feel sober enough to drink more. At last the group gathered around in a big circle, everyone together. Anglor supposed he was having fun, but it was such an odd feeling he didn't know how to appreciate it. He didn't have fun very often, mostly he just worked, so in a way this was a welcome diversion.

With them at last gathered around in ne big group they at last began to talk to each other, though Anglor mostly just sat back enjoying his brief, fleeting high until he had to snort another line again. Liza began to pontificate more.

"You see, after the holocaust we were hoping that God would punish us by ending the world. But God didn't do shit, so we took matters into our own hands, we created the nuclear bomb, and we didn't end the world with it, but since then every generation has threatened it, and it's a possibility, an imminent threat, that we live with always now. But we still haven't done it and hopefully we never will. I hope we don't…at least I think I hope we don't. In a way it would solve a lot of our problems."

"The problem of ourselves?" Maria said. Liza nodded.

"I don't know what I want," Liza said. "I don't know if I want to live forever or die right now."

Anglor nodded to her. This was a problem he understood. This was a problem he thought everyone understood.

"And I feel the same way about the whole human race," Liza added glumly.

"What?" Anglor said. "If you have to go we all have to go, and if you have to stay we all have to stay?"

Liza shrugged. "Well, I don't want to be lonely."

"That's childish," he said, "and particularly sad because I think everyone in the world feels that way."

Liza nodded at him in concordance, a sad, solemn look in her eyes.

"You'd still be lonely," Anglor added. "Whether you are with everyone or no one, both are lonely."

"How'd we get on such a sad subject?" Liza said with forced bonhomie. "This is a party!"

"We could do more coke," Anglor suggested.

"Wait a minute," Liza said. "I don't have that much."

"It's never enough, is it?"

Liza groaned. "Nothing ever is. I feel like the more we have of anything the bigger the hole inside us gets to swallow it all, so we are still hungry."

"That's why it's important to renounce the world," Anglor said while Maria rolled another joint. "That's what Christ and

Kierkegaard said, though they promised that if you renounce the world you'd be given another one, Heaven, in other words. But that's not true. This is the only world, if you renounce it you have nothing. But it's better to have nothing, that's the only thing that can fill the hole. Nothing means more than the whole world. The world in comparison to it is nugatory, *sinnlos*. It must be renounced, that's what I mean by killing history."

"To renounce the world," Maria said musingly. "How can one do that without death?"

"You can't," Anglor said. "But some people really can do it when they're alive."

"Very few people," Maria retorted back quickly.

"Yes, but these people do change the world that they've renounced. The world they've renounced never forgets them."

"It's easy for you to say," Maria grumbled under her breath. "You're not even from this world."

"What?" Liza said, and looked at Maria wild- eyed. The coke was making her look that way.

"Nothing," Maria said weakly and waved a lazy hand of surrender in the air. Everyone shrugged, continued partying, and didn't say anything. They didn't get to sleep until about seven in the morning, and Anglor thought due to all the alcohol he would have a long, mercifully dreamless sleep, but he was wrong. He had a brief dream, but it was memorable. He was holding the piece of art that had frightened that woman, but it was a little different. On the first world that was enclosing all the other worlds there was a sign Anglor had not put there. It said *alethes lanthanei*, truth hidden, and Anglor suddenly felt panicked at the words. He tried to open up the world, but it was closed tight. He did many things to try to open it. He hit it with a hammer, he threw it against the wall, but still it would not budge. He began to cry because he couldn't open it, because he realized that man who was buried in there under all the worlds, that man was the truth, he was the *alethes lanthanei*, and not only could he not get out of his layered prison, he could not be found- the truth was a prisoner and it was also unseen, buried underneath the worlds within worlds, buried within the nothingness that is greater than all these worlds and is always surrounding them and is always burying the truth that is intricately hidden, kept prisoner, left unseen within them. But this nothingness is the truth, this nothingness is the same as the man buried within it along with the worlds that are also within it and intricately layered within themselves. The man is the same as nothingness, and it is not nothingness that hides him, it is the illusion of something that he is buried under, concealed by, *vershuttet*, but really he is the heart of nothingness, trapped within man's inventions, his own inventions, longing for the truth which man likes to cover like a wound, that it keeps as a leper in a sanitarium- truth is the outcast, truth is the prisoner, truth is the man we try to write out of history, truth is the man we ignore, who we cut out of the human race, and instead leave buried under the wreckage of our inventions, our fabrications and our failures, our worlds within worlds that is in one world that is in nothingness, that is in truth, and that truth, the nothingness, is the one we can't conceive of, and because of our inability to conceive of it we cannot hide it. It surrounds us, it hides *us*, two different truths constantly trying to erase the other, while the man who tells the truth is trapped so deeply under history we cannot hear him, and we were the ones who inhumed him there.

We are the ones who bury truth and therefore we are the only ones who can find truth, it is within us somewhere, an engram we forced in the unconscious that some of us, through time, wish to emerge again, that we search for all the Earth wide not realizing it is somewhere in the hinterland of our memory, that it is inside us, not outside of us. We are the ones who put ourselves in the proverbial cave where all we can see is shadows and we are the ones who can let ourselves out of this cave to see the light and the world, as it is, not as we'd like it to be. We are the ones who endow ourselves with ignorance and then we are the only ones who can erase it with knowledge. Maybe that is the point of this ignorance, so we can choose to rise above it like some choose to rise above evil, for it is the root of evil, and the truth, though it may be awful, is necessary to building a good character. We walk through the Earth partially blind to it, and we are the only ones who can return our own vision, and we may not like what we see, but we must see it first in order to change it.

Truth and the search for it are important, though few take part in it, few try to shed the ignorance that comes from being a part of a large population, few people want to be alone that much, for truth only comes to you in solitude, the masses are the obscurantism of it, they are the ones that buried the man so deep within the worlds within worlds and who will not let him out. One has to escape them to find truth, and one has to escape them to be themselves, for the first step to truth is being who you truly are, not what others would like you to be. I can understand why many people don't want to go on such a quest, but for some of us it is compulsory, for some of us it has been calling to us, a noise coming from the Earth, since we were born, and so we do it, we search for truth not caring that it may be nightmarish, not caring that the mere search for it is indeed a burden, and it makes you strange, it makes you alone, still we cannot help it, it obsesses us, it is, to us, the only reason to live, for really it is life's great odyssey, its hidden meaning, buried like truth, waiting for these eldritch few to uncover it.

Anglor woke up and groaned a little bit. It was a frightening dream, but he had learned something from it. He got up to use the bathroom. In Liza's bathroom there were more paintings on the wall. Anglor saw a re-print of Joan Miro's "El Segador," and laughed to himself.

"So she is educated," he said. Then he thought about death. It is with us everyday and everyday we ignore it. We are alive everyday and so we forget that we're going to die, we erase our knowledge of it with daily routine, and yet in this routine is the everyday presence, the *zugegensein* of death, waiting for us. Each day we forget we are going to die and yet each day we are closer to death. But no one can think about it all the time, or eventually the combined anxiety and curiosity about death will overcome them and they will try to force death, they will try to commit suicide. That's what this daily routine is for, to forget death enough not to commit suicide, to think there is something important to do everyday and because everyday is so casual, so regular, we can forget the knowledge that is somewhere within us that each of these regular days are one step closer to the last. But really there is no regular day. Everyday someone is born and someone dies-everyday there is a war and an atrocity, a genocide, a bombing, a migration of refugees, everyday the world itself is dying.

And all we can do is try to forget and to live our lives as normally as possible. So we do. When we are children we divert our existential angst with a number of activities- swimming, ballet recitals, school, etc. Then we grow into adults and all we're allowed to do is work and then go home and drink- the job, the family, the kids and the alcohol are supposed to be enough to distract us, and they do in an unusual way. They exhaust us until we can't think anymore, and this makes us slaves but at least we have avoided the fear of death in the average everydayness again, have buried it in the normalcy that says "you are alive today and you will be alive tomorrow, you will be alive to work and drink and take care of the kids." Anglor didn't want to live that way, it was too boring and it was also draining, though people, after their enormous powers of the ability to adjust, had forgotten that so long as it made them forget death, but Anglor would prefer any other lifestyle even if it meant he would be more aware of death than other people, and as an artist and a philosopher he certainly was, but somehow it was better for him this way, again for only a few certain people, the people that seek after knowledge seek even after the knowledge of death, they hold it with them at all times, like all people do, but they are more aware of it, and still they live, they also live an average everydayness though it is a different average everydayness, they also forget for a moment they are going to die because of the work they do, though it is a different kind of work, a work that really can make you immortal, or at least make your mind immortal, though the spirit and the body still have to die no matter who you are, the fact that the wise person knows this and accepts this without too much grief, without too much existential angst, and a willingness to remember it, not to try to forget it with the diurnal ennui, is what makes their minds immortal in the end.

People want to be immortal but they are still too frightened of art to realize it is the only thing that could ever make a person immortal. They are still too frightened of it because it reminds them of death, because it speaks of death so often, and the immortality it offers is of course paid for with death as well. Anglor thought perhaps they were afraid of immortality, he thought perhaps it wasn't death they were frightened of but eternity, for death is eternal, much more eternal than life. But eternity was daunting to everyone, even the philosopher who tries to understand it and to make it a part of themselves. But it is a part of us all, because we all die. That which is everlasting in us is always waiting for death so it can emerge again. But all human beings can recall is being temporal, they do not remember what it's like to be eternal, and this forgetting is what makes them frightened, it is their ignorance that causes their fear. Ignorance engenders fear and then fear engenders evil, that's how it works, that's why human beings, who are sometimes willfully ignorant, created evil, that's why evil exists, to replace ignorance with knowledge is to replace evil, fear, with goodness and bravery, for evil is always afraid, that's why it does the things it does, that's why it kills those it kills, because it is frightened of them. Fear is the root of all evil, fear of other people most of all, and even fear of death can create evil, too, even though we are all afraid of death, even the philosopher who is perhaps less afraid of it, is still afraid of it, so we all have a little it of evil in us, created from the ignorance of the eternal, of having forgotten what it's like not to be, and resigning oneself to the temporal, being intimidated by anything else, by making oneself finite.

Good is eternal, truth is eternal, and they are often rewarded only with death, but that is what makes them eternal. Ignorance, evil and fear are temporal, though they never die on Earth, they are bound only to the Earth, they do not exist in eternity, they only exist because of time, which does not exist in eternity, and so they are bound to the temporal, so they are finite, and often extinguish themselves with their folly. Fear of death belongs to life only, death actually relieves it, for the dead are not frightened of being dead any more than the living are frightened of being alive. I suppose it's like anything else that you adjust to. And you can adjust to anything when you're dead, the same as you adjusted to anything when you were alive. I don't suppose the two are really that different, except death has less anxiety.

Anglor finally woke up at around two in the afternoon with a raging hangover. He got up amidst all the bodies on the floor, all that were still asleep, and got a glass of water. The water felt good going down his throat but as soon as he swallowed it he was thirsty again. He grabbed another glass of water, then another, and another, and he felt like Tantalus with his face only an inch from the water and not being able to drink it, though he was drinking it, he was still incredibly thirsty, his mouth went dry again as soon as the water was done. He kept drinking profusely until he hard someone stir on the floor.

It was Liza. She went up to him and smiled weakly. "Hangover?" she asked.

"Yes," Anglor said through another large gulp of water. "Very much so."

"I have some asprin I can give you, and I'll make coffee."

"Coffee and asprin sounds good, thank you."

"No problem. I strive to be a good hostess."

"It was a hell of a party. I overdid it a little bit."

"Well, you're supposed to. You think a lot don't you?"

Anglor shrugged. "I suppose so."

"I could tell because of how hard you partied. The deep thinkers always get the most drunk, their minds are too sober the rest of the time."

"I can see how that would be true."

Liza put a couple of asprin on the table in front of Anglor, and he smiled weakly at her and took them with yet another glass of water. Liza began to make coffee.

"I don't want to do that all the time, though," Anglor said. "Party."

"Why not?"

"I feel like I'm wasting my life."

"Hmm," Liza said. "Most people feel they're wasting their lives if they don't party."

"There's too much to do," Anglor said absently. "I don't have the time."

"So you like your sober mind?"

"I have a diseased mind."

"Some minds are sober and diseased at the same time. They are the most brilliant ones."

"And the most onerous," Anglor said with a sigh. "Even when I feel fine I'm a little sad."

"Some people are like that," she said and patted him on the shoulder. "Coffee's done."

"Thank you," Anglor said as Liza poured him a hot cup of coffee.

"We'll probably be the only ones awake for awhile."

"What time is it?"

"A little past noon."

Anglor grunted and drank his coffee. It was warm and smooth and went down his throat easily. It wasn't exactly hydrating but it was what he needed right now, to sober up his diseased mind.

"What if someone were able to make you happy?" Liza suddenly asked. Anglor looked at her strangely.

"What if?" he responded. "What if someone made me happy? Would I still have a right to my despair?"

Liza laughed and Anglor raised an eyebrow. He didn't think it was any laughing matter, it was how he really felt, it was a legitimate question.

"You know," Liza went on, changing the subject again. "We are history, it makes us. If we kill it what will we be?"

"It makes us victims and oppressors," Anglor responded back stiffly. "We have to be a little bit more than that. History hasn't made us well, it has held us back in its image when we're supposed to be made in God's image."

"Maybe God is history."

"Then I want to kill God. There is no changing my mind, Liza. Do you know what's going on at the border right now?"

And now at last Liza was sobered, her entire face dropped. "Yes," she said through a shaking voice. "It's horrible."

"Children are not only being separated from their parents and being kept in cages, they're being given to *traffickers*, traffickers Liza. You know why I want to kill history, because it kills children, and not just now, it always has. Our children are supposed to be the most important thing to us in the world, but every epoch we sacrifice them to the vagaries of our politics and violence, every generation we abandon them for the sake of our own historical vanities, to our organized murder, our bullshit, and so I really do want to kill history, because it has slaughtered billions and all these billions were innocent, and they were sacrificed to a lie, they were sacrificed to nothing, and so many of them have been children, so many children have died because to us war is nothing more than a game we play to alleviate the boredom!" and he slammed his fist on the table. By now he was shaking with rage, his face rubicund and sweating. "And to everyone else it is sure death, destruction of their families, their homes, it uproots their whole lives and they are left with nothing. All these children die for the sake of bigger children who want to put their mark on the Earth, even if they have to do it by violence, these bigger children to whom the whole world is a playground they want to be the ruler of. Children are at the mercy of these bigger children who will destroy the whole world just to be remembered, real children who have nothing to do with such vanity, real children who certainly have not done anything wrong, who are far more innocent than the bigger children who are constantly sacrificing them to their politics, real children who do not even understand yet what history is, are being sacrificed to it like the children in the fiery furnace."

And now tears were streaming out of his eyes, tears of rage and also great sorrow. Liza put a hand on his shoulder. "I'm sorry, Michael" she said. "I didn't know."

And now Anglor broke down sobbing, his emotions addled by the drugs. He dropped his head on the countertop, covered it with his fists and wept. Liza kept her hand on his shoulder. "I'm sorry," she said again.

"So am I," Anglor groaned. "I'm sorry history even began, and each generation it gets harder to end. It never really ends. Its effects go on for millennia."

"It's nice to see someone who really cares," Liza whispered, because at the sound of Anglor's sobs people were beginning to stir from their beds on the floor.

"I have no choice but to care," he said. "It's my job."

"As an artist?"

He nodded. "Indifference kills," he said, "but it cannot kill history. In fact it feeds it." Maria suddenly stirred at the sound of his crying and got out of bed and walked over to him, also putting a hand on his shoulder.

"What's wrong?"

"It's nothing. It's the drugs."

"They do that sometimes the first time," Maria said consolingly, rubbing his shoulder in a wide, counter- clockwise circle. "Let's go get something to eat, there's a diner around the corner."

"I'm so hungry," Anglor said rather pitiably.

"We'll go get food honey," Maria said, still in a maternal manner. "Wanna come, Liza?"

"I appreciate the offer, but there are ten people asleep on my floor. I can't really leave."

Maria nodded. "I'll go wake up Mark," she said.

It took some effort to get Mark off the floor, he was probably more hungover than anyone else, which was pretty usual.

"Let me have some of that coffee before we go," he pleaded.

"There's coffee at the diner," Maria said like a frustrated parent talking to an unruly child.

"I'm telling you, Maria," Mark responded with equal frustration. "I'm not leaving this place until there's some coffee in me."

"I have half a pot left," Liza said, and generously poured him a cup of coffee, to which Mark was relieved.

"I'm sorry," he said. "I can't get out of bed without it, especially when I'm hungover."

"It's fine," Maria said stiffly, and had Liza pour her a cup as well. "I of all people should understand."

"Then why don't you?"

"I don't know," she said. "I feel a little restless right now."

"I told you," Anglor said. "Partying is a waste of life."

"But so is not partying," Maria put in miserably.

"Just enjoy the coffee," Anglor said. Liza looked at them strangely.

"You're a bit of a depressed bunch, aren't you?"

"Aren't you?" Anglor said. "You're an artist."

She shrugged. "Usually I'm able to drink it off."

"That doesn't work forever," Anglor said. "And there's always the morning after."

"You guys are the ones who have issues the morning after…"

"We're mentally ill," Maria suddenly said. "We can't help it."

Liza looked at them consolingly and then other people began to wake up, so she went to make more coffee. Some people left immediately which was a relief to Liza. She realized more and more with these damn parties that she didn't really like the people who attended them. Michael, Maria and Mark were okay, though, in spite of the fact they were always glum. 'The three M's,' Liza though to herself. 'Melancholy, Malaise, and Maudlin.' She laughed to herself privately at her little joke. 'I can't wait to have this house back to myself,' she thought. 'I can't wait to be alone. Then as soon a I'm alone I'm going to want to have another party. What's happening to me? I'm becoming one of those vacuous extraverts I hate, or at least I'm pretending to be one. That's what the cocaine is for, to make me become someone else, to make me that person I've always hated, the person that always told me I wasn't good enough, but who I've always envied.' She sighed to herself. 'I feel like I've swallowed a worm,' she continued to think. 'And now it's crawling all around inside of me like I'm a grave. And it's eating everything, it's eating my ability to love, it's eating my ability to feel, to do anything that's important to me, but I can't get rid of it. I can't stop.'

Mark drank his coffee as quickly as he could knowing Maria and Anglor wanted to leave. He finished it and slammed it down on the counter like it was a shot at a bar, and he grinned peevishly at Anglor. "Alright," he said. "Let's get some food in us."

They were all three relieved when they left Liza's house, because they got the feeling that if they'd stayed any longer they wouldn't be able to leave. It's a difficult life, the one that disguises itself as fun, and it's very difficult to abandon, it keeps pulling you back in with its promise of eternal youth in rebellion, its promise of freedom, all promises you realize quickly are empty, but it feels like there are no other alternatives, so you keep doing it, you keep going to the numb and empty parties, you keep drinking, you keep snorting cocaine, because it feels like all the world has got to offer, and it is another blatant nothingness, another artificial happiness, another lie one tells oneself to keep going. It is a prolonged and undignified suicide, one in which all the while you are enduring it you are pretending to be happy, pretending it is a choice you made gladly. Anglor didn't want to live that way, but now he also had taken a bite of the worm, and he wondered if he would want to go back for the rest, though he would only find that it doesn't end. It would be particularly easy now that he was famous, and nothing else was easy, in fact fame wasn't even easy- it was so facile it became difficult. Anglor thought perhaps the parties were the same way, after they had gone on too long, after you were a guest in your own life that had worn out their welcome.

At the diner our three glum friends did not talk to each other much, and they hardly ate their food because all three had stomachs that were riled up, but they tried, they tried to be regular humans for a moment, ones that ate and went out but did so in a healthy manner. They were all hiding the fact that they did not know how to go out and do so in a healthy way, that as three die-hard introverts it would always be difficult, and an excess of social lubricant would have to be involved, be it alcohol or cocaine or whatever the hell was around.

"Did you guys like Liza?" Maria asked, breaking the silence.

Mark simply shrugged and continued shifting his hash browns around his plate with his fork, staring at them and not eating them.

"I think she's a little ostentatious," Anglor said.

"Yea. She's smart though."

"I suppose, but she advertises it too much."

"Is she supposed to hide it?"

Anglor sighed. "It's nothing to brag about."

"Well it's not shameful, either," Maria quickly riposted.

Anglor shrugged not only with indifference but also without knowing. He thought intelligence could be quite beautiful, particularly when translated into art, but he didn't feel that way about his intelligence, his art, and while he wasn't exactly ashamed of it he knew it made him harder to reach, he knew it was a large wall erected between him and other people, and he would not tear it down because it was such a good defense, as he always had the feeling that people approached with weapons, especially when they fell in love, which Anglor had never done for it being foreign to his alien race, but with the wall up he didn't have to worry about it. People could shoot at his heart but they would always miss because his big mind had already swallowed it up, it was no more. it rested with his intellect now, which means it had been annihilated, devoured by his intelligence, so well hidden that one day it finally disappeared somewhere deep into the unconscious where he didn't have to notice it anymore, didn't have to feel it anymore, and he was glad. That was one good thing about intelligence, it made it easier to be alone.

"We should go to Paris," Mark suddenly said out of nowhere, and Maria and Anglor looked at him with raised eyebrows. "They understand better there."

"You speak French, don't you?" Anglor said as he drank his black coffee, the third cup already today.

"Somewhat," Mark answered. "I can read it and write it a lot better than I can speak it." He paused for a second, laughed to himself and added: "That's kind of symbolic. I've always been better at reading and writing then speaking."

"Same," Maria said. "If only we could speak as we wrote, people would fall in love with us all the time, but we hide our eloquence, our talents, and no one bothers to read them when we write them down, because we can't speak it."

"People like to listen just as little as they like to read," Mark said without emotion, as if it were only a simple scientific fact. "It would be no different."

"Then what the hell do people like?" Maria said.

"Ask Anglor, he's the famous one."

So Maria turned to Anglor with an inquisitive face. He shrugged again. "Don't ask me," he said. "I'm supposedly a genius, which means I have no idea what people like, and after awhile I don't care either."

Mark threw his head back with laughter. "That's rich," he said.

"All I know is what I like," Anglor said. "That's enough for me."

"You guys are depressive," Mark said. "I know why. It's because you both have pure hearts, pure hearts are always depressed, lonely in a world that is corrupt. So you become depressed, and then eventually your depression corrupts your pure hearts, and you are no longer pure hearted. It's a great tragedy what the Earth does to pure hearted people: it rips their pure hearts out!"

"That's not true for all the pure hearted people," Anglor said. "Many become depressed, but many do not let this depression get in the way of them making the effort to create a new world that is just as pure as their hearts, people like Martin Luther King Jr. He never gave up on his pure heart, and he never gave up on the idea that one day the world could match it, so he really did change things, and he will always be remembered. People like him will always be remembered, because they didn't slump into a depression because they didn't like the world, instead they actually fought to make it a safer, more moral place."

"You need to become one of those people," Mark said. "Don't let the world rip out your pure heart by letting it make you depressed. Fight it. Make the world a mirror of your heart."

"It's already a mirror of everyone's hearts."

"But not yours."

Anglor smiled. "What about you, Mark? Why are you so depressed? Were you also once pure hearted, and now mourning the death of your pure heart?"

"No, I have a different problem," he said.

"What is that?"

"I am too 'grounded,' I am too 'down to Earth,' and now I am chained to the Earth, now I am melded to the ground, and I can't get up, I can't feel like I'm flying the way I used to. I am stuck to the ground permanently- I am part of the Earth and I was once part of the sky, but that is the part of me that has died."

"You're getting old," Maria said mysteriously.

"Yes," Mark said. "Every year I get closer to this Earth that I am chained to, every year I'm closer to being under it, and time is going so fast." He sighed, and to Anglor and Maria's shock tears were welling in his eyes. "I just wanted to be good," he whispered.

"Do you believe in good and evil?" Maria asked.

"I do," Mark said, wiping the inchoate tears out of his eyes. "But I think people have perverted both of them terribly. I think what they perceive as good is hypocrisy and what they perceive as evil is merely misfortune."

Anglor nodded, having understood. He and Maria were so young, they could never at this stage in their life understand Mark's struggle of being bound to the Earth, particularly not Anglor, who was only visiting it, but they could understand his fear of both good and evil, and the feeling of wanting to be good even while knowing you're a human and therefore innately inadequate, the feeling of wanting to be good in a world that was so perverse you weren't even sure what good was any more, knowing in your heart it isn't what your parents and elders told you it was when you were a child, but still not sure what it is exactly, only knowing it is the opposite of this world, and that is why it is important to renounce the world, even if there is no heaven after it, for in this abnegation you will find the good, in this nullity you will find the truth, in this freedom you will know what is worth knowing, that there is good and evil only on the Earth, they don't exist anywhere else, so to renounce the world means to become free of this moral schism, this extremism that ruins humans and their narrow world that is obsessed with good and evil, and is easily swayed by evil. All three of them, Anglor, Mark and Maria wanted to find the good that was buried beneath the hypocrisy and the misfortune, but they thought it was more likely to be amidst the complete ruin and desperation of the misfortune, the everyday tragedy that people have become so inured to they ignore it, even when it is right in front of them, every time they see a homeless man on the street and drive or walk past him as if he doesn't exist. Anglor could relate to this. Even now that he was famous people still looked right through him, and not at his heart, whether it be pure or not, but at the nothingness he consisted of, which we all consist of, but was more obvious in people like Anglor. They looked at him like he wasn't there, because truthfully he wasn't, everywhere he went he was always somewhere else. They looked through him as if his flesh were but a mere hunk of transparent ectoplasm, they didn't ever look at him because he was so strange, and the words he said, the lesson he had to teach, they did not want to hear- they looked at him like he didn't exist because they didn't want him to exist, they didn't want him to be real and they didn't want the words he said to be true, and they found he was an easy thing to erase. What they didn't know was that people like this, the easy to ignore, the ones you want to write out of existence because they secretly intimidate you, one day rise above the invisibility people have forcibly imposed upon them and cry too loudly not to be heard "I exist nonetheless, whether you want me to or not!" and at last they eventually become remembered, these seemingly meek, inconsequential people that are so anathema to the masses they rise so far above them, become so singular, that the very history that tried to make them vanish then bows in obeisance to them, and offers them the only onerous prize it has to offer, memory, and being part of it, not just it being a art of you- the rare gift of being remembered and not simply remembering, and eventually the people who tried to erase you are erased themselves, for they were the inconsequential ones, they were the ones that did not truly exist. Anglor was only so invisible because he existed too much, was too real, and that's why people couldn't see him. But they would remember him.

Eventually the trio left the diner, they dropped Mark off and then when Anglor and Maria went home they immediately went back to bed. Anglor's brain chemistry was addled by the drugs still, and he had trouble going to sleep. He was waiting for the solemn sound that is often so elusive, the *higgaion*, the rare peace that comes after you have thought so much you cannot think anymore, and your soul in its restlessness at last goes to sleep. It took an hour or so, but the peace that was almost like nullity eventually came, which can only be followed by sleep, the hollow sound in the soul, the ancient echo of the past, saying nothing but blowing through you like the most harrowing wind. At last it came, and Anglor rolled in the bed with ecstasy, his mind that was always tired but always awake at last ready to ease into sleep, into the diurnal impermanent oblivion that prepares us one day for the eternal oblivion, he at last found it in the depths of his soul and it swarmed and covered him like a blanket, like the night sky wrapping around the Earth. Higgaion. Selah.

Chapter 8

Finally Anglor and Maria moved to New York. They got a place on Waverly, it was expensive, but Anglor could afford it. Mark helped them move. They rented a Uhaul and drove all the way to New York City in Maria's tiny car and they smoked joints all the way there to keep their calm. They had fought almost the entire time. They had been using cocaine fairly regularly now, and Anglor got the feeling that once they got to the city it would be even worse, but he didn't care, he just had to get out of Miamisburg. Maria had never really wanted to move, though, she just wanted Anglor to be happy, and she resented him for this, because no matter what she did she couldn't make him happy, and couldn't make herself happy. She agreed Miamisburg was not exactly the optimal place to live, particularly for someone who didn't drive and had a higher intellect than most of the people in that small, two hundred year old ghost of a town where most people actually made an effort to be deliberately simple, and they despised the complex, and people who read were strange to them. They didn't understand why anyone would need to know more than how to work, how to change a tire, how to mow the lawn, the bare essential tasks for living in normalized society. And Anglor had grown to hate them, had grown to hate so called simplicity in general, particularly when it was forced like this and considered the highest virtue in the town, to love God without thinking about it, to love life without thinking about it, and to love nothing else, because after these two thoughtless loves there was no more love left- none of them actually loved people, none of them were actually compassionate, they just tried to avoid the complex, and they did not see people, neighbors, or even lovers, as anything more than people to engage in useless palaver with to pass the time which was agonizingly slow in Miamisburg because it was a town that did not exist, and because it did not exist it did not change, it was preserved by two hundred years of time that was mostly immutable, by a long history of nothing but racism and a flood, by its obdurate refusal to change or ever be a part of the modern world.

Anglor just felt more free in New York City- he felt like he was in the center of the world there, he felt as if he actually existed in a place that certainly existed, that wasn't buried under years of the complacency of numb habit and mindless, even often times barbaric tradition. This city throbbed with life, to the point one thought it would explode, but it never did, it was a bomb full of people that never detonated, it just went to work, caught cabs, trains, the subway, drank, went to the stock exchange, and lived with an enormous amount of people almost peacefully, perhaps the only place in America that was used to being a melting pot and wasn't bothered by people who were different, wasn't even bothered by people who were strange, for New York City had seen every possible eccentricity, and it had grown to learn that all people were strange, and this was a city that made them even stranger, which actually made people happier, the freedom to be strange, and not alone in your strangeness like you would be in Miamisburg where normalcy is practically worshipped like an idol.

Something about this city filled Anglor's soul with immense joy, even exhilaration, to know he could be a part of the heart of the world, the intense, packed, ululating, throbbing center of this corner of the universe that seemed to contain all the world's people- a place where there was a home for everyone, though it may not be a loving home. Anglor realized New York City was a bit like beauty- it was an easy thing to idealize, but it could be very cruel.

New York was a bit like a femme fatale, something you were all too willing to fall in love with, to give up everything for, even knowing that it would destroy you. But Anglor didn't care. He couldn't imagine loving another woman, as men often are when they meet such a femme fatale- spellbound, captivated just as much by their cruelty as their beauty. But Anglor thought there was a kind of ancient wisdom in this city, that maybe their was even an ancient wisdom in beauty though it could be so thoughtless, and that's all Anglor wanted out of life was wisdom. He felt without wisdom there was no point of growing old- without wisdom there was only death, and even dying is supposed to provide a bit of wisdom, the final wisdom, the ultimate wisdom, that death though it seems so atrocious is perhaps the only normal thing in this world, and all things must die in order to live, and all things must live in order to die, both life and death are one another's true purpose, the purpose of dying being to live and the purpose of living being to die. And without this wisdom you cannot except either of them. Without wisdom there is only life and death, and neither of them mean anything, and wisdom is knowing this to be true but still loving them anyway, still accepting them as the natural balance of all things here on Earth. Even things that are not truly alive die, even stars die, the sun, and eventually Earth, and eventually the galaxy, and probably eventually the universe. It's only natural. Forever is allotted to nothingness, the only thing that's built to last, everything else, all the somethingness, can endure time for as long as necessary but cannot live forever. Time endures them in return, but it cannot endure them always, just like they cannot always endure time. We bend time like it is matter, but not to our will, out of the necessity of nature, and in return time ages us. In return it leads us slowly and rapidly to our deaths. And without wisdom, what was its purpose? What was its design? Why did it even happen at all?

Even the universe, the only reason it lasts so long is because it is mostly nothingness, that is the past of it that is eternal, and it was born beyond time, before time existed, and then it *was* immortal, but now it is like the rest of us, bound by time, which means you only have a limited amount of it, which means you have a death sentence just like almost all things now that time exists. Perhaps that is the only reason that time is necessary, just for the purpose of killing things, because few things can really be immortal, and usually they become immortal by dying.

Anglor and Maria's new apartment was nice, quite a bit bigger than their apartment in Miamisburg, and there was a hell of a view of the Village from their upstairs window. Maria did not like change much, but she looked around at the place and began to slowly adjust.

"It is nice," she admitted.

"I think we'll bee quite comfortable here. Besides, it's easier to be famous in New York City. In a small town it doesn't make any sense."

"At least in Miamisburg no one knew who you were."

"I want a link to the world," Anglor said. "This city is it."

"I thought you hated the world."

"I do, but I want to be a part of it. I have to be a part of it, I can't imagine not being so."

Maria laughed and started unpacking things. "Maybe we will have a better life here," she said.

"Even if we don't," Anglor said "It's always nice to run away."

Maria smiled up at him and continued working. Anglor did the same thing. With the mess of moving he was unable to draw for a couple days, and his neuroses were suffering for it, but at least there were still things to do, there were always things to do, be they predestined or not, no one should ever be bored. And Anglor was not the kind of man to just surrender to fate like so many other people did, attached to their clichés which were nothing but "lazy sophisms," *logos argos* that people grabbed onto tenaciously as if they were rocks in the midst of a violent ocean, and all of them were fatalistic, all of them spoke of what little control we have, so one must fall down and passively accept misfortune without doing anything to change it, everyone must accept the will of God and nature without thinking about it but boiling their complex ideas into simple aphorisms that prevent one not only from acting amidst the vicissitudes of fate, but also not thinking about it- it was a lazy resignation without remonstrance to something that supposedly couldn't be controlled, but Anglor found that fate or God or something blessed in nature had indeed given us free will almost to spite itself, and while you cannot change the past, and you are always blind to the future, it is possible to make your own fate, to change God's supposed plan. You will suffer dearly for it, but Anglor thought it was worth it. He was grateful that since Earth he had gained some kind of driving conatus, a resolute will, *ratzon*, the will to fight fate, to work against it, and he found fate always rewarded its adversaries in the end, after punishing them dearly, still in the end it does recompense those it tried to destroy simply because it did not destroy them- fate eventually rewards those who fight it, it eventually rewards the bravery of those who will not let their lives be controlled by a blind destiny, and try to control it themselves instead, whereas most people are relived at the thought that fate might make their decisions, so they do not have to take responsibility for either their suffering or their joy, these people want the responsibility which is the freedom of being the master of your own life.

These people are all about the present, the nonce, the *tantisper*, and *unumquicquid*, all the little things, all that subsists in the present though it is only for a moment, they perceive every detail of the moment to forget it for the next moment, which they also must perceive every detail, and they learn never to reflect on it, ever to reflect on anything lain life unless its actually happening right now. They know the past is a dead man who shouldn't even be mourned, that it is the death of a tyrant or some devil, a necessary death, as all death is, and the future is just thin air one cannot grasp at- all that exists happens in only a moment, a second, then it passes back into non-existence happily, having had its one moment of life and ready to retire, and the future, the future doesn't exist, not until it becomes the now. The now is the only thing that exists, and to recognize that is how you become the master of your own fate, by realizing only the present matters, the *gegenwart*, to be obsessed with either the *vergangen* or the *zukunfst* is to waste what little life is granted to you and which only exists in moments, in the present, in something which is passing. And you cannot hold onto it, you must just recognize it as it is passing and then let it go.

Anglor and Maria's place was on the third floor, so it was difficult moving everything. They found to both their surprise and their dismay that the aging Mark was actually more fit than they were. Neither of them cooked, so they mostly ate out, they had the money to do so, and either really exercised, either. They found out Mark did, because he was awfully afraid to die, and yet he wanted it at the same time. He thought of death as that eldritch and special depression that occasionally comes over you that is a solemn depression, a wise depression, and can actually be dignified. He was no stranger to this kind of depression, the most merciful of all depressions, but he had not experienced it enough, and he knew this time he experienced it would be the last time, and this time it would actually end, completely, and his entire life along with it. He didn't know whether to run from it or run to, because even though it was the most pleasant depression there was, it was still grief, and he didn't know if he wanted it to be the last thing he ever felt, but he thought there was nothing else to feel while dying. And this just made him depressed simply, without the solemnity, without the wisdom, without the dignity, and he was certainly frightened of that being his last feeling. Any feeling could be his last feeling at any moment. He would like to die in a moment of joy, if that was possible, but he realized few people, especially in the modern world, die without first having to contemplate dying, and that's probably the worst part, worse than the dying itself. He thought of an Andre Vesalio illustration he had seen. It was "Man Contemplates Himself." It was a drawing of a skeleton holding a skull, contemplating it, contemplating himself, contemplating death. That was what dying was like, being the remnants of what once was a man contemplating the remnants of what was once a man. He tried to shake the image off, the image of him holding his own skull, opening it up to find his brain, and in there finding the knowledge of death that life had worked so hard to keep hidden.

"I'm gonna miss you kids," he said to Anglor and Maria after they finally finished getting everything up the stairs.

"I'm sorry," Maria said. "We shouldn't have made you do this. Sit down, you look pale."

Mark sat down and Maria quickly ran to get him a glass of water. "I'm fine, really," he said. "It is just hard to be an old man and still have to say goodbye. Young people do it all the time, but they have the rest of their lives, don't they? Then again, what else is there to do when you're an old man but say goodbye?"

"I'm sorry Mark," Maria said again.

He waved her off flippantly. "It's fine. Do you mind if I stay the weekend with you? I'm awfully tired."

"That's fine, Mark," Anglor said. "Really. We're grateful for everything."

"I'm so tired of goodbyes," Mark whispered to himself, then fell asleep on the couch. Anglor and Maria still had a lot of work to do, but they did it as quietly as possible after taking a brief break to smoke a cigarette and a joint.

"Do you think he's alright?' Maria asked, gesturing towards Mark comatose on the couch.

"I don't know," Anglor said, concerned himself. "We shouldn't have made him do all that work. I don't know why, maybe it's just because I'm young, but I forget that he's old."

Meanwhile Mark heard everything from the couch. He was only half asleep, therefore in a state of peaceful delirium, contemplating, consumed by *betrachtung*, wondering what he would be like when he was dead, if he would change at all or would still be the same person only with a dead mind. He couldn't stop thinking about it, but eventually the solemn depression lulled him into sleep, a long dreamless sleep that resembled death, that prepared him for death. He thought perhaps death was just like going to sleep drunk, though you didn't wake up from it. 'No hangover' he thought to himself with glee, and then went completely into sleep.

He slept for over fifteen hours, with Maria and Angor alternately checking on him to make sure he wasn't dead. Anglor soon had an interview with the Today Show he was certainly not excited about, but it was a good way to spread his message. For some reason reporters made him hostile, though. He wasn't one of the NRA alt- right lunatics that wanted to kill journalists (after members of the Capital Gazette had been killed in a shooting,) but he didn't like the enfilade of questions they asked him. Still he realized the press was important, and they weren't all lying like the alt- right assholes continued to claim, getting all the conspiracy theorists behind them, the so called "free thinkers," and that they were and always would be an integral part of society- the press was important, we need to know what is happening in the world so if it does all end like we unconsciously want it to, at least we will know how it happened, and we, if we don't all die, will have to take up the burden of collective guilt, because history is a painful charade we have all taken part in, even by doing nothing.

When Mark finally woke up he was weak. Maria quickly made him some food and he groaned as he woke up and looked at Anglor.

"I keep sleeping so I don't have to think," he said. "But I am thinking in my sleep."

Anglor smiled at him weakly. "You are dreaming?"

"No, I am too old to dream. Now all I can do is think."

Maria brought him his food. He barely ate it but it seemed to strengthen him a little bit.

"I don't want to drive home," he groaned. "I want to stay with you."

Anglor was shocked. Suddenly Mark, whom he just realized was old, seemed like a child again, a child frightened of what was under the bed, a child frightened to say goodbye.

"Are you alright?" Anglor asked again.

Mark smiled at him mysteriously. "I'll be alright soon."

Anglor prepared for his interview. He put on nice clothes, a suit and tie, but he didn't bother with his hair and face because he knew they'd do that at the studio no matter how nice he looked, but he never looked too nice. He looked at himself in the mirror briefly and realized he was awfully ugly to be a star. Luckily he was an artist, a field where it didn't matter a whit what you looked like. Anglor had never really looked at himself. Being an alien he was not familiar with the concept of a mirror, and still today he didn't understand it. He thought it was a tool for the very few to validate themselves and for the many to hate themselves. And it was just a piece of glass. It was so fragile, our appearance is so fragile, it doesn't mean anything. Anglor was amazed that people were judged by this, their visage in the mirror, the reverse image of themselves that was their appearance like their soul inverted and pulled over their skin, like another mirror. People only wanted to look at you to see themselves, and that's why they wanted you to be attractive. Anglor couldn't believe it was so important in America. A person's appearance literally tells you nothing about who they are, and yet it is what we are all judged on in America. Anglor thought it was more laziness, the unwillingness to truly know someone or god forbid you might truly know yourself- it is easier to just look at someone and hope they look back at you, as if we are all mirrors, as if we are all reflections of nothing in an endless carnival hall of mirrors, as if we are just echoes of each other in a void. Anglor shuddered at the thought of it. He was glad he was ugly, he was glad no one looked at him and therefore never tried to get to know him. He had his friends, and he wasn't human so he wasn't attached to the idea of romance like all humans were-always hoping they got someone good looking, always searching the skin and never the soul, which was bartered off to big business and capitalism in America, even if you were just a worker, they still took it. Some people here good looks were all they had, all they were, while the rest of them was hollowed out, spread thin, dead.

Anglor again realized how lucky he was that he got to do the work he loved, even though he did not love it all the time, but no one truly loves something or someone all the time. He understood this, he understood reality in spite of his insanity. He recognized that on Earth he was lucky, unlike the moon where no one was lucky or unlucky, people all had the same life there, they just were. But on Earth he was lucky. Still he was not happy here, but the more he pondered he realized he was not really happy on the moon either. He belonged to no world, that was where he was unlucky, but that was what had made him the artist that brought about his fortuitous position in this paltry, fleeting Earth life. He supposed fortune had to be paid for with misfortune, just like good had to be paid for with evil. He looked in the mirror one last time, and to his great shock and dismay, he saw a human being.

The interview went as it usually did. The interviewer had a sickening pseudo interest in him that was certainly overplayed, and of course she didn't understand him. Why would she?

"I have to ask," she went on, "about the manifesto you wrote at one of your first openings, the one where you compare history to the devil…"

"Qoud scripsi, scripsi," Anglor said. "Tolle, lege."

The interviewer laughed nervously. "What does that mean?"

"What I have written I have written. Take it up and read it."

"I have read it."

"And you didn't understand it?"

"No," the interviewer admitted. "I mean, history is who we are."

"I know," Anglor said. "I've heard this argument before. But I think we need to be someone else, without history. Then we will be forced to make ourselves."

"Don't you think your quest is a little naïve?"

"Of course it is," Anglor said. "But it is naivete with conviction. That kind of naivete can save us."

"I think I understand where you're coming from," the interviewer said. "But most people think it's impossible. Do you feel alone in your argument?"

"I always feel alone," Anglor said. "And the fact that I'm alone in my argument is probably only more proof that I'm right."

"Your art is very interesting."

"Thank you."

"What is your biggest inspiration?"

"Killing history," he said with a smile. "Art can exist without it, though art is often political, based on history. But art is about everything. There will still be enough nihilism in the world without history that art can still be created, art is independent of history, it is independent of everything except life, and we would certainly have more life if there was no history."

"But won't we be overpopulated then?"

"Don't be Malthusian," Anglor admonished gently. "It's casual cruelty, which is the most cruel kind, the one that is so easy, the one that you have to merely speak. I'm not one for sacrificing anyone for the so called greater good. The greater good is that we all have the right to live until we die of our own accord, none of us deserve to be killed, none of us deserve to be sacrificed, particularly no to history, which can never have its fill of corpses."

The interviewer nodded, having understood. "You used to live in a place called Miamisburg, Ohio. Now you live in New York. Why did you leave?"

"Miamisburg is a very small town. No matter where you go you're always almost home, and I wanted to be far away."

The interviewer nodded again. "You want to make people think, don't you?"

"I do."

"Do you think there's more evil in the world than good?"

"No," he said. "I don't. That's why I don't think my quest is impossible."

"Do you think there's more good than evil?"

"I'm not sure. I just think it seems like there's more evil because even the world's optimists pay more attention to the evil than the good. The good goes mostly unnoticed."

"I think you may be right," the interviewer said. "So, if history will no longer make us, what will?"

"Like I said, ourselves. Then we will have to be something more than a barely put together hodge podge of moot velleities and false ambitions. And we will have to be less cruel. It is so easy to be casually cruel. People who foolishly think they're regular do it all the time. This will have to stop. We'll all have to be a little strange, a little eccentric, because it is easier to be kind that way- it is much easier to be kind when you yourself have also been stigmatized."

"If we all become eccentric that will be the new regular. Then eccentricity will be cruel."

"That's already happening. Truthfully everyone is strange, but the people who live for themselves, not as their told to live but how they wish to live, are considered markedly strange. But I think we all need this independence, because honestly it makes people happy, eccentricity makes the eccentric happy, and happy people don't feel the need to be casually cruel. That's what history is built by and abetted by, the casual cruelty of regular people who are secretly bitter that all their lives they had done what they were told because the people who were telling them what to do also told them this would be the key to happiness, then they find they were all lying, but they won't admit it, they won't admit that they wasted their lives being the servant of some higher order that was a false idol whose promises were empty, they will not admit they are unhappy, so they are cruel instead."

"Hmmm…"

"I think too much," Anglor admitted. "But it passes the time. I work in solitude, I am always in solitude, and I am very lonely, but it helps me get my work done. Work you do alone is a lot easier to become dedicated to, because it is making you feel less alone, or at least giving you something to do when you're alone. It makes being alone bearable."

"You work a lot, don't you?"

"Yes."

"Have you ever been in love?'

"No."

"Really?" the interviewer said, shocked. "Perhaps that's why you work so much."

"I prefer it that way. I think my work is more important than love, and I have learned to live without the latter."

"You are strange indeed," the interviewer let slip, then a look of mortification came over her face. "I'm sorry," she then blurted out next.

Anglor shrugged. "I don't mind," he said. "I know it's true. I'm a lunatic."

"And what does being a lunatic consist of?"

Anglor smiled almost wickedly. "It means everybody needs me but nobody wants me. I am a foul tasting medicine."

Chapter 9

There are two different possibilities of how the universe will end. There is of course "the big crunch," where the universe will suddenly stop expanding and start contracting- time would go backwards, and everything and nothing would equally implode. The other theory is this: the universe is perhaps almost 99% dark matter. It's possible the mere one percent of matter will burn out its energy completely, and all that will be left is dark matter, a universe that ha gone from 99% nothingness to 100% nothingness. It will be what the Hebrews called *"effes"* a darkness that cannot be comprehended by human beings. As I am sitting here writing about it I am realizing I not only can't describe it, I can't imagine it, a universe that is almost infinite that is filled with absolutely nothing. All I can imagine is black holes zipping around this universe sucking the nothing into its singularity, an infinity of void eating more void, so it will never be full. All I can imagine is nullity upon nullity, and I can't really imagine that. But this possibility is quite likely I believe, though it is anathema to my imagination. Anything that is anathema to my imagination, to my opinions, to my beliefs, is probably the truth. What I can't imagine must be real. What I can imagine is purely fiction, the delusions of my own prejudiced fancy. I can imagine love so it might not be real. I can't imagine nothingness, I can't even imagine the universe, so they must be the only truth, these things that are beyond my comprehension.

The universe doesn't give a damn about us, the only time it even deigns to recognize us to mock this, and it does so unconsciously, as most cruelty is. I call it reverse synchronicity, when the universe mocks you, when after you lost what you thought was your one true love you suddenly see their name everywhere, in the fabric of the universe, an irrevocable part of nature. Synchronicity is meaningful coincidence, so reverse synchronicity must be meaningless, and it is meaningless because it is so cruel. Momus is the God of mockery. Momus is the indifferent universe that only mocks us unconsciously, on accident, still without noticing us, and it is often the only time the universe ever calls to you. And one day when the universe is complete nothing and we along with it, if we could possibly live through such an event we would miss the universe ribald lampoons against us in the most minute folds of synchronicity. When it is absolute nothing the phenomenon of life will pass like it was the universe's dream, and then when it is filled only with dark matter is when the universe had woken up, woken up to its own desolation.

That was how Anglor felt after Mark died. Everything he saw was some kind of cold hearted reminder of him. He saw the name Mark everywhere, he heard people say the same things he used to say just walking on the street, he saw his face in the sunrise and in the sunset, in the eventual nothingness of the universe that would someday match his death, his eternity. He saw him even in the stars, for the stars are nothing but the past, a pre recording of light, dead things shining at us as if through a mirror, and Anglor could even see Mark's face in the mirror, he could see himself becoming Mark, he could see himself becoming dead.

They buried him on June 22nd, the year of our lord 2018. There was no one else to show up at the funeral. It rained that day because it always rains when someone dies, and someone always dies, that's why it always rains. The Earth itself is weeping that she could not give immortality to her creatures. Anglor left roses on his grave, Maria put a picture there of the three of them together.

And then of course life went on, though it had lost what little meaning it had to begin with. But it did go on. Anglor drew more than ever so he did not have to confront his grief. His facture was ever growing, it was more than the world would ever be able to keep up with, and Anglor was proud of himself for this, though he knew he was only working so hard to make up for the rest of his life that was empty, that he was forcing himself into a state of mania so he did not have to be in a state of depression, little did he know that a state of mania is not much different from a state of depression, it is simply a state of depression that is trying too hard to avoid itself, that is over-compensating more than it need be for the feeling of loss, that it was still grief but violent grief, and like any violent emotion it could not last for very long, it was energy that was meant to burn itself out and explode at any moment, then he would be only left with the dark matter, the knowledge of death he was trying so hard to suppress in his mind.

He thought a lot in this state, though. He thought about the cross on top of Mark's allocated bit of Earth and he thought about how the sacred and the profane are not much different from each other. Death is profane, and the sacred is always dead. He tried to describe this in pictures. He made a series of art called "The Sacred and the Profane," that came to be almost twenty drawings long, the topic obsessed him. Even Maria at last thought that he was working too hard, but the way she was dealing with her grief wasn't the healthiest, either. She had taken up cocaine as a regular habit because she could not force out mania from within like Anglor could, she only knew depression, so she had to get her avoidant mania in a powder. Anglor joined her for these long bouts of substance abuse because he didn't care anymore how manic he got, as long as he was not depressed, as long as he could hide from himself the fact that he also wanted to die.

They went on a week long cocaine binge. Anglor drew the sacred and profane with rabid speed now, trying to illustrate how similar the two were. He felt like Francis Bacon and his insatiable taste for drawing crucifixion, it was the same kind of mania, it was a thing he could not get off his mind. The profane is desperate, so is the sacred. The profane is in mourning, so is the sacred. Anglor just couldn't figure out which one he was, he was hoping the drawing would tell him. He only guessed at last almost to his dismay that he was indeed like other people, so he was both. But maybe all that has been sacred has been both, and all that has been profane has been both as well. Anglor didn't know why but it certainly aggravated his mind, it was like a question he could not solve, it was like the universe itself, it was like dark matter, he didn't know what the hell it was or what the hell it was made of, he only knew it existed.

With his combination of the mania and the cocaine, Anglor did not sleep at all that week. Maria barely did, only a couple of hours at a time, and they were both on a very short road to ruin; they knew it themselves, and they did not care. The first thing they had ever loved was dead, and one day everything they loved would be dead, and then one day after that, they would be dead, though they had never much loved themselves. They wished the process could be reversed, that they could be the first to die. The cocaine might help with that. They could have a heart attack and they would never have to watch anything else die again, except themselves. They simply wanted to speed up the process of nature. But it wasn't long until the hallucinations came, and they always resemble death without giving you the succor of actually dying, they just remind you it will happen one day, and the rest of life is just waiting, and suddenly you feel this waiting stretch out before you, expanding like the universe, and it seems like it will never end, it seems like though you will not live forever you will still live too long.

Anglor was still awake at five in the morning. Maria was finally asleep, and all the lights were out. Anglor found a random scrap of paper on the kitchen table, he was thinking about drawing. He opened the piece of paper but there was already writing on it. He pulled his phone out of his pocket so he could read it in the dark. It was in Mark's handwriting, it said "*haine et mepris*," French for hate and contempt. It was another of Mark's brief poems. Anglor read it quietly. It said:

Haine et mepris somme le roi du monde,
Et nous sommes leur desherite.

Anglor put it down and noticed on the back it said "kill history!" also in Mark's handwriting. Anglor couldn't take it anymore. He at last broke down and wept.

In the dark it was hard not to see, to see the things we normally ignore. Anglor wept and saw a shadow pass across the wall, but it was not his shadow. It was running, as if it were escaping something. Anglor at last stopped crying to feel fear instead. The shadow ran around on the wall for a few minutes, looking dangerously free, then it jumped off the wall, and Anglor was too frightened to even gasp. The shadow had a sign around its neck, it said "the sacred and the profane." Anglor cowered before it and it rose much higher than him, like a subject he would never be able to tackle, something that was much too big for him. It grew taller and taller until it was curving around the ceiling and then it screamed, approaching Anglor slowly, and as Anglor slowly backed away he suddenly hit the wall, he had nowhere to run. He realized he was under a small table, his knees to his chest, trembling all over and whimpering low like a dog. There was a book under the table. It was Nabokov's "Bend Sinister." He picked it up. He thought perhaps it would save him, but he looked up once again at the ever growing shadow and saw now that the sign on its neck said *haine et mepris*. He looked up at it and it had Mark's face.

He tried to scream but he couldn't, so he just backed further against the wall, growing smaller and smaller, like he was becoming a child again, while the shadow just grew taller. Its sign said the sacred and the profane again. Then it said *haine et mepris*. Anglor put his head in his chest and picked up his copy of Bend Sinister. He began to read in the dark, but still the shadow was moving ever closer to him. He tried to read but the word's didn't make sense. Something about a hair in soap. Something about the traces of an old love, something about ghosts, then he looked at the words and all he could see were the words "the sacred and the profane," written over and over again. He tried to scream again but he was too frightened to even speak, let alone shout. He turned the page. The next page were the words haine et mepris over and over again. Anglor threw the book angrily at the approaching shadow, but it just went right through it. The shadow then lowered itself from its great height and crawled under the table with Anglor.

He wanted to tell it to go away, to leave him alone, but he was stunned speechless, he could not even move. The shadow put its arms around him like a mother, and it was cold and Anglor shivered. It lifted his face up, forcing him to look at it. It had Mark's face again, but the face was decaying and when it opened its mouth maggots came out of it. Anglor shuddered. It leaned down to kiss him and Anglor still could not scream and he could not get away, the shadow was all around him not, and it kissed his with putrefied, awful breath, Anglor could feel its poison and toxicity seep into him as if he were catching a bad cold, and he shuddered all over. It was cold, so cold, it was the coldest embrace he had ever known, the embrace of the sacred and the profane, of hatred and contempt, the embrace of death.

At last Maria came I into the living room, having heard some whimpering and wondering what was going on. All she saw was Anglor huddled into that corner underneath the table, shuddering and with a look of terror in his eyes Maria had never seen before and would never be able to describe. It was as if he had come across some terrible truth no one wished to know, as if he had seen into everything and found only the worst rotting core at its center, it was as if he had seen a great atrocity first hand, not on the television like everyone else, and Maria could only hope it wasn't real. That inexplicable look in his eyes would haunt her for a very long time.

She went over to him, touching him gently on the shoulder. "Anglor," she said softly. "What is it?" but he could not speak, his eyes only widened with that wild eyed, incomprehensible terror and he shook his head mutely back and forth.

"Do you need to go to the hospital again?"

He only whimpered. "What is it?" Maria asked again, "What is it that you see?"

He whimpered more and pointed to a vague spot on the wall, his finger shaking as he did so. Maria had seen enough. She called 911. And that look in his eyes did not go away, whatever it was he was seeing would not go away, and it only got worse when the ambulance came. Anglor tried to run from the paramedics, knocking the table over as he did, and they chased after him and grabbed him. Luckily they didn't call the cops, and Anglor looked like a trapped animal, Maria had never seen something so helpless and so alone. He would never be able to tell anyone what he had seen, and it would haunt him for the rest of his life. He would only be able to draw it, and these drawings no one else would understand, no one else would understand what he had been through, few people have ever been that afraid, and Maria knew that terror would not cease until they had got him to the hospital and given him some medication, shaken him back to reality, which was mercifully less terrifying than psychosis, though perhaps psychosis is just reality amplified, it is the things we do not normally see because we have defensive barriers against them, and psychosis was simply no longer having these barriers, what defended the brain against too much perception, so he was seeing everything that usually goes unnoticed, and it was indeed terrifying, the things our own perception hides from us, and with good reason, for if we could see them all the time we would not be able to live, Anglor could barely see it for more than a week without it driving him to suicide. That's why Maria knew she had to call the ambulance.

But it did not stop there. When they arrived at the emergency room Anglor was catatonic. Whatever he had seen was too much for hiss perception and at last the defensive barriers had come back, but they over compensated, they shut his body down completely. And he was still hallucinating in the motionless, hallow shell that had become his body. As Maria looked at him, completely motionless but still with that look in his eyes that said he was plagued by demons he could not hope to describe, she imagined a man who was on fire, but not moving, just looking dazedly into the empty space with an acute look of fear, but having no defense against the fire that was consuming him, barely even noticing it for the things that did not exist that were hurting him more than the flames licking around his body. He looked like some kind of crazed Joan of Arc, and his eyes, besides the pronounced terror, were otherwise completely dead. She ran to him to put her arms around him and weep.

"We have him on intravenous drugs," the nurse said coldly. "Hopefully that will end the catatonia soon. We will have to take him to the psyche ward. Tell me dear, did he express any inclination towards suicide?"

"No, or at least he didn't tell me if he did. He's been sad. A friend of ours died recently."

"Yes," the nurse said. "People who have his disease find grieving particularly difficult. They can not do it like other people can."

"No," Maria admitted. "He can't."

"Has he expressed any homicidal thoughts?"

"What?!" Maria said, bewildered and offended. "No, of course not. He wouldn't hurt anyone."

"He's that artist people talk about, isn't he?"

"Yes. Do you like his art?"

"No, not really. Do you think he is a danger to himself or others?"

"No," Maria said tetchily. "He's not. He's not a danger at all. He's the most peaceful person I know."

"Alright. We will still have to take him to a facility, but I don't feel the need to pink slip him."

"Thanks. Whatever he saw…"

"Yes?"

"It really frightened him."

The nurse simply nodded and walked out.

Anglor was escorted to the mental hospital shortly after. Since he was catatonic he didn't put up any fight, he couldn't have even if he wanted to. That was the really scary part- his own brain had stripped him of his own will, and made him a prisoner of both his own body and his own mind, and what was worse, he did not even notice. He could not notice anything except whatever horror was going through his head that he would perhaps never be able to speak of, and was perhaps even more terrifying because it was imaginary, because it was in his head, the one place he would never be able to get away from- even sane people can't get away from their own head, no one can, our whole conception of the world is in there, and without a conception of the world there seems to us to be no world at all. Maria thought that was perhaps what was happening to Anglor, that whatever had invaded his head now, something that was not his own invention but his mind's own invention (and that's what made it really tricky, the fact that his mind now seemed to be another entity than himself, that it was in complete control now, without the body and without the ego, and it was the master even as it was broken) was distorting his conception of the world so much that it seemed there was no world, only the mess that had become of his head, nothing else existed, and so the world had ended. Anglor probably thought he was the last man alive on a completely dead planet, and he could not move or speak, he could not exist without some dim image of the world in his head as if in a mirror, as Ecclesiastes said. Now instead the mirror was broken, and he could not see the world in it anymore, he could only see the refracted broken pieces of his ego and his will surrendering to a mind that was at the moment ruined with disease, that was a complete tyrant, subjecting its sole citizen to the worst torture, the worst degradation, having taken his will as all tyrants and tormentors do. All he could see were the smashed and vitiated little pieces of his ego before the unconscious had swallowed it whole- who he really was was a distant memory right now, he did not feel as if he even existed, he felt as if he was in the vaguest world possible, the world human beings cannot know, and that's why his mind was rebelling against it so even after his body had surrendered to the razing and wreckage of his mind.

He was catatonic for about a week. They gave him his drugs intravenously at the psych ward as well, so eventually he snapped out of it, but for the first week he sat bolt upright on his bed, his eyes painfully open, more open than any pair of eyes should be, and he was put in isolation so no one would see him. When he did finally awaken from the sleep he was awake for, he looked around dully, docilely, like a caged animal who has given up on the prospect of being let out. He looked around and wondered where he was, so he at last stepped out of his room.

"Michael!" the nurse cried. "I'm glad you're up!"

"Where am I?' he asked, still dazedly, perhaps due to the drugs.

The nurse explained to him the name of the hospital and what had happened to him.

"I was catatonic?" he asked, confused

"Yes, dear."

"I don't even remember it and it happened just a moment ago."

"It's probably good you don't remember it."

Anglor nodded. "Yes," he said. "I don't want to remember it."

But you cannot forget something like that completely.

Chapter 10

After Anglor finally "woke up" so to speak, Maria was able to visit him. He had been alone staring at the wall the first three days he was there so he hadn't made friends with the other patients yet, and he and Maria so far didn't have any friends in New York. It was hard for regular people to find friends in a new place, let alone two people like them. Anglor was convinced it would be easier than in Miamisburg, though, there were more like minded people here, but to their dismay they only found out people like them were intolerable too, and they weren't really like them, they just liked the same things, they didn't actually know how crazy you had to be to be a legitimate artist, they didn't know what it was like to be alone, they were constantly adulated for being so indifferent, they didn't know what it was like to be so indifferent you were actually indifferent to both life and death, so it would be easier to die when it didn't scare you and life no longer interested you. They all seemed like models and actors, modeling and acting the role of the art savvy intellectual, but they did not know what it was like to be an actual artist, not someone who pretends to be one, but someone who was born so alone they had no choice but to take up some pursuit of the mind for a lack of anyone else to talk to. That was the problem with people. Most of them hadn't talked to themselves like Maria and Anglor had, so they didn't really know themselves, they had never been alone enough to know themselves, and that's where their false notion of superiority came from, the fact that they had never delved into themselves and seen the equally potential good and evil buried there, they cared only about their practiced indifference, only about the adulation, they wanted to be actors and models, they didn't want to be real people who had to be alone often, had to live alone, had to work alone, and had to think alone, therefore had to know themselves, and then had to become somebody, somebody unusual, somebody people never liked right off hand, an actual person, not an easy to mold yourself unnoticeably into stereotype. This was too difficult for most people.

So when Maria visited him Anglor was glad. He knew once he got out of his shell he would make friends with people in this mental hospital, they were all real people, too, which means you don't belong anywhere. They were all like that, but unfortunately you cannot speak to these friends after you leave the hospital, everyone just wants to move on with their life and pretend it never happened. That's what you have to do. Anglor didn't like being so dependent on Maria for company, as she didn't like being so dependent on Anglor, because they both knew at any time their friendship might fail, and then they would be left with nothing, truly alone, a state of existence no human can actually bear, even though we are all alone from the minute we are born to the moment we die, none of us can live truly alone. It is impossible. It always ends in death.

Still Anglor was happy to see Maria, and she him. They were all one another had, and it was a tenuous position but it was better than having nothing, although having nothing is far less tenuous.

"I finished that series," Anglor told her.

"What series?"

"The sacred and profane."

"I didn't know about that. You never tell me about your work."

"I'm sorry," he said. "I just assume it's boring to everyone else."

She smiled at him weakly. "Few things are more interesting," she said. "That's the problem with people, they find the truly interesting boring and the meaningless exciting."

Anglor nodded. "You think for yourself," Maria went on. "That must be difficult."

Anglor shrugged. "It's easier when you're an oddball and are alone most of the time."

"So, you finished your series?"

"Yes. I finally solved the riddle. Here is the last drawing."

He showed her the drawing and Maria shuddered.. It was a picture of a standing, towering corpse that looked disturbingly like Mark. Half of its face was decaying but there was a halo around its head, it was carrying a cross on its back with a scythe in its hand, and one half of its face, the one that wasn't decaying, looked sad and blessed, while the decaying side of the face looked menacing and mocking, as if it was mocking everything on Earth.

"I solved my riddle, God's riddle," Anglor went on. "The sacred and the profane are both death."

Anglor was let out of the hospital a week later. Luckily no one else had seen the drawing, but it would become one of his most famous, it was called "The Sacred and the Profane Final," and people were equally disturbed and delighted by it. Anglor went home and back to his life that was totally numb except for his work. He stopped using cocaine, realizing it was detrimental to his mind, and eventually Maria stopped as well, realizing that though it made her far less depressed only for a moment, the next day she would be more blue than ever, her serotonin completely drained on a night of nothingness, of just listening to herself talking rapidly.

Anglor, now out of his state of mania, did not work quite as much, but he still worked indeed, at least thirty hours a week, because he realized it was integral that he work a lot, though he could not be manic. Still he had to be productive, still he could not waste anymore of this brief human life he had been forced into and feel right about himself. He had to work. There was nothing else to do. But he had a little more leisure time now, he was not working constantly, at a level that was disturbing and super- human, at a level that was actually bordering the suicidal. He was able to watch more movies. He had found a copy of Jean Cocteau's "The Human Voice," a DVD copy of the play with Ingrid Bergman playing the sole character. And the sole character in this play is suicidal, she has just woken up from a failed suicide attempt, and Ingrid Bergman plays the role with disconcerting accuracy. For people who had been through this thing, which Anglor was realizing more and more that though it was a lot of people, was still an incredible minority, enough to be stigmatized on all levels of society, it was difficult to watch, it brought back memories of an incredible darkness that at the time seemed like it would never end, that it didn't matter if one died, because life had already turned into death, it was endless nothingness like death, so, seeing no difference, one chooses to die, but people who had never been through this could not possibly understand it, empathy could not reach that deeply into the darkness.

But Anglor knew what it was like, he could empathize completely, and he felt like he knew some dark secret about humanity that he had to keep to himself, that there are indeed things life harbors that are worse than death, and the feeling that death is the only answer to them, the feeling of life being so unbearable and unnatural, as if it were the profane, and one had to exit it to keep their dignity that life has destroyed. He felt like he knew something only the few knew and which none of them could speak of: It was knowing life's evil too well, and this knowledge, if it were shared with everyone, would kill off humanity, that is why it spares most people, but people like Anglor, people who have to know everything, it seeks them out and teaches them how to know nothing, an incredible emptiness that makes life resemble death so much one can never have the luxury of being frightened of death again. It felt as if he knew how to make an atomic bomb, that if he shared his knowledge with the general public they could use it as a tool for Earth's total destruction, and that's why only so few people knew it, so they could kill themselves and not the whole world. It was an outré experience that one can eventually get out of, having barely escaped death and having known death too well for a living thing, but it never completely leaves you, it changes you irrevocably, it makes you wise and distant, knowing this thing you must hide from others, this knowledge of living death, and being grateful that not everyone knows it, because you would not wish it on anyone, and yet you think to yourself "why did it happen to me? Why did I have to know what others cannot know? Why didn't knowledge spare me like it does so many others?" but you must leave these thoughts behind, realizing this knowledge still wants to make itself known so it gladly exposes itself to people who are far too curious and have to live through everything, people like you.

Anglor scoffed to himself. 'That would account for the strange look in my eye,' he thought. 'That will never go away.' He watched the Human Voice in silence, and realized he was one of few people who had actually seen a void in life, not just in the distant reaches of space that is comfortably far away, but right up close. He had looked into it as if he were looking into someone's eyes, and then he looked into his own eyes, and they were just as empty. This void had sucked out what was in them, and he became blind to anything else, all he could see was that void. It seemed to consume everything and he was amazed that no one else noticed it when it seemed so obvious. That's what was so lonely about it. He was blind in all ways but the one thing he could see others were blind to. And it was the same way now, now that he knew this dark secret of creation, that it can undo itself, it was still like he had seen something no one else had seen and which he could not explain, and he could not talk about it because human beings cannot bear it, he himself could not bear it either, and only survived it out of dumb luck, because eventually it did spare him, but not without him first knowing this truth that must necessarily be hidden in order for life to go on. He knew what it was like to be truly alone, he knew what it was like to be dead. He knew a state that few people survive, and he survived, almost miraculously, but now he knew something he shouldn't know, that no one should know, but still people discover it just as clumsily as they escape from it, and you cannot talk about it. To talk about it would be to bring it back, to delve into the far reaches of your brain and dig out something from what seems to be an immense, endless hole in your mind, where few things escape but when they do…

It all felt incredibly strange to him, and it was a stark reminder that it could happen to him again anytime, as when any atrocity makes its first appearance, can easily be repeated. He had to try to keep himself together for this to never happen again- he had to work even when he was depressed, he had to work through the immense gloom to abate it, he could not vegetate like he often wished to, for then he would not get out of bed for months, for then he would experience it again, the knowledge he couldn't share, and he never wanted to experience it again. He wanted to live life as normally as was possible for such an anomaly as him. That was his one true wish, even more than fame, which he already had, even more than love, which to him was only a vague hallucination in a utopia that could not exist, more than anything- he just wanted his right to live a quiet life, to be a compulsive homebody, and to be left alone, left alone to work. He was in a good place at the moment, and he was often afraid that it would get no better, but if it didn't he would still live. There's only so much you can ask for when you're insane. Peace of mind has to be good enough.

And Anglor realized, even though people didn't know he was an alien, they still treated him like one. People did not want him to exist. And he realized solemnly that he shouldn't exist, that he was absurd in every way, a *Lucus a non Lucendo* and there was no reason for him, but he felt it wasn't just him- the entire human race was like that. We shouldn't exist, but we do, by accident, and we must make the best of that, we must try to do good towards the world that invented us by mere chance but harbors us even at our most violent. We must try to escape this violence. We are an accident with incredible potential, and we have shown our potential, we have harnessed the Earth and sky, we have eradicated disease, we have learned how to fly, but we also learned in our infancy organized destruction and murder, we learned how to regress just as much as we learned to progress, and our instinct for both seems to be equal. When we see an opportunity to make the world more bearable we grasp it instinctively, but when we see an opportunity to destroy the world, we grasp it just as instinctively, yearning equally for both. That is the machine that moves history. It is people's instinct for self- destruction that allows people like Hitler and Donald Trump to take office. We want the world to end just as much as we want it to go on forever, it is a universal cognitive dissonance, the wish to be immortal while being suicidal at the same time.

People didn't want Anglor to exist, and yet the world was in love with him. Everything was an incredibly dichotomous contradiction, that's how the human mind works with its two halves, the desperate wish to love along with the off handed instinct to hate. It is a strange place, the human mind, and Anglor often wondered if it was not humans themselves that shouldn't exist, but perhaps consciousness. Perhaps consciousness was another absurd irrationality, rare in a universe that is also irrational and absurd. Perhaps the Earth was better off without its dichotomy. But Anglor realized it was too late for that. A cosmic accident had created consciousness, an accident formed from the ashes of an accident from an accident from an accident and so on until the moment of creation, the biggest accident of all- birth itself is an accident, and the birth of consciousness is no different. But Anglor realized that though consciousness was formed blindly like anything else, and could be a torment, we were still lucky to have it. Lucky accidents, that's the make-up of our entire existence. We ourselves are lucky accidents, but we are only lucky to ourselves, to the rest of the Earth we are a bane, and we seem to predate ourselves almost as much as we do the animals. I wonder what force passively allowed us to exist, but it must have been one without much foresight, something similar to us, just as aleatory and blind, and just as trapped in the present, something that was just as unknowing of the future. That could have been anything.

Anglor finished watching The Human Voice. It was only about an hour long anyway. He felt strange after having watched it, though, after having remembered that time. He sat down on his desk to work. Recently he had been experimenting with digital art. He though if one used their own photography and if it were well thought out enough it was still art, and there were indeed some things he could do with it he couldn't do with the pen and paper. He felt a little bit limited as an artist, that he was stuck in his own style. Though it was his style, the fact that you could tell his work was indeed his work, having an almost inimitable quality, he also wished he could do more than that. He had another gallery opening in a week. He had plenty of pieces to put in it, but still he felt like he needed more, still he felt it wasn't good enough. He was pushing himself too hard again, and though his imagination seemed to always be fertile, he was exhausting himself, and he was terrified of the thought of eventually bleeding the well dry, of running out of ideas. It was in that state that he was most likely to become suicidal again. Without ideas he didn't have anything else, in fact his mind became completely empty, hollow.

But still he worked. There was nothing else to do. And he thought to himself sadly that it is those we can't control that we always call mentally ill, that whatever is free has to be an outcast, an alien. The rest of people wanted to be enslaved. Anglor only wanted to be enslaved by ideas, and he was, he was completely possessed by them, but he felt he owned them just as much as they owned him, as long as he was able to articulate them, as long as he didn't just leave them to rot in his head, because then they really would become the sole master, and they in their anger would manifest themselves as disease. He was free, so he was alone, and he could not change it, because he was a slave to freedom, it owned him. It was far more indomitable than his will, and though it made him indomitable as well, he was completely dominated by *it,* the feeling of freedom which you constantly have to work in order to maintain, and which naturally makes you feel alone. That's why the whole human race is alone, because it is free, and it finds to its great displeasure that there are limits to freedom, it cannot extend past your body and mind. That's why it's lonely, because everyone else is free, too, which means they are confined to a certain individuality, and can understand no one except themselves.

It's perhaps the loneliest world, this one that is full of life.

Maria at last came home and Anglor felt better. She was the only companion he had in the world, but her eyes looked swollen and watery, and Anglor approached her cautiously, with a questioning look in his eyes. She dropped herself onto the couch with a loud thud, then stared dazedly into the mostly empty room.

"What's wrong?" he asked.

"Do you remember Zeke from back home?"

Anglor nodded. Indeed he remembered Zeke. Zeke was a schizophrenic that lived in their old apartment building in Miamisburg. Poor Zeke, he had been more stigmatized than anyone Anglor had ever known, and vilified as well. The neighbors often spoke ill of him, for he was the first person they'd ever seen undergo psychosis, and they could not understand it. Anglor realized the only reason they were kind to him was because they had never seen him in a similar state, simply because he hid it better, but Zeke had no hope to hide it. Like most schizophrenics he wouldn't take his medication, and he was far less fortunate than Anglor and Maria were, for the last few years he had actually been homeless, a fate many schizophrenics wind up in.

"He's not dead is he?" Anglor asked with trepidation.

Maria shrugged. "I was the last person to see him about eight months ago," she said. "Since then no one's heard a word."

"Well, our friends were never particularly kind to him. He's probably still alive."

And now Maria was silently weeping, the inchoate tears forming around her swollen eyes at last coming out in a subtle microcosmic deluge, but she made no sound. "I was the last person to see him eight months ago," she repeated again. "And I ignored him. He tried to talk to me but I just disengaged heartlessly in the book I was reading."

"What? Why?"

"I don't know," Maria said through tears. "I didn't want him to ask if he could stay at out place again," and at last she sobbed. "I am so cruel."

"It's ok…"

"And I am a hypocrite. I am mentally ill and have always been lonely, I of all people should have understood. All Zeke has ever wanted was a companion. He is truly alone, and that's the worst state any human being can be in, and I helped orchestrate his alienation." She sobbed more and Anglor put his arm around her. "Poor Zeke!" she cried. "Everyone, including me, has been trying to write him out of existence!"

She then violently threw her weeping face into Anglor's chest and he held her uncertainly. It was true what she said about Zeke. People really were trying to write him out of existence, that's why no one was sure if he was dead or not, because if he were dead they would not notice and they would not care, and Anglor realized with great sadness that this is probably what happens to many schizophrenics, that they walk the Earth like ghosts and then when they are gone people are secretly relieved because they were always afraid of them, afraid of something that itself was incredibly afraid, in unspeakable agony, just trying not to be so alone in a world that forced them to hide themselves for the inconvenience of their abstract terror. A tear at last came to Anglor's eye as well.

'How many?' he thought to himself. 'How many people live and die like this without anyone noticing they are alive or dead?' And then he thought to himself sadly that people do this to these unfortunates on purpose, and completely without a conscience, assuming their victim deserves it, and why, even they do not know, they just assume it's true to justify their cruelty. Anglor shuddered for a moment when he thought of Mark's poem *haine et mepris*. Hate and contempt ruled Zeke's world, he was the butt of it everywhere he went, and he was its *desherite*, its disinherited, its dispossessed, its forgotten and disposed, its victim. Anglor rested his head on top of Maria's head. "It's ok," he said. "It's difficult not to be cruel when it comes so easily."

"It seems to come easier than anything else."

Anglor nodded against her head and for awhile they were silent. Hate and contempt were easy, it was so much easier to disinherit someone from the Earth even as they wandered it than to dare have to for a moment see through their eyes. That's what people were really afraid of, that this absurdity was a part of them, and part of the world they lived in, inextricable from it, a condition for it to live. That's why people were so cruel to Zeke. They were afraid they could easily become him, because they could see a part of themselves they had hidden from themselves reflected in his eyes, the part they had buried underneath their work and their hollow success, the part that was confused, alone, and frightened, just like Zeke. They were not only trying to erase him but that part of themselves they could only half recall but which they recalled with violence. They knew they could not change the world, so instead they decided to obdurately ignore it or try to erase the things that reminded them of the truth of the world's absurdity, these poor objective people who were at the mercy of the subjective, who secretly envied abstract people because they were more in harmony with the world as it is and as it will always be, not trying to work against it by forcing purpose upon it, purpose, a thing it had never known and never wanted to know. It was like the universe, it simply wanted to be, it was not bothered by the existential paradigm that had to exist in order for it to be. Only humans were bothered by that, and people like Anglor and probably Zeke too not only accepted it but found it fascinating, while the average people were so frightened by it they would not even recognize it. They got by in the world by ignoring the world completely.

"I'm sure he's not dead," Anglor said. "He's a survivor."

"I hope one day he can get better like you have. Of course, you're not really a schizophrenic, you're just out of this world."

"I can't wait to be out of this world," he said. "Everyone here is afraid of it."

"We're afraid of everything. We're so afraid of ourselves we decide instead to become afraid of other people, without reason."

Anglor nodded and at last they parted their embrace. Maria dried her eyes and attempted a smile. Anglor smiled weakly at her in return.

"I'm gonna start cooking dinner. I think it's my turn."

Anglor nodded. "Thank you," and then in the meantime he departed to his room. The solitude wrapped all around him and he sighed with relief. Often it felt better to be alone.

Chapter 11

More bad news from home, it seems after they had escaped the place it began dying. Aaron, a young boy, twenty two years old, who had grown up in the house next to the house Maria had grown up in, had died in a particularly atrocious car accident. Anglor never knew him well, but he was glad he had gotten the pleasure of meeting him the few times he did, even when he was alive. Anglor could tell he was a man who wished no ill will on anybody, and in fact hoped only to make everyone happy, and he did. Maria could recall with intense clarity when she had been in a horrible mood and Aaron would get her out of it almost immediately, with just a smile and wisdom beyond his years and his words that were always at once witty and kind, a feat that Maria had previously thought was impossible.

So they would have to return to Miamisburg for the funeral. Anglor didn't mind. He knew the boy had meant something to Maria, and it was all the more proof that the blind randomness of life is so unfair, that it can kill you at any possible moment in any possible way, even if you are a kind hearted, talented young man with their whole life ahead of them, capable of great things, a person that loved everything they touched and whom everybody loved in return, a comet in the sky, something that should live forever, should have to die so soon, before even Maria, who was older and not as vital to life as Aaron was, who seemed to embrace it too much for him to have died so suddenly, someone who was happy but did not condemn the sad- that is incredibly rare. Maria thought it would be much more fair if she had died. She was older and she had lived more life, and she had wasted it profligately, in sorrow and cynicism, though her life was probably much easier than Aaron's- she had burned her days with a despair that bordered on the narcissistic, and she was partially already dead, while Aaron seemed more alive than life itself. Perhaps that was why he had died. Perhaps life envied him and his easy smile. Life was a bastard then, and death colluded with it to kill a boy, a man who had only barely just stopped being a child, for having beaten the vicissitudes and cyclical despair of the rotating process of life and death, that moves with the Earth as we do, that is the essence of the seasons. The seasons are something that die over and over again, and that's how they seemingly live forever. Maria was grateful humans were not like this. She would hate to see Aaron die every year.

She called her brother, he was closer to Aaron than she was, and he had the same naturally depressive nature that she did. She called him and he told her with woe that he could not cry.

"You will," she said.

"The funeral is Saturday," her brother said stiffly. "Can you make it?"

"Of course."

She put down the phone and walked away. She couldn't cry either, and it was a mockery of Aaron, who deserved the whole ocean, not just a few tears. Someone that had been around for almost her whole life, who she had taken for granted for his stable ubiquity and youth, was gone, and it didn't seem real. She had seen him just before she had moved to New York. She remembered he had told both her brother and her that he loved them, and they of course told him they loved him in return. She was glad of that. She was glad she had even known him.

She felt hollow inside, as she often did, but now she noticed it. Anglor gave her his sympathy but she wanted to be alone as well. She packed up her purse and went to Central Park. It was completely empty, which was strange, she had never known any part of New York City to be empty, but she was glad, she was glad to be alone. She sat down on a bench and began chain smoking. She really needed a drink, but for right now she wanted to be in this empty, lonely place, the only somewhat bucolic place in New York City, with the animals and the pond and the grass beneath her feet, she did often miss grass beneath her feet. Whether you are in the city or the country it doesn't matter, you are still alone, but Maria was glad to be alone right now. She was facing death again, and she had faced death many times before but it still seemed foreign to her every time it happened. It was perhaps the only thing in life that one did not get used to, that felt like the proverbial first time every time, but not in the way one wants something to feel original- it was a unique pain each time. And Aaron's death particularly knocked her to her knees, because he was so young and still in love with life, his youth seemed immortal, but his youth died, and not with the passing of time, as most people, but in a single violent moment, in an accident of fate that did not give a damn who lived and who died. That was the hardest part of it for her to face, the fact that anyone can die at any moment and with any cause, it does not matter that they are young, kind, in love or anything. It was easier when it was expected, but often it came so suddenly one could not even comprehend it, it was like trying to see light travel. There was no logical consecution to life and death, it all happened as randomly as the stars. 'I have no control over anything,' Maria thought to herself. 'That's freedom.'

She finished a cigarette and inhaled the last bit of smoke slowly, then put it out I the ash tray. She had one more thing she needed to do. She always did this, it was her way of praying when someone died. She would repeat over and over again the Heart Sutra mantra, she thought for some odd reason that if helped souls reach wherever they go when they have become liberated from their bodies. She said it quietly, under her breath, but she chanted over and over again: *Gate, gate, paragate, parasamgate, bodhi shava.*

"Gone, gone, completely gone, all the way over." She chanted it in a rhythmic repetition for about fifteen minutes or so, and she pictured Aaron in her head in a small boat, moving towards the horizon, but the horizon was actually infinite, he would be travelling forever, he would go everywhere. He was smiling in this picture she had in her mind.

The wind blew as she did this, a merciful wind, since it had been so turgidly hot recently. It blew and it seemed to bring everything to life as it did, the tress, the grass, and it went through her hair and she felt as if some gentle ghost was saying a final goodbye to her. She wished she could look at the wind, really see it, for suddenly she felt as if the wind were souls traveling the Earth, at last happily incorporeal, invisible, but still restless wanderers, *planetas*, still wandering the Earth, but part of it now. The wind rustled and made everything that was standing still move. It wandered all over the Earth, but it was entirely free, barely even subject to the laws of nature because it was an aspect of nature- the dead are human beings at last coming to terms with nature, not trying to fight it anymore, and then when they die they can go anywhere, they are entirely free like the wind. It blew more through Maria's hair, playfully, like a younger brother that was much older than her, that had been around since the Earth itself. She wanted to look at the wind but she could not look at the wind, but she could feel it. She was glad she could feel it, though she could not touch it, it could touch her. She smiled to herself, and just simply watched the wind blowing, bringing everything to life, singing us nature's song. She opened her hand and let the wind blow through her fingers, as if she really were touching it, saying goodbye to something that always had to be necessarily leaving. She felt the wind through her fingertips and she smiled again, a mysterious smile, the smile of someone who knows something most people don't. "So that is where the dead go," she said.

In line at the BMV. Maria's birthday was coming up and her id was about to expire. The line was long as it always was, everybody staring at their phone like a great congregation of zombies all letting the government know they were still alive, that they existed as a long series of documents, and the world was in their pockets, in their phones- they could look at it whenever they wanted out of this limited telescope as if they were aliens on their own planet, studying themselves, casually of course, not with real interest, as they got the huge computerized mirror out of their pocket. Maria felt out of place because she didn't have one. She opened a book instead, content to know that she was doing the right thing even if no one else realized it, even if it was something only an outcast would do nowadays.

She briefly looked around her. There was an electronic marquee advertising organ donation. It read in violent flashing lights, "YOU'RE NEVER TOO YOUNG TO DIE!" Maria shuddered. There was a mirror right under this sign, and she saw herself in it, holding a book, young and dying. She looked for a moment into her own eyes. Surely this was the same as looking into some void we're not supposed to see. She looked depressed as always, but it was a solemn depression. It was wisdom. Wisdom is just a solemn depression, that's what death teaches us. She shuddered once again, looking at herself in the mirror and realizing she was never too young to die. She thought of Aaron, she thought of her brother. Her brother was grieving much more deeply than she was, and he did not have that solemn depression Maria recognized as wisdom- his depression was violent, intense and afraid, very afraid, of something it was still too young to name, and that was what was so frightening about it, that death can take you long before you've even begun to know it well, to have had it in your life. You're never too young to die, at a time when you don't even know what death is, when it is a complete stranger to you.

But Maria did what she always did, she disengaged into a book, escaping reality through reality, for all the books she read were realistic about life, though they were only an imitation of it, a mere contemplation- but often the contemplation of life seemed more real to her than life itself. Pondering a dream once you are awake, that is what philosophy is. Wisdom is just a solemn depression. Wisdom is being forced to know you're never too young to die. Wisdom is knowing you could have died any second of any day, and having to be grateful that you didn't. Wisdom is realizing every second of your life is a reprieve, even as it brings you closer to what it is a reprieve from, death.

Maria thought about Anglor. For someone so depressive he seemed naïve at times. She didn't think his dream of an apokatastasis without history would ever be possible, but she already knew his rebuttal, and perhaps he was right- perhaps the fact that she wouldn't try made her part of the problem. She felt sorry for Anglor. He had become inextricable from the art world, a world full of narcissists and people who worshipped narcissism. She knew well what a narcissist was. A narcissist was someone who was delighted by the idea of solipsism, not crushed with fear and loneliness by it, in fact, solipsism, which has thankfully been disproved, was actually true for the narcissist. They looked at he world and saw themselves, they could stare at the horizon for thousands of miles, and all they would be able to see was their smug grimace which supposedly didn't mar their face but enhanced it. Maria wondered if they were ever lonely, or if they enjoyed the world this way, full of nothing but their casual disinterestedness, their scathing refusal to believe in anything but themselves, and in a way they were right, their was nothing else to believe in, but Maria realized she didn't want to be a part of it anymore. She didn't want to be an Egon Schiele or an Ezra Pound, she wanted to be a Jean Paul Sartre, a Thomas Mann, someone who looked at the world and saw themselves in other people who were in great pain, and wanted to lend a hand, not someone who was compulsively alone because they loved nothing but themselves, because they were so damn cool. They knew all the good music first, they were more talented than you, they were more beautiful than you, but they were terrible people, and Maria felt bad that

Anglor constantly had to be surrounded by them, him being a Thomas Mann, a Jean Paul Sartre, someone who gave a damn about the world he lived in and not just his own image supposedly imprinted on it.

The line was moving steadily and Maria kept reading while she got bits of conversation around her as if it were bits of information flying randomly in the wind. She heard the two men behind her, talking about nothing:

"You can't know everything," one of them said.

"No. I don't even know all the things I know."

Maria chuckled to herself and moved an inch in the line, never lifting her face from the book. She saw the sign again, the one that reminded her you're never too young to die. That was the only thing we all had in common, that we all die, it was the only destiny we all ubiquitously shared, *mektoub*. And then life was spent waiting in line, waiting in line for death, in a crowd full of people one had nothing else in common with, all staring numbly at their phones, waiting, wasting away in anonymity, complacency, and the mindless self indulgence that in America was offered to you in every corner, and which most people could not resist because it made them forget life and death, it made them forget they were waiting. But really it was just more waiting, waiting disguising itself as a diversion from waiting. The world had turned into a waiting room, each of us blindly taking a number and waiting for God to finally call it out, but it was of course not that organized. Maria's number was called out.

They were back in Miamisburg, back for the funeral. They had experienced a lot of death recently, first Mark and now this young boy, this young boy who deserved to die far less than Anglor and Maria did, who were aging and whom it was an effort to love, something Aaron did just as easily as he smiled, just as easily as he walked always in style, just as easily as he loved life no matter how poorly it had treated him. Maria had never met someone who loved not only easily, but profusely, as if he included the entire world in it, and he did. There must have been over one hundred people at the funeral, and every sort of person, young, old, of every race, age and creed, Aaron had managed to touch so many lives in his mere twenty two years, Maria was actually jealous. She hardly knew anyone and hardly cared. She had never even touched her own life, she had never even inspired herself, let alone over one hundred people in a long line crying and waiting to see his body.

The viewing was horrible. As soon as she saw the coffin she shuddered. "Jesus Christ," she groaned.

"What?" Anglor said.

"I don't want to look at the body."

"You don't have to." But immediately as she got further up in the line she saw it out of the corner of her eye, that's when the tears, buried under years of insensate cynicism, at last wrenched themselves out of her eyes. She was grateful. She did not sob, she just cried silently, realizing there were people here who were far more bereaved than she. Her father and brother were there, too, standing with her and Anglor. Her father saw her tears and placed his hand on her back gently. She realized how selfless he had always been in loving her and Justin, her brother, and she realized how he was feeling. He knew Aaron well like they all did except Anglor, and after he had heard the news he had cried and began drinking heavily, but Maria realized what harsh reality he was living, what rude awakening had struck him, the fact that he realized it could happen to his children, too.

Her father cried when he saw the body as well. They went up in the line to hug Aaron's parents and grandparents. Aaron's grandmother held her and Justin for a long time, weeping on them, and Maria tried to make her arms stronger for her, and she kissed them both on the cheek, then turned to their father and said "hold onto them." Then Maria's father also held her and kissed her on the cheek, tears streaming out of his eyes. Maria, Justin and Anglor did what they always did after that, they went to go smoke a cigarette. They smoked in silence. Justin was particularly heartbroken, and still he could not cry. Anglor put a hand gently on Maria's shoulder and they sat there saying nothing. because there was nothing to say, death made everything silent.

They went back inside the funeral home, Maria got a cup of coffee and they sat down. Many girls were crying in the bathroom and Maria looked at them in the mirror when she went in. She hated to see young people in pain, young people do not deal with pain well, because they have never been given any instructions for it, and the grieve violently, passionately, and older people who have long learned to accept death cannot understand it. Maria tried to soothe the girls in the bathroom as best she could. She had never been competitive with other women, it had never struck her as strange that most of them were more beautiful than her, she just wanted to help them, because she knew they felt the same way she did, she knew all women, especially young women, feel like outcasts in a world that has always been catered towards the needs and desires of men, that pushes women violently into the background, behind the stage, where they do everything and are never thanked for it.

Maria, Anglor, Justin and their father sat alone, away from everyone else, in the corner where the coat room was. Maria got up to get a cup of coffee, Justin went to smoke again, but luckily in only a few more moments the funeral started, and they migrated to the large room with several chairs (though still many people had to stand,) to attend. A band came on, with Aaron's father playing the tuba, and a man singing. They played "No Woman No Cry," and Maria of course cried. She cried throughout the whole funeral, silently, with dignity. She did not sob, she just let the tears flow gratefully from the corner of her eyes. Justin still could not cry, but he was obviously upset. Throughout the service people came up to the pulpit and described their memories of Aaron, all of which were lighthearted and witty, like Aaron was, and Justin would not even laugh at the jokes. Thankfully the coffin was closed now.

Maria cried all throughout, still silently, but it was strangely an uplifting funeral. Aaron's mother spoke of an instant where there was a meeting about diversity and inclusion at her church, and she asked Aaron what he thought. Apparently all he said was "love," and Maria at last came to the realization, she formed a minor insight, that he was right, that in a universe that was mute except the Earth that was always screaming, the only thing you can really say is "love." Maria realized at last after twenty seven years of obdurate cynicism that the scriptures, the songs were all right, even though it had seemed like such a cliché at the time, there can be truth in clichés as well, though often it was upsetting that truth could be so trite. But this was not trite. Maria finally knew, she could feel it in the very foundations of her soul, that it was true, that love is the only possible answer in a world that is otherwise completely bereft of them, that in a world that otherwise has no meaning, not even in art, the only meaningful thing is love, the only true thing is love, everything else is a lie and a diversion. And Maria felt incredibly lucky, she felt the whole human race was lucky, that the only answer we have is more than adequate, it is abundant, kind, compassionate true, it never turns the lowliest beggar away, it never turns anyone away, and we are lucky that our sole answer is so profound in a world that is otherwise completely without purpose, where everything else is an illusion, everything except love, and we are lucky not only that our only answer is so grand, so beautiful, so tangible and which is the enemy of cruelty, it is also incredibly simple. Maria couldn't believe she had dedicated so many years in philosophy to find the answer, when it was so simple, it was only human beings that made it difficult, but in its essence it was the most easy and natural thing in the world, the fact that we have complicated its truth so much is the reason we have damned ourselves. Love itself is simple, it is only human beings who find it difficult to love, but it is not difficult, and even if it were, still it would be the only conceivable reason to be alive, it is the sole truth in the entire universe, except nothingness, which human beings must necessarily reject, but then why do we reject love, when truthfully we have nothing else?

Anglor also thought it was a lovely funeral, and as more and more people shared their memories of Aaron he wished he had known him. He was tired of death. It was good for the works but it took the flavor out of life. Everything that was good for the works was bad for life, he realized. Sometimes he wished he wasn't an artist at all, though he thought art was the only answer, that it fulfilled the needs that science, philosophy and religion could not meet- but he did not realize it was another version of love. It was a deep love for all humanity, presented in the form of criticism. It was saying to everyone in the world "I love you, and because I love you I want you to do better. I know your potential, and I believe you would be a lot happier if you lived up to it." It was about trying to make humanity as a whole happy by recognizing not only its shortcomings, but the fact that it could overcome these shortcomings, and then the world could be as it should be, not as it is. There was a great deal of hope in art this way, though it often depicted despair, it also stated that we are the cause of our own despair, and therefore only we can ameliorate it. The fact that many people weren't interested in art was what made the artist misanthropic. They think to themselves "I love you so much, and you will not even listen to me." In many ways humanity fails the artist, though the artist doesn't fail humanity. That is what is Christ like about it, the immense love and then the rejection of your love, then many years after your death the real fame, when you become a memory that haunts the Earth, when humanity tries to compensate for rejecting your love by putting you in the textbooks, and then they pretend that they didn't hate you. But that is what we must do. We must love all of humanity even as it is rejecting us, even as it is burying us in obscurity, even as it is wishing we didn't exist and trying to erase us.

Anglor put a stiff, heavy arm around Maria's shoulder as she was crying. Neither of them said anything. Anglor thought not about humanity, but the individual. The individual is dividual, he or she is divided into many parts, along with id, ego, and superego, there is also soul, body, and mind- we are full of many different parts that barely reconcile with one another, enough so we can go on living, not noticing the constant internecine inside us over what will control it all- the heart, the soul, the mind, the ego, the superego, the id, but none of them ever win, and the war doesn't stop until death, the best we can do as humans is to ignore it, realizing we are an amalgam of parts that are barely in cooperation with each other, and not one sole thing can be master of us, not even ourselves. Thankfully that even as we are divided within ourselves we still have free will, and if we are slaves to the body or the mind or the id or anything else is because we choose to be. In reality though no one and nothing is master, their isn't even a master of the individual, because the individual is not even master of themselves with the many divided parts within themselves, but the many parts cannot be master, either, because they are all equally useful, we need a little bit of all of them and that's why were built this way, constantly split inside ourselves, with no master.

Anglor realized in even the most simple things, even the most plain and uninteresting rock, there is an enormous web of complexity behind it. In everything we do, in seeing, in hearing, in feeling, there is a labyrinthine mechanical process. That is why we do not understand ourselves. Nothing about life is simple, not even the universe, which is mostly dark matter, is simple, for dark matter isn't even simple. Matter is not simple. Atoms are not simple, the things we cannot even see are not even simple- absolutely everything in this world and what it is made up of is complex, and we are the only creatures that can attempt to understand it, therefore we are incredibly complex as well, so we have to study ourselves, we have to look in the mirror and wonder how. How was I made? What am I made up of? Why am I alive?

The only thing that's simple is love.

After the funeral Maria and her father felt alright. It was an optimistic funeral, as far as these things go, and Maria was glad because she felt that was what Aaron would have wanted. All he had ever wanted was to make people happy. That's what real love is, wanting to make people happy, even if you have to go by way of criticism, pointing out what people are doing that's making them unhappy, like Anglor did, that is still the essence of love. Artists love and hate humanity at the same time, and they only hate it because they love it. When they got back to Maria's father's house Justin immediately went to his room to sleep, and the rest of them of course drank, the prescribed "adult" way of handling grief.

Maria was mostly silent and went outside to smoke quite a bit. Then she went upstairs to listen to a Ryo Fukui album. The first song on it was called "It Could Happen to You." Maria scoffed to herself. 'What are you talking about?' she thought. 'It is going to happen to me.'

Anglor sat alone smoking outside. Maria's father had been kind enough to give him a glass of wine. He looked at the glass of wine suspiciously and thought to himself, 'I really shouldn't be doing this anymore,' but even as he thought it he was drinking the wine. 'At least it's not cocaine,' was how he justified it. But this was part of being human, particularly an American human, being subject to addictions and violent desires beyond the control of your free will, which should be impossible, one would think desire and will were the same thing, but Anglor had learned from being human that desire is often the opposite of will. He looked up at the sky and wished it were night, he often felt better in the darkness, more at ease, which made sense because he was born in the darkness, in the intangible mostly void of outer space.

He thought about the universe. It could have a beginning and end or it could have no beginning or end. Anglor thought it probably had a beginning, and before this universe another one had a beginning, and before that one another one had a beginning, and so on and so forth. That's how Anglor assumed infinity worked, through an unending series of beginnings. And of course all things that begin end, even most likely the universe, so infinity is made up of finite things. Or maybe our universe is the sole universe, and once it ends nothing will exist at all. Perhaps nothing is infinite, except the damned event horizon, which turned all things into nothing. Or the theory that there is no beginning or end, that seems truly infinite, but then if you traversed the whole of the universe you would end at the beginning, and have to do it again, as the Earth moves around the sun, it would never stop moving. Perhaps it is orbiting around something else.

Anglor finished his cigarette and went back inside. In this house everyone was separated. They were all the same. They liked to be alone when they had lost something. A house full of introverts, of strange creatures that didn't seem to belong anywhere, not even at home. Anglor walked up to the room that harbored the computer where he knew Maria was. She was still listening to the Ryo Fukui album and numbly scrolling through Facebook, a glass of wine in her hand as well.

"You alright?" Anglor asked.

"I'm fine."

"You cried a lot."

"It felt good though."

He put a hand on her shoulder. "What's going on in the wide world of Facebook today?"

"Nothing as usual. It makes me wonder…"

"Yes."

"Egon Schiele was such a narcissist because he painted over one hundred self portraits, but today, with Facebook, almost everyone has done over a hundred self portraits. We're all that narcissistic."

"It's because we are living in the end times. We're full of ourselves because we're the last remaining people on Earth, and if we don't have to care about anything else but ourselves we don't mind that the world is dying."

"It's been the end times for the last forty years…"

"Yes," Anglor said. "The end is long. Perhaps much longer than the beginning. We are very tenacious creatures when it comes to life."

"Maybe people do care that the world is ending, but they're afraid to admit it because then they would have to admit the world is ending. Maybe narcissism is just a coping mechanism."

Anglor smiled. "I suppose if you tell yourself you're the greatest you don't need anyone else. Maybe that's the coping mechanism part, deciding to live alone because one knows they're going to die alone- a mental preparation."

"We all live alone, though," Maria said. "The narcissist is very lucky to have themselves. It's more than most people have."

Anglor leaned down and kissed her on top of the head. "We go back to New York tomorrow."

"I know. I've missed it, it is starting to become home, but it's just as hard to be strange in the big city as it is in the small town."

"I know it is. It's particularly hard to be strange on the Earth, where people have worked so hard to normalize everything. They do not realize they are living in a strange universe and a strange planet. They do not realize that the odd is much more natural than what they have called sane."

"I don't think anyone can fit into the modern parameters of 'sanity.' It's impossible, it's cruel and unfair."

"Many people believe they're sane. They're the really crazy people."

Maria smiled at him and exited out of the internet. They went back to their hotel room, now they could afford it, and they slept in separate beds just like they did at home. Maria couldn't stop thinking about love, that perhaps it was the strongest force of the Earth, perhaps it was the real *vis viva* Leibniz was talking about. And it was a strange thing. It was ultimate forgiveness, maybe even it was the only forgiveness, but it was the most unforgiving thing the world had ever known as well. It would not forgive hate, it would not forgive violence, it would not forgive indifference, and it would not forgive hypocrisy perhaps most of all. But in the end it did forgive these things, but by trying to annihilate them, and at the same time knowing it could not annihilate them completely, but fighting it in battle (and many people still to this day do not believe this though it has happened over and over again,) love usually wins, then it forgives its opponent, and that's how it really vanquishes them. But of course they are reborn, but love is reborn as well. This is a battle that must be fought constantly, through every epoch and all the annals of history, up to the present day and certainly in the future. It is a timeless battle, so it must be fought throughout all time, but love always wins and it always will. It is insurmountable, it is intense, it is unimpeachable, it would be the true ruler of the world if only it didn't believe in kings, but it is an incredible authority, the only authority that's not corrupted by its own power, that is another great thing about it- its own power never gets to its head, because its power is humility.

In the other bed Anglor thought about death. He thought it was strange that everything was created from nothingness and everything will end by nothingness. And it was the great evil of life, the fact that it was everywhere that life was, life's shadow, waiting like a spider for its prey to come into its web even though it was what gave birth to this thing it shall eventually devour- nothingness invented us just to kill us, it made us into its prey because it was bored and it was lonely and it was *hungry*, and wanted to make life so one day it could devour it, as it devours every life, as it is life's shadow, stalking us our whole lives, until at last we fall into it and there is complete darkness, like what it must have been like before creation, and what it will be like when the universe ends, uncreated by what created it, just like human beings. Eventually we will remember what it is like to have never been born, when we die. The shadow is much bigger than us and our lives. We step out of it to be born and then one day at last critically stumble and fall back into it when we die- it is what allows us to live, it allows us to exit it into the brief arena of life, and it then forces us to die, to come back into it, where we came from, the only thing on Earth that is truly home. And we perceive it as our enemy, as part of the conditions of living is you forget what non- existence is like- we fail to realize we have been in the state, for much longer than we've been alive, and we will have to return to it. The only reason we are frightened to return to it is because we have no memory of it, but it is where we all have spent eternity except for the succinct time that we were alive, a time we will forget with death just like we forgot non- existence with birth. It did not frighten Anglor, he realized this was they way things had to be. We cannot have an Earth full of immortal people propagating more immortal people. The Earth could not hold it, and I think the universe, which, like the nothingness it's made of, only allows life begrudgingly, and only so one day it might reclaim it, could not fit it as well.

Often Anglor thought perhaps death was more essential than life, which is an accident, though in many ways death is an accident, too, one that will certainly happen. He looked over at Maria, who was pretending to sleep in the next bed, her head being crushed by thoughts just like Anglor's. He knew she was building a new and soon to be immutable moral hexis based on love. He was proud of her for this. The more he thought about it, the more he realized love was the only thing that could kill history. And history like all things must die, Anglor just wanted it to die before human beings did, not at the same time. He rolled over in bed, facing away from Maria and thought more about nothingness. It was a lecton, something we can only thing about abstractedly, but it was a reality, perhaps even more of a reality than existence, which was based on universal objectification, in other words, on universal illusions, of hallucinations of life without nothingness following close behind it. Anglor found it much more unreal than the subjective. Everything was subjective, the way the universe ran itself was subjective, totally random, it was only human beings that wanted to objectivate everything, and Anglor, perhaps because he was an alien, perhaps because he was an artist, perhaps because he was a lunatic, not only did not feel the need to do this, to a certain extent he couldn't.

He knew the reality that was only an inch beneath the surface of human objectification of reality, and though it had often made him sad in the past it had now ceased to bother him, and he had never been frightened of it. He accepted it as essential. He did not want to change the metaphysical laws of the universe, that would be entirely impossible, he simply wanted to change the hearts of human beings, who had given up love for it being too difficult and traded it for a cold indifference in their hearts that was much easier to manage and so they didn't mind that it made them empty. Love was the essence of freedom, and they did not want to be free, because freedom is very intimidating, it often tells us there is not a God- freedom comes with the condition that the world must be completely arbitrary, which it is, but many people have given up freedom for the thin, fragile patina of illusion from human objectification that lies to them and tells them the world isn't completely arbitrary. But Anglor did not understand this. He would never give up freedom just for the opportunity to deceive himself, like so many others have. Freedom has been sacrificed completely for a lie, and it was already limited to begin with due to external objects, due to the universal objectification of reality that tries to make it less chaotic, but which is only a mere appearance. Freedom, however limited, however intimidating due to the fact that it implies abstraction, at least is real.

Anglor was free, so he knew it was lonely, but once you become free freedom is a compulsion, along with the loneliness it implies, as well as the knowledge that all things are arbitrary, which is perhaps what creates loneliness, being one of the few people who do not try to mask an often harsh reality. Anglor supposed if being free was a compulsion giving up freedom and becoming un-free was too. But it abetted history, so it had no place in the world he was trying to build. History tried to destroy our freedom, it tried to make us all mere pawns in a greater scheme that had no meaning, and when go along with it each epoch because we have given up our freedom, though many people throughout history have been brave, selfless, and a testament to the love Maria was now also fighting for. It was those people who loved freedom not only for themselves, but all people- they were other people who where also trying to kill history. Anglor was relieved at this, he at last realized he wasn't the first one. Freedom is important even though it implies a world without meaning- without freedom there is even less meaning, there is only the blind and senseless mass violence of history.

And we are also free to not be free, to shed freedom like it is a nuisance and prefer illusion. Anglor would never be able to stop people from doing that, but he thought perhaps he might be able to convince enough people to make a difference. It was a sad world at the moment. Even the intelligent people chose no longer to be free, but instead to be slaves to media and popular culture. The Earth was a strange place, much stranger than outer space, which was an I credible anomaly, which followed its own laws that were so contrary to the norms of human beings. But still it was the Earth that was the most odd. In space everything is ruled by abstruse, aleatory laws that are hard to comprehend, but on earth is where the true atrocities existed. People thought space with its hard to comprehend nature was intimidating and depressing, but nothing so depressing had ever occurred in space as the things that occurred on Earth regularly, that one saw in the television over coffee each day. Anglor thought it was time to accept that the Earth was bound by the same absurdities as the universe, but perhaps even worse, because some of these absurdities were cruelty, violence, atrocity, history. No such things happened in space, which accepted and was happy with its absurdity, the fact that it was an anomaly, that it was something that shouldn't exist but did nonetheless, and whose laws were so strange it was mostly lawless. The Earth is the same way, but it's people cannot accept that, and yet that can accept the horrors that are entirely their own making, that they have become inured to.

Anglor rolled around in bed, still unable to sleep. His back was hurting him a great deal, something that had never happened until he reluctantly became an Earthling. He thought all earthlings were perhaps reluctant to become so- no one really wants to be born, we stay in the safety of our mothers wombs for as long as we can, afraid of what's outside of it. Anglor, of course, being a Selenite, was born a different way. A Selenite is always born after someone's final suicide, out of their head, so Anglor had no parents, and he remembered it a little bit. He also reluctantly crawled out of the felo de se's head, having been happier when he was a mere idea. And on Earth he had learned what it was like to be a failure. It was pitiless but it was also idyllic. Many failures are the only people capable of true idealism, because they are failures, and they have nothing to lose, so it is easier for them to dream when they are unencumbered by worldly goods or bourgeoise "respectability." Failures dream more than anyone, it is once a person is successful that they are stripped of all their ideals because success teaches them they have everything and too much to lose to dream or to care about the freedom of others, at whose lack of freedom they partially owe their success.

But failures are different. They are idealists through and through. They still have the ability to desire goodness in the world because, being unsuccessful, they know how dark the world can be. Still, failure is tirelessly disheartening and unkind, very hard to live within its confines, (though its confines are what make its dreamers dream's boundless, because they are confined, because they don't already have it all, and one can dream endlessly when they have nothing) but it is perhaps because it is so disheartening and glum that failures are able to be such idealists, because the harsh reality of their world gives them an idea of how the world could be otherwise, and idea successful people have absolutely no notion of, because success has made them too indifferent to have ideas of a better world- for them the world is fine as it is because they are successful in it. Failures, however, would change everything about the world because they really know it, and because they are idealists- an idealist is a person who wants to change everything about the world. Anglor was proud of himself that he was successful and still an idealist, but that was because he was an artist, so he was a black sheep no matter what, no matter how successful he became, so he always had the failure within him, because he was unusual, because he was still an outcast though now he had money. So he could afford to be an idealist, because something of him would always be so free it could fail, a luxury un-free people have never had, they have always had to succeed, only free people can fail, and that's why failures are such idealists, because they are free. They are a wonderful minority who instead of sacrificing freedom for success, sacrificed success for freedom, and their lives are very hard because of it, but it was a choice they always knew, no matter how grueling failure became, they had to make, in fact they were not free enough to choose to be un-free, to them freedom was an obligation, they had no choice but to be free, so it was a choice they would have to make over and over again, being unable to choose anything else. That's idealism, being enslaved to freedom.

The failures had no future because they knew there was no future. The present is but a second and then everything else is the past, the future becomes the present for a moment then quickly fades into the past, like anything else. And one day the human race shall die, then the universe shall die, and everything will be past, there will be no present or future, and this will be truth, because really already there is no present or future, really the past is the only reality, in other word's, dead things are the only reality. Protention was completely blind. We live in regards to the future as a blind man in complete darkness, but because he is blind, he does not realize he is in complete darkness, complete darkness is the state of his eyes, he is already always in complete darkness, too much to realize that he is in complete darkness.

Anglor rolled over in bed, troubled by these thoughts. The final realization came to him and he sighed as he considered what he believed to be the truth, that truth is just a belief, an opinion, most of the time it isn't apodictic or empirical, most of the time it was just a fancy. But this was what Anglor believed to be the truth, a truth that made him sad just by its essence, and a truth that had always alienated him because it was so anathema to the beliefs of other humans, they would socially crucify him for it, they had done so to everyone who had discovered it, but Anglor knew it was the truth, and he didn't like it either, but still it was the truth: Everything is not.

Chapter 12

Maria and Anglor went home the next day after having one last lunch with Maria's father and brother. They fought the entire way home. Maria blamed him for dragging her to New York, if he hadn't she could have spent more time with Aaron.

"You can't stay in Miamisburg the rest of your life," Anglor said tetchily.

"Lots of people do."

"Yea, and they're miserable."

"As if we're happy!" she scoffed.

"I'm content," Anglor said emphatically. "That's even better."

"You're content because you're rich. I can't stand it. Ever since I met you all I've done is what you wanted to do. I went to your faggy little art shows and then you took me out of my home…"

"I didn't understand why you didn't want to move on with your life…"

"Because I was happy!"

"Bullshit! You're the most brooding, sulking, depressive person I've ever met, no matter where the hell you live."

"I hate New York."

"Why?"

"Because it's dirty."

"Everything is dirty. You're going to have to learn to live with it. Miamisburg was never exactly clean either."

"It was cleaner than New York."

"No it wasn't. It just pretends to be. You're smarter than this, Maria! Why would you want to live in a town of old racists and junkies? Why would you want to be surrounded by people who are dumber than you?!"

"Because they understood me."

"No they didn't."

"They understood me better than you do. Besides, Aaron lived there. He wasn't an old racist or a junky."

"I'm sorry I wanted better for us."

"You wanted better for you."

Anglor didn't say anything but sat back angrily in his seat. Maria kept driving.

"We should have gotten a plane," Anglor said stiffly.

"It was too short notice."

"We could have afforded it."

"I get it," Maria said sardonically. "You're rich."

"I give half my money to you."

"Oh, thanks daddy."

"Bitch," Anglor whispered under his breath and Maria became startled. He had never called her hat before, Maria didn't think he ever would. She opened her mouth to make a rebuttal, but then just as quickly closed it. She did however glare at him with dagger point eyes for the rest of the way home. When they finally got home after several hours of irascible silence Anglor threw his suitcase roughly on the couch and immediately started to walk out of the door.

"Where are you going?" Maria asked.

"Out."

"You're acting like the typical man right now. That's not like you."

"Just leave me alone."

"No…" Maria said, then faltered. Anglor looked over her and there were tears in her eyes. "Bleibe, bitta," she said.

Anglor moved out of the doorway and came closer to Maria. He gently put a hand on her face. "Okay," he said. "I'll stay."

"I'm sorry," Maria said. "I was grief stricken and I took it out on you."

"Do you really not want to live here?"

"I didn't," she admitted. "But soon enough it will become home. Anywhere where you are is home."

They embraced and Maria wept into Anglor's chest. "It was Aaron," she kept saying. "It was Aaron."

"I know sweetheart."

"I watched him grow up. He was practically another little brother."

"I'm so sorry."

"I didn't think someone like that could die."

"I know," Anglor said. "I know."

The next day Liza came from Dayton to stay with them. She was in New York because she had won some art competition, and she was happy to brag that while she was in New York she was staying with the great Michael Smith, that they were friends. Anglor would have hardly called the two of them friends. He knew she only said that because she thought he might help her get ahead in the art world, but he wasn't. He hardly understood how he had "made it" in the art world. He just woke up one day and he was famous, but he had not forgotten the struggle, they years of being a "loser," of being hungry and sick in the mind, and having nothing else at all but art. But things hadn't changed that much. He still felt like a loser and still the only thing he had was art, even know when he had much more than the average person.

"I don't want her using any cocaine in this house," Anglor had told Maria. "I hate that shit."

"Don't worry, she won't." Then the knock on the door came. They all had to pretend they were happy to see each other, though for some strange reason Anglor couldn't understand, Maria was happy to see Liza. Perhaps it was because they still didn't have any friends in New York, but Maria seemed to legitimately like Liza, and that was what Anglor didn't understand. To Anglor Liza was just another self- obsessed narcissistic art whore from Dayton. She was what Anglor referred to with vitriol as a "counter cliché," the cliché that was the opposite of the most accepted cliché, but a cliché nonetheless. But Anglor put on his fake smile anyway and grabbed Liza's luggage like aa fake gentleman, as so called gentlemen often are in the modern world. They went into the living room and all sat down.

"You guys got any booze?" Liza asked.

"Yes!" Maria said with too much enthusiasm, then grabbed her a whiskey and coke.

"I brought a little something for us," Liza said cheekily and pulled out a bag from her suitcase in a clandestine manner. Anglor guessed it was drugs.

"I have mushrooms," Liza said. Maria looked to Anglor.

"It's ok," he said, flippantly waving her off. "As long as it's not cocaine."

"Yea," Liza said. "Maria told me you're off of that now, which is cool, but you can still trip, right?"

Anglor shrugged. "I suppose."

They all three got a cocktail then and sat on the living room floor. Liza took the mushrooms out of the bag and portioned them out so they would all be even in between them. Anglor ate his surreptitiously, chewing slowly, which only made the rotten taste linger.

"These taste like shit," he said.

"Wash it down with your whiskey," Liza instructed and Anglor did so.

It took awhile to hit him, and at first it was innocuous enough. He just seemed to find everything funny. Liza and Maria were trying to have a faux deep conversation and every word of it made Anglor laugh uproariously. They looked at him strangely, which only made him laugh more.

"You guys," he said. "You think you can plan to have a meaningful conversation. It has to happen on its own, like an unplanned pregnancy." He laughed more at his own joke and took another sip of whiskey. Suddenly he got dizzy. He tried to steady himself on the coffee table but the coffee table leaped away from him, and he looked at it and it was a mile away from him as he was stretching his arm for it. He felt like a child again, too small for everything. And yet we are always too small for everything, even when we grow up. Anglor thought perhaps we are always children and we can only ever play at being adults, that it is a role like any other, made for an audience, with a mask one must wear. But no one can wear a mask for long. That's why shortly after adulthood we die, when they play of being an adult is over. Anglor couldn't reach the coffee table so he very shakily got up on his feet. Now he was as tall as a skyscraper, the ceiling almost couldn't contain him, but he still felt small even when he was a giant. That was how he always felt. He could reach to the sky and he would still be just a little child, playing at being a giant, playing at being taller than others, wiser than others, and now he had to bend down to reach the coffee table and still his incredibly long arms could not reach it, still it was a mile away. There was nothing to steady him. He would just have to walk through life with nothing to hold onto, with his gangly limbs and his vertigo, feeling as if he would throw himself off his own great height.

Liza began to laugh. "I think it's working for Michael, there."

Maria laughed as well and drank more whiskey. It had hit her as well, but she was more sane than Anglor and could therefore handle drugs better. Anglor plopped back down on the floor, still trying to reach for the coffee table.

"Why is it so far away?" he whimpered.

"What's so far away?" Maria asked.

"Everything."

Maria just shrugged. She felt like no one knew the answer to that. Anglor then laid back on the floor and his enormous body began to shrink again, making him child sized this time. He felt as if he were on the Procrustean bed, but he didn't mind. It didn't matter whether he was small or huge, he could only be relatively huge, compared to others, in reality he was still small either way, and either way he could still not reach the coffee table, which he felt was a symbol for something but he didn't know what. He didn't even know what this thing that he was trying to reach but couldn't was. That part was eve scarier than being unable to reach it, not even having the foggiest notion what it was.

Suddenly Anglor looked down and he saw himself, as if looking into a pool of water. He stretched his arms out and looked at them. He could see his own arms, but they were different from the arms of the himself that he was observing, in fact, he was observing two himselfs. He wanted to scream, but as he tried to make sound he realized he was completely mute. He watched himself, as if looking in the mirror, but the other self he was looking at seemed to have its own volition independent of him. He looked down at himself, though he wasn't sure it was himself. He looked exactly the same, he still had basic proprioception, but he noticed there was a sign hanging off his neck. It said "The Other." He took a step back and looked at himself, the other self that he was watching outside of himself, though he was watching both of them. He saw the man he thought was him. He was still trying to reach for the coffee table, but he had the sign on his neck also, he was the other other. He could not tell which of them was his real self, or if both of them were his real self, or more disturbingly, if the sign was correct, if neither of them were himself, and both were only the other. He shuddered. Liza and Maria were continuing their ersatz profound conversation.

"I'm a lesbian," Liza said, while gently stroking the side of Maria's arm, "I am one of those people who are persecuted for love."

"Is it really love if you're not being persecuted?" The Anglor watching the other Anglor said, but no one could hear him, no one could see him except himself. Then the other Anglor looked at him. He made a start with terror in his eyes, as he saw the mirror image of himself only wearing a sign that said "The Other," then he made another mute start as he looked back at himself and saw the sign on him too. Anglor just shrugged at himself, and so the other had to shrug back. The other Anglor, whether it was the original Anglor or not, stood up to get a piece of paper. Anglor had no choice but to follow him. The first Anglor sat down, and did what he always did when he was frightened and confused, he began to draw.

Anglor watched over him like his shadow. He drew a strange picture, and it only took him les than half an hour though it had felt like hours, as it did for the Anglor watching him.

"What you drawing, Michael?" Liza asked.

"My ekstasis," Anglor said, and as he said this the other Anglor was mouthing the words.

They all looked at the drawing curiously. It was a two paneled drawing, almost like a comic book strip. It was a picture of two men who looked exactly the same, both wearing a sign that said "The Other," but one of them was walking out of a mirror, and they both were looking at each other bewildered. The Other stepping out of the mirror was bewildered because he thought he was the original, but he was stepping out of the mirror, so how could he be real? He did not realize he was in a mirror this whole time. But then the other other, who also thought he was the original, was confused as well, wondering if perhaps he was not the original self, and perhaps all these years he had just been a reflection of this reflection that had its own volition. Then in the second panel there was a panoramic view with the Other who had not come out of the mirror looked at in wild confusion. They were both in a mirror. So who was the original? Were they both just reflections, each thinking they were different from the thing they observed on the other side only to realize they were one in the same, just observing themselves the whole time? And yet were either of them real, or had they both just hallucinated each other, and therefore hallucinated themselves? It was a strange predicament. They both needed each other to exist, and they both destroyed each other's existence.

Liza eyed the picture with a raised eyebrow. "You're tripping pretty hard, aren't you?"

"Yes."

Anglor looked down at himself and the drawing, then he looked wildly around the room. The Other was gone, he was just himself again. Then he looked down at himself. The sign "The Other" was still around his neck. Perhaps it wasn't gone. He swallowed uneasily.

"I need a glass of water," he said, but as soon as he stood up he fell back down.

"I'll get it for you," Maria said. "Just stay there."

Anglor was amazed at how calm Maria and Liza were being, when his whole existence had come into question. It was always watching him, it determined who he was. And yet it was just him. He decided what he was to a certain extent, the rest of it was assigned to him by opinion and censure. He was a lunatic simply because people told him he was. But it wasn't what he really was, it was just what people degraded him to, forgetting all his other redeeming qualities. But then he felt all he was, all he's ever be, were what people thought of him. But that couldn't be true. He was never what people thought he was- he wasn't even a lunatic, he was only insane sometimes, and the rest of the time he felt like he was actually more in touch with reality than most people, *because* he was so strange, because reality is so strange along with him.

Maria came back with the glass of water. "Are you having a bad trip?" she asked, as she gently handed him the water and kept one hand on his shoulder.

"I'm just coming to terms with reality," he said. "So yes, it is a nightmare, but it's necessary I experience it."

Maria didn't completely understand him. "Why?" she asked. "Why is it necessary?"

"Because it's the truth."

"It's a hallucination, Anglor."

"Exactly," Anglor said. "It's reality, it's the truth, it's a hallucination."

"Just leave him be," Liza called.

"I don't know if we should have given him the mushrooms… He's struggled with psychosis before…"

"I'm fine, Maria," Anglor echoed hollowly. "Reason always sounds like madness."

Maria plopped down on the floor very abruptly. She was beginning to get dizzy, and everything was reflecting off each other. She supposed it could happen that one might find reality in a hallucination, but she felt Anglor was acting strange. 'Of course he's acting strange,' she thought. 'He's on hallucinogens.'

"He's a grown- up," Liza said. "He'll be fine."

"He's a child," Maria whispered under her breath. "I read in Jean Cocteau's 'Bacchus' that the word demented, or lunatic, comes from the French word demure, which means to remain a child."

"That would explain why he's so wise," Liza said cheekily.

Anglor sat there and listened to them talking about as if he wasn't only a few inches away and he rolled his eyes. He turned on the news.

"Oh no, Anglor," Maria protested. "You're already having a bad trip, that will only make it worse."

"I want to know the truth," Anglor said stiffly.

"Anglor?" Liza said with questioning brow. "I thought his name was Michael."

"It is," Maria stammered. "That's just a little nickname I have for him."

The news went on anyway, in spite of Maria's protest. Their was coverage of the alt- right protest and the liberal counter protest in Portland. Police were everywhere, hosing people down and using rubber bullets. One of the groups on the alt- right side, "The Proud Brothers," had signs that said "Immigrants Get Out." The reporter mentioned that the Southern Poverty Law Center had labeled this group, The Proud Brothers, as a hate group, and they certainly were.

"Please turn it off," Maria begged. "I don't want to think about this right now."

Anglor saw the pained look on Maria's face and did as she told him, though secretly he thought she was a coward for it.

"I just want to feel happy right now," Maria said. "Don't you?"

"Happiness doesn't concern me much," he said lissomly. "There are many things that are more important. The truth is more important, and the truth can often make you sad."

"What is this obsession with the truth?"

"I've always been like that," he said stiffly, irascibly. "You just never noticed it before…"

"Wha…"

"I finally accept that my life is supposed to be hard," he said distantly. "There is dignity in it, and there's probably almost a billion people whose lives are even harder than mine. By comparison I'm lucky. But that doesn't make me happy. It's the truth, and it makes me sad."

Liza looked at him with a wicked spark in her eye. "Pity for mankind is difficult," she said. "Especially since we do it to ourselves."

"We do it to each other," Anglor said.

Liza shrugged. "Same thing."

Anglor smiled at her gently and spread out on the carpet. He lit a cigarette but it vanished as soon as he lit it. He lit another one and the same thing happened. He sighed. Liza and Maria were still talking, and Anglor watched them talk but he couldn't hear a single thing from their mouths, he just saw their mouths groping around air, struggling like little children in the darkness to put words to their thoughts. He didn't feel the need to do such a thing, not right now. He just lay their and thought, without opening his mouth, and that way thought slipped into language easily, so long as it did not leave his head. He thought about himself, as we all think about ourselves, the way we pay narcissistic attention to our own being, the phenomenon that we as an individual somewhat separated from other individuals exist in this world, the way we reflect on the reflections of ourselves that we have in the mirror of our head, which is perhaps always inaccurate, a fun house mirror, making us either better or worse than what we are, but then again we are only what we say we are, and even more, what we think we are.

Anglor thought about how no one noticed him, even now that he was famous. It had been that way his entire life. He had always been a shadow in the incredible darkness of swarms of life so no one could see him. They didn't want to see him. They realized unconsciously he was a person of some talent and they wanted to suppress it, because his main talent was presenting the world to people as it is, as they don't wish to see it. He realized he was hard to notice because he was something of a pragnanz. He was not the whole that most other people were, the easiest thing to notice, he was the little parts that made it, the labyrinth of interconnectivity that made it work but which is to most people only a small detail. People did not notice him because he was too complex, they could not see him because he was one of the parts that were difficult to describe, a complex organ, but not a body. He was not the easiest thing to see, one had to look for him, and most people were not looking for him, most people were far more content with the more obvious whole he helped produce, and yet this whole, humanity, they knew nothing about, because though it was so conspicuous as a multitude, that was just a mere appearance. If you do not know what it consists of, what makes it up, you do not know it, and that's why people did not look much at Anglor, because he was the key to a riddle they did not want to solve, they wanted the whole, humanity, to be a mere appearance, so they did not have to try to understand it, or to understand themselves- that would mean to have to admit there is not only evil in them, but evil in all of us, that the human race is crippled as a whole more than it is of its parts.

But Anglor was grateful that to be so small and hard to see, it was easier to make almost the entire planet his hodological space. His ideas were everywhere, stretching across oceans, whispering to people continents away, whispering to all of the human race, but in a voice that was too quiet to hear. But he decided that the hodological space, the pathways and physical manifestations of ideas, were only a querencia- it was a place to bleed. The whole Earth was a place to bleed, and Anglor bled profusely in this querencia, in this hodological space, his ideas being the blood, his opening of his skull so one might peer into his soul having an inner eye on the Earth. The sad thing was, no one stopped by to look into his open head to peer at the soul, they didn't even see him as they passed by the Earth, his place to bleed, and though he bled for a lifetime that by death and memory turned into eons, no one ever noticed. He didn't mind though. He just liked to bleed for the catharsis, for bleeding's sake, and he knew one day, though it was perhaps a long time in the future, one poor fool would become curious and peer into the gapingly open and begging skull, and find the soul there, so Anglor could at last know it truly existed with confirmation from The Other.

Maria and Liza were talking to him, but he still couldn't hear what they were saying.

"What?" he asked pathetically.

"Morality," he at last heard Liza say sharply. "What do you think about morality?"

Anglor sighed. "It's like wisdom," he said begrudgingly. "You can never really be wise or moral, you can only *try* to be wise and you can only *try* to be moral. But it is important that you try."

"What are you talking about?" Maria asked.

"You asked me what I think about morality."

"Oh, man," Liza said with excessive risibility. "He's tripping hard. I asked you if you wanted another drink."

"Oh," Anglor said. "Sure."

He lied back down on his back on the carpet, staring at the ceiling that now seemed excessively tall. He looked down at himself. He was mostly translucent now and he was still wearing the sign that said "The Other." He realized he really was translucent, that everyone could see his insides, and so he was lucky that everyone ignored him. "Get this Other away from me," he said pitiably but he was ignored. It was quite a travesty, he thought. If solipsism were true life would be unbearable, but the existence of others was alienating, too- in a world full to the brim with people we are all nobodys, and we all enforce our nothingness on each other, we all alienate each other with the fact that we are all mostly strangers and that we are all just a *flatus vocis* to each other, and immediately in the presence of an other we are both others and we both instantly put on a show for each other, we all confirm each other's existence and the existence of the world and then we all turn ourselves into something we are not, and the world along with us. It was almost just as lonely as solipsism, being in a world packed with others, we alienate each other merely by our prodigious contingent existences and the fact that there are too many of us to know, but still we change in a stranger's eye, still we are not ourselves when we are together, and we even feel this strange presence, the fear of censure, when we are alone; even when we are alone we are acting, pretending to be socially acceptable. Even when we are alone we are trying to please somebody. And in the end there is not much difference between being alone and being around others. In the end there is not much difference between solipsism and a world full of many people, because even in a world full of other people, we are constantly projecting ourselves onto them, and they are doing the sane to us in return, until we cannot tell the proverbial "where I end and you begin," until we lose ourselves into the great sea of anonymity and the casual censure of others, and with so many strangers it is hard to remember who we are, if we ever were anyone.

Anglor again thought of the people who were lost by the world, whom the world had rejected and yet they had no other place to go but the world, but in this world they were *heimatlos*, without any world even as they were in the world and if the world had ejected them, if they were not harbored by their planet even as they still existed there, their sense of existence, their very being, must have been destroyed. They must have felt like absolutely nothing, no one, and they died in unmarked graves that if they were marked would say "nobody," once a human which other humans had degraded into the mere refuse of the planet, forced into being ghosts before they were dead- people who no longer had the luxury to be afraid of dying.

Anglor felt immense sadness for these people, and he realized they existed perhaps by the millions, and it was not the world itself that had rejected them, it is far too indifferent to do that, it was other human beings, what the world consisted of and was semi mastered by even though the world mastered them in return. No one who had not been through this could imagine the pain. Most people's pain to us is only a vague idea, a passing nightmare we try to convince ourselves is not real, which we feel we must ignore in order to carry on with our own senseless lives, which are dominated by false purposes so we may forget their senselessness- these people did not have that option. All illusions were forcibly stripped from them, they knew their lives were completely senseless, without the patina of ersatz security, of ersatz purpose, of thinking their nightmares were only nightmares, not the truth, not the world as it was.

Anglor was becoming very depressed as he thought of this. So many people in this world without names, so many people forgotten before they were even a memory, so many people barred from being a memory, who were ghosts that had no love to haunt.

When you become truly lost everything is lost to you, and no one decides to become so lost, it happens on accident, but these people, they were forced into their lostness by other human beings, other human beings that needed to make their fellow man stray in order that they should be found. It made Anglor sick, but he realized he participated in it, we all participated in it by doing nothing, but what else can we do? He heard an echo in his head. It was someone screaming for help, but he could not help them, all he could do was pity them, which did not help at all. All he could do was pity the whole human race, he could not help it. He scoffed to himself. 'This must be the way God feels,' he thought.

"What?" Liza said.

"What?" Anglor repeated back at her, still communicating as if in a mirror.

Liza smiled at him warmly. "You just said that out loud," she told him.

"Oh," Anglor half whispered, then turned over on his side. He hoped he would stop speaking out loud, all he wanted to do was think, he did not want to be heard at the moment, he did not want anyone eavesdropping on his mind. But in this moment he knew what was really wrong with humanity, its modern phenomenon, its current *mal de seicle* being itself, but maybe it had always been that way- maybe humanity has always been its own disease and its own cure. But humanity's real problem, its current disease, was this- it had started to believe its own lies.

Chapter 13

Anglor got up to go to his room. He knew he wouldn't fall asleep, but he at the very least wanted to be alone in bed, something many other people fear but which to single people eventually becomes a comfort.

"Where are you going?" Maria asked

"To my room."

"Hey wise man," Liza called, drinking bourbon directly out of the bottle and laughing uncontrollably. "What's the responsibility that comes with freedom?"

"That you have to use your freedom well," Anglor said stiffly, then departed to his room. He could hear Liza and Maria laughing in the other room, so he turned on some music. He put in Aaron Copland's "Fanfare for the Common Man." He lied back in bed and let the music sweep over him. The crepuscular gloom was coming in from the window, the general darkness, the Ta Olon that surrounds everything. Anglor sighed. He began to consider himself. He had always been somewhat of a loser, even on the moon. That's what made him such a mystery. People we call "zeros" we only call them because we do not understand them, not because they are truly nothing, they just might as well be nothing to other people because other people can't grasp them like they can't grasp nothingness. It was different with successful people. Successful people are always conspicuous, translucent, they always made themselves obvious and there was not much to them. The loser, the zero, the cipher, the fool, however, was veiled by a strange obscurity that frightened people. Their whole lives were obscure, and so were they themselves. They were obviously strange but hard to get to know. They looked like nothing but there is a profound depth underneath this gaping hole in existence, in supposed nothing, because no one can truly be nothing, they just seem to be nothing in the eyes of others for their lack of so called important stats and appurtenances. They were nothing because they did not recognize society, because society did not recognize them.

Anglor realized people were actually just as jealous of this as they were frightened of it, because they knew it was freedom, and they were frightened of freedom, but they also envied the losers attachment to nothing, not even to himself. People were jealous of Anglor, but they did not use their jealousy to emulate him, they used it to condemn him, because even while they were jealous they were angry that they had worked so hard for everything and this loser, this cipher, was perfectly content with nothing, and these people in their envy would not even acknowledge their envy, because they knew they had much more than the cipher, the zero, so why should they be envious? They had everything. But deep down they knew in their hearts that this everything they had amounted to the same nothing the loser had, and somehow the loser made it more fulfilling. And the loser didn't exactly have nothing. They had one thing the successful man will never have, though no one in the long and also brief history of humanity has ever been able to name this thing, not even the loser that has it, but still they had this nameless thing that the successful person would never have, and the successful person wants absolutely everything, even the things he cannot name and does not understand and which actually frightens him. But this is the one thing he cannot have, and he should be thankful, because it is just as much a burden to bear as it is an enviable commodity. Anglor had whatever this thing one, and it was no consolation, but he could not be like the successful person simply because he had this thing, and had always had this thing. It was forced upon him at birth. And he realized he, on the other side of the hill, was no different than the man looking in at him. He also wished he could be the people he hated and condemned.

He rolled over in bed. He could hear Liza and Maria having sex rather loudly. He rolled his eyes. 'What weirdoes have sex on mushrooms?' he thought. He could not sleep, and knew he would not be able to because of the drugs. Still, it was better than cocaine, and he had to have fun sometimes. His problem was that he didn't really find fun to be fun. Often he preferred work. He lit a cigarette. This one at last didn't disappear as soon as he lit it. Still he could not really savor it, time was moving too fast, and he was grateful, because he wanted it to be over. He looked down at himself. The sign that said "The Other" was at last gone. He sighed with great relief. Perhaps that was when the other left, when he was alone, but even as he thought this he could see the bastard out of the corner of his eye grinning at him in the mirror. He rolled over on his other side. "Is it possible to ever be alone?" he asked the otherwise empty room, and he could feel it shrug at him in response, it didn't know either. He didn't want solipsism to be true, but he did want to be alone every now and then, without an Other peering out at him through his own eyes, eavesdropping on his mind, as he put it. Maybe when you're alone there are always others, and when there are others you are always alone. Maybe that's the way to be alone, maybe a world full off too many other people is more solipsistic than solitude, and maybe solitude, pure solitude, does not truly exist, or perhaps it cannot exist without others. But we are always alone, we live and die that way- there are just other alone people around us as we do it.

The Aaron Copland album stopped. Anglor got up to put in another CD. Maria had recently introduced him to Radiohead, and he was actually quite fond of this group. There was one thing that was much better on the Earth than it was on the moon, and that was the music. Anglor realized he had become almost too accustomed to being an Earthling, in fact, he had entirely forgotten what it was like being a Selenite, as if it were some dream that meant nothing, that was neither frightening or pleasant, that he forgot as soon as he had woken up. It wasn't that being an Earthling was better, in fact it was much worse, but it was so much more real, and now Anglor, who had become obsessed with wanting to know the truth, felt like you had to be human to do so, though humans can never know the complete truth that is nothingness, their minds necessarily must it from themselves, still the closest any thing can ever get to truth Anglor was suddenly feeling had to be discovered by a human. So he chose to be human, in spite of the pain, and besides, he was in a new world with new aliens, he would have to adjust to their world and to them as well.

He listened to Radiohead. He hoped one day he could meet them, now that he was famous, and tell them how moving he thought their music was, that it spoke to his introversion, to the large part of him that wanted to simply crawl into itself until finally it could not be seen, and then by degrees, no longer existed, that devoured itself while it was sinking back into itself, that buried itself until it was dead. He listened to the music. It was particularly good at the moment, because his brain had no defense against sensation right now, and he was particularly sensitive to the music, he could hear its every subtle nuance, and it felt as if his whole life there was something standing between him and the full glory of music which was now gone, the only problem was that now he could feel everything else along with it- it was not a position his mind could maintain forever, but for the moment, in the face of music, it felt quite good, it felt like the music was piercing his bones.

He lit another cigarette and reached for the ash tray that was at the side of his bed. The nightstand moved all the way to the other side of the room when he tried to reach for it, so he got up, then it moved further away. He shook his head and gave up. He decided to smoke by the window and just ash outside. The breeze felt nice. It as a hot August night but it had been raining quite a bit, so it cooled a little bit, and there was the breeze, the tantalizing, playful wind in the air. He thought more about humanity. It was strange to him that he had so much pity for something he actually somewhat hated. But that was the only way to look at humanity, the only way to approach it, with disappointment and love, with censure and pity. He looked out of his window upon Waverly. That was the nice thing about New York, that it was never quiet, that anywhere you looked there was life, at any hour, the city never slept, which was good for an insomniac, one almost felt at home here.

He thought about that long documentary he had watched about World War II only a few days ago. The documentary had made him incredibly sad, and not because it had happened, but because it was always happening. There were many things in that documentary, many basic truths about human behavior, that were timeless with man, and that was what had made Anglor so sad, these timeless faults were what allowed it all to happen in the first place, and if they remained timeless, would allow it to happen again. Man must stop being timeless, he must be temporal again, and not just roll with the punches of the epoch, but attempt to control them. Anglor knew this well by now—mankind had to change, it could not continue to allow its timeless faults to remain timeless, because it is just the mock infinity of the *gehemmte mensch* that creates and then abets history. We would all have to change, we could not continue living forever through our ineptitude, we could not make an eternity out of repeating the same mistakes with complete blindness. We would have to make ourselves eternal in another way, not through the repetition of history, which is really just the immutability of history, which is really just the immutability of man, who recreates his same flaws with every generation, but through something else, something less unconsciously destructive, that is always waiting to passively allow disaster until it is the perpetrator of disaster, something that would be much more difficult to attain.

Anglor dropped his cigarette off the fire escape right outside his window and watched it fall to the Earth the same way he did. He had fallen into a deep grave, a deep grave wrapped in darkness and stars, the Earth, rock bottom. At the moment he felt strange. He mused about his fall with nostalgia, he wanted to fall again. It had felt nice. It was not the falling that was bad it was finally reaching the place that he was falling to, to come to the Earth a complete stranger and ask the impossible, that something which has never changed since its inception to change, to ask something that perhaps cannot change to become its own radical opposite. It was a fool's errand he was running, but it was that of the holy fool, the ultimate reject, society's unwanted cure, a prince dressed in rags, a genius that appears to be an idiot. And often Anglor didn't want to do it anymore.

He still could not sleep, so he got out a book to read. He could still hear Maria and Liza in the next room. They were no longer having sex but they were giggling profusely. Anglor didn't fit in with them, he didn't fit in with anyone that was supposedly like him. Perhaps because there was no one quite like him, perhaps because he was an alien. But he didn't feel welcome in their world just as he didn't feel welcome in the world. He was a stranger everywhere he went, a stranger no one wanted to know, a shadow briefly passing through humanity that humanity willfully left unnoticed. He couldn't connect with anyone, not even Maria. So he just read instead. He could connect with dead writers at the very least.

Writers were a strange anomaly, perhaps eve more than artists. Many artists feel they have the right to be obsessed with themselves, but writers, they are too reclusive and too intelligent for such a luxury. Their heads are always full, and it is their job to bring the common man out of the darkness, out of the dense fog of anonymity and into the printed page where everyone can see their words, their behaviors, their dreams, and of course their faults. The writer brings humanity to light, but they get no special compensation for this, in fact, humanity still hates them, even many years after they have already written several books and they are at last discovered, when people begin to recognize their talent, they are still treated like something that one takes out of a box occasionally and then puts the back in the box for the majority of its life, writers are very lonely, being exiled from mankind for having understood it too well, for understanding themselves too well, and that is the cardinal sin, one isn't supposed to look within themselves that way, not with vanity, but with realism, with displeasure, with heartbreak, with criticism. Writer's are supposed to record humanity, but they are not allowed to be a part of it.

Anglor thought of all of this while he was reading, so, of course, he wasn't really paying attention to the book. He was reading "The 42nd Parallel" by John Dos Passos, but he was too intoxicated to truly retain anything- in fact, in the morning he would forget all these thoughts he had, it would be just like the end of a bad dream, and then one day he would die, and never be able to recollect his thoughts ever again. They would be gone completely. That was what made them so immaterial, but in Anglor's eyes the immaterial was much more valuable than the material, though at the end they both melt away, at the end it is all immaterial. He set the book down. He liked Dos Passos. He certainly did write with a kind of style. He heard a knock on his door.

"Yes?"

"It's me," Maria said. "I just wanted to make sure you're okay."

Anglor smiled warmly at her though she couldn't see him. "I'm alright, Maria," he said. "For some reason I just wanted to be alone. But it's wearing off. That or I'm just getting used to it, I can't tell."

"Okay," Maria said. "Let me know if you nee anything."

"Maria!" Anglor called as she was walking away.

"Yes?"

"I'm really not a child."

She sighed and relaxed her whole body with it, looking at once dejected but at peace. "I know," she said. "I'm sorry I said that."

"It's alright."

"What are you doing in there?'

"Mostly just thinking."

Maria smiled. "You always were strange," she said. "I suppose that's why I thought you were a child, most people, their authenticity wears off in adulthood."

Anglor smiled at her through the door again. "How long do you think I'll be tripping?"

"It should wear off by tomorrow morning."

"Good night, Maria."

"Good night, Anglor." And then she walked away and Anglor was left alone with his thoughts once more, as he wanted to be, but he didn't know why, he had already wasted so much life this way. But he didn't think it was a waste of life. Contemplation was much better than action, and if it were possible to have both contemplation and action at the same time, the world would perhaps be a safer place. But guilt always takes place in the mind in hindsight, never foresight. That is one of the many flaws of this overly complicated contraptions we carry around in our heads and which might also account also for soul and body, which might be the whole of what we are, something that is very susceptible to disease and violent emotion, that was built to break, and often breaks even before we die. Anglor's mind had broken many times, and he was always the lonely one to pick its pieces back together, working alone and doing a haphazard, shoddy job of gluing his mind in place, and every time he did a worse and worse job so he knew the next time his mind would break would be coming soon, because he was having so much trouble holding it together by himself. That's the problem, they tell you to get better but they do not realize that most of the time you have to get better alone, that the cure is just as lonely as the sickness was. And one cannot get completely better that way, because one cannot feel complete at all that way, even people like Anglor, who used solitude for fulfillment, there is only so much emptiness it can fill as it creates new holes.

But he was used to it now. He assumed this was the way things had to be. He smoked another cigarette by the window and when he finished it and watched it drop he wondered if he should drop out of the window as well. He watched the cigarette butts rapid descent to the ground and envied it. He wished he could fall again. Falling was easy, it was being on the ground that really hurt. *Facilis descesnsus Averni.* The fall to Hell was easy, it was then being in hell, having landed at the destination of your downward concatenation, then not being able to fall in reverse, not being able to rise back up for perhaps years after falling in only a few decisive moments, that was the hard part. Anglor closed the window and decided not to throw himself out of it. It was too short of a fall anyway, and he was more ambitious than that.

Anglor finally got to sleep at about six in the morning the next day. He then woke up at around three in the afternoon. He got up groggily, his head feeling like it had imploded, like it were empty and yet still full of pain. He was the only one up. He got to be alone for longer. He made coffee as he always did. He made more than usual today because he felt like shit. He felt like he had just woken up from a Rip Van Winkle like sleep, like he was someone who ignored the world and just went to bed, someone he hated and yet had also been. That's the biggest thing that feeds history though, ignoring it. Anglor drank his coffee. It was strong and bitter. He saw on the counter top the dregs that were left of the bottle of bourbon and he poured a small shot of it into his coffee to make it taste better and to ease the hangover a little bit. He sat down on the loveseat in the living room and smoked a cigarette.

He quietly put on some music, Paganini's Caprices. The music made his head feel a little better, it always did. He smoked the cigarette languidly, glad to have at last one that lasted for a normal period of time, that wasn't undergoing time dilation. He savored it as best he could, though he was never good at savoring things, because he was always foolishly thinking about the future, because he was like many people for whom the present wasn't good enough. He heard a phone ringing in Maria's room where he was sure Liza was sleeping as well. It was Maria's phone though. She ignored it at first but the caller called persistently, until she at last rolled over in bed and answered it.

Anglor couldn't hear the conversation, he assumed it was nothing. He rested his legs on the coffee table, fully enjoying his relaxation as he rarely relaxed, he was in fact a little intimidated by relaxation, he felt it was a little bit like death. Maria talked on the phone for about five minutes then emerged from her room with tired eyes that also looked like they were carrying a rather large weight, the weight of the world in her eyes, Atlas eyes, eyes that had to see everything. She looked at Anglor with those eyes and he suddenly stopped the brief bit of relaxation and tensed up under her gaze. He knew that look. That look knew death.

"What is it?' he asked.

"My mom," she half stuttered, half whimpered out.

"What about her?"

"She's dying," Maria whispered.

Anglor put out his cigarette. "Jesus, Maria I'm sorry."

"I have to go back home," she said. "Everyone is dying there."

"That's why you had to get out of it."

"We have to go back, I have to say goodbye to my mother before…"

"Yes," Anglor said. "Yes you do."

"Is there more coffee?"

"I made a whole pot."

"Cool," and Maria departed glumly to the kitchen to get her cup of coffee. She also put the last bit of liquor into hers, none was left for Liza. Liza roused from sleep only a few moments later where she found Maria and Anglor sitting on the loveseat smoking and drinking coffee. Liza went up to Maria and hugged her.

"I'm sorry, dear," she said.

"It's ok. It's no one's fault."

"But I'm still sorry. I have a joint, would you like to smoke it?"

"Yes please," Maria said almost greedily.

"Michael?" Liza asked.

"No thank you."

Liza plopped on the floor at Maria's feet and the two smoked a joint while Anglor smoked his cigarette and tried to enjoy his coffee. He looked at Maria. Her face looked very serious but calm, as if she were at last coming to accept something that had irked her for her entire life, even at the times when she yearned for it. He wondered what she was thinking. On the moon no one dies until their final suicide, and no one really mourns it. He had never quite understood death, not until he had come to Earth and lost Mark, but he realized on Earth it was everywhere, and no one managed to escape it, and you no only had to mourn your own death, but the death of your parents, your lovers, your friends, in fact everyone you know. That's why Earthling's were so sad, self destructive and confused. They were trying to avoid something which for their species was unavoidable. So history was easier. It was easier when a mass of strangers on the other side of the planet died- with history they had not escaped death, because they couldn't, but had made a Faustian bargain with it. But it was a fool's bargain like any Faustian bargain- everyone you loved still died, after death had first cheated you.

They all smoked in silence. Maria was having her own thoughts. She was trying very hard not to think of her mother, so she could still go about her day. That was one thing you had to do when you had just barely escaped the death grip of clinical depression, you have to assign yourself daily tasks, and you have to force yourself to preform them, and this means not thinking about many things in order to just keep going, in order to endure. She thought instead about Christ's parable of the seeds and where they might grow. She remembered he had said the people who knew the world and mourned its evils, who mourned its very existence, were like seeds growing among thorns. Maria didn't know why, but Maria thought there was something poetic about it, about growing among thorns. It was certainly hard to grow that way, but Maria liked being a sole rose in an otherwise desolate field of thorns, a field of something that was unfriendly and desperately trying to protect itself, that did not want to be touched. And meanwhile she was in the midst of that begging to be touched, but one would have to bleed to touch her, one would have to reach into the defensive things, the things that were untouchable, to try to touch what was buried underneath them, the heart of the Earth that mourned the Earth's very existence, its potentiality, what it could be if only it weren't surrounded by thorns, what it could be and not what it was. But as she thought of this, though the idea seemed poetical, she realized it meant she would always be alone, and the thorns would eventually suffocate her and she would wither before she had even blossomed. This was something of a wake up call for her. She needed to abandon her depression, abandon her loneliness, because she realized at last in this moment that the poetic martyrdom of it was a lie, and if she let herself grow among the thorns that was her negative perception of the world, the sun would do no good for her, happiness would do no good for her. But it was awfully hard having a positive perception of the world, especially when one reads the newspaper everyday, it is hard not to mourn the Earth.

Maria looked over at Anglor. He was right, she now knew. To have a positive perception of the world was something reserved for the future, it was to completely disregard the past and the present, to throw them away like refuse. To have a positive perception of the world means to hold out hope that one day it will be better, one day it will change, one day the meek will really inherit the Earth, and at last she knew what Christ meant by that parable, that to mourn the Earth was not to change it, one had to actually have hope for it, that's what would change it, it took a bit of tragic optimism, but then one could grow free in the open field, and reach towards the sun, the sun being the future of a renewed world, of a world that would at last reach the final step in its metamorphosis, which is not only to be forgiven, but to be able to forgive itself, then it could start a completely new life, one, as Anglor posited, without history. Maria could see why people found it to be a foolish hope, but there was nothing else to hold onto in this world except the almost naïve belief that it can be saved, but if more people believed it it would be less naïve- if more of us choose to grow this way, not in the midst of the thorns, though they protect you from being touched, your aloof weltschmerz keeping you defended from all outsiders, and therefore protected from the very world that has made you so nauseous, so full of dread, but in the open field where you are always vulnerable, people wanting to attack your hope in every corner, but free and wild and true to something, true to the Earth, and a testament to its real beauty, the real beauty of the Earth that even human beings cannot bury. This hope, once you have it, cannot die.

So Maria decided to leave the thorns behind, for though they protected her from the very world they represented, they could not protect her from themselves, they pricked her and made her bleed, they closed in on her until she could not grow or breathe, they tried to make her potentially pure soul die in her body. She looked at Anglor and smiled. At last she understood him. And at last she understood her mother who had never abandoned her faith no matter what sorrow visited her and hung on so tenaciously, not a mere visitor, but something that would stay as long as it could, wearing out its welcome while it wore out its victim, and this was the hope Maria was now starting to contemplate and which she thought was so foolish before, but now she was beginning to understand. Giving up was the only foolish thing. If you give up you will get what you want, death will come to you early, but at last Maria no longer wanted that. She suddenly grabbed Anglor's hand and squeezed it. He squeezed it back with equal vigor.

"I'm going to be alright," she whispered. "It's going to be hard but I can handle anything."

Anglor smiled up at her and patted her on the shoulder. "Good," he said. "I know you can."

"You can't break that which was born broken," she said with a fragile smile and a forced laugh and both Anglor and Liza looked at her sadly. Then she started to laugh genuinely as she smiled at both Anglor and Liza and said acerbically, "to be an artist is to be so fake."

Anglor nodded, because he knew it was true, and Liza squirmed a little and blushed, also knowing it was true and having to face the discomfort of knowing herself perhaps for the first time in her life.

"And yet it is also the most authentic thing in the world," Maria added.

Anglor nodded again, knowing this was true as well, knowing truth was often a contradictory dichotomy of everything and nothing, that often both sides were right or both sides were wrong, that all opposites have a dialectical similarity, that they fall back in on each other, and this is our shoddy version of truth. He finished his cigarette and began to draw.

"How long are you staying Liza," he asked absently as he sketched.

"I don't know," she said. "Not much longer."

"I'm sorry, Liza," Maria said consolingly, "but we have to get back to Miamisburg soon, before…before, well, before she dies."

Liza nodded, having understood. "I won't get between you and your grief," she said.

"It's strange," Maria said musingly. "I've never fought it before, I usually just give in to it immediately, and now I am fighting it, I must have more free will than I used to, but it's much harder, it's much harder to fight it, and I am tired everyday of as soon upon waking I must fight this invisible, immaterial thing that exists in my head only, but it puts up a hell of a fracas, often I think it's stronger than me. It was much easier to just let it win, but it was also worse that way, because it would not be expelled that way. Now I can possibly expel it, but, like I said, it is a formidable opponent."

"I know," Anglor said from his drawing. "But it does lose if you fight it, though it seems so strong, it cannot possibly be as strong as human free will. Once you decide to engage it in battle it will fight tooth and nail, but it cannot possibly win. It seems like a formidable opponent but really it is just like a child. It only wins if you let it."

Maria smiled. "I'm proud of myself," she said. "I've never been so exhausted in my entire life, fighting this ghost, but at least I am not passively allowing it to haunt my head anymore."

"I'm proud of you, too," Anglor said gently. "It takes a long time to get to that point, and I am sorry to say, it is a lifetime battle. You will have to fight it and beat it over and over again, it is just like the fight for liberty, it is escaping a fascist that always seems to manifest itself repeatedly, throughout history, but it must be defeated every time, though it will of course return, still we cannot possibly live with it."

"That makes sense," Maria said.

Liza lit a cigarette and was silent, and Anglor kept drawing, mostly ignoring both of them. It didn't matter that it was the weekend and he had a vicious hangover, it was still a working day. He was not looking forward to going back to Miamisburg again but he understood they had to both times. It was too much death, it was enough to even drive a sane person mad, let alone two people who were already mad. But that was life, which is so difficult to the insane person because they know it can't be taught and that they can't learn it, that life is nowhere near as natural as most people think, in fact, often Anglor felt death was more natural, and that's why it was everywhere, that's why we mass produced it, because in our hearts we know it makes more sense than the repetitive diurnal heartbeat whose action we mimic, doing the same thing tomorrow as we did yesterday, and finding there is only yesterday, for that is what today and tomorrow always become, just like us they must die, they die with us, and meanwhile we waste them in numb routine, in our own inanity and life which we have made inane to handle better, as if we were taming a lion, as if we were taming something that should not be tamed, and which will one day resent us for our cruel supposed mastery over it, as we as human beings think we have mastery over everything, and yet we cannot master ourselves, we cannot tame ourselves, and it is our very inanity, our supposed domestication that produces all the death, all the massacres- atrocity is created by boring people who are bored, too bored to mourn a tragedy and instead produce it will nilly, without even considering it, without contemplation, for though they are bored they still do not dare to think, and certainly not about their actions, which they assume are few and have little consequence, but these actions are massive, affecting the whole Earth, and they are the actions of inaction, of not giving a damn which group of real human beings dies on the tv today and tomorrow- the more bored we get the more we kill, so we should have never tamed life so, degraded it into such numb banality, because it has only made ourselves more baleful.

Anglor was thinking of a way that he could put this into art. He drew a picture of a man sitting at a television set, and in that television set was the world burning, while the man looked at it with lassitude and disinterest, and the more he did this the more the world burned in the television set. Liza looked over his shoulder. "Your art is too complicated," she said. "I try not to think about it.

"You try not to think about anything," Anglor whispered under his breath and Liza looked at him quizzically.

"What did you say?"

"Nothing. I create art differently, I guess. I have to think about it before during and after. I have to think all the time."

"Sounds exhausting," Liza said sardonically, but Anglor ignored her. He knew she was jealous, jealous that he was crazier than she was. Then the day started. Maria showered and got ready while Liza started packing her things. They were going back to Miamisburg today, and they were dropping Liza off in Dayton on the way. Maria cried in the shower where no one could hear her. She had always hated crying in front of other people, she didn't know why, she didn't care if people thought she was weak, and she didn't think people would take advantage of her if they saw her real emotions, she merely thought it was a part of life, and life was a series of religious experiences, and religious experiences had to be experienced alone. Life was just wondering in a desert alone hearing God or something like Him speak to you in whatever way, and only you could listen, and then only you could do whatever this divine impulse had bidden- it was actually quite lonely. And death was another religious experience, it was God speaking to you of your finitude, and one had to bear it alone, one had to bear everything alone, in the desert where the angels only spoke to you occasionally and it was only a mirage.

She didn't cry for long, she never cried for long, and as soon as she got out of the shower she continued her day as usual. It was a day like any other and certain things had to be done, no matter what tragedy had struck, she was learning that from Anglor. Most of life was pretending, pretending your world wasn't imploding, for if you pretended it wasn't eventually it really wasn't. It all depended on what you we rei the eyes of the Other. If to the Other you appeared alright then you were alright, even if truthfully inside you felt like you were dying, once the Other deems you sane you are sane, you can be secretly mad as you want to, as long as no one else sees it then it doesn't exist. But Maria wasn't sure she wanted to live like that, though as an American, a populace that was particularly dependent on the opinions of the Other, she didn't know any other way to live. But she knew to be privately mad was quite painful, and it comes out eventually, naked and bare for the Other's eyes, s truth always has a way of surfacing, no matter how you try to stifle it with pretending, with putting on another casual societal role.

So she didn't know what to do. She was becoming afraid of the mental hospital as well, though she had never been to it, at least not yet. Mercifully Anglor decided they would arrive at Miamisburg by plane, for which Maria was incredibly grateful. She could just sleep the whole way there and pretend she was dead. Everything is alright when you're dead, isn't it? And the nice thing about it is there is no Other. Maria thought sadly that even friends were the Other, even lovers, though lovers are usually much more plastic. The problem with lovers is that they are pretending to you, as well. And if you don't pretend it is impossible to find a lover, because no one really wants someone as they really are, for to expose yourself means only to prove to everyone that you are incredibly flawed, are often mean, and almost always afraid. People trying to find a lover try to find someone who isn't any of these things, though such a person does not really exist, they exist only in the mind, and in this way we have turned love into a hallucination, into a form of madness, one does not want to be cured of, but they are eventually, because the truth always surfaces, because no one can wear a mask for long, and that is what is so difficult about the Other, that we wear a mask before them and eventually truth and gravity make the mask fall off, then the Other leaves us, and we are relieved and heartbroken at the same time, finding it just as difficult to be alone as it is to be around Others, finding we pretend to ourselves as well, finding we are our own Other, and never feeling free to be ourselves who are incredibly flawed, often mean, and always afraid.

They got on the plane the next day. Maria sat next to Anglor and Liza sat across from them, feeling alone, feeling as if she wasn't part of their grief. Maria slept the whole way as she planned to, while Anglor of course drew and read, never taking a single day off, but of course it wasn't his mother that was dying- it wasn't a pain he could understand, because he was from the moon and had no mother, but at the moment he did feel incredibly sorry for humans. Even the thing that gives them life must die one day, and then they must die, and they are lucky if the mother dies first, for losing a child is a pain that cannot be described, whereas almost everyone loses both their parents. There is a lot of death in life, humans all being potential bearers of life who all must die. Anglor thought it was better not to have children, but then the whole human race would die. Somehow that seemed less painful, though. One cannot possibly mourn everyone, though the writer's and artists try, in their hearts when they mourn for their species they are really mourning for themselves, but that's the way it has to be, we have to identify all of mankind as ourselves, that way we might protect it and love it as we love ourselves, as something you love begrudgingly, because you have no choice, but which you want to keep alive. But if the human race is to stay alive it also requires death. It requires lovers who turn into mothers and fathers who then turn into corpses, then children who become lovers then fathers and mothers then corpses, and on and on. It was dizzying. Human life not only required death, it required the constant reproduction that created life but which led to death, it was Sisyphean, it was trying to push a rock up a hill into infinity but the rock could only move back and forth, and that was its version of infinity, it involved a kind of cosmic repetition, through love and death, love being what creates death and death being what creates love.

The plane trip was not long, and everyone except Anglor mostly slept it off. They landed in Dayton and parted with Liza. Maria gave her a kiss and she nodded abruptly to Anglor and then was off to her artist dream life that was no life at all, only a dream. They took the bus from the airport into Miamisburg and went to the hospital Maria's mother was staying in. It was a sad scene. She was in a tiny room with a bag collecting her urine on the side of it and a retablo above the bed of St. Denis carrying his own head. Maria shuddered. Her mother was on a bi pap mask and could not speak, she just kept breathing violently every few minutes. Maria sat down by the bed and held her hand, and her mother squeezed her hand in return, and Maria was relieved. She was still lucid. In about a half an hour she was allowed to take the bi pap mask off to eat. She still struggled to speak and did not say much, and did not eat much either, saying it was too difficult to eat and breathe at the same time. Maria wanted to cry but still couldn't.

"I signed a do not resuscitate order today," her mother said weakly. "I hope you don't mind."

Maria shook her head. "I would have done the same thing," she said.

Maria's brother Justin walked in the room, looking melancholic and harried as always, but he sat next to Anglor and Maria and managed to give them a quick, flippant smile.

"How you doing, mum?" he asked.

She barely moved her head and managed to get out a weak "I'm comfortable," and then Justin and Maria grabbed both of her hands and silently wept. She had to put the bi pap mask back on. When she did this she couldn't speak, but merely lay down as passively as she could and gaped for air like a fish out of water, trying to swim upstream into the arms of God. Maria hung her head. All she could think about was the Hyeruranion, the place beyond the sky. Her mother had always been a hyperuranion thinker, an idealist through and through, like Anglor but not quite as depressive of an idealist, not an idealist who knew they would probably fail. Maria thought about the hyperuranion, the place beyond the sky. It was outer space, it was blank dark matter and lightyears of nothingness stretching out like a blanket over the scant stars in between- that was the empyrean, and that was the primal mover, nothingness, it was the God the created us and it was the God that her mother was slowly slipping back into- a blind, cruel God, and a God that could never know it was cruel, that wasn't so much cruel as it was arbitrary, and it gave us our freedom as it gives us our death, when we are truly free, becoming nothingness again, going beyond the sky by being buried in the Earth, becoming God.

Maria had always been critical of her mother for her almost obdurate optimism, but she realized ow it was only because she was jealous, and soon it was going to be very difficult to live without this tragic optimism, but she seemed to still posses it on her deathbed, and that was something good to die with- that was Christ, not God, not the son of nothingness but the son of man, someone who perhaps really did exist beyond the nullity of the creator. Her mother particularly disdained the bi pap mask. Maria didn't blame her. The nurse came in and said she could take it off and then she would just slowly fall asleep into death, the easiest way to go. But her mother didn't want to do that. Maria knew that this tragic optimism of hers meant she would fight to the bitter end, that she felt she had to remain alive at all costs, and fight the inevitable as she had been doing for years, and this would be the final battle, and everyone knew she could not triumph, but hopefully her tragic optimism would follow close behind into the grave, the shadow of a ghost, and the only light in the midst of a world that was ever narrowing and darkening, into a small tunnel that was long and lead to nowhere, much like life. And Maria was glad she had this tragic optimism, as a light to get through the tunnel, the burgeoning nothingness, that she would eventually have to bury herself in, no matter how hard they fought.

The nurse when speaking of taking off the bi pap mask said "they just fall asleep." Maria thought it was curious. Everyone refers to the dying as "they" when it should be "us."

Anglor put a comforting hand on her shoulder, and rubbed small circles into it. They were in the house of death, which though extremely lugubrious is also a house of love, love and death being inextricable as always, and this woman who was dying with the dignity of her hyperuranion mind, was the love that created both Maria and her brother, the first love they had ever known, the love that yanked them out of nothingness, out of the hyperuranion, and into the world of the living, and now that she was dying, still this love that she had given and made would follow her into the grave even as it lead her, a shadow but also a guiding hand, and this would exist still past the decaying flesh, this would remain until all their lives had ended, this would remain until all the lives in the world were ended. That is what we have that is truly hyperurnaion, that is truly beyond the sky, and this is because it is of the Earth.

Maria's mother's condition only drastically worsened. They let her leave the ICU in the next couple of days but she had to return almost immediately. They sent her back home so she didn't have to die in the hospital, and she was put in hospice care in the nursing home where she had been living for the past few years. She went a couple days mostly asleep, unable to speak, and not responding. They all kept vigil over her deathbed and Maria grew restless and uncomfortable. She felt terrible even for thinking it, but she just wanted it to end, she didn't want her mother's suffering to be so prolonged. The nurses kept her as comfortable as possible, giving her an oxygen mask and loading her up with morphine. She fought to the bitter end, but at two seventeen in the morning, August 23rd, the year of our lord 2018, she died in her sleep.

The nurse stood by her bed and timed how long she had stopped breathing. Once it was two minutes they knew she was dead. Justin immediately began weeping. So did Maria, and she threw herself on her Mother's deceased chest one last time and wept there. Then she ran outside for a cigarette. Justin followed an threw himself on the ground, screaming the word fuck and sobbing until he curled up in the fetal position on the asphalt, saying he was nauseous, shaking, and couldn't breathe. Maria just smoked her cigarette ominously and didn't say anything. She couldn't feel anything, her defense mechanisms were already well in place.

"I thought I was ready," Justin moaned, and Maria smiled up at him sadly. Their father, who had been divorced from their mother for years, was crying as well. But Maria just curled up in the fetal position in her mind, buried there as she always was, just thinking. She thought about the problem with human beings. Our problem is that we think without ever thinking about it. And then of course she thought about the dead. She thought about how there's a great spanning abyss between perception and reality, of our perception of reality and reality as it actually is, and she thought the dead, and now her mother, were on the other side of this abyss, trying to call out to us through a thick layer of black nothingness, trying to scream to us the truth, but even as we are mourning them we are completely deaf to them, we are built not to hear them even as we weep from them and they are completely alone, trying to stretch their hands to us across a chasm that is insurmountable and which the living are not even completely aware of (they think without thinking about,) and even if they were aware of it, they could not cross it either, especially if even the dead cannot cross it. And that was where her mother lived now, calling pitiably in a blackness the human mind cannot imagine, and the human mind imagined everything, but it could not imagine nothing, it could not even imagine death though life is penetrated by it in everything, though we all eventually die.

It was strange, but as Maria watched her mother slowly died, she couldn't help but wonder what was going on in her head the whole time, what she saw and heard, what she perceived as she got closer and closer to that chasm that the living cannot conceive of. She hated herself for this curiosity, but she was curious. She wondered what it was like. She looked over at Anglor, whom she did not realize had her arm around her this whole time. She looked in his eyes. You could see there that he was insane, but she didn't feel sorry for him for this anymore. She now thought the insane had a wealth of perception and intuition that the sane could never possibly have. They could grasp death. They were cursed and lucky for this, incredibly lucky.

Maria put out her cigarette and they all went back to her father's house. She didn't cry again until the morning, and she did her death ritual that she always did, her mantra. She felt alright, but only because it hadn't truly sunk in yet, because their was a barrier between her and her grief, one she had put in place deliberately, as she always did. But it wouldn't last for long. Due to the delay once it hit her it would knock her out, but she couldn't get too depressed, she didn't have the time and she had already squandered so much life that way. And yet she felt like it was an insult to her mother, that she was barely weeping, but Maria had always been a little cold, at least outwardly. In the face of death she dealt with it in a certain epoche, suspending her judgment of its very existence, merely knowing that it existed but not caring anymore about it than that. She knew to be angry at death would only prolong the agony, that you cannot be angry at something like that, that is to be angry at life itself, at a God that does not exist, the only things that truly exist on the Earth being life and death, and in between, thankfully, love, and one cannot be angry about any of them, for that is only to rage against yourself and your solus ipse place in a world that for the most part does not know you, and you cannot be angry at it either, though it forces anonymity and loneliness on everyone, you cannot fight these things, and to be angry with them is only an unproductive waste of what little breath, what little ability to emote, we are almost begrudgingly offered- it will only make you more anonymous, it will only make you more alone. So Maria decided not to rebel against metaphysics, for it determined everything, and was somewhat like justice, although a blind, cruel justice, still justice nonetheless, and fate had deemed that we had no choice but to agree with it, because to disagree with it meant to disagree with the entire universe that does not argue and does not listen to human objections or objections of any kind, that is an iron, relentless God, the entire eidos of what few things are alive, are fortunate enough to be eidos, though vague, abstracted eidos, but still this force we cannot bend our minds around as easily as gravity does is justice anyway, though it is a justice that does not work in accord with our idealism, our naivete.

So Maria would not scream, she would not rent her hands, she would not tear at her breast, she would not fight the God that one cannot fight, death. Peaceful acceptance bordering on passive resignation, that is the only way to deal with the things higher than us that operate in such arbitrary, cold ways. It was pointless to hate them, it was pointless to hate anything, Maria realized. Her mother was the first person who taught her love, the first person that loved her and who created her from love. That taught her that it is better to react to death with love by continuing to love the dead, and this is surely painful, but love is often painful, but it is the sweetest pain in the world, a medicine that makes you ill but tastes like honey going down, and eve as it is making you ill it is curing you, it is erasing all the pain through pain. She thought about Christ. "Lord, I do not want to drink from this cup any longer." But there was no other cup to drink from, everything else was poison, though Christ's cup was poison as well, but poison that was a remedy, a mixture of Paracelsus, a mixture of God.

In the morning Maria's father took everybody out to lunch and they all tried to pretend the world wasn't ending. But the world is ending all the time. One adjusts to it. Maria was having severe depression pains in her back and kept gulping down four ibuprofen at once every few hours. Anglor tried to rub her back, but it only made it worse, it was her body rebelling against the harsh facts of the present, it was her mind rebelling against reality, and forcing her body to go along with it. That is the sad thing about perception, it is the only possible reality, in fact it is what creates reality, but it is always inaccurate, it skews reality, it mutilates it, and yet it is all of reality we will ever know, it's what makes reality able to exist for us, and it is a complete fiction. Everything is so complicated, and therefore everything is a pragnanz- we have our perception which is the only hope of reality, and yet we don't notice most things, and things can only truly exist if we notice them. So these incredibly complex things that always escape our notice do not truly exist, not without confirmation from Others, and yet they are most things, most things go beyond our perception. Most things do not exist. And then we, where do we fall in all of this? We are all Sisyphus. We all live and die under a rock.

But they were cremating her mother. Maria felt guilty about it. She thought if her mother had any say about it she would have preferred to be buried, but she had never spoken about it with either Maria and Justin, and on her deathbed it was much too late to ask, for most of it her mother was asleep and when she was awake she could not really speak. Maria knew she understood, though. When the priest had read her last rites she had seemed comforted, when her favorite nurse Sarah came in and said "Lucy, it's Sarah," her head had perked up a little bit. One thing Maria thought was blessed, on the way to her end she was a child again. But her and her family could not afford to have her buried. Anglor of course had offered to pay for everything, but her father declined due to his pride. He was paying for everything. And she was glad. On her deathbed Maria's mother and her father had at last forgiven each other, and remembered that at one point they were very in love. That is one good thing about death, it produces forgiveness, at a time that is almost too late, but not quite too late. Not only Christ's death, but all death produces forgiveness, His was just the universal one. And Maria at the same time was glad that her mother was being cremated, because she would be the one to own the ashes when it was over. Her and her mother would at last be able to live together.

Maria went on as best as she could. She got manic a couple times but everyone told her that was to be expected, so she scrubbed the baseboards to her heart's content, but a heart can never be content in mania. A heart can never be content in life, life is what makes it ravenous, growing starving even as it feeds, it is death that stops this hunger. Maria was going to have to do the positive identification of the body, because she didn't want her brother to do it and for an odd reason she didn't want her father to do it either, she felt he had already done enough, and now it was at last her turn to be selfless, as her mother was. She hoped her other was in the Hyperuranion world where her ideals belonged, she hoped she was beyond the sky into something far more expansive, less limited, more free, and yet she also hoped the *toto caelo* was hers as well, that she now owned all things earthly and unearthly. She hoped her mother had inherited the sky, as she left the Earth behind.

Chapter 14

The funeral was held on Tuesday, and there was a memorial at the nursing home where Maria's mother lived on September 7th. Anglor knew they would have to stay for that, as well, but he was anxious to get home. He asked Maria.

"Do you want to go back to New York after the 7th?"

Maria looked like she was choking back tears as she hanged her head and looked at him very seriously. "Anglor," she said.

"What?"

"I have to stay here. My brother is losing his mind, my father is now our sole caregiver, I need to help them. I need to be with what remains of my family."

Anglor nodded his head, also choking back tears. "I understand," he said. "You're right. I will stay for the memorial service then on the 8th I'll go home, without you."

"I'm sorry," Maria said.

"Don't be."

"I know this is the way it has to be," she continued. "For both of us. New York is your home, I can tell, you love it there and you belong there. But this is my home. There are plenty of things I would change about it, and I'm not sure I belong here anymore than I belonged in New York, but this is my home."

"I know," Anglor said, nodding his head vigorously. "I'm sorry I made you part from it."

"You're exciting, Anglor," Maria said. "You are full of purpose and ideas, and you have well earned your fame. I went with you because I wanted to follow you everywhere, but now I realize, I cannot be someone's shadow. I am more tame than you. The only person I can follow behind now is my mother."

Anglor smiled at her sadly. "Well, thank you for following me the time that you did. I'm sorry I dragged you through my world, when you wanted your own world. But I am extremely grateful to know you for the time that I did."

Maria smiled. "Me too." Then they both leaned in and briefly kissed one another on the lips.

"Will you write to me?' Maria asked.

"Yes."

"I feel like I've lost two people…"

"These things do tend to have a domino effect."

*   *   *

So things took their course. The funeral happened rapidly and at a dizzying pace Maria had trouble dealing with. She read the eulogy and the ashes were released to her. She moved back in with her father and brother and Justin would never enter her room because the ashes were in it, and he was somewhat frightened of ghosts. Maria wasn't. She had been around ghosts all her life, she thought they were just like aliens, most of them were pretty nice, and she wanted her mother to haunt her. She had told her on her deathbed, at one of the times they were alone together, that she wouldn't mind her mother haunting her. But she was going to no matter what, it was called memory.

She and her brother dug out the photo albums in her father's basement. It was fun but it hurt. It was nice to see pictures of her parents when they were young and still in love. They traveled the world together. Maria was actually jealous. Her youth was spent battling addiction and depression with a series of unhealthy and sometimes abusive lovers. But she was glad her parents had that, that time of pure youth, where the world seems to be yours, a period Maria had never had, and which Justin had never had either. Their mental illnesses had gotten them early, and they were landlocked in Ohio for most of it. But it was nice to see that once her parents were truly alive and truly happy. They seemed like two different people then, and Maria supposed they really were.

Anglor went home Spetember 8th. Maria said goodbye to him at the airport, in the midst of the hustle and bustle, the anxiety of adulthood that wastes us all away slowly it seems, but truthfully it is rapid. She put her arms around him in a solid embrace, and at last she wept, something she was only able to do late. Anglor put a pair of strong arms for his asthenic body around her and let her weep unrestrainedly. He was sad about their diremption as well. He had spent all his time on Earth with her, and she was really the only friend he had ever had. When Anglor got on his plane they both said goodbye without looking back at each other, as if they were both running out of hell, and besides, they had both learned a long time ago not to look back, and not to look forward much either, to just try to be in what little remains of the now, as it is always elusively making its escape into the past, the past that Anglor and Maria necessarily couldn't recollect if they were expected to go forward, though each step forward goes back in an instant, one could be aware of this, one had to be if they wanted to be a philosopher, but one couldn't think of it much if they wanted to life, even as life was escaping them like sand falling inevitably through the fingertips, as if we were foolishly and tenaciously holding onto the grains of sand in an hourglass as they plummeted rapidly into what has been, into time that is no more, the sorites paradox.

When Anglor got home he immediately got to work. He had to meet with Adam Zweifle. Zweifle wanted him to give a speech about killing history, as if he hadn't done that a thousand times already.

"I suppose I could bore history to death," Anglor said acerbically.

Zweifle smiled at him mysteriously. "You know," he said. "That could work."

So Anglor took up the podium again, and looked at a restless and he assumed probably indifferent crowd as he forced the words out. "The only thing that can kill history is love," he started. "Love is the only thing of this world that is other worldly, it is the only thing in this world that is eternal, and history, thankfully, is not. Love remains even after bodies decay, it is the spirit that remains, and universally, it is the holy ghost, and Christ said you make renounce the father, you may renounce the son, and still be forgiven, but you cannot be forgiven if you renounce the holy ghost, you cannot be forgiven if you renounce love, for love is forgiveness. I beg you, humanity. Do not renounce love, for we have an awful lot to be forgiven for, history being our biggest crime, do not let Christ die in vain.

"But love is difficult. Truthfully it is a cross to bear, and in the end we all must die for it. Love means you will be persecuted, love means you will be mocked, love means you must wander the Earth alone with nothing but love, and realizing that is enough, that it is a defense against the world as much as it is an embracing of the world, and wishing to save it. All things of this Earth are hollow and dissatisfying, all things of this Earth are like a handful of dust we cling to and yet still lose someday, the only exception to this rule is love. Love is the only thing of the Earth that is more than just ashes and dust, for it is not only of the Earth, it is of whatever antecedes the Earth as well, though we may perhaps never know what this is, all I know is that like any world it must be found on love if it is to survive. Only love can kill history, only love can forgive us of our crimes, and only love can make us forgive ourselves.

"Love never forsakes anyone, though sometimes it feels like it, that is only because in our darkness we are often blind to this light that never goes out. But it does not forsake us. It remains even in our blackest darkness waiting to be seen, waiting to wake us up from a wretched sleep, waiting for us to become enlightened through it. From love we are all created and back into love we must leave this world, as well, but that is the only dignified way to go. Perhaps if we kill history the world will stop turning, but at least we died for love instead of war. Too many people have died for war, not enough people have died for love. We cannot leave it all to Christ, who has now died for us too many times, we cannot continue using Him as a scapegoat even as we worship Him. We must take up the errand ourselves, we must arm ourselves with the holy ghost, with love, and fight war, fight genocide, fight atrocity, fight history, and in the end slay it like Michael and the dragon…I thought I had something more to say, but…"

Suddenly a shot rang out so loudly it seemed to split the air, and a deafening flash of light, and suddenly Anglor, too suddenly for him to understand, was on his knees bleeding. Someone had shot him. People in the crowd screamed but did nothing, and the assailant disappeared into the crowd like something dissolving in thin air, unseen. Someone called 911 and while Anglor was on his knees bleeding he couldn't help but think of how inauthentic this all was. He was no Martin Luther King Jr. He thought about what Karl Marx said "first as tragedy then as farce," then he thought of what Maria had said, "to be an artist is to be so fake." The ambulance came and rushed him in, but the worst part was not being shot. The worst thing was that now he was a part of history, the very thing he had tried to destroy.

Maria had been staying at her dad's for a couple weeks. She was already desperate to get her own apartment, she hated living at home, though her brother was always fun and her dad was perfectly hospitable, she just didn't feel like she belonged there, and she was dying for her old independence back. She walked to the gas station to get a newspaper, cigarettes and a cup of coffee. She felt like an old man, so dependent on creature comforts, but that was the way she had always been. It was a long walk from her dad's to the gas station, but she didn't mind. Fall was at last coming in, so she could wear a light jacket as she liked doing and the air smelled crisp and fresh and it was pleasant out. It was a long walk but she had always been someone with a lot to think about, so she could always occupy herself. Long walks are good when you have a lot to think about.

She got to the gas station, got her cigarettes, her coffee and her newspaper, and she decided to sit outside for a moment and smoke one of the cigarettes, enjoy the coffee, and read the newspaper. It wasn't the first headline, the first headline was of course about the death of John Mccain, but as she got further into the newspaper she finally saw it. **ARTIST MICHAEL SMITH SHOT** it said in bold, conspicuous print. Her head reeled for a second and then she rested it back on the wall, dragged on her cigarette, and calmed down. She read the article he was not dead yet, and besides, he wouldn't die, he would just go back to the moon. She supposed that was the good thing about being an alien, about being an outsider, in the end you just go home. It must be terrible to have to leave a world you belong in, but one you don't…Yet Maria was sorry Anglor had to suffer like this, murdered by the very people he was trying to save. But she supposed that was just part of it. Try to kill history and history will try to kill you, and usually it does, but it is strange, that's how you win. To kill history you have to sacrifice yourself to it. To kill history you have to let history kill you. But he wouldn't die, he would just go back to the moon.

She finished her cigarette and lit another one. She couldn't take anymore death but she paused for a moment and smiled. The wind was blowing through her hair.

Anglor woke up slowly, at first his eyes would not open. He peered out through half slits. He saw himself surrounded by doctors and nurses. He looked down at himself. He saw himself bleeding, and it was an oddly cathartic sight. He thought this whole time that's all he wanted to do, to bleed. But he knew what to do. It's what all Selenites do when they're wounded. He put his chin against his chest and a light shined there. The doctors and nurses stepped back. Anglor thought it was at last time that people knew he was an alien. Then they would really want to kill him, but perhaps they already knew, and that is why they had killed him. The bright light shined in his chest and he kept leaning his chin on it. It was his heart keeping him warm, and slowing the blood down.

The nurses and doctors stood back in shock. Anglor knew it was only a matter of time.

"I'm sorry," he said to them weakly.

The nurse looked at him wild eyed, but managed to say in a trembling voice, "Why are you sorry?"

"I'm about to scare you," Anglor said flatly. "I always scare people in the end, though I really don't mean to. But I'm a lunatic."

And then it happened. The spaceship landed right in the hospital room. The nurses all gasped and recoiled, while the doors to the spaceship opened. Bogomil stepped out and looked at the hospital staff confusedly. They looked at him confusedly, as well, they were all aliens to each other. It was like Anglor's experience on mushrooms, it was like looking in the mirror and finding a different reflection of yourself, one you'd never seen, it was like finding the Other. One of the nurses screamed and was about to call for help when Bogomil stretched out his hand with the long fingertips and all of them froze where they were standing, like riga mortis had just set in. Anglor coughed a little bit but his wound was beginning to heal. "Did you know?" he asked Bogomil.

"Know what? That they would shoot you?"

"Yes."

"I did. It's all part of the process."

"What's it like to know everything?"

"It's terrible. It's time for you to go home, Anglor."

Anglor rolled around in the hospital bed. "I have no home."

Bogomil extended a hand. "Come with me," he said.

"Yes, sir, and Anglor grabbed his hand and they boarded the spaceship. Bogomil was watching Earth on the television as the spaceship drove itself. Anglor looked at Earth curiously, as if he was seeing it for the first time. Bogomil looked at him curiously.

"Do you miss it?" he asked.

"Not at all."

They were silent and watched the Earth as they were departing into space.

"By the way," Bogomil said. "You did a great job."

Anglor paused and looked at him quizzically, in deep thought. "What do you mean?" he asked, confused. "Nothing's different. The Earth never changes and history never dies!"

End.